TOAST

Hells Salvation

BOOK 2

Rick Allen

A catalogue record for this book is available from the National Library of Australia

NATIONAL LIBRARY OF AUSTRALIA

First published 2021 by Rick Allen

Copyright © Rick Allen 2021

A Catalogue record for this Book is available from the National Library of Australia

Publisher: Inspiring Publishers P.O. Box 159, Calwell, ACT Australia 2905 Email: publishaspg@gmail.com http://www.inspiringpublishers.com

Publisher:
Inspiring Publishers
P.O. Box 159, Calwell, ACT Australia 2905
Email: publishaspg@gmail.com
http://www.inspiringpublishers.com

National Library of Australia Cataloguing-in-Publication entry

Author: Allen, Rick

Title: **BOOK TWO : TOAST - Hells Salvation/Rick Allen**

ISBN: 978-1-922618-44-3 (print)
       978-1-922618-45-0 (eBook)

The Author

Rick Allen lives in Woodsdale, Tasmania, with his wife Lesley. Rick is a, 'born and bred' Tasmanian (1956), with a keen interest in naval history, military horses, saddlery, long equestrian journeys, and the history of his profession; that of a saddler. He started his education at Cosgrove High School, and with his father a merchant seaman and professional fisherman, grandfather a master mariner tug skipper in London, and his great grandfather a master mariner Thames Barge sailing Captain, it was a natural progression for Rick to join the Navy at the age of 15 and complete his education at HMAS Leeuwin.

Rick then went into the Electronic Technical Weapons branch of the Navy and served on many ships and support depots. Upon discharge from the permanent Navy, Rick then served another eight years in the reserves on a Patrol Boat. Some of the hats that Rick has worn since those navy days include those of qualified electrical fitter, workplace trainer and assessor, ship's master, marine engine driver, saddler, and horseback tour guide; just to mention a few. Rick's passion to write comes from a desire to pass knowledge and stories on to others.

Table of Contents

Dedications

I dedicate this book to my father, who sadly passed away in March 2021. He lived with Lesley and I during his palliative care phase and used to love my updates each night about what I was writing about.

Fair winds and a following sea sailor.

Rest in Peace.

Acknowledgements

COVER DESIGN

Photos of HMAS Fremantle by LS/ POETP Gary Haigh.

Other photos used in this book were copied by me from my photographs.

'No copyright infringement is intended.'

Statistics, where appropriate by Wikipedia.

Those people in my life who inspired the main characters in this book

Even though this book is fiction, it is based on real life characters. Their names have been changed to protect their privacy, and I would like to formally acknowledge them here.

MY EDITING TEAM

I would like to formally recognise my other
half of my editing team, Lesley Allen.
Thank you for your many long hours of dedicated work.

Prologue

In the year 2000, after ten long years spent designing and re-designing it, an international law was eventually passed to help combat climate change. All vehicles manufactured from that point on were to have the E1 (Engine 1) modification; a device which successfully reduced emissions to less than 1%.

This revolutionary device was an accumulation of twenty years of painstaking research, involving scientists from all major countries. The device was eventually perfected in 1996. It took four long years before all nations world-wide would agree to its instigation; this was largely due to concerns over who would manufacture the device and who would get the profits. Eventually China won the rights to produce the E1, and it was agreed that the profits would be split between all those countries that had a hand in its design. The E1 was considered to be the one major coup for mankind since the beginning of time.

To assist with emission reduction, every country in the world agreed to get rid of all pre-2000 vehicles. This type of world-wide co-operation in itself was a never before heard of event. At the time of this world-changing legislation there were untold numbers of pre-2000 vehicles in operation; it was left up to each individual country to develop its own unique way of dealing with the problem. In Australia alone, there were literally millions of pre-2000 vehicles in use. Vehicle owners were given two years in which to decide, they could either sell their pre-2000 vehicle to the government for bugger-all coin, or they could choose to have them modified.

To choose modification was not an easy option, the cost was exorbitant, and most governments were against the idea anyway. It was easier for governments to simply turn these vehicles into scrap.

The, 'Dob in a Dirty,' program was introduced in Australia in 2002. Service station proprietors, mechanics, panel beaters and everyone employed in vehicle related industries were 'encouraged' to advise the authorities when a customer brought in a vehicle with a pre-2000 manufacturing plate for repair, refuelling or re-registration. The reward for this was a $1000.00 bounty paid to the 'Dobber,'

Once advised of its existence the authorities would simply confiscate the rogue vehicle and scrap it. In return, they would recoup the scrap metal price, and on top of this the owner of the vehicle incurred a hefty fine of $1000.00. As you can imagine, this was a very popular program which had the potential to generate large amounts of money for those who chose to 'Dob in a Dirty.'

Within a couple of years this program alone had seen the destruction of nearly three million 'dirty vehicles' throughout Australia. By 2005, statistics gathered world-wide showed that all engines remaining in use were in compliance with the less than 1% emission output ruling.

The world was a different place following the events of 9/11 and the consequent 'War on Terror.' ISIS had become without doubt the most well-known participant in terror activities world-wide. There were multiple suicide bombings in most terror-threatened countries on a daily basis, resulting in the formation of an elite sub-committee of the United Nations for the sole purpose of dealing with this problem. The heavy-handedness of the major powers was seen as an excuse for some of the more extreme nuclear equipped countries to sit up and take notice.

While the rest of the Western world was thoroughly engaged with the 'War on Terror,' they focused their efforts on planning their revenge against the major powers. Unbeknownst to the rest of the world, in 2012 North Korea, Indonesia, India, Pakistan, Turkey and Iraq banded together to form an alliance. Although invited, China was reluctant at first to become involved.

However, after much deliberation, and believing that the Alliance would eventually achieve global domination, China joined in 2013. None of the other major non-Alliance players were aware of what was going on.

In mid-2014 a united push against ISIS took place, with all the major countries throwing everything they had at the 'War on Terror.' After more than a decade of terrorist activities, the United Nations sanctioned a show of force which it hoped would finally annihilate the enemy once and for all. The one stipulation was that only conventional weapons would be used.

At the highest level it was agreed without doubt that there would be collateral damage; however, this was considered acceptable in light of the ultimate aim of ridding the world of terrorists. In essence, all non-Alliance nations, (including the United States of America, the United Kingdom, Russia, France, Germany, Australia, Japan, New Haka, Saudi Arabia, the African Nations Group, Italy, the Scandinavian Group and Canada), agreed to deploy 95% of their ground troops; backed up with 95% of their navy and 100% of their air force, to get rid of the menace once and for all. It was decided that the only way to rid the world of these constant threats was to simply kill them all.

In August 2014, Iran accused the United States of spying on their nuclear facilities, this made world-wide headlines after Iranian forces confiscated two US Patrol Boats and their entire crews after catching them out. This was the catalyst that convinced Iran to stand alongside the Alliance against the Western powers, and especially against the United States of America.

In November 2014, North Korea added fuel to the fire by testing its own nuclear capabilities; a nuclear device was deployed as a 'test,' in preparation for possible world-wide conflict. This action in itself stirred the old feud between themselves and the United States. With 90 to 100% of the military might of the world's major countries focused on Syria, Iraq and the Middle East, it wasn't long before tensions reached boiling point.

Too late, it was discovered that it was a monumental mistake to place all your eggs in one basket, so to speak. With the 'War on Terror' at its peak, tensions boiled over on the 17th of December 2014. North Korea pushed the button to unleash its nuclear arsenal on Central Europe and the United States.

Simultaneously, all other countries within the Alliance did the same; targeting all strategic satellites, including the E1 Master Satellite that controlled the E1 components, along with many non-Alliance nations, including the Middle East, United Kingdom, and U.S. Bases in Northern Australia and Russia. Needless to say, the Western world had been expecting action of some sort and was not caught entirely with their pants down.

Swift retaliation came within thirty minutes. Unbeknownst to the majority of Alliance members, a small number of countries within the Alliance had predicted this retaliation and had secretly formed a pact to identify a safe haven where they could start again if the world as we knew it was obliterated. North Korea, Indonesia and India were the three break-away Alliance members who shared this vision.

It was obvious that, in the event of a world-wide nuclear disaster, all countries in the Northern Hemisphere would be wiped out in a very short space of time. After meticulously working out the global weather patterns and predicting the areas where they believed the majority of the nuclear fall-out would settle, the break-away Alliance agreed that the only two possible regions in the Southern Hemisphere, where a new start could be made were New Haka and Taswegia.

Within twenty-four hours of the first strike, all digital E1 compatible electronic components world-wide were rendered totally ineffectual. Every aircraft world-wide simply fell out of the sky; the E1 device in every post-2000 vehicle exploded and disabled the unit, all digital satellites were destroyed, and all digital transmissions became non-existent. The world, as we knew it at that point in time, simply ceased to exist. In Taswegia, this catastrophic event occurred at 0235 AEST.

The flow-on effect was extreme, with no transport, power, planes, or combustion engines of any description able to continue to operate. The most immediate impact on the local inhabitants was that within two days all supermarkets ran out of fresh produce. Those people who were able to access grocery stores on foot or by other means went into panic mode, and within five days, this resulted in the stocks of tinned and dry goods being almost totally depleted. The roads were littered with abandoned vehicles and trucks. Displaced people could be found everywhere, trying desperately to get home, and all business was stopped in its tracks.

All pleasure and commercial vessels ceased to operate, and the main passenger ferry between Devonshire and Millburn was rendered powerless and left to drift with the tides. On the positive side of things, (if it could be considered positive), because the effects of the strike hit Taswegia in the early hours of the morning, only a few freight planes fell out of the sky, however, all aircraft on the ground were immediately rendered unusable.

In the majority of northern hemisphere countries, the impact of losing all modes of transport was the least of their problems. The citizens of these nations were either killed outright in the blasts or were dying due to radiation fall-out. Within 24 hours life had ceased to exist on mainland Australia, and even the Boss Strait islands just north of Taswegia suffered limited fallout. In Taswegia itself, within a few weeks of the first strike, the new Alliance invaded the State with an unwritten mandate to annihilate every Taswegian, with the exception of the doctors.

The invasion date was Friday, 2nd January 2015. This was part of their plan to re-populate Taswegia and New Haka with their own people, and to eventually rebuild their empire. There was simply not enough room for the native Taswegians and their invaders. It was literally, 'them or us!' Twenty purpose-built super tankers powered by old steam and fuel oil engines had been filled with the invading force some six weeks before North Korea pushed the button.

The first ten tankers held over two million North Koreans who, along with their accompanying troops, were planning on becoming the new inhabitants of Taswegia. They brought with them countless quantities of aging machinery, which, being non-E1 compliant, would enable them to spread out and occupy their new country of residence.

The first four super tankers started departing Haeju Bay on 5th November: with regular sailings every week. Fights for survival broke out when loading the last two tankers, every person there was desperate to be among the privileged few to board. The President, his family and his North Korean naval escort were included as part of this last convoy; it was felt that the first four convoys would have drawn too much attention if escorted.

No-one was certain on which date this last tanker sailed. During this time, a second fleet of ten tankers were sent to New Haka with the same plan of action. In addition to the fleet despatched by the North Korean invaders, Indonesia despatched one tanker and four old navy vessels containing 275,000 invaders. In the end India was not able to finalise loading their forces in time and left it too late. Although they finally set off on 15th December, in the ensuing blasts their fleet of vessels and the one million invaders aboard were ultimately destroyed.

Upon reaching Taswegia, knowing that their own medical staff would not arrive until the landing of the third convoy, Alliance skirmish parties quickly rounded up all the medical doctors they could find. They also started their push to gather up all remaining fuel. This was needed to run the antiquated generator sets and their aging military hardware, as well as keeping essential buildings such as the hospital and headquarters operational.

All their military vehicles were pre-2000. In a well-thought-out plan, the Alliance forces landed simultaneously at Kings Town, Bull Bay, and Devonshire.

With all conventional communications lost across Taswegia, the few news broadcasts still running post-holocaust could only be heard on the old UHF radio band through the repeaters around the island state; although the prevailing atmospheric conditions meant that even these were intermittent ...

... Following the invasion, ex-navy Clearance Diver, Dick Mann and his wife Patch, together with four of their closest friends, (an ex-navy CD Sniper, an ex-army Sapper and their loved ones), found themselves fighting for their lives against unbelievable odds, as they desperately tried to get to Hells Beach; the one place from where they might be able to make contact with and enlist the help of other Taswegian survivors to rid their land of the Alliance.

A danger-fraught week of travel began, with Sarge, Patch, April and Annie on horseback, and Dick and Jack travelling by road and sea. Along the way both groups encountered Alliance troops more than once, only narrowly escaping with their lives. They eventually managing to reach the relative safety of Hells Beach, where they set up camp, thinking they were well out of reach of the Alliance at last.

However, their reprieve from danger was brief; awakening one morning to find that a Fremantle Class Patrol Boat had appeared at the entrance to the bay. Realising they were about to be discovered, they worked together to overpower the Alliance crew and take control of the Patrol Boat. However, the skirmish left one of their number seriously injured, and in urgent need of medical help ...

TRF Vessel FCPB Fremantle, 137 foot ex- RAN and Indonesian Patrol Boat Twin 3200 HP MTU's
Photograph compliments of LS/POETP Gary Haigh

Chapter 1
Wounded

1700 Wednesday 14ᵗʰ January 2015... Hells Beach ... through Dick's eyes ...

After moving everyone ashore I suggested we should work on a plan to repair the 40-60 Bofors, and then take the *Fremantle* to Kings Town to try and find Doc.

"The first thing we need to do is get hold of a pushbike brake cable, so that we can fix the firing mechanism on the gun. I think I saw one at old John's farm; we'll just have to be careful not to draw any attention to ourselves when we ride in. We might have to kill the 'new inhabitants' there. Unfortunately, this could bring inquisitive troopers to check things out; it wouldn't take them too long to discover our tracks and eventually our camp."

Sarge scratched his three-day-old stubble, the ex-Sapper looking a little unwashed, and his clothing starting to show signs of negligence, "How do you suggest we go about it Dick?"

"I reckon we should just go in, stealth-like, and steal the whole bike mate!"

I added that I thought with future raids we should turn right when we enter the plantation, riding all the way to Bronze; that way they wouldn't know what direction we'd come from.

Scran was fresh pork chops accompanied by some of those lovely veggies Annie had acquired for us two days previously. Once the vegetables were in the pots, with the chops sizzling away on the steel plate, Sarge mixed up some gravy, while we got April settled more comfortably. Patch and Annie had made a lean-to seat by using a single swag, a bit like a chaise lounge. The French woman was feeling a lot happier by now; at least until she needed to go to the loo. It was a two-person job to carry her there; something she found really embarrassing.

Once we'd enjoyed our meal and cleaned up, I explained my plan in more detail.

"Jack, can you go aboard tomorrow and strip the firing cable out of the Bofors. You'll need to patch up any issues from when you shot it up. I checked the 40-60 spares cupboard and found a replacement hydraulic joystick control unit but definitely no cable. Then maybe you can give yourself a rub around in the engine room. You know the routine ... valves, start-up procedure, generators, paralleling, tools, fuel transfer and so on."

"No problems Dick. I should be right down the hole, just a matter of checking where the specialist tools are kept and sighting all the relevant valves etc. While I haven't served on F-boats, I've been on plenty of other vessels with a similar engine room layout."

"What's paralleling Dick?"

I had to admit that I'd always loved it whenever someone gave me the opportunity to share my knowledge.

"Well, I'm glad you asked Annie! Normally the Patrol Boat would operate on one generator; this would carry the normal electrical load of life on board. When the boat leaves harbour or weighs anchor, it needs to put power onto the windlass to hoist the anchor, or when leaving harbour stations in an emergency it might need the windlass. One generator is simply not able to supply enough current, so two are used for this, to run two generators simultaneously they have to be in parallel. Does that sound about right Jack?"

"Couldn't have put it better myself Dick!"

"So, Annie," I continued, "in order to do this, we have to control the cycles and watch the two synchrometers. You have to hit the 'parallel' switch when the needles are travelling at the same speed and in the same direction, this gives you the capacity of both generators at the same time. It's a bit like having two twelve-volt car batteries hooked up in parallel; you still only get twelve volts, but you've got a heap more grunt!"

I looked around at the group, pretty impressed with what they had been through over the last week or so.

"Patch and Annie, I'd like you both to run the camp and look after April please. You'll have to be on your guard though; if any intruders appear you'll need to fire off a few rounds to alert Jack. Sarge and I will do the raid, if we leave around 0200 that should get us to John's around 0530. Patch, are you still happy if Sarge rides Zen?"

"Sure thing Hon."

I paused, drawing a plan in the sand to show them the layout of the farm.

"Sarge and I will need to leave really early. We'll take the NVG's, although I'm not sure how they'll go, or even if we'll need them. I'm thinking we should leave the horses at the edge of the plantation and go the rest of the way on foot. Next, we'll have to find the bike; from memory, I think it was in one of those sheds on the right. On the way back to the horses we should take the opportunity to grab some fresh veggies out of the garden."

"Are you going to strip the brake cable off the bike or bring the whole thing back with you?"

"I've been thinking about that Jack. By the time we get there it will be almost daylight so we might not have much time. I figure the NK Nationals will possibly start work on the farm as soon as it gets light. It will be a bit awkward to carry, but better to bring the bike back here; I dare say we'll be able to use the other parts off the bike at some stage."

"You mean like making a cart for collecting firewood Dick!"

It was good to see a smile on the injured woman's face.

"Exactly April!"

Patch always smelt fantastic to me. It didn't matter how long she went without a wash; it must have been her natural scent. She snuggled up to me as we lay in our swag later, quietly talking about everything that had happened since we'd first heard the broadcast. It was hard to believe only twelve days had passed since then; at times it all felt a bit surreal, although April's injury was a constant reminder of the bloody fire fight earlier in the day.

Two weeks ago, we had been simply going about our own business and getting on with life. Of course, we'd all known about the nuclear holocaust, but we'd had no idea of the invasion or the bloody wrath that was coming. Everything since then seemed like a blur; from struggling to feed ourselves and not knowing when or if our beautiful State would get back on its feet, to having to kill people to defend ourselves. I felt a bit sick as I thought of the horrific sights our women had been confronted with. I could feel Patch's body trembling as she sobbed gently, trying to come to terms with it all.

"Are you all right Chook?"

I hugged her tightly as we talked about everything that had happened. We had no idea whether our plan to get the analogue phone going would work or not; the brick phones had become outdated by new technology years ago, so it was quite possible that these days there would be nobody who still had one lying around.

Was it even possible for us to beat the Alliance? We had absolutely no idea how many troops they had; although, because of the rate of dispersion I suspected they had shitloads! What I was certain of was that we would not be able to do it on our own. We were going to have to find other pockets of resistance like ourselves and the people at Benowa, and maybe Doc, if he was still alive; that's if we could find him. I was sure hoping that he still had his brick phone.

What we did have now was one very powerful tool of persuasion, the *Fremantle*. Jack and I were able to operate the boat, and I could train the others to assist. I'd need to work out who to send down the hole with Jack, the others could help to steer the boat and Sarge was perfect to man the 50-calibre machine guns and assist with the 40-60 Bofors.

Patch asked sleepily,

"Could I learn how to steer her Dick?"

"Too bloody right Chook! I'll even give you a go on the 50-Calibre."

The reality was that it would take a miracle to get the jump on the Alliance; although finding Doc and getting that round out of April's shoulder would be a damn good start. It was even possible that Doc might know of other pockets of resistance.

It had started to drizzle with rain, the sound of this on the overhead tarp was comforting and familiar. Patch had always liked the sound of the rain on the tin roof.

"I know it's not a tin roof darling, but it's nearly as good isn't it," I grinned.

There was no answer from Patch, she was sound asleep!

Thursday 15ᵗʰ January 2015 ... Hells Beach through Dick's eyes ...

I wasn't sure whether I'd heard a voice or whether I was dreaming.

"Dick, you awake?" It was Sarge.

"Yeah mate, I am now. What's the time?"

"It's 0130. Billy's on."

I quickly dressed, trying not to disturb Patch, although I didn't quite make it. As I climbed out of the swag she grabbed my leg, and after pulling me back down, gave me a hug.

I kissed her, telling her, "See you in a few hours Chook."

Although she smiled, I could see her top lip quivering; I knew she was worried.

The one thing you could depend on was that Sarge would always have the billy on and the fire stoked up. He handed me my hot coffee, and we both collapsed into a couple of the folding chairs we'd carried from our place. As we sipped the hot drinks, we thought over the possible dangers ahead.

"Maybe the Alliance hasn't taken over John's place yet Dick."

"Shit, that would be good mate!" I think we both knew that this was unlikely.

"What are you thinking of taking in the way of weapons Dick?"

"I thought I'd take the silenced .22 cut down rifle, along with my 9 mm Browning. What about you?"

"SLR and 9 mm Browning mate."

After finishing my coffee, I made my way to the 25-man army tent, thinking what a good thing it was that I'd thought to splice a rope sling onto the .22. It was way too big to fit into the wither bags. I switched on the 12-volt light inside the tent flap and looked around, puzzled.

"Where are the saddles Sarge?"

He pointed to the horse paddock. I could just make out Annie, who was coming back leading Bob and Zen.

"All saddled Dick!"

I gave the twenty-eight-year-old a hug. "You're amazing Annie!"

Patch and I had always loved Annie as if she was our own daughter. This scrawny kid who'd come into our lives now looked like she could have just come off the model catwalk. There was not an ounce of fat on her, just pure muscle. Her facial features under her blonde hair were fine, almost like a Nordic goddess, and her smile was infectious. The holocaust had only served to increase the bond between us; we had no idea what had happened to our own children, so for all we knew she was the only child we had left.

We grabbed the weapons and our NVG's and double-checked the ammo. After quietly leading the horses away from the camp we mounted and set off. From the bottom of the track, leading up away from the beach, I turned and looked back at our new home. I felt a bit in awe of what we had created.

"Mate, is that some campsite or what?"

Chapter 2
Hot Town

Wednesday 14ᵗʰ January 2015 ... Kings Town General Hospital

As Doc and Nari walked to the hospital they realised the *Warrnambool* was not at Queens Pier.

"Nari, can you find out where it's gone without drawing too much attention?"

"I will try Doc."

When the pair entered the staffroom to report for work, they were bombarded with questions. It was quite obvious that by now everyone had heard about the information Doc had shared with Ted Green, Les Solomon and Helen Smith in the operating theatre the other day.

"When is the convoy getting here?"

"How do you know we will be killed?"

"Will it hurt? Why do I have to go?"

Although he understood their fear, Doc couldn't help thinking they were a bit like a bunch of whinging school children, complaining about going to the dentist for the first time.

"Look! We've only got about five minutes before Li Chun arrives. Nari overheard Jun Lee and the runt discussing our incompetence after their first officer died on the operating table, and how this would change after the arrival of the next convoy."

As he spoke Doc was doing a head count, trying to work out whether or not they were missing another staff member. As the days passed it was getting more and more difficult to remember who was left and who had disappeared. There were ten of them present, plus Nari and himself.

Les snorted, "That's not many of us when it comes to running the whole hospital Doc!"

"I agree, although I don't think they really give a toss! We have to remember there are small medical centres in every district; they'll be operating the same as us with maybe one or two doctors doing the job of ten or twelve!"

Doc held up his hand to warn the others as Li Chun opened the door.

"Good morning doctors. We want two of you to go to outlying medical centre and work there."

Doc was hoping the 'two' would not be himself or Nari.

The runt pointed to Les Solomon from cardiology and Dave Reddy from renal.

"You and you! You go now!"

"Where are they going Li Chun?"

"You no worry Doctor Roger. They take over main medical centre at Soothe. We have need of their services there."

Doc sighed, wondering to himself just how good a Cardiologist and a Renal expert would be as far as fixing wounded troopers went. Les and Dave were just standing there, obviously thinking the same thing.

Motioning for the newly appointed Soothe physicians to follow him, the runt headed out the door.

Turning he grunted, "You go work! Now!"

The stress was starting to get to Doc, and he was finding it harder to concentrate on what he was doing. He almost made a fatal error when he was extracting a round from the groin of a young trooper; accidently nicking the main artery. The blood shot high into the air, like a fountain. Pat and Reg saved the day by applying a quick clamp.

"Shit Doc! That was close. Are you all right?"

"Sorry Pat; just a mental lapse. I'll be fine. I'm just not used to all this surgery!" Reg agreed.

"Neither are we mate; at least you did a bit of this before changing over to ENT!"

It was a long, long day, and one Doc was glad to see come to an end.

As they walked home, Nari could tell that something was wrong. Holding the aging doctor's hand, she asked, "What's wrong Doc?"

Doc was feeling too stressed to say anything. Putting Nari off for the time being, he told her he would tell her later, and that he just needed some time to clear his head.

After the meal, he collapsed into his favourite chair; feeling exhausted and defeated. Nari, still in her light blue scrubs held him tight as the sixty-five-year-old unleashed the torrent of thoughts and emotions he had kept bottling up inside himself since the arrival of the Alliance.

"I'm not sure I have what it takes to continue love!"

Nari, who was facing him while sitting on his lap, slapped him across the face ... hard! She screamed at him, "You NEVER ... NEVER ... NEVER give up!"

The shock of the slap and the abruptness of her words had the desired effect, jolting Doc back to his senses. Nari kissed his face, apologising over and over again for hitting him.

"No, you were right Nari. I was behaving like a wuss!"

He kissed her back saying,

"Let's go down to *Footy* for a while; think it's time for a cigar."

As the pair approached the marina, they stopped, horrified at what they saw. The marina was in one hell of a mess! The fuel truck had obviously done the rounds; siphoning all the fuel out of the vessels. Over half of them had been destroyed, possibly by grenades. These now sat on the bottom; some of them barely visible at high tide.

Doc's heart sank, as he and Nari desperately scanned the tangled masts and rigging, trying to work out whether *Footy* was still in one piece. The feeling of relief when he finally caught sight of his beloved yacht was almost overwhelming.

"She's still afloat love!"

Climbing on board, they checked her over, realising that she hadn't been touched. Nari looked into Doc's eyes as she lit his cigar.

"What will you do my man?"

He looked at her, appreciating her concern. She was really just a kid, but like him, was dealing with some really bad stuff. On top of that she was stuck in a foreign country and had no way of going back home. Hell! She had no home anymore!

Puffing on the NK cigar, Doc pulled her closer to him.

"I think they must have only destroyed the cruisers and left the yachts: I'm hoping we might be okay, at least for the time being."

Grabbing the brick phone, the solar charger, and a few personal belongings he added, "Maybe we should sleep in a real bed for a while!"

Thursday 15ᵗʰ January 2015 ... Doc's Place, Chook Point, Kings Town

He slept well that night, waking just before the alarm went off at 0500. It helped that Nari brought his body back to life; every time he thought he was too tired, she proved him wrong. As he started to climb out of bed he heard the unforgettable sound of an F-Boat.

Watching the *Warrnambool* come up the river as he ate his breakfast of vegemite on toast, which had been toasted over a small butane burner, he wondered where she'd been for the past two days. More importantly, which way was she going next.

Upon their arrival for the morning muster, they found that their number was now down to seven; Doctor Alex Wallace from endoscopy simply failed to turn up for work. This did not impress Li Chun one bit! He already had more bad news to tell them. It seemed that the medical centre at Dove, south of Kings Town, needed two replacement doctors; apparently the two who had been working there had been shot!

With no explanation forthcoming, the runt chose Reg Miles from urology and David Benson from haematology. With their removal added to that of Les and Dave, things were really getting busy. Those remaining had to not only perform their own tasks, but also had to cover surgery, change bed linen, clean bed pans, dress wounds, clean patients, do their own blood-works and x-rays and move the patients around as required.

Doc met Nari in the hospital canteen at lunchtime; over a dish of hot rice and vegetables she quietly told him about the latest news. The *Indo Maersk*, an Indonesian Super Tanker, had been spotted off the southern tip of Taswegia; they had contacted the Alliance via signal lamp from a point near Dove.

The news of her imminent arrival had caused a great deal of excitement, because it meant the arrival of another 75,000 troops and 200,000 Indonesian Nationals; apparently these had been allocated the East Coast from Barracouta, north through to St Anne. During the time leading up to the invasion, those in charge had realised the potential logistical nightmare of transporting 200,000 Indonesian Nationals up Taswegia's East Coast, so had added an additional 100 vehicles to the tanker's load. However, the reality was that even these 244 vehicles, comprising of 200 trucks and 44 jeeps, would simply not be enough to carry out the exercise in a timely manner.

Jun Lee was well-aware that he was supposed to have the areas cleared of Taswegians by now, and that the clean-up crews should have been through the entire area, making it ready for Indonesian occupation. His troop numbers had continued to dwindle since the invasion, meaning that he was struggling to get any further north than Benowa.

"Did they mention the eta of the Indonesian Super Tanker Nari?"

"Sorry, I don't know that Doc; and I don't think they know either."

"I reckon at a rate of five knots they should be here some time tomorrow.'

Nari told Doc that she believed, from what she'd overheard, that Jun Lee was more interested in the 75,000 troopers than the civilians. It was his intention to commandeer some of these, to bolster his own dwindling forces.

"Good luck with that!" snorted Doc, who had worked with the Indonesians during his time in the Naval Reserves.

"From what I know of the Indonesians, I reckon he could have a real 'barney' on his hands if he tries that!"

Doc had been growing increasingly worried about the dwindling staff numbers at the hospital, and it took considerable persuasion before he was able to convince Lee Chun to allow him to speak to the General about it. By now they were down to five, and things were desperate; he wanted to ask the General whether he would allocate some of the Alliance troops to help them with body removal and transport, as well as general cleaning duties.

Lee Chun, smartly dressed as usual in his dress uniform, escorted Doc to the General's office. Although Jun Lee motioned for him to speak, he could see that the General was only half listening; obviously distracted by the fact that things were not going to plan. This made perfect sense now that Nari had told him about what was happening; the late arrival of the second convoy with its much-needed reinforcements. With nearly 400,000 NK Nationals being deposited into Taswegian homes, even at an average of six people per household, this would occupy over 66,000 troops with escort duties; when the numbers needed for the kill and clean-up squads were included, it was obvious that the numbers of troopers were getting thin on the ground, and that the NK Alliance was stretched to maximum capacity.

Doc couldn't help wondering how many of his troops the General had lost to firefights from desperate Taswegians wanting to defend their homes. Jun Lee's face reflected the stress and worry he was dealing with.

"You ask for too much Doctor Roger!"

Doc was past the point of caring, and persevered, ignoring the look of annoyance on the General's face.

"We have to have more help if you want us to keep running the hospital General. Can't you see it's impossible for us to do everything that needs to be done? We simply can't do everything!"

The sixty-year-old General looked intently at Doc; realising how serious he was, he sighed, replying,

"Very well! I will give you only ten more Doctor Roger! No more!"

Nari was also under immense pressure; there were now only two of them left to run the outpatient and triage departments, which meant she was constantly exhausted. Every day brought the arrival of between twelve and twenty new patients. Even though some of these only had minor ailments, they all still had to be processed. Pressure was also put on them to return injured troopers to active duty before they were ready. Nari couldn't help thinking this was not going to end well for the Alliance. It was all becoming too much for the South Korean triage nurse; but somehow Nari summoned the strength to keep going, while keeping her ears open for any talk that might be useful to report to Doc.

That night, they sat in front of the huge window overlooking Kings Town Harbour. This had always been Doc's favourite spot in the house; even though things were so different now, the harbour still held that special magic for him, and he loved watching the water, the boats and the people going about their jobs. Nari had listened to a lot of talk that day and couldn't wait to report to 'her man'. Doc smiled wearily at her as she offered to light his cigar. Millie had always hated him smoking inside and had absolutely forbidden it. 'What a joke' he thought.

"Yeah, light me up love. No point worrying about a little smoke is there."

"I have a lot of Intel for you Doc!"

Nari went on to tell the tired doctor about the snippets of conversation she had overheard. It seemed that the *Warrnambool* had been on a test run for the past two days; concentrating on coastal towns and seeking out any vessels that might be holed up in secluded bays. From what she'd heard, it had been a successful mission, with over one hundred Taswegians killed, and forty-three vessels sunk.

They were planning on sending the *Warrnambool* out again in a few days' time. Apparently, there was a fair bit of bickering happening between the Indonesians and the NK Alliance. The Captain of the *Warrnambool* was worried that his sister boat hadn't turned up yet and wanted to go and search for them. However, the General had refused him permission to do so;

saying they were required to run important sorties out of Kings Town, and that this was to be their priority.

Nari also told him that by now the Alliance had made it all the way to Lakeside in the midlands, and that they had full control of the Channel and as far as Kings Bridge towards the west coast. They had also developed a garrison at Barracouta on the East Coast. They were restricted at the moment because of the current lack of manpower. The main topic everyone was talking about was the imminent arrival of the third convoy any day now.

Doctor Alex Wallace seemed to have disappeared; apparently, he was nowhere to be found. Nari had overheard Li Chun and another officer discussing the possible whereabouts of the doctor. It seemed that they had searched his home, but to no avail; although they did find evidence that the good doctor owned a yacht.

"Do you know Alex, Doc?"

"I don't know him that well, although I do remember Dick and I sailing against him in the twilight races a few years ago."

Nari gazed at Doc; her deep brown eyes reflecting the trust she had in him.

"Maybe we can sail away and team up with Alex?"

"Maybe love," replied the sixty-five-year-old, who was trying to remember the name of Alex's yacht.

"Mind you, I have no idea where he would have gone, or even whether we could track him down."

With a satisfied grunt, Doc exclaimed, "That's it! *Rumble!* That's the name of Alex's yacht! It's a fifty-foot fibreglass if I remember correctly, a Roberts design. I think he keeps it over on the far walkway."

Keeping their eyes out for any sign of danger, Doc and Nari carefully made their way down to the Marina, and crept quietly back along their walkway, along the main pontoon, and past the next five walkways. Nari could not believe how many boats there were in the Marina.

"I know love; there's a lot of money tied up here!"

They arrived at berth number 122, finding it empty.

Doc said with a satisfied smile, "Looks like he might have got away; this is where she was when I last saw her."

Friday 16ᵗʰ January 2015 ... Footy, Chook Point Marina, Kings Town

It was after midnight when the pair returned to *Footy*; both feeling excited about the possibility that Alex and his family might have given the Alliance the slip. To celebrate, they 'spliced the mainbrace' with a bottle of Royal Swan rum that Doc found tucked neatly away in one of the compartments on board. He poured Nari and himself a large tot, adding a dash of room temperature ginger beer he had, which took care of half of the bottle in one go. Any remaining inhibitions were quickly thrown out the window. The sex that night was fast and furious!

They both slept so soundly that neither of them heard the alarm. Doc woke with a start at 0600 and shook Nari awake.

"Shit! That's torn it!"

After throwing on their clothes, they ran to the hospital, anxiously hoping that the runt would not be waiting in the staffroom. Finding nobody in the room, Doc gave Nari a quick hug before heading off to theatre, hoping desperately there would be no repercussions for being late to work.

"Where were you at muster Doc? The runt's furious!"

"I simply slept in for once Pat; although I know that's no excuse for missing muster."

As he worked through the morning, Doc kept a watchful eye on the door; feeling sure that at any moment Li Chun would come bursting in and drag him out for punishment. Nari told him at lunch time that she too had been worried, but nothing had happened so far. Later that afternoon, Li Chun entered the scrubs room, where he found Doc scrubbing down from surgery.

"Doctor Roger! You come with me to see General!"

As he stood nervously in front of the General, Doc felt like he was back at UTAS; standing in front of the Chancellor and about to be dressed down for one of the many pranks he had been accused of.

"Doctor Roger! You late this morning! Why?"

"I'm afraid I have no excuse General; I just slept in."

"Why did your whore not wake you when she left to go to work?"

It was with a sense of relief that Doc realised both the General and the runt must have thought Nari had turned up on time. This was great; if someone was going to be punished, Doc was glad it was only going to be him.

Thinking quickly, he answered,"We sleep in different rooms; she probably thought I had already left for work."

Doc winced to himself, thinking how ridiculously feeble that must have sounded to the General. He braced himself, ready for whatever would come next.

"Very well Doctor Roger. I give you this. But only because I am happy for what you did for my son. Now tell me Doctor Roger; what do you know about this Doctor Alex Wallace?"

Doc was puzzled, wondering to himself, 'Son? What bloody son?' He'd have to figure out what the General meant later. Aloud he answered, "All I know is that he didn't turn up for work. I didn't really know him that well General."

Jun Lee nodded, dismissing Doc and the runt with a wave of his hand. After being escorted back to the hospital, Doc concentrated on the usual afternoon duties; bed pans and washing. The hours passed slowly, and it was a relief to be able to enjoy a hot shower when 1730 finally rolled around.

As he walked home with Nari, he told her about his visit to the General; knowing how relieved she would be to find that she hadn't been missed. They were careful to always keep their conversations to a whisper whenever they were on the streets; the place was filled with constant streams of NK foot traffic, and they were both extremely aware that they could be overheard at any time.

"I can explain about the General's son," said Nari, giving Doc one of her special hugs, before going on to tell him how the General's son had come into the outpatients' department for a check-up, following the surgery on his hand a week before.

The penny dropped at last, as Doc remembered the emergency amputation he and Pat had performed on the farmer, whose hand had been mangled by a threshing machine.

As they rounded a corner they were confronted by the sight of the *Indo Maersk*, which was now berthed at Governor No 1 wharf. Unloading of vehicles had already begun; the pair could see the huge on-board cranes lifting the six metre containers housing the jeeps. It looked like the troops were being billeted in the old Chevron Hotel overlooking the wharf. The sheer bulk of the Super Tanker was astounding; she was the same size as the first two arrivals, which were all now riding at anchor down the river, well out of the way to allow room for the third convoy.

Later that evening they relaxed on *Footy*, letting the stress of the day fade away. By now they were starting to run out of food; dinner consisted of braised steak and onions out of a tin, which they spread onto toast they'd 'borrowed' from the hospital kitchen bakehouse. As Nari placed the messy feast under the gas grill, Doc poured them each a glass, or shall we say, mug, of red wine to wash it down with.

Nari playfully protested, "No more rum for you Doc; you were very bad boy today!"

Doc retaliated by tickling her under her breasts, as he laughed, "Who, me? It wasn't only me; you were a pretty bad girl yourself!"

Nari was starting to find her way around the thirty-three-foot steel yacht reasonably well. Doc asked her to switch on the UHF.

"Now hit 'scan' love."

Nari did what he'd asked, and they both listened intently for any response; however, the only thing they heard was static. It was almost 2300.

"Might as well leave it on for a bit Nari."

Doc had bought the brick phone back to the yacht with him.

"I thought I'd try and call Dick again while we're at it."

Brrr ... Brrr ... Brrr ... Brrr ... Brrr ... Click!

Both Doc and Nari looked at the brick phone in astonishment as they heard, "G'day Doc, you old bastard! So, you're still alive!"

*Currently the largest containerships on the seas, they were
designed to carry more than 11 000 six-meter containers–
144 containers on deck, now carrying vehicles, (44 Jeeps, 100 trucks)
converted below decks to house 275,000 personnel
(75,000 Troops and 200 000 Nationals).*

*The Indo Maersk, at 397 metres long and 63 metres wide with
an engine that produces the equivalent output of 1,156 cars.
The anchor alone weighs in at an impressive 29 tonnes.*

Chapter 3
On the Scrounge

Thursday 15th January 2015 ... Hells Beach

Heading up the path with Sarge and Zen in front, Dick donned the NVG's just in time to see Zen knock a log off a rock.

"Stop Sarge!"

"What is it, Dick?"

"The log mate! Wasn't that your early warning sign for the Claymore?"

"Holy shit! I must have been half asleep! That could have been ugly."

After dismounting and disabling the Claymore, Dick led Zen to where Sarge had reinstated the deadly trap. The pair had found it was usually better not to use the NVG's when on horseback as this seemed to affect their equilibrium; Dick thought it had something to do with the movement of the horses.

By the time they found themselves approaching the edge of the plantation and the paddocks leading to John's farm it was almost 0400.

"This is where I thought we should probably leave the horses mate. We'll proceed on foot; only need to find the bike, and then see if we can pick up a few veggies on the way back."

The 45-year-old ex-Sapper looked at Dick.

"Are you sure we can't kill anyone this time mate?"

"I'm quite sure Sarge! Remember if we start shitting in our own neck of the woods it wouldn't take them long to track us down. Mind you, as it is, we could still be in deep shit; it's only going to take one inquisitive NK National to come out to the end of the farm and start following the track."

Sarge was hoping this wasn't going to happen.

"Surely they're not going to try and walk the twenty-seven kilometres through to the beach Dick."

"Well, let's hope not mate!"

They found a selection of bicycles, just where they'd thought they were; in the hay shed hanging on the wall. After a brief discussion they decided the mountain bike would be the best choice; the brake cable certainly looked to be long enough. After slinging it over his shoulder, Sarge headed back towards Bob and Zen, with Dick covering him from behind. Pausing along the way, the ex-CD stopped to pick some spuds and carrots. They found the horses were restless and quite fidgety.

"They weren't very happy Dick."

"Probably because there was no feed for them to pick at Sarge."

"I have an idea. We're ahead of time; we could go back to the old fellow's farm up the road and take another look in his kill shed. Last time I was there I noticed a couple of huge meat safes hanging up in the corner. What do you reckon Sarge?"

"Sounds good to me mate!"

The two men rode back through the plantation to the beginning of the tree line. Sarge dropped the bike there, figuring it would be easier to pick it up on the way back through. They turned left and continued parallel to the road that ran from Julie Beach to Bronze Road. It wasn't too long before they could see the back entrance to the old fellow's farm.

Sarge looked at his watch.

"It's 0525 Dick, nearly daylight. What do you reckon?"

"It'll be touch and go mate; it's going to depend on whether or not they get up early."

Both men spent a few seconds just soaking in the view; at this time of the day, with the early morning mist just starting to come in from the sea, it had a special beauty all of its own. Dick looked at the faint plume of smoke which was only just visible as it snaked its way out of the chimney.

"It doesn't look like they've kicked the fire in the guts yet."

After tethering Bob and Zen, the pair made their way to the back of the house, where they grabbed a couple of hessian bags from the stash the old guy used to keep outside the back door. The kill shed was only twenty metres away from the back entrance to the house. Sarge winced and sank to his knees outside as Dick opened the very squeaky wooden door to the shed. They inspected the contents of the two meat safes, discovering a hindquarter of lamb in one and three chickens in the other.

They were only halfway through filling the bags, when Sarge motioned to Dick to stop. They both froze at the unmistakable sound of the flyscreen on the back door to the house banging noisily. Sarge held the kill house door ajar with his foot and kept his weapon ready to inflict its wrath; whispering to Dick that in the moonlight he could see a NK National standing near the back door, stretching. They could just make out his clothing. The National was dressed in what looked like peasant pants and a loose-fitting shirt with no buttons. It looked like the pants had no fly; he was pulling them down to pee much like you would with a pair of track pants.

Dick whispered urgently, "If he sees us, he's dead! Then we'll have to kill everyone else who's inside!"

They could hear the trickle of water splashing on the slightly frosty grass, followed by a few grunts and the bang of the fly screen again as an unmistakable aroma drifted through the open door of the kill house. Sarge whispered,

"He was taking a bloody piss!"

After securing the bags they made their way back to where they'd left the nags. Sarge swore.

"Shit! Where's Zen?"

Dick, feeling quite frustrated, asked, with tongue in cheek, "Didn't you tie him up mate?"

"I thought I did!"

Bob was not happy; obviously wondering where Zen had gone. After a quick look around, Sarge discovered the missing Zen twenty metres away, happily munching on grass.

"Mate, that could have been disastrous, I'll have to give you some lessons on knots." Although Dick was grinning as he spoke, they could both see the potential problems that losing a ride home could bring.

Dawn was almost upon them as they made their way back along the plantation track. There was still a slight frost and a little mist hanging in the air; left over from the light rain shower that had fallen earlier in the night. Unfortunately, this made for very poor visibility. Sarge broke the silence.

"Sorry about Zen Dick."

The ex-Sapper was frustrated with himself, knowing he could have jeopardised the mission with his mistake. Not only would he have had to walk back, but Bob would probably have started calling out after Zen; this would surely have alerted the occupants of the farmhouse.

"It's obvious we would have had to kill them all then Dick."

"Yep!"

"How far do you reckon Zen would have gone?"

"Not far unless he was spooked; like he would be when we opened up with the weapons. Even then he would probably head back towards the beach."

"Like I said mate, I'm sorry."

"Hey! It's all good, don't worry about it."

Ten minutes further down the track Sarge held up his hand, signalling to pull the horses up.

"Can you hear that mate?"

Dick cocked his ear. "Mate you know I'm nearly deaf! Hear what?"

"I thought I heard a vehicle."

"What, on the road? That's got to be a couple of clicks away! Who'd be out at this time. The kill squad maybe?"

"No. Whoever they are, they're coming up behind us!"

After a minute or two, Dick saw a faint light appear in the distance, although he still couldn't hear anything. He thought it might have been coming from the road, but it was too far away to be certain. Sarge was pretty sure they hadn't been seen by anyone at the farm, so it was most likely a coincidence.

"The bloody track isn't wide enough for a vehicle Sarge!"

The pair spurred Bob and Zen on, and cantered around the next bend, looking for a suitable ambush setting. Finding the perfect place, they dismounted and hid in the scrub.

"I can hear it clearly now mate! It sounds more like a bike than anything else."

By now Dick could hear it too.

"You'd know Sarge; you're the bike man. I've never been on one in my life."

Sarge was astounded, "What! Never?"

They looked at each other when the sound of the approaching bike stopped.

"I can't see the light anymore!" whispered Sarge.

They listened intently, shivering slightly in the crisp clean early morning mist, as it deposited a light coating of moisture over them both. Nothing! Mounting again, they continued at the trot along a straight section of track for some 900 metres. Pulling up again, they both turned in the saddle to listen again for any sound.

Sarge shook his head.

"I can't hear anything now Dick."

"Guess it must have been coming from the road Sarge."

They set off again at the walk; only to pull up some 600 metres further down the track, as they heard panting, and the faint mumbling sound of a male voice. It sounded like something heavy was being pushed through the scrub. They dismounted quickly and tethered the two horses, then hid behind a thicket of dense bush to wait for whatever was coming.

Dick slid the cut-down silenced .22 rifle off his shoulder; Sarge, after sliding the safety catch forward on his L1A1 SLR, was already scanning the immediate area, with his rifle held up to his shoulder.

Through the mist they could just make out the blurry shape of a person who appeared to be pushing a heavy motorbike along the track. Sitting on the pillion seat of the bike was a second person, with some sort of huge roll sitting behind them.

"I've got a clear shot!" whispered Sarge, easing his finger off the guard and onto the trigger.

"Wait!"

Dick placed his hand on the SLR's barrel, signalling Sarge to wait. As the moving bike drew closer, they could clearly hear the huffing and puffing of whoever was doing the pushing.

"200 metres. Still got a clear shot."

Watching the silhouette drifting in and out of the mist, Sarge whispered,

"100 metres! Still a clear shot!"

Dick was straining his eyes, trying to make out the blurred figures.

"30 metres!"

Dick whispered urgently, "Wait mate!"

Dick pushed the barrel down; indicating Sarge was to stand down. Smiling he pushed through the bushes onto the track in front of the bike.

Sarge thought he'd lost the plot completely, thinking to himself, 'What the fuck do you think you're doing Dick!'

As the 'bike pusher' saw Dick emerge from the bushes he pulled what looked like a rifle off his arm; bringing it up to his shoulder, ready to fire.

Just in time, the ex-navy CD yelled out, "Don't be a dickhead, Vince! It's me!"

"Bloody hell mate! You scared the shit out of me!"

Sarge emerged from the bushes, giving Vince, who was struggling for breath after pushing the bike, an even bigger scare.

"Where on earth have you two come from?"

"We've been looking for a way into Hells Beach for a week now mate!"

Dick introduced the pair.

"Sarge, meet our neighbours; Vince and Laurel Bradley."

"We've actually met before Dick," Sarge told him.

"It was about six years ago; at a barbeque at your place."

After introductions and handshakes all round, Vince and Laurel quickly gave the other pair a brief run down about what they'd been doing over the last twelve days or so.

"We've got about three kilometres to go before we get to the edge of the plantation, so we'll lead the way while you two follow us on the bike."

Vince shook his head.

"No can-do Dick, out of petrol!"

Dick thought for a minute.

"Maybe take what you want off the bike Vince, and then hide it in the bushes. Make sure you'll be able to recognise the spot; you never know when we might need it again! Sarge, I'll get you to dink Laurel behind you on Zen. Unfortunately, Bob's probably a bit too old to dink you Vince; you must weigh about the same as I do!"

After boosting the slightly overweight ex-security guard, Laurel, on board, Vince strapped the swag onto Zen's back. They then walked the three kilometres back to where they'd left the mountain bike.

"Your new ride Vince," declared Dick.

"We've only got about fifteen clicks to go now."

By this time, it was 0745; the mist had completely disappeared. The soft sandy track proved to be a bit of a problem for Vince, who had to constantly stop the bike and carry it over the really soft parts. The slow going meant they didn't come out into the open high above Hells Beach until 1355.

Laurel was in awe of the sight.

"Wow! What an amazing view!"

Vince was more interested in what he saw moored in the bay.

"Mate, what's the *Fremantle* doing in the bay?"

"Oh, she's just something we picked up along the way!"

Dick grinned as he halted the group while Sarge disabled the Claymore.

"Nice!" Vince was smiling.

As Sarge reinstated the device, Laurel asked, "What would have happened if we had made it through to here without running into you two?"

Sarge was grinning.

"No invite … no welcome! As you can probably see, we don't want any unannounced 'guests' Laurel."

As they descended the track, with Dick taking the lead, they could see the campsite open up below them. Patch and Annie came running out to meet them, glad to see them back safely.

"We'll de-tack for you Dick."

"Geez thanks ladies! Oh, and look what we found!"

Dick grinned and moved aside, revealing Sarge dinking Laurel, and Vince bringing up the rear on the mountain bike.

Patch exclaimed, "We thought you'd both been killed!"

"Nearly Patch," responded Laurel. "Believe me, it was touch and go for a while!"

Vince still had his mind on the *Fremantle*.

"What's the story behind the 203 Dick?"

After filling the newcomers in about the events of the last couple of days, Dick asked Jack how April was and how he'd gone with doing the repairs on board.

"Not ready for the cable yet mate. I reckon there's about four hours of work still to fix the hydraulics where I hit it!"

Vince smiled. "Ah! Now the penny drops Dick. I wondered what gave with the mountain bike!"

Sarge slipped over to the CJ while the rest of the group settled the pair in and sorted out some bedding for them to use.

"You can use one of the single swags; all you have to do is to slide the mattress in alongside of yours and zip the two together. Hey presto, a double swag."

Sarge had pulled a dozen crayfish out of the wet well.

"Reckon we should have a feast tonight people, in celebration of our new recruits!"

Once the banquet was prepared, the group sat around the campfire, tucking into crayfish tails and salad; with the exception of Annie, who was enjoying a pork chop. As they ate, Dick went over the newly revised plan for the following day.

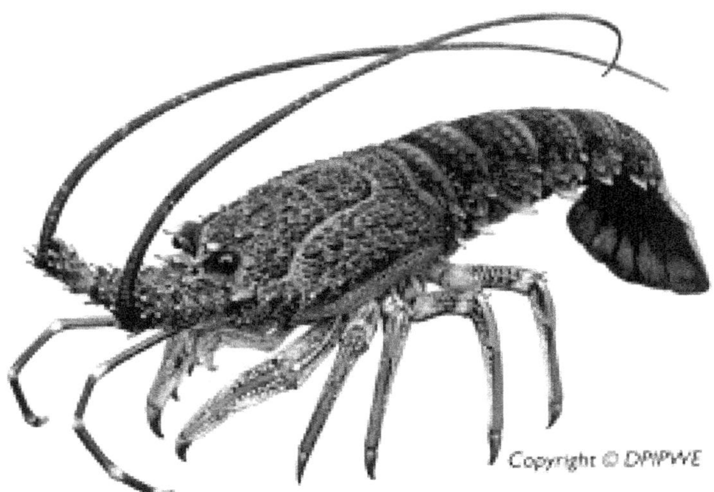

Taswegian Rock Lobster or Crayfish

Chapter 4
Vince Bradley

Vince Bradley, son of Norma and Fred Bradley, was born in 1969 and was raised in Port Adelaide. Fred was a milkman, and Norma assisted in the business by doing the books. Vince's upbringing was based around sport and all things IT related; he was a keen ice hockey player, eventually rising to state level competitions.

Vince had always displayed an avid interest in computers, so his parents were somewhat puzzled at first when he told them he wanted to join the Navy. However, Vince knew which branch he wanted a career in. After completing his basic adult recruit training at *HMAS Cerberus* in early 1987, he moved straight from recruit training into electrical training and from there into the electronic communications branch. He was in his element, serving on numerous ships over his twenty-year career.

In 1989, he met Able Seaman Communicator Laurel Bennett while he was on shore leave in Darwin serving on the *HMAS Hobart*; the pair were married a year later.

In 2010, Petty Officer Vince Bradley and Leading Seaman Laurel Bradley moved to Taswegia, hoping to enjoy a somewhat quieter life after purchasing a property from Bill Green. Their new 250-acre spread shared a border with Dick and Patch's place, just outside of Twaddle; they planned to use it to run sheep and a few head of cattle, as well as Laurel's couple of horses. It didn't take Vince long to find a new job with Eye-Tech, the leading Taswegian communications company, as a communications technician; this provided the extra dollars needed to cover the mortgage on the property.

Dick and Patch met their new neighbours soon after they moved in, and the four soon became good friends.

The Alliance

Friday 2nd January 2015... Kings Town

Once General Jun Lee Sung had instigated the invasion of Kings Town, his troopers spread out like the ripple of a wave across a lake. By the end of the first day, they had not only successfully cleared the general hospital of patients but had also sorted out the doctors from the other staff, killing the latter as they went. A major coup had been stopping the UHF broadcast from alerting the Taswegians of their arrival, which meant that within three days they'd cleared the town of its normal inhabitants. Body disposal was going well, with the bodies being burnt at the South Kings Town refuse site.

The General had appointed an Alliance Captain as his 2IC, or next in command.

With the hospital on his agenda, Li Chun, a career soldier always immaculately turned out, was kept extremely busy.

Setting up the headquarters in the Taswegian House of Parliament on the wharf was one of the General's first priorities. This gave him easy access to the wharf areas, and meant he was also close to the town and the hospital. To keep abreast of the progress of the invasion he demanded daily reports from all area officers; however, the ongoing communication problems meant this was impossible to maintain. The main issue was simply that there were no communications. In order to get reports back from a particular area, Jun Lee had to wait till the officer-in-charge sent a messenger back to Kings Town to report in person.

His irritation at these delays showed itself clearly during one of the pair's situation reports.

"I am not happy about this Captain Li! It annoys me that our communication specialists were on the 3rd convoy!"

"Yes General. This seems to have been an oversight on the part of our esteemed President!"

Both Jun Lee and Li Chun were well aware that it had been the President himself who had laid out the main plan; including logistics of who would be travelling and when. It was the same with the marine engines they had designed to go into the huge alloy catamarans manufactured in Kings Town; these would be coming with the last convoy. This meant that the Alliance would have no control over the water until after the arrival of the Indonesians and their Patrol Boats, and also after the arrival of the Alliance Navy, which would be convoying the President and his party to their new home.

Jun Lee had received a report from the Lakeside Commanding Officer, Captain Tun Kim, to the effect that the work of the 'jug-eum-ui-bundae' (death squads) was progressing well with minimal resistance, and that the 'bundae leul jeongli' (clean up squads) were on track and managing to keep up with the death squads.

Unfortunately, they had lost one 'bundae leul jeongli' already, and had put this down to the work of a few isolated resistance pockets. However, the rest of the squads were going well. Within three days they had worked their way through to Twaddle, and had met up with the Soothe squads; completely covering everything in between the two townships.

Monday 12ᵗʰ January 2015 … Alliance Headquarters Kings Town

Sitting in his office staring out at the magnificent Kings Town Harbour as he waited for a staff meeting to begin, the General felt pleased with the knowledge that the first of the Indonesian Patrol Boats had arrived that morning. He had requested the captain of the 204, Commander Suprapto to attend the meeting. There was a knock at the door.

"Everyone is here General."

"Thank you Li Chun. Is the Patrol Boat Commander present?"

"Yes Sir!"

Jun Lee made his way to the lushly carpeted former chamber of the upper house; a room decorated with the finest of Taswegia's ornately and beautifully made timber furniture.

"Good morning fellow officers of the Alliance! For those of you from the 204 my name is General Jun Lee Sung, Supreme Commander of the Alliance troops in Taswegia. I welcome our Alliance brother, Commander Suprapto, Captain of the Patrol Boat 204. I request that we speak in English only please gentlemen."

Commander Suprapto had brought his second-in-command Lieutenant Joko with him, along with his engineering Chief, Aide.

"Tell me Commander Suprapto, when do I expect the other Patrol Boats?"

The Commander, a small man about five foot six in stature, and dressed in Indonesian Navy camouflage fatigues, looked at him, startled by the question.

"Boats! I am sorry General, there is only one other Patrol Boat coming. That is the 203."

Jun Lee was furious! He had been promised at least four of these Patrol Boats to assist him to rid the land of Taswegians.

In reasonably good English, the veteran Commander went on to explain that the other two Patrol Boats had been allocated to go to New Haka instead, and that 203 was coming down Taswegia's East Coast, and should be arriving any day now. The General exploded!

"How can I be expected to control the waterways with only two boats Commander?"

"I am sorry sir! This is not my concern. Once my Supreme Commander arrives on the Super Tanker, along with the 203, I have been ordered to patrol the upper East Coastline. We are to cover the placement of the Indonesian Nationals."

The General was already conjuring up a plan.

"And when do you expect the tanker to arrive?"

"Once again General, that should be any day now. Oh, and General, I expect to be informed once the 203 is sighted off the East Coast."

Ignoring the Commander's last statement, the General stated,

"I expect you and your crew to prepare for a patrol the day after tomorrow."

After bringing the meeting to a close, Jun Lee dismissed all of them except for the Commander, calling him into his office to discuss the patrol.

"You are to patrol around Frog Island, weeding out and destroying all vessels and killing everyone you come across."

"You want everyone killed General? You take no prisoners?"

"This is correct Commander!"

"It was my belief that the original invasion plan was to round up all the Taswegians and to hold them prisoner on Frog Island."

"Plans change Commander! We cannot afford to house or feed the prisoners, and to be perfectly honest there will be no room for them."

"I will have to clear this with my Commander in Chief when he arrives, Sir."

The furious General stood over the smaller Commander, glaring down at him.

"You no listen! I say kill them all! And what I say goes! If you disobey me, I shall have you executed for treason!"

After taking his leave of the General, Suprapto headed back to the 204, feeling angry and more frustrated than he had ever felt in his life. In his thirty-two-year navy career he had never before come across a more arrogant senior officer. He was not at all happy about his new orders, but being a career navy-man, he also understood that orders needed to be obeyed.

After giving his crew the bad news about the patrol, he informed them of the new orders.

"Chief Aide, is everything ok in the Engine Room?"

The Chief nodded, "All ok Sir."

The Commander continued.

"Lieutenant Joko, please make plans for getting underway at 0600 on Wednesday. We will refuel first then head to Frog Island. Set a course down the outside, around the bottom and up through the channel. We must inspect every bay!"

Friday 16th January 2015... Alliance Headquarters, Kings Town

"Admiral Adi Atmadja from *Indo Maersk* is here to see you Sir."

The General waved his hand.

"Show him in Captain Li."

The Admiral was veteran navy with some forty years' experience behind him and spoke excellent English. He was dressed in his best dress uniform, something that was a rarity these days, and he smiled to himself, knowing that under normal circumstances he out-ranked the General. He held the position of Supreme Commander in Chief of the Indonesian Alliance, as well as tanker skipper; he was here to sort out the logistics of moving the first 200,000 Indonesian Nationals up the East Coast, and to make sure that Jun Lee had done the ground work, clearing the Taswegian homes ready for their new occupancy. Jun Lee began to explain the reasons for failure in this area.

"We have been understaffed Admiral, due to the non-arrival of our third convoy. Despite this, we have started the cleanout and are now past Barracouta. I anticipate we will be at Benowa shortly, although some of the back roads may have been overlooked because of our low staff numbers."

The Admiral looked at the sixty-year-old.

"This is not good General! This will slow us up, which means that the Nationals will need to stay aboard the *Indo Maersk* more days than we had expected."

Jun Lee told the Admiral that he would need some of the Indonesian troops to assist to get the area ready; what he didn't tell him was that he actually intended to use them elsewhere until the reinforcements arrived.

"Taking into consideration that you are so short-staffed, I can spare 10,000 troops General, but no more than these. They are to join your 'jug-eum-ui-bundae' (death squads) and 'bundae leul jeongli' (clean up squads) only above Barracouta."

With a smile, the General replied, "You have my word Admiral Atmadja."

The logistics required to carry out such a great task were to transport fifty Nationals in each truck, along with one jeep per five trucks for protection purposes. Unfortunately, this meant they could only disperse 10,000 Nationals with their accompanying guards to their new homes each time; it also meant the return journey would take around five days. All in all, this time frame meant it would take over three months to unload the Super Tanker. Admiral Adi Atmadja had anticipated that the General would by now have almost one thousand trucks at his disposal, instead of the original two hundred (or even less, once those that had been destroyed by the resistance were taken into account).

The logistics of keeping the Indonesians on the tanker so much longer than first anticipated were daunting; it meant a huge amount of additional supplies, such as food, water, and sewerage facilities, would need to be resourced. Added to these issues was the fact that conditions below decks were not the kindest for the Taswegian invaders.

Jun Lee continued.

"We will be better placed Admiral when our third convoy arrives."

"Let's hope that we are not kept waiting too long General!"

Jun Lee knew the Indonesian Admiral was not happy, but there was very little he could do about that. It wasn't his fault that the third convoy had not yet arrived; and after all, he could only work with what he had at hand. He had to admit to himself that he did like the sound of an additional 10,000 troops though!

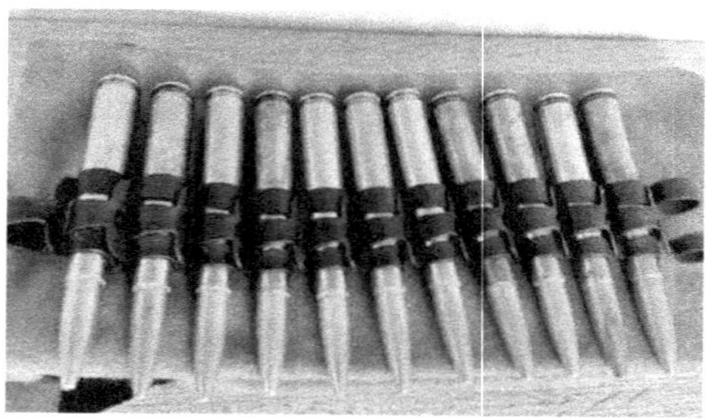

50 Calibre Hollow Point Rounds

Chapter 6
40-60 Repairs

Friday 16th January 2015... Hells Beach Campsite

Life in the Hells Beach camp started that morning at 0800. Once breakfast was over Dick, Jack and Vince cruised out to the *Fremantle*, leaving the others to get on with normal camp chores. Dick and Jack wanted Vince to look over the Comms Centre, while they continued with the hydraulic repair and fitted the new brake/firing cable. Sarge, Patch and Annie showed Laurel around, and then introduced her to her chores; starting with helping Patch to collect the firewood for the camp. Laurel was obviously not happy.

"Vince collects the firewood at home."

"The problem with that is that you're not at home now Laurel. Everyone has to help out, especially with April out of action at the moment. Believe me; Vince will have other chores to do."

Sarge was trying to be polite, knowing that if he said things the way he wanted to say them, the fireworks would really start. Ignoring the look of annoyance on Laurel's face, he continued.

"Unless there are other duties Laurel, this is the usual routine. First up is firewood collection; that's you with

Patch, and April when she's able to. Cleaning the dishes and prepping for the next meal is done by Dick, Jack and I. Annie tends the horses, and the cooking is done by Dick, with me assisting. Dick, Jack and I take care of the cleaning of the weapons. After 1000 we all have free time unless something is happening. For the rest of the time, we all just help out where necessary; although things change whenever there's a raid happening."

"Who goes on the raid Sarge?"

"Whoever Dick decides Laurel."

"Oh! And who made Dick the boss?"

The others responded in unison. "We did!"

"Another thing Laurel, we all have responsibilities. For instance, April is in charge of the food stocks and self-sustainability. Sarge the defence perimeter and campsite in general, Jack the weapons. Patch in conjunction with April work out the menu, and Annie looks after the saddlery, tack and horses."

Laurel pushed the point a little more.

"What about Dick? What exactly does he look after?"

"Everything, including the two boats!" informed Sarge.

Back on the FCPB, Dick stepped back to admire the pair's work.

"Fits like a new one Jack!"

The ex-Sniper smiled.

"Yes! You would have thought it was made for the gun, Dick."

They topped up the hydraulic reservoir with oil found in the stores compartment, then, after closing the electrical breaker, gave it a test run. The pair were happy with their handiwork.

Dick added, "At least it fires Jack!"

The ex-sniper smiled again from under his signature cowboy hat; his wrinkled face, weather-beaten after all those years living rough as a sniper, now partially hidden by his longer than usual hair.

"I can't wait to try it out, proper like!"

Joining Vince in the Comms Centre, Dick asked, "Give us the bad news Vince."

The ex-navy Communicator scratched his head.

"Well, I reckon you already knew that most of the communications are stuffed after the holocaust."

Looking puzzled, Dick exclaimed, "Most!"

Vince filled the pair in about what he had found.

"Well yeah! The FCPB's had an analogue system fitted when they were first built; aerial and amplifier are both still good."

Thinking sideways, Dick asked, "Could we plug my brick phone into her amp and aerial Vince?"

"Don't see why not mate. What did you have in mind?"

Dick went on to explain about Doc and his obsession with the old phones; he hadn't had much luck getting out and thought the boosted signal might help.

As they headed ashore in the RHIB, Dick asked, "Did you serve on the FCPB's mate?"

Vince replied with a laugh.

"Yep, sure did! Even did time on this one!"

Dick was smiling, so was Jack.

"Great mate! Welcome to the crew of the *Fremantle*."

Once back in camp, Laurel and Vince went for a swim. Sarge called Dick aside.

"Watch your back Dick!"

"In which way mate?"

Sarge told Dick about the challenge from Laurel and warned that it might get uglier if Vince happened to think the same way.

The 61-year-old nodded.

"Thanks for the heads-up mate."

He knew what the ex-Sapper meant, and decided to file the warning away for future reference.

Patch looked at Dick.

"What time are you going to leave Love?"

"Well Chook, I reckon late this afternoon. Don't want to delay it any further with April's wound the way it is."

Vince, fresh from his swim, asked what the plan was.

Sarge pointed to Dick and the ex-CD explained the way they saw it unfolding.

"We'll leave at 1600. Kings Town is 120 nautical miles from here; at 15 knots it will take us 8 hours, putting us in Kings Town Harbour at around midnight.

"They are expecting the 203 to turn up at some stage, so won't be too concerned when we do. I'll try and get us close to the Chook Point Marina, then we'll tie up while Vince and I slip up to Doc's place. Let's hope he's home!

"I'm hoping that he will have the appropriate supplies needed for April's operation. Depending on how things go along the way we might see if we can re-fuel either out of the tank at the marina, or if this has been sucked dry, even up at Fel's Point.

"Just in case we can't, how are we off for fuel usage at that speed Jack?"

"10,000 litres should give us 25 hours; at full noise 30 knots."

Jack continued, "So at 15 knots, we will have better than 50 hours' steaming time; good for a few trips in and out if necessary."

Vince asked, "Who's going Dick?"

Vince was still trying to come to terms with the knowledge that Dick seemed to be making all the decisions.

Dick replied, "Jack in the Engine Room, you on comms and .50 calibre, and me on the wheel; although, apart from Jack, we'll both do a trick on the wheel. If we get into a scrap, you can take the wheel while I operate the 40-60."

Pushing a bit further, Vince asked, "Can Laurel come? She's a good Communicator and could be handy if we have to run lights or flags."

Dick couldn't see any problems with this and said yes; he could already see Sarge smiling, knowing that she would be out of people's way if she was on the boat.

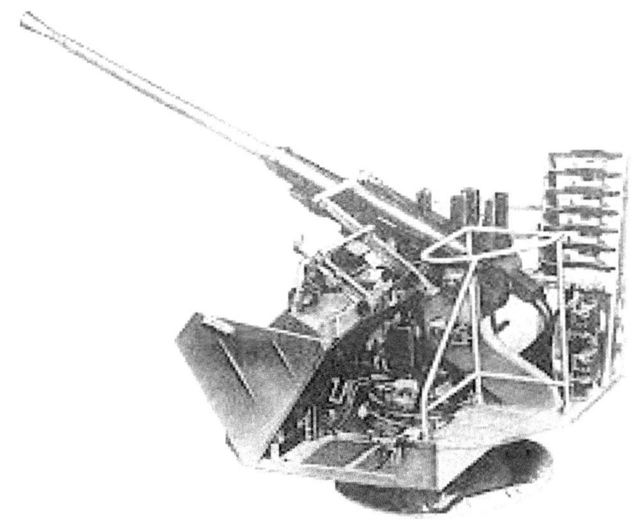

Mk 7 40-60 Bofors

Chapter 7
The Bradley Story

Monday 5ᵗʰ January 2015 ... Vince and Laurel Bradley's Property, Old River Road

Getting to the driveway, it was obvious to the ex-Pussers Communication Technician, that the old Bedford look alike truck was definitely not one of their neighbours. The officer on the running board brandishing his Type 54 pistol was a dead giveaway.

Vince made it to the back door under a hail of bullets; grabbing his .243 deer rifle inside the door, he yelled at Laurel to duck. He hit the driver first, killing him instantly. The .243 round entered the trooper's neck at the larynx, and he bled out immediately.

Killer, Laurel's German shepherd took to the officer as he dismounted from the running board, dragging him to the ground. Killer was shot by a trooper emerging from the truck's canopy, but not before he tore the officer's throat out.

Vince got his next shot off as Laurel made it back to the house. This shot connected with the last trooper, hitting him in the chest. This left the one who'd disposed of Killer still aggressively firing his Type 68 assault rifle at the pair.

Laurel was hopping mad at the death of Killer; she grabbed her snake gun, the double barrelled 12-gauge shotgun. As the trooper appeared from behind the bird aviary, she let him have both barrels.

Vince quickly checked the bodies; thinking fast he remembered what Dick had said. This was obviously a kill squad, which meant a clean-up squad was going to follow.

"Shit Laurel! Let's get these bodies out of sight and ditch the truck."

Laurel dragged the bodies into the duck pond while Vince drove the truck behind the shearing shed.

"What are we going to do now Vince?"

"I reckon the only thing we can do is for me to finish the motor rebuild on my bike, and we get the hell out of here."

Vince had been working on a pre-2000 motorbike engine and was almost ready to install it into his 900 Yamaha.

"You work while I get some stuff together Vince."

One hour later he was still no further advanced. Defeated for now, Vince suggested,

"Can't take the risk of staying here. Let's load all the tools and the bike on to their truck and disappear up into forestry so I can work on the bike."

Twenty minutes later they were up on top of Poultry Hill looking down on their farm. Vince pointed to the farmhouse.

"Lucky we moved when we did Laurel! Here comes the clean-up crew."

It didn't take them long to find the bodies and set about sweeping the farm.

"All the more incentive to finish the bike," said Vince as he started work again. Exactly one hour later he fired up the aging 900 Yammy.

The sound of the bike starting gave their position away. With the troopers closing in fast, Laurel strapped the swag on to the back of the bike. The saddlebags were already full of tucker; they set off down the bottom track just as the troopers appeared. Vince yelled over the exhaust,

"Shit that was close Laurel!"

Gripping her husband even tighter she agreed.

"Not wrong there Vince! Where are we off to?"

Vince went on to explain the conversation he'd had with Dick and Patch earlier.

"Do you know where this Hells Beach is Vince?"

"I've got a rough idea."

They only made it about a kilometre before the bike gave up the ghost.

"Bloody hell! This is the wrong time for this to happen."

After pushing the bike off the track, Vince started stripping the engine down.

"You keep guard Laurel; this could take a while."

Tuesday 6th January 2015 ... Twaddle State Forest

Vince spent most of the day working on the bike, while Laurel kept him fed and hydrated. The only conversation was an occasional swear word and a lot of mumbling. From the vehicle sounds, it looked like the Alliance clean-up squad had given up with their chase. Towards the evening Vince announced that he thought he had fixed the bike but needed some oil before he fired it up. Laurel stood with her arms crossed and looked at him.

"And just where are we going to get that from Vince?"

Vince, already detecting some agro in her voice, answered, "There's a farm on the other side of the hill Laurel; I'll get it in the morning."

0610 Wednesday 7ᵗʰ January 2015 ... Twaddle State Forest

And what a shitty night the pair had; trying to squeeze into a single swag and having to move a couple of times because of the leeches. Vince yawned, folding back the weather flap to reveal a damp morning.

"I'll get a move on Laurel; do you want to come with me?"

Laurel was only half awake.

"How far is it Vince?"

"Not far, probably 5 kilometres. In this terrain it should take us about two hours, although I'm not sure what to expect when we get there!"

After a breakfast of cold meat, the pair made their way up the tail end of Poultry Hill. Laurel, who was finding the slope a problem, grumbled the whole way. The dampness underfoot didn't help. The track brought them out on the Old River Road to Meed-Stead Road junction, overlooking the back of a farm.

Vince stepped over the fence.

"You stay here Laurel and I'll take a look in that shed."

Carefully moving forward, Vince was fully aware that he was becoming more visible by the second. He shouldered the .243, scanning the back of the farm through the scope for movement. The machinery shed was a mess; it looked like the Alliance had torn through it like a tornado. There were upended paint tins, old car parts pulled off the benches, and tools everywhere.

At one time this would have been a pretty tidy shed, thought Vince, finally spying what he was looking for: a 4-litre container of two stroke engine oil.

"Perfect," he murmured.

As he secured the container, he was alerted by a noise coming from the little shed next door. Before he could exit the way he'd come in, the door between the two sheds opened, and before him stood two kids. They couldn't have been more than five or six years old.

His mind went into overdrive. 'Do I shoot them? Do I just run?'

What he did do was to put his finger up to his lips, as if to say 'shush'. He pointed for them to go back into the next shed, and then shut the door behind them before running flat out; clearing the little fence surrounding the house yard without even noticing it.

"Let's get the fuck out of here Laurel!"

"What's up Vince?"

"I was seen by a couple of gook kids," panted Vince.

"You didn't shoot them?"

"No! I didn't shoot them! It all happened a bit quick. I told them to piss off and then I bolted."

It took them till around lunch time to make it back to the bike; mainly because Vince took a wrong turn, taking the left track instead of the right. He quickly set to filling the engine up with oil.

They got under way at 1300. It felt good to finally be moving again, although they were not all that confident about which track to take. If they'd taken the D2, and ultimately the Red Mountain track, they would have been able to give the farms a wide berth, but they missed them both, and ended up at the end of the D Road.

"Which way Vince? Where is this beach again?"

Vince, who was becoming more and more annoyed with her digging, blurted out, "It's called Hells Beach! I think Dick said they got to it from Willy Town."

Laurel, who was trying to get a handle on just how lost they were, asked, "And the quickest way there would be?"

Vince, figuring he'd worked it out, answered, "Probably through Oxford and on the Oxford Bronze Road. We'll have to go through Bulldust and then Oxford; could get a bit hairy Laurel!"

She smiled.

"What, you mean? Hairier than troopers shooting at us and killing our dog?"

He gave in with a sigh. "No, not really."

After turning left, they only had to travel half a kilometre to the back Bulldust Road turnoff; this would eventually bring them out on the Bulldust Road. They would be passing about two dozen farms, with the first three being overrun with activity; there were NK Nationals everywhere. Vince thought it better to wait till dark, and then try and get to Willy Town before daybreak.

0018 Thursday 8th January 2015 ... D Road, Meed-Stead Road Junction

"Shit! Are these bastards ever going to bed?"

"It looks like the noise has subsided Laurel."

Vince and Laurel had been waiting since dark for the new occupants to go to bed. He clunked the 900 into gear and advanced to the turn; it was two clicks till the next farm. Slowing down, they could see no form of activity. They continued on, travelling past the rest of the properties and on to the approach to Bulldust.

"Well here goes nothing Laurel."

Vince gave the big bike some stick, and before Laurel knew it they were travelling along at well over 130 kilometres an hour. Laurel was used to this, but with the addition of the swag and the bags on board, the aerodynamics were not quite right.

At that speed it didn't take the two ex-Pussers long to get through the dangerous area alongside the Oxford River. They found themselves in downtown Oxford at 0330; the streets were pretty quiet. Turning right at the bridge, they headed out of town and to the Oxford to Bronze Road. Vince was now sure of which way they were going.

"Got about 50 kilometres to go to Willy Town Laurel."

Laurel was still not certain he knew the way.

"Do you know where the turnoff is?"

"On the left, just at the town. Well, that's where Dick used to go. Then we follow the forestry tracks to the coast."

After slowing down to avoid getting hit in the ribs again, Vince kept the bike at a reasonable 70 kilometres an hour. For a very loose gravel road this was plenty fast enough. Just before 0500 they stumbled upon the nearly hidden Willy Town.

"Shit! Nearly missed it," swore Vince as he pulled the bike to a stop, sliding in the gravel just a bit.

"What's with the punch in the ribs Laurel?"

"You know I don't like it when we lose traction in the dirt! Remember the last time when you dropped it!"

Vince did remember; they'd been touring on the mainland. Coming off the bitumen at 120 clicks he'd hit the dirt, which would have been fine if, in a momentary lapse of concentration, he hadn't forgotten he had Laurel on the back.

He had not anticipated her added weight when entering the turn. As he headed up the nearest track the ex-navy Communications expert, cringing a little, replied, "Yep! I remember Laurel!"

The partially overgrown forestry track was slow going and there were lots of holes. In some places it was not really passable for a large road bike.

"Should've bought the dirt bike," grinned Vince as he narrowly avoided yet another trench dug across the track.

Forging their way through the state forest toward the coast, at times they had to dismount and walk the bike over the obstacles. They eventually reached the coast at 0835. Unbeknownst to them they were 20 kilometres further north, having taken a wrong turn up a non-existent track.

This was because Vince just took the path that he could negotiate the bike over; not really thinking to follow the hoof prints.

"It's no good Laurel, we'll have to turn around!"

Laurel, who was feeling more confused than before, asked, "Which way then Vince?"

"We'll go back to Willy Town, wait just outside till dark and then turn left. I know the road eventually comes out at Bronze, but I haven't driven it, so who knows what we'll find along the way."

"You look buggered Vince. We should get some sleep."

"A good feed wouldn't go astray either!"

"Sorry," Laurel replied. "The only food we have is some tinned fish and a few cold chops."

Friday 9th January 2015 ... Forestry track outside Willy Town

Vince was dreaming of playing ice hockey. Just as he scored the winning goal he was slammed into the fence.

"Wake up Vince!"

Realising it was Laurel shaking him, he came to, crying, "Bloody hell! You're a bit rough Laurel."

She was mad.

"A bit rough! I've been shaking you for five minutes; its already 0200!"

"Shit! We must have been more tired than we thought."

The weather was cold and misty, and it was drizzling with rain. The previous few wet days had left the road very slippery, with a layer of soft mud some 100mm thick. This made the bike slide from side to side and meant speed was down as low as 20 kilometres per hour.

"What's happening Vince?" enquired Laurel as the 900 Yamaha's lights dropped out.

"Shit Laurel! I don't fucking know!"

Pulling up he rummaged through the bags, trying to find the torch.

"Where did you put it?"

After thinking hard for a minute, Laurel smirked, "Shit Vince, I think I left it on the side of the track where we slept so I could go to the heads during the night."

"Bloody lovely! How am I supposed to fix the bike if I can't see?"

Beginning to crack, the ex-navy Communicator spat back.

"Don't yell at me! It's not my fault I forgot, all right? Life's a bit stressful you know!"

After pushing the bike off the track, they waited till full light to have a look at the problem.

"Looks like the globe assembly has vibrated out of the fitting."

"Can you put it back in?"

Vince, who was feeling just a little annoyed with the whole thing advised her, "No! It's smashed the globe, meaning we can only travel in daylight. Otherwise, we run the risk of travelling these dirt roads at night with no lights."

It was now 1000. Giving up, they continued on. As they slowly made their way round a corner, they were confronted by two NK Nationals and one Alliance trooper standing square in the middle of the road. They startled the trio as they rode through the middle of them; it didn't take the trooper long to shoulder his weapon and get a few rounds off.

Behind them they could hear numerous shouts, and what they assumed to be abuse coming from the two NK Nationals and their guard as Vince gunned the 900 gingerly in the mud and rounded the next bend.

"Glad they don't have any vehicles!"

"You're not wrong there Laurel!"

Up in front, Vince could make out a vehicle pulled up on the side of the road. As they got closer the pair could see it was a hire camper.

"Must have been exploring when the E1 hit Laurel."

Stopping the bike, they carefully peered inside.

"Yep! It's just the way they left it. Must have legged it up the road; they obviously didn't even know what happened. I reckon they were camped here on the side of the road for the night, they probably woke up the next morning and just thought it was a breakdown."

After putting the kettle on the little gas stove inside the camper, Laurel made them both a drink.

Handing the steaming coffee to Vince, she told him, "They have a fully stocked pantry, although the fresh stuff is obviously no good now. We can sure make use of some of the staples though."

Vince just nodded, not really listening. His brain wasn't functioning properly; he was frozen to the core and cupped the hot drink with both hands. He'd reached the point where he just didn't care.

"I'm just panging for a hot drink; seems like a month since the last one."

Both of them were enjoying the warmth of the cuppa, accompanied by a handful of biscuits. Laurel scrounged up a few things to take with them, a kettle, matches, tea, sugar, biscuits, instant noodles, spaghetti and some tinned baked beans. Vince loaded it all into a saddle bag.

"Shit! We won't know ourselves Vince. We should be able to make a feast now, as long as we can light a fire."

Their thoughts were disturbed by the now familiar sound of the look a-like Bedford truck coming up behind them.

"Looks like we spoke too soon Vince!"

They only just made it into the bushes in time. From their hiding place they watched the truck come to a halt alongside the camper. After dismounting from the cab, one of the troopers inspected the vehicle before lifting the fuel lid and giving it a smell. After yelling something at the others, he rifled around inside again. He must have touched the gas stove and realised it was still hot. After emerging from the camper, he pulled the pin on a grenade, then jumped back on board the truck as it continued down the road, in hot pursuit of the Taswegian bike.

'Whoomph!'

The camper was quickly reduced to a smoking pile of tin and ashes. Vince pointed out the obvious.

"Shit! It won't take them long to realise we're not in front of them."

Vince and Laurel waited about half an hour and then headed off after them. With no side tracks to divert into, they were stuck; the only way was to either keep going forward, or turn around and go all the way back through Willy Town, Oxford, Bulldust, Meed-Stead, Soothe and eventually on to Bronze.

"It's too far Laurel, and way too risky. I suggest we keep going and deal with any trouble when we find it."

The trouble with trouble is that it has a way of finding you when you don't want it to; and that's what happened, not 5 kilometres down the road. It looked like the truck had stopped in the middle of the road; its occupants were obviously clearing a property. The sound of gunfire was loud and rapid, accompanied by yelling and a few screams. Vince thought he could detect return fire.

"That sounds like a 12-gauge Laurel."

Laurel, who was feeling just a little scared asked, "What will we do Vince?"

"We could stop and join the fire fight, although that's probably not a good idea. Or we could use the distraction to speed past. hoping they will be kept busy long enough for us to do this."

"Let's do that Vince."

They moved slowly towards the truck. All went well until the troopers, who had obviously killed the occupants of the farm, saw the ex-Pussers on the bike whilst returning to the truck.

This bought a hail of bullets in their direction. Vince felt one hit his motorcycle boot and take a graze out of the side at about ankle level.

"Shit!" Laurel exclaimed, as one round came a little too close for her liking, leaving a bloody trench in her shoulder and hitting the bike's right-hand side rear view mirror.

"You all right Laurel?"

Feeling blood running down her shoulder, she replied breathlessly, "I'll live!"

Just as they rounded the next bend, the pair ran out of petrol.

"We're not having a good run Laurel!"

As they pushed the bike off the road, they could see the next property a click in front of them.

Vince suggested, "We'll get some fuel there."

Laurel was more concerned about what they could hear coming up behind them.

"Shit! Here comes the truck again Vince!"

They helplessly watched the kill squad as it moved on down the road to the farm.

"Poor bastards don't know what is about to hit them Laurel!"

It didn't take the troopers long to clear the farm; just three shots. After spray painting a cross onto the farm ute, they sped off.

"What do you reckon they did that for Vince?"

Vince, using his logical brain as usual, suggested,,"I reckon they've marked it for diesel collection. We'd better get there quickly, just in case the clean-up squad is fast on their heels."

Vince and Laurel pushed the bike to the farm. Upon inspection they found the now-dead occupants, an old couple still sitting in their chairs; the family dog had been shot at their feet.

"Bloody bastards," Vince whispered to himself as he scavenged through the owners' shed.

Finding a drum of what looked like chainsaw fuel he yelled out, "She will run a bit smoky, but what the hell!"

While Laurel grabbed some extra food, Vince got the 900 operational again.

"You know we could run into them again Laurel," he warned.

"Shit! Here comes another one!"

This of course was the clean-up squad. The pair took off, attracting a few more bullets as they tore down the road.

Over the roar of the bike, Vince yelled back at his wife, "This is a real nigger's bum Laurel; we're caught in-between both of them!"

They pulled off the road at 1945. Laurel, who was feeling near exhausted, asked, "What do you reckon about lighting a fire?"

After thinking about the possible consequences, Vince answered with a shake of his head.

"Might wait an hour. If the clean-up crew hasn't passed us by, then it's probably not going to tonight, so we will light one then."

Dinner, courtesy of the camper, was a concoction of instant noodles and tinned baked beans, along with a few herbs and spices Laurel had packed from home; tossed in with some tinned fish. Later, as they lay there in their swag, the pair recapped on the events of the past seven days.

Laurel was the first to say what they were both thinking.

"I don't believe that it's really happened; it all seems like some kind of bloodthirsty dream."

Vince was thinking he should have taken his neighbour up on their offer.

"Yeah! I thought Dick and Patch were pulling my leg when they came over. I feel really bad about the way I reacted; looks like they were genuine about the whole thing."

Laurel looked at her husband, asking, "Do you reckon Dick's plan will work?"

"At the moment Laurel, any plan is better than none!"

Changing the subject, he added, "If the fire's hot enough, do you want another tea?"

"Yes please!"

0723 Saturday 10ᵗʰ January 2015 ... Willy Town to Bronze Road

It was like Pitt Street; each time Vince and Laurel tried to get the bike out onto the road, another truck would go by. There wasn't much time to look, but they assumed the first one was the clean-up squad, then realised that one coming the other way could have been the same truck.

Laurel exclaimed in frustration, "Geez! I'd kill for a cuppa!"

Vince was concentrating on the road.

"You know we can't risk it Laurel."

The pair were stuck; they sat there in the bushes for most of the day. It was late afternoon before they worked out the reason for the traffic; it was the clean-up squad taking bodies back to a dumpsite near Willy Town.

Laurel looked at Vince.

"All this traffic means there must have been a lot of people in the farms in front of us."

The ex-navy Technician agreed.

"It would seem so Laurel; I didn't really know how many farms were in front of us."

They spent another night in the same spot, too scared to make a move.

Vince's stomach was groaning.

"What's for scran Laurel?"

Laurel looked through their supplies.

"Well Vince, once again we'll be eating courtesy of the camper; this time it's tinned spaghetti with tinned snags thrown in."

"Great!"

Vince decided he'd had enough.

"Let's make a move Laurel."

After rolling up their swag, Laurel tied it onto the Yammy. Carefully, they moved off into the early morning frost. The pair travelled a couple of wind-chilled kilometres before coming across the first farm. All was quiet now; the only evidence of anything that might have gone on was the sight of a few blood stains in the kitchen, as well as just outside the front door.

After helping themselves to more food, they continued on their journey.

It wasn't far to the next farm, and they found almost the same scenario there, except that there was evidence that the gunfight had been even bloodier. Vince came to this conclusion because of the shell casings on the ground. A mixture of 12-gauge and the Alliance Type 68 assault rifles had left plenty of 7.62mm casings; this weapon was a common modernised variant of the AK 47 rifle and had been developed in the 1940s.

"Shit! There has to be a hundred casings!"

Laurel nodded, adding, "And based on the amount of times the truck went backwards and forwards, there must have been a lot of bodies too."

Vince nodded, sadly agreeing with her.

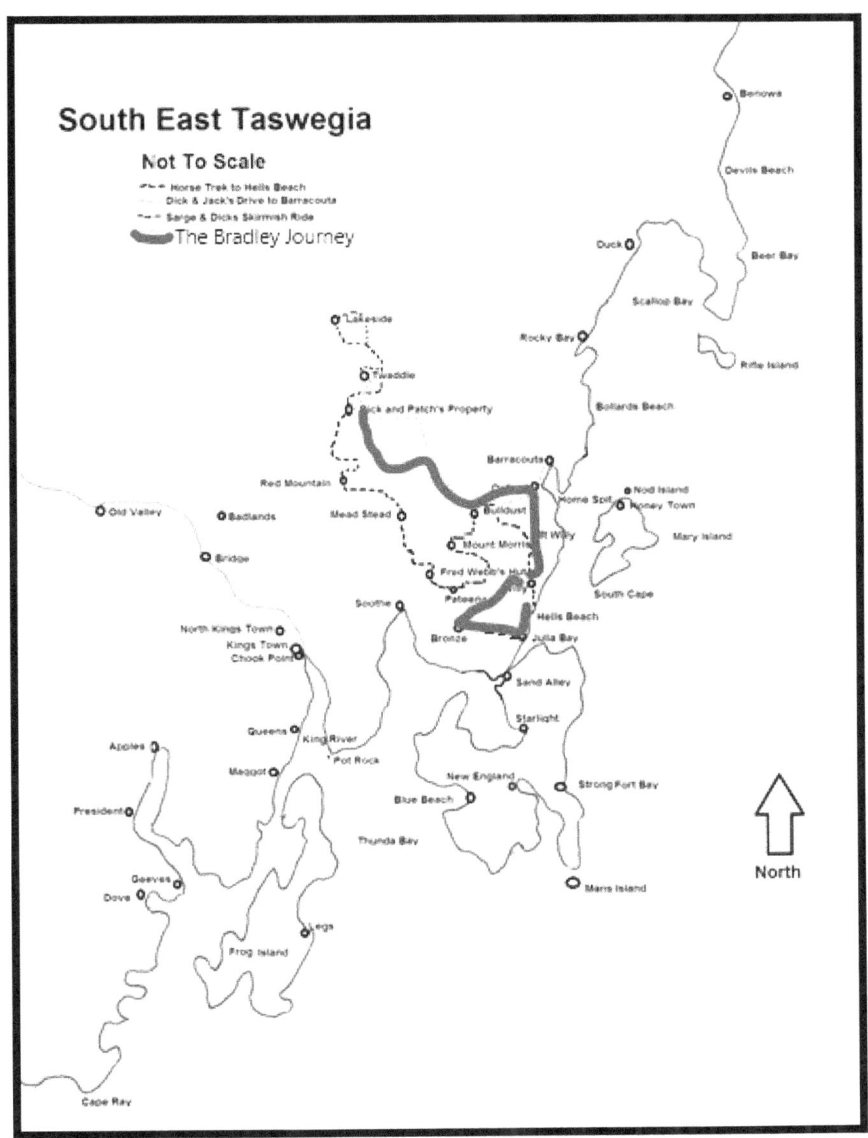

Vince and Laurel Bradley's journey
0502 Sunday 11th January 2015 ... Willy Town to Bronze Road

"Those poor bastards didn't stand a chance against trained soldiers."

As they travelled further down the road, Laurel leant in close.

"Do you think we stand a chance against trained soldiers?"

Vince laughed.

"Shit yeah Laurel! That's because we have our own trained soldiers."

"What? Do you mean Dick and his mate Jack? And that bushman, what do they call him, 'Sarge'?"

Vince took a little time to fill his wife in about just who they were going to be meeting up with.

"Dick was a Clearance Diver, specialising in covert operations in Nam, sort of like a SAS Specialist. I googled his old team. Quite the explosives expert is our Dick!

"And Jack was also a CD, except this bloke was a Specialist Sniper. Served in the Ghan, and holds, or should I say did hold, the longest confirmed kill for a sniper in the world. All I know about Sarge is that he was a Sergeant Sapper."

Laurel was quite impressed with the bios.

"You mean like an Engineer? Blowing shit up and stuff?"

"Yep, you got it!"

"Well Vince, I feel safer already. How far to go now?"

She hugged her man tightly as they continued, wondering who'd thought of making a record of the longest kill by a sniper.

Smiling Vince added, "He's a member of what they call, The Mile Club. His kill was logged at 2815 metres; it well and truly qualified."

Vince frowned.

"I need more fuel Laurel! The bloody bike seems to be going through it like I don't know what!"

Pointing to a building just ahead of them, he added,

"Looks like we're almost at the next farm."

It had started to rain harder and harder, and by now the pair were saturated.

Vince asked with a bit of a shiver, "Didn't think to pack a coat Laurel?"

Looking somewhat like a drowned rat Laurel spat back, "Well, we didn't have much time to think about it Vince!"

After stopping at the next farm, Vince pushed the bike around the back and into a shed. He grunted with satisfaction when he came across a stash of fuel after a short search. This time it was straight unleaded. 'Great,' he thought to himself, no more smoking.

After shutting the shed door firmly behind him, he made his way into the house and placed the .243 and shotgun on the kitchen table before quickly surveying the rest of the house. Once again, he found some signs of resistance; there were shell casings outside, as well as a few .22 cases inside.

Laurel had been rummaging through the cupboards in the kitchen; after sourcing some food she put the kettle on, then lit a fire in the open kitchen fireplace while admiring the ornate brick hearth with its Blackwood mantel piece.

The pair stripped off and hung their clothes over the fire guard in front of the fire to dry. Among other things, Laurel had found some vegetables and half a chicken, and after making sure the bird had not gone off, she quickly put some dinner together while Vince went to get a couple of warm beers which he'd found stored in a cupboard in the hall.

"It's home brew Love; looks like he bottles them in long necks."

"I think we'll risk staying here tonight. I'll set the watch alarm for 0600; based on what happened yesterday, hopefully they won't be back before then."

0200 Monday 12ᵗʰ January 2015 ... Reynolds' Property, Willy Town to Bronze Road

Vince woke to find Laurel shivering; the main bedroom sported a grand old queen size bed, but there wasn't much linen on the bed. The fire had done its job; they'd both been feeling toasty when they retired, but now that the temperature had dropped, she was freezing. Vince scrounged around, finding a couple of bedspreads in the second bedroom.

It was still raining heavily outside. After placing another couple of pieces of wood on the fire in the kitchen he returned to bed. It wasn't often they went to bed stark naked; but then it wasn't often they had to dry the only clothes they had with them either. Slipping under the covers and snuggling into Laurel, Vince warmed her up the best way he could. They both fell back into a deep sleep.

Waking suddenly, Vince yawned.

"Shit! It's 0600 and still raining! I slept like a log Laurel."

She agreed.

"Yeah, me too. It must have been the company!"

Laurel had one hell of a smile on her face as she added, "I'll see if I can rustle us both up a decent breakfast."

Vince thought it would be a good idea to make sure the old girl would start after all the trouble they'd had the day before. After pulling on his rather smoky dry clothes, Vince ran outside to the shed and started up the bike before going on the hunt for some wet weather gear.

"Come and get it," yelled Laurel from the house. "Eggs, ham and stale bread turned into toast."

As he headed back into the kitchen, Vince sniffed the air in appreciation.

"Geez that smells divine Laurel! Look what I scrounged!"

He triumphantly showed her an old oilskin coat and an old bluey, concluding, "I reckon the oilskin will fit you, and I should be able to squeeze into the bluey if I don't do it up."

"What do you reckon he had the bluey for Vince?"

"Looks like it was an old PMG issue. They are as tough as nails; pure wool, tight weave, heavy and waterproof."

Dressed in her new attire Laurel climbed on board the Yammy while it was still in the shed. Peering through the open doorway Vince exclaimed in his usual logical way, "Looks like it's still pissing down Laurel!"

"No shit Sherlock! Let's hope the Alliance don't work on rainy days."

"Better still," retorted her husband, "let's hope we come across some live Taswegians!"

It was 0730 by the time they set off; the Yammy spluttered a bit as they made their way down the road, although that didn't worry Laurel, who was crouched behind Vince, with her head down and pressed hard up against his back. Vince was finding it hard to see. They were riding into the weather; the raindrops felt more like tiny hail stones as they hit the ex-navy Communications expert in the face.

"Wish we'd had time to find the helmets before we left Laurel!"

Laurel laughed.

"Now that was a great idea Vince! Why didn't I think of that!"

Laurel grinned to herself; still digesting the events of the past week, and thinking to herself, 'Cripes! Is that all it's been!' She didn't want to think about the rest of their families on the mainland, or rather, what might have been left of them.

Vince whinged in disgust.

"It's no good Laurel! This is bullshit; I can't see a thing. We'll have to look for a spot to pull over."

As they coasted down a bit of a hill, they could see the next property gate coming up on the right.

"Can't see the house; maybe that's a good sign they might still be intact."

Laurel looked at the ex-pusser with that, 'Do you reckon?' look.

"Well maybe not!"

After riding up the drive for some 400 metres they came across an old weatherboard farmhouse. As was the usual case with old buildings, the paint was not weathering too well, and was peeling off all over the place. The house had probably been built in the 1930's. There was evidence the kill squad truck had been there also; there were tyre tracks everywhere, although there were no obvious signs of bloodshed.

Vince rode the bike around the back, pulling up under a carport.

Thankful to finally be out of the rain, Laurel said to him, "Bloody hell! That's better Vince."

He agreed.

"Yeah! No rain under here Laurel."

After turning the Yammy off, Vince shook off what water he could as he took off his ill-fitting bluey. His legs were saturated, along with a strip down the front where the jacket didn't quite do up. Hanging it up under cover, he turned to his wife.

"You stay here Laurel while I reccy the place."

Laurel peeled off the aging oilskin coat and did the same, thinking to herself that it must have been really old; it was obvious that any waterproofing it might once have had was long gone now!

After entering the house by the back door, Vince found himself in a little back room, a sort of lean-to full of boots and coats. He thought for a minute about removing his boots but thought better of it.

Like most old houses of this era, the ceilings were 10 or 12 feet high, except for where the lean-to had been added much later. The original back door opened up into a hallway; the first room he found to his left was the toilet. This was an antique by today's standards, with the cast iron header tank high up on the wall above a newish porcelain bowl. Vince moved the .243 to the ready position, keeping his finger lightly resting on the trigger guard. He'd never forgotten his weapons training; 'only put your finger on the trigger when you want to use it!'

The bathroom was on the right; a bit like the toilet it was a combination of old and new, with a claw foot ornate cast iron bath alongside a modern vanity. Then came the main lounge room, where he was confronted by the sight of the first body; a male aged around 60, who'd been killed by a good working over with a bayonet.

To his right was the large kitchen/dining room. One of the windows from this room overlooked the driveway while the one at the rear overlooked the lean-to.

There were signs of blood on the kitchen table, which was an ornate Baltic pine table measuring eight feet long and surrounded by no less than twenty chairs. 'Bet this has seen some family gatherings' he thought as he carefully made his way to the bedrooms. These all ran off the hallway; in front of him he could see six doorways.

The first door led into what had once been a bedroom but was now just a storeroom. Next came a bedroom with twin single beds; the decoration would suggest it was a girl's bedroom. Next the mirror image of this in a boy's theme, followed by a double guest room with plain décor and no personal belongings. He wished he hadn't seen the next room, the second last. The old lady was obviously bedridden; he put her age at about eighty.

They'd used her as a pin cushion, repeatedly stabbing her with their type 68 bayonets.

He almost vomited at the sight and didn't really want to look at the last and master bedroom, which was at the front of the house and alongside the front door. However, he knew he had to. He was horrified to find the body of a woman who he assumed was the lady of the house, stripped naked and tied spread eagled across the queen-sized bed. After, or possibly while they were having fun with her, they had cut off the woman's nipples and butchered her genitals.

He wrapped the woman's body in the blanket that was on the bed. He was doing the same to the old lady next door, when he heard Laurel coming in the back door.

"What's taking so long Vince?"

"Wouldn't look in there Laurel! It's a bit blood thirsty!"

Hearing the urgency in Vince's voice she decided to take his word for it, and asked, "What will we do with the bodies?"

"The problem is the clean-up crew will be here soon; probably today. Things could get quite confrontational, especially if we're still here."

Laurel pushed the point.

"So, what do you want to do?"

After thinking about all their options, Vince finally decided.

"There are three choices the way I see it. We could leave now, and still end up wet and in-between the two crews. We could move the bodies out the front and heap them up somewhere down the driveway. Maybe they will be dumb enough to think the kill squad has done that for them. The final choice is to wait and ambush them."

His wife asked, "How many do you think will turn up Vince?"

"Based on what we have seen so far, I reckon three or four troopers at most."

"Do you think we can kill them before they get reinforcements?"

"Maybe. We have your 12 gauge and my .243, and I've got around twenty-two rounds left. How many have you got?"

"Half a belt full Vince; that's twelve."

After deciding to move the bodies out the front, the pair used the blankets to lift them. Taking them the 400 metres to the front gate was quite a chore.

"We can't leave them in the blankets Laurel," said Vince, rolling them out onto the verge.

Laurel fe t violently ill at the sight and had to make a dash into the scrub inside the gate to throw up.

"That's disgusting Vince."

Vince couldn't bring himself to comment, knowing full well that if they were cornered that could well be the way they would end up.

After throwing the used blankets and bloody sheets into a bin out the back and thoroughly washing his hands, Vince set up a watching post at the front of the lounge room, opening the window six inches, which would give them just enough room to push the weapons through if necessary. Laurel found enough food to put together a feed. Vince, who'd discovered a welcome surprise in the bathroom, yelled out,

"Look at this Laurel! The old fellow has rigged up a twelve-volt caravan pump to run the shower. Looks like its gas as well!"

"You bloody beauty Vince; I'd kill for a hot shower!"

"Hold that thought; you might just have to!"

By now it was nearly 1030. Vince kept guard while Laurel had her first proper hot shower since the Holocaust. They hung their wet clothes over the gas hot water system that just happened to be situated in the lean-to room.

"We can't run the risk of a fire yet, just in case they see it."

At 1145 Laurel took up position at the front window while Vince enjoyed his shower; the hot water was almost to the point of causing pain, but it sure took the sting out of his cold body.

"Are you hungry Vince?"

Laurel had heard him turn off the water, and by the time Vince appeared in the kitchen doorway, she was sorting out some food on the gas stove. Vince gave his usual reply,

"I could eat the crutch out of a low flying duck, Laurel!"

After heating what appeared to be a lamb casserole, Laurel added boiled spuds and carrots to the feed. They ate while sitting on the big plush lounge suite and washed it all down with a cuppa. Vince, patting his bulging stomach, belched loudly.

"Bloody top feed Laurel."

Laurel responded, "My pleasure Vin ...," pausing as she heard a noise coming from the front of the house. "What's that? Can you hear that?"

It sounded like the clean-up truck was changing down in gears as it approached the driveway, and the spot where they'd dropped the bodies. They knew it would have to stop and move them first before making its way up the driveway. With the rain easing they could first hear chatter, but then ... silence. Vince was the first to speak.

"They're loading the bodies I reckon!"

The Kia-built Bedford started up and drove along the road. Laurel was ecstatic.

"Dickheads fell for it!"

"Well, it's about time things went our way."

After spending the afternoon inside enjoying the break, Vince decided to take the risk and light the fire in the wood heater. It was already set and just needed a match. Vince went scrounging again, finding half a box of 12-gauge shells, as well as the matches he was looking for.

"What number 12-gauge?"

"Couldn't see one Laurel. I reckon it's worn off with age."

After deciding to stay there until the rain subsided, they made themselves comfortable. It didn't take the wood heater long to heat up the room and for their wet clothes to finish drying. Laurel boiled some spuds, mashing them well, then added a couple of tins of fish and an onion to make fish patties. Carrots and dried peas accompanied them, finishing off the feast nicely. All Vince could find, alcohol wise, was an old bottle of unopened tawny port.

Pouring a couple of shots, he said, "Probably a gift."

Laurel was still trying to get her head around things.

"Do you reckon they suffered Vince?"

Vince spluttered, nearly choking on his port.

"Don't think we'll go there Laurel!"

Tuesday 13th January 2015 ... Granger Property on the Willy Town to Bronze Road

Their breakfast over, the pair headed off at 0700. The weather was a lot better, with no rain, a clear sky and just a light breeze. They passed three more properties but didn't bother to go in and investigate. They wanted to get past Bronze and on their way to Julia Bay.

They say all good things come to an end and this was the day! As they approached the junction with the main Peninsular highway, they could see a constant stream of traffic heading south.

"Must be the NK Nationals being deposited into homes. There's got to be twenty trucks, and five or six jeeps."

Vince brought the 900 to a stop but miscalculated the grab of the brakes. The bike skidded, and because of the added load on the back he dropped it. The sound of the motor revving up as that happened caught the attention of two truck drivers who were having a chat while they were waiting at the junction.

Vince scrambled to get the bike upright, yelling, "Shit, they've seen us!"

It seemed to take forever for Laurel to get her gravel-rashed leg cocked over the swag, but she finally did it. Vince mounted the bike.

As he started it up, he dropped the clutch on the Xj900. Then they were off, with bullets again whistling past the pair as they accelerated back the way they had come. Vince could hear the truck clunking through its third gear change, thankful that he knew they would have no way of catching the much faster bike. It was all he could do to resist wheel-standing the Yammy but thought better of it because of Laurel sitting on the back. It took no time at all before they found themselves pulling up where they'd started.

Vince grunted breathlessly, "We'll make a stand here!"

After dropping Laurel off to hide in the native bushes near the front of the house, he left the bike in full view in the carport and skirted around the other side in typical ambush formation. The plan was simple. He would wait for them to get out of the truck and then fire; any retreaters would be covered by Laurel's 12-gauge.

Vince had not seen action in his career. Well not like this anyway. He'd been on a couple of boarding parties in the Gulf War but compared to what was happening now, they seemed pretty lame. He found himself breathing quite erratically, and the adrenaline was pumping wildly. He hadn't felt this sensation before, but realised he rather liked it. He was on a high, but still able to concentrate on what he needed to do. Focussing on slowing down his breathing, he made sure the magazine was loaded and that he had another ten rounds in his pocket.

Finally, giving Laurel the thumbs up signal he wondered if they would come. They didn't have to wait long; the truck stopped at the gate, brakes squealing.

'Bastards are coming in on foot!'

Sure enough, the first trooper came into sight, scanning the area as he went. After sighting the bike, he signalled the next trooper, then moved towards the carport. Vince waited as number two emerged, but there was no sign of a third.

'Damn! Maybe the last one is staying with the vehicle.'

The first two troopers entered the house and were having a good look around when ... *Boom!* Vince realised he was hearing the 12-gauge open up. Let's hope that took care of the third one.

The two troopers appeared in the carport. Vince took aim, pulling the trigger. The .243, 100-grain hollow point round entered the first trooper's temple just above the left eye, literally removing the back of his head as it exited.

The sound of an AK47, (or in this case the NK knock off Type 68), is not that exciting when it's being fired at you! As the blast sprayed the ground to Vince's right and across in front of him, he took aim at the perpetrator. Knowing he didn't have enough time to get clever; he simply aimed for the biggest target, his torso, and squeezed the trigger. At the precise moment Vince's round blew a hole in the man's back, Laurel's 12-gauge took his head off.

She'd moved in closer, and because she was to Vince's left and to the trooper's right, he hadn't seen her coming! Laurel broke open the gun and dropped two new cartridges in before giving the corpse another blast. By the time Vince got to her she was reloading again, seemingly in a trance. He carefully took the weapon away from her as she sank to her knees, sobbing, then sat alongside his wife, cradling her in his arms.

"It will be all right Laurel."

All she could do was spit out, "I hate them!"

She was obviously distraught. Vince decided it was time to change the subject.

"Come on Laurel, we'd better move that bloody truck before anyone comes looking for them."

Snapping out of it quickly, Laurel dragged the bodies away from the front yard, while Vince climbed into the Bedford look-alike and hit the start. The old truck wound over once and fired. Vince drove it into the yard and around the other side of the house, up and over a neat garden bed.

"Sorry!"

He realised he'd spoken out loud, as if to apologise to the owner for destroying what looked to have been her pride and joy!

"It's a pity the bloody truck has bugger-all fuel in it; otherwise, we might have been able to commandeer it. I'll give you a hand to move that last body Laurel."

Laurel looked at what was left and said, "Can't really be called a BODY Vince; its head is only held on by a few sinews."

Smiling he replied, "Well Laurel, SHIT happens when you fuck with us!"

Vince suddenly realised how hungry he was.

"Shit! It's almost 1400! No wonder I'm starving!"

Laurel wandered back towards the house, smiling to herself as she went. Sometimes food was all Vince seemed to think about.

"I'll see what I can round up. Might put the kettle on as well; we should make the most of all the modern conveniences while we're here."

After watching Laurel disappear into the house, Vince went down to the front gate and shut it, thinking to himself, 'They were dumb enough last time. Maybe it will work again!'

The first cup of tea went down so fast he didn't even taste it. As she poured his second cup, he tucked into dried biscuits and tinned spam.

"What next Vince?"

"Same as this morning I suppose, but we'll wait till dark now that we know how far away the main road is."

Vince knew that from where they were now, they only had twenty kilometres to go to the Julia Bay turnoff.

Dinner was chips, along with Spam fried in breadcrumbs and a couple of semi ripe tomatoes Vince had found in the garden.

"Might get our head down in shifts Laurel. We'll head off at midnight. I'll take first watch; you get your head down first."

0027 Wednesday 14th January 2015, Granger Property, Willy Town to Bronze Road

"Brew's ready, Vince."

Vince woke from a really intense dream; a combination of his old Pusser's days and his work now as a Communications Technician.

"Oh ... thanks Laurel. Wow! What a dream!"

The fire had died down; kicking it in the guts while they enjoyed the drink helped to make them more comfortable.

Vince knew the wind chill factor meant it would be freezing outside at this time, especially on the bike, with no headlight. Shutting the gate behind them, they headed off.

"Makes the place look the same Laurel; as if nobody's been here."

"Good move Vince! You are definitely the brainy one."

Five minutes later they arrived at the junction. After turning left, and in the better moon light, the Xj900 ate up the bitumen, and they arrived at the Julia Bay Road at 0140.

All was quiet. It was obvious that all the homes were now occupied by NK Nationals.

As they turned left the bike coughed and then came to a halt. Vince pushed it off the road, then, with the aid of a torch they'd acquired from the last home they'd stopped at, managed to sort out what the problem was. He explained to his frustrated wife that, due to the age of the bike and the amount of work they had given it in the last few days, the carburettor had blocked. He was pretty sure the contaminated fuel had something to do with it as well. He knew it would take him around three hours to rectify the problem.

This would have been fine if an Alliance jeep hadn't arrived on the scene about two hours into the repair. It seemed that the Alliance had made the former café, come service station, into their Bronze headquarters. Unfortunately, this was right where Vince had pulled off the road.

The backpackers' accommodation behind the café had been turned into trooper's accommodation. After checking it out, he cursed, "Didn't see that coming Laurel!"

"Are you nearly finished Vince?"

"Nearly. The problem is that they are all getting ready to start work."

The pair could see the kill and clean-up squads were prepping for the day. This could be a problem for them any minute now. Vince made a quick decision.

"Bastards are up early! We might have to take to the plantation to avoid them."

After moving out at 0450, they made their way down the Julia Bay Road. They hadn't gone far before they realised that heading left into the plantation would be a lot safer than staying on the road. The track was narrow, and about two kilometres from the road, but it would be a lot safer for both of them.

The Yammy was playing up again!

"I think it's going to shit itself again Laurel!"

Laurel, straight to the point as always, asked sarcastically, "We're not going to run out of fuel again are we? And look! Nowhere to find any out here in the sticks!"

"Afraid so!"

It was nearly daylight now. The track was more than a little lumpy and finally, as expected, the bike died.

"Shit! Yep, you said it, we've run out of fuel!"

Vince started running alongside, pushing the bike along the track as he went. Although he found himself huffing and puffing more and more, he tried his best to keep his momentum going. It was clear that he was definitely not as fit as he once was. Despite this, something urged him on, and with Laurel leaning forward to help with the aerodynamics, he refused to give up.

Just when he thought he could go no further, a menacing figure suddenly loomed out of the morning mist in front of them. Whoever it was, they were standing in the middle of the track. Vince realised they were armed.

While Laurel crouched down on the bike, unsure of what was going on, Vince shouldered the .243. Just as he was about to fire the figure spoke ...

"Don't be a fuckwit Vince!"

Chapter 8
The Run In

Friday 16ᵗʰ January 2015 ... Hells Beach

Life at the Hells Beach camp started like any other day; with the sounds of surf crashing on the sandy beach, birds calling, and of course, the constant sound of numerous seagulls interrupting the silence, obviously squawking over some tasty morsel. All of these were seemingly competing with the distinctive song of the Wattle birds. Then there were the murmurings coming from the direction of the swags, the sounds of Sarge bringing the fire to life and putting the billy on, and the ever so familiar crackle of the kindling as it heated up in the fire.

With the introduction of two additional players, it was inevitable that there would be problems. Hell! It's human nature. Dick was usually up next, and really cherished his morning coffee with Sarge. Next came Annie, close behind Dick, then Jack. They usually let the other women sleep in a little. The routine was a little different now, with Laurel up at the same time as Dick. Vince was not a morning person, and because of the amount of shift work Laurel usually did she was always up before him.

Jack, Dick, and Laurel sat around the fire. Annie, as always, was preoccupied with the horses. Laurel asked when the F-Boat was likely to sail.

Dick replied, "If we can get ready in time Laurel, we will probably leave about 1600."

She told the ex-Sapper and CD about the past four to five days and all the killing that Vince and she had to do along the way. This made her seem just a little more human, and the men sympathised with her.

Once the chores were out of the way, the group discussed the day, the main priority was to make sure that those staying behind were well prepared for whatever turned up while the *Fremantle* was away.

"The crew for the journey will be Jack in the Engine Room, Vince on comms and weapons, Laurel signals and weapons, and me Bridge and weapons," declared Dick, adding, "and everyone takes a trick on the wheel except Jack. Vince, Laurel and I will handle weapons if it comes to that."

Jack spoke up.

"I need a couple of hours to complete my look at the Engine Room Dick."

Nodding in agreement, the sixty-one-year-old ex-navy CD continued.

"Vince and Laurel, can you both familiarise yourselves with the weapons systems and comms on board. Vince, can you set the brick phone up to the analogue system and fire up the 916 radar. Jack, can we have both generators paralleled by 1545, ready for a 1600 weigh anchor.

"Sarge, you're in charge of the camp while we're away. If shit happens, you'll have a couple of outs. The main one is the CJ. I've shown you how to get her going. You'll need to get April, Patch and Annie on board and get out of here. No heroics! We don't want anyone to die. Oh! Nearly forgot. If any of us happens to be where there are any supplies of ladies' sanitary items, we need to increase stocks of these; with no more suppliers they could become a rare commodity."

Patch made sure that there was enough food on board. After getting Sarge to take her out in the afternoon, she found Dick looking over the navigational charts. She watched him draw a pencil line along their intended course, then run the roller ruler from the line to the compass rose on the chart and jot down the course. He explained that doing this at every turn, would give him the course to steer. He would then set the dividers at the distance of each leg, measuring off on the scale at the side of the chart. This would give him the distances.

The fifty-four-year-old asked, "Is everything ok darling?"

Grabbing her around the waist, he gave her a huge kiss; his grey beard tickling her face.

"Couldn't be better!"

"So, this is where it will all happen?" asked Patch as she surveyed the Bridge of the FCPB.

Jack appeared, catching them in a passionate embrace.

"Sorry Dick, Patch!"

"No probs Jack!" said Dick, grinning. "What's the problem?"

"No problem mate, all good to go. The gen set's up and running, ready use fuel tanks are full, and the main's ready when you give the word."

"Thanks Jack. You may as well grab a brew. We still have thirty minutes."

"You want one mate? You Patch?"

Patch replied with a laugh,

"I'm good Jack; I have to leave soon anyway. Sarge should be here to pick me up any minute now."

"Yeah I'll have one mate," replied Dick, kissing his wife hard, like he really meant it, and saying, "I love you Chook."

"Oh and I love you too, you bastard!"

"What do you mean, bastard?"

"Oh, just because."

She was smiling, he knew she was jesting with him.

Patch had brought Dick's overnight bag with her. This was his original navy echelon bag, or Pusser's grip, as it was more commonly known. Inside was the usual stuff: his bath bag, his small drug bag, a change of underwear and a couple of tank tops, which he really loved wearing.

"Oh, and Dick, the other thing you wanted is in the bottom of your bag."

Sarge emerged from the upper deck.

"All weapons ready Dick! 50 Cal's rigged and loaded; one box on each."

"Thanks mate."

Patch reported to Dick that there was enough food to get them through a week if necessary.

"Plus, you have shit loads of stuff in the freezer love. Having said that, you'd better be home before you need to start on that!"

"Thanks, Chook."

Sarge took Patch ashore in the RHIB. They'd decided the best plan was to leave this with the group at Hells Beach. It had been a hard decision to make, but one that Dick thought was paramount to ensure the group's safety.

The Indonesians had changed the layout on the stern; previously she had carried an alloy dinghy mounted alongside the RHIB. It looked like when they had retro fitted the torpedos, they must have scrapped the alloy dinghy, opting for the twenty-two-foot

RHIB to be mounted amidships, and what looked like spare torpedo mounts on the port side where the alloy was.

Dick looked at the clock on the Bridge.

"1545! Start main engines. Vince, can you and Laurel man the windlass please."

Vince replied, with just the slightest hint of sarcasm, "Aye, Aye Captain!"

From the shore, Sarge, Patch and Annie watched on as the exhausts of the 137-foot Patrol Boat, began rumbling underwater. She was an awesome sight!

Patch looked at Sarge.

"Are you jealous Sarge?"

The forty-five-year-old ex-Sapper replied, "Well Patch, if you're asking if I wanted to go, the answer's a big, YES!"

On the forecastle of the FCPB, Vince gave the signal.

"Anchor chain upright."

With the anchor stowed, they turned to port. Dick eased the throttles to slow ahead both and gave a couple of quick blasts on the ship's horn. With the anchor chain lashed, Laurel and Vince made their way to the Bridge.

"Brew Skipper?"

"Love one Vince! I've even brought my lemon juice."

Jack appeared beside him, reporting, "Mate, back on starboard generator set. I'll have a brew as well thanks Vince."

They cleared the entrance to the bay just as Laurel and Vince appeared with steaming brews and a tray of biscuits. Dick and Jack nodded in unison.

"Great! Thanks troops."

Dick eased the throttles up to half ahead. The *Fremantle* looked the perfect picture. They were now making fifteen knots, and the bow wave was foaming from each side as she rose and fell in the half-metre swell.

Vince took a look at the 916-radar screen, reporting, "All clear Dick."

After switching the UHF on and handing Laurel the wheel, Dick looked at Vince.

"Better slide those rotting bodies off the arse end. Can you give us a hand mate?"

They punched their way south on course, *one six five*. The *FCPB Fremantle* loved the slight swell. Two hours into the journey Laurel came up with scran.

"Ploughman's dinner I call it," she announced with pride. "Cold meat, cheese, biscuits, olives, sundried tomatoes, pickled cucumber and tinned salmon."

Vince was first to acknowledge his appreciation.

"What a feast Laurel!"

Everyone agreed with Vince; too busy eating to say much for a while. Dick plotted the course and took another fix on the radar.

"Vince, can you take the wheel?"

Dick descended into the Engine Room, where he found Jack in his element, with machinery purring, and the mains sounding great for their age and the gen set with a little load. Jack was continuously oiling, greasing, and tinkering; this was truly his domain! Jack who had his earmuffs on, looked up as Dick approached. Dick gave the thumbs up signal, along with hand to mouth, meaning it was scran time.

Back on the Bridge, Vince suggested, "Why don't you get your head down for a couple of hours Dick. I just turn right when we run out of land right?"

Dick grinned.

"That's right mate, will do. Shake me in a couple of hours, and of course, if anything happens that I should know about."

Sometime later, Laurel tapped on the Skipper's Cabin door.

"2200 Dick. Just about to enter Thunda Bay. Looks like you needed the sleep."

"Thanks for that Laurel."

After a well-earned shower and feeling a whole lot better after a solid sleep, Dick grabbed a coffee before entering the Bridge. Vince was still on the wheel, with Jack relaxing in the captain's chair. He checked the 916 and hit the scan on the UHF and VHF radios.

"ETA, Chook Point, 0100 from what I can make out team. Jack, are things okay down the hole?"

"Yeah mate! All good. I even had a bit of shut eye myself."

"Vince, if you and Laurel want to get a bit of kip, that's all right with Jack and I; we'll handle things for a while. I'm thinking the Chief's mess would be more comfortable for you two."

"Cheers mate. You up for a bit of rack time and a shower Laurel?"

Laurel's face was looking rather pale in colour.

"I reckon that would be good," she replied. "I don't feel all that great in this swell."

Jack and Dick chatted about the events coming up, and what it would be like to just pilot the 203 straight into Kings Town Harbour. Jack was worried about April and whether she could cope with the pain of her wound.

"What happens if we can't find your mate Doc?"

"Honestly Jack, I don't know. Let's just hope he's around somewhere. Otherwise, we might have to resort to kidnapping a doctor from the hospital."

It was 2300. Dick was puzzled by a sound he couldn't identify.

"What's that noise Jack?"

Jack pointed below.

"It seems to be coming from the Comms Centre Dick."

Dick gave Jack the wheel and entered the comms room to find his brick phone ringing.

Brrr ... Brrr ... Brrr ...

As he picked up the handset, he could see the incoming number. Knowing exactly who it was, he answered with a grin,

"G'day Doc you old bastard! So! You're still alive!"

He could hear Roger (Doc) Johns laughing on the other end of the line.

"Mate! I was wondering whether you would answer this old thing. Are you and Patch all right?"

"Yeah mate, we're ok. What about you and Millie?"

There was a moment of silence before Doc spoke again; Dick could detect a slight quiver in his voice.

"Dick, Millie's dead."

"Shit Doc! I'm so sorry! Was it the Alliance?"

"No mate. The cancer got her in the end. Well sort of anyway; tell you about it some other time when we're having a beer or something. I've got so much to tell you, don't know where to start. First up, where are you?"

Dick was smiling; he knew his mate would have a heart attack when he found out.

"Well Doc! You're not going to believe this, but we are just entering Thunda Bay on *HMAS Fremantle*."

The sixty-five-year-old ENT Specialist couldn't believe his ears.

"Fucking hell mate! Where did you get that? And how?"

Dick laughed.

"So much to tell you; we'll do it later over a beer. What's important is that we're coming to get you. We need a surgeon who can take out a round that's lodged in Jack's missus's shoulder. So, grab your black bag and we'll meet you at the Chook Point Marina."

Doc, trying to think fast, said, "Shit Dick! The bag's at the hospital. Nari and I will have to go get it, along with whatever else we think we will need. It could take us a couple of hours."

Jack looked at Dick with a quizzical look, as Dick asked, "Nari? Who the fuck is Nari?"

Dick filled Jack in with what Doc had told him.

"Better slow her down Jack. Change of plan."

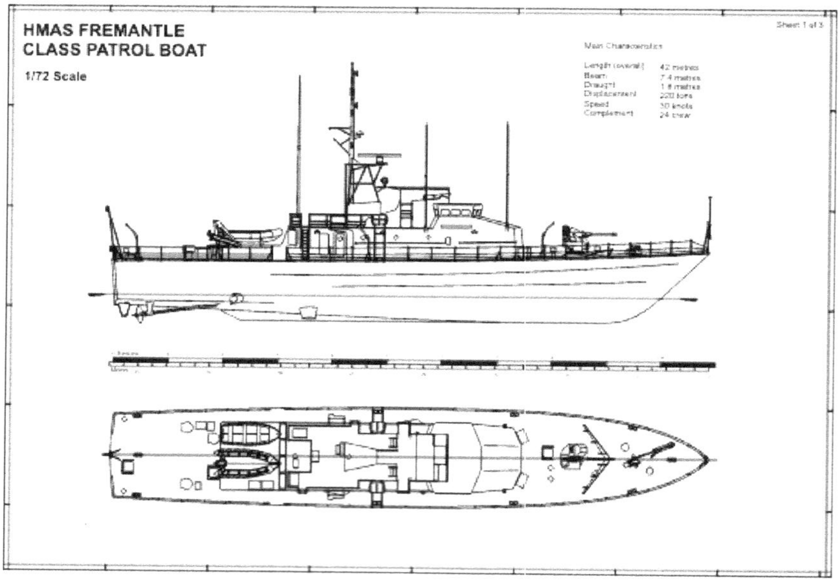

Chapter 9
Doc and Nari's Raid

0001 Saturday 17th January 2015 ... Chook Point Marina

The 25-year-old South Korean triage nurse, Nari Kim, looked at Doc.

"Do you really think we can get your bag and stuff?"

The 65-year-old replied, "Good question love. There shouldn't be too much activity happening around town at this hour. I know a way in the back so to speak; it will save us having to go past the guards at the front door."

The pair quickly made their way out of the marina and towards the town centre. The streets were quiet until they reached the Old Anchor Hotel, where it seemed a few drunken revellers were still sitting outside.

"Shit Nari! We'll have to go the long way round; back one street and around the block."

Nari was puzzled.

"Where do we get into the hospital Doc?"

He cringed in concern as he replied, knowing he was about to remind her of something they'd both rather forget.

"You remember where the Alliance officers were holding you captive?"

Nari knew how hard it would have been for him to say that and smiled at the worried man in front of her.

"How could I forget Doc."

She blushed as she remembered the sordid details of how they'd repeatedly raped and humiliated her and abused her with objects unimaginable.

After giving her a hug, Doc continued.

"There is a door into that level; it was once the entrance to the expansion of that floor when they excavated the lower level, making another twenty-four rooms."

Nari was concerned.

"But how? It will be locked Doc."

Doc held up his key ring.

"Ah, but I have a key my darling!"

"You are a clever man Doc!"

At 0135 Doc and Nari approached the lower-level door. Making sure they both stayed in the shadows, Doc unlocked the huge emergency door, desperately hoping that it wasn't alarmed. Once they were safely inside, they found it was pitch dark; possibly that area was powered by mains electricity and not batteries.

Nari held his arm tightly.

"I can't see Doc."

After fumbling in his pockets, Doc produced a stainless-steel Zippo cigarette lighter. He ran his fingers over the familiar Navy crest on the front as he flipped the Zippo's top; flicking the flint wheel and igniting the fluid filled collection piece. This gave them more than enough light to safely make their way to the stairwell.

"Where is your bag Doc?"

"It's in the staffroom love. I think we should first get some supplies from the utility room alongside of the theatre. Dick mentioned they needed sanitary items; he said to bring all we could find."

Nari suggested, "I could also get an emergency triage bag or two from outpatients; I know they keep more sanitary supplies there."

Doc was worried about her.

"No, it's too dangerous love."

Nari persisted.

"Doc, you must let me help. Please!"

Doc savoured the moment, as he gave her a quick kiss, before letting her go.

The corridors were really wide, leaving Doc feeling on edge, and glad there was very little lighting. The bad thing was that he was on the wrong floor.

'Shit!' he thought. 'I may as well get my bag anyway.'

After picking up the black Gladstone bag, he descended down one floor to the utility room.

He ran his eye along the shelves, instinctively selecting the items he would need, and taking as much of each item as he could carry. Last but not least he found the ladies department, with its hundreds of boxes of tampons and sanitary pads.

'Well,' he thought. 'Dick did say to get what there was!'

Finding a large clear plastic bag, he filled it to the brim, thankful that the sanitary items were not too heavy. Armed with his Gladstone bag and the now bulging sack, he looked rather a lot like a grey-haired version of Santa Claus.

Nari had almost reached the outpatients department when she heard a guard coming. After quickly ducking behind a curtain, she climbed on to a bench, making sure that her feet weren't visible from under the curtain. The triage bags were made up for outside visits; these would normally have been in the ambulances, but now they just sat there, waiting for an emergency visit away from the hospital. They were kept in the supplies annex alongside of the main triage room.

Nari frequented this room, sometimes up to fifty times a day, and knew it well. After opening the first bag, she proceeded to fill it with vials of morphine, syringes, packets of needles, scalpels, staples, stapler, bandages and tape. By the time she'd finished the rotten things were very heavy and were full to the point of not being able to close them. For a moment, Nari wondered if she would be able to manage it on her own.

'I'll just have a look outside the door …!'

Before she could finish the thought Nari felt a sudden sharp and painful blow to the back of her head before blacking out completely.

Doc knew he had to make his way two floors down to emergency. To do this he could head straight down the corridor, although this meant he would have to pass the guard station. The other alternative was to go back down to the basement where Nari and he had parted and approach it from that angle. He chose the first option, thinking to himself that the other would take too long.

He sneaked his way along the main corridor, fully aware of what he would need to do if a guard came into view. Doc glanced sideways into the rooms as he passed them, checking that no one was visible through the glass panels. He could hear voices and excited laughter coming from somewhere ahead of him, and frowned, realising there was something rather unusual about that. The one thing he did remember from when he was an Able Seaman, was that doing duty was something that most people were definitely not excited about. It was one of the most boring times in the military and most people found it hard to stay awake at times.

Nari woke to the sounds of laughter, realising that her head was thumping heavily. Opening her eyes just a little, she realised she was tied spread eagled on the portable bed trolley facing down, and that she'd been stripped bare from the waist down. Nari felt angry and disgusted; there were two of them, both night guards. The older one was trying to encourage the young boy, who couldn't have been any older than 17, to rape her. At first, she thought they might have already done it, but, telling herself to keep calm, she listened carefully to what they were saying. She was thankful to realise she felt no trauma below, and that nothing had happened yet. The two had mistakenly thought she had escaped from where the officers kept her for their pleasures, and they figured it was time they got their fair share!

The young and inexperienced trooper was so excited that he shot his bolt too early, all over Nari's buttocks. Embarrassed, the young lad fled the room. The older man's reeking breath stank as he leant up close to her face, taunting her as his fingers did their evil work on her body.

He untied one side and turned her over, saying he wanted the whore to witness him having his way with her. She struck out at him as soon as her hand was free, but he was too quick, smashing his fist into her face, stunning her. This gave him enough time to retie her hand and foot. He was quite shocked when she started yelling abuse at him in his own tongue. He stifled her voice with a roll of bandages, and proceeded to spread her thighs, ready to begin his violent assault.

As the tears streamed down her face, she saw the pig open his mouth to taunt her again as he was about to thrust into her. He didn't get a chance. Nari watched in shock as the end of a scalpel erupted from the man's throat.

Doc pushed it through from the right-hand side! The trooper's body slid to the floor in a red puddle as his blood spewed out over the linoleum.

"Sorry I was late love!"

Doc untied her and she collapsed into his arms as he continued urgently.

"No time for sentiments love; he might have a friend."

She replied, "He has, a kid. He was here earlier."

As she dressed quickly, she forgot for a minute the reason she'd been there in the first place. Recovering her thoughts, she grabbed the emergency bags, surprised to find that they seemed to be a little lighter now, before realising the reason for this was probably adrenaline from the anger welling up from within.

After grabbing the trooper's weapon from where it had been left leaning against the wall, Doc checked the magazine and pushed off the safety.

The sixty-five-year-old warned, "It could get a little noisy love as we leave."

Nari gritted her teeth and hissed, "That's fine by me my man. I would love to kill someone right now!"

They opened the door and peered carefully out into the main corridor. They could see the kid coming towards them. Doc whispered, "Looks like you'll get your wish my love!"

Doc pulled the trigger. The Type 68 assault weapon unleashed its deadly arsenal of lead in the young trooper's direction. Firing off the hip is not all that accurate, but Doc did manage to hit the kid with all three shots. The first got him in the groin, sending arterial spray everywhere, while the second hit his chest. The third shot went straight through his neck. The 7.62 mm NATO rounds pretty well chopped the young trooper's body to bits. He made a kind of gurgling sound as he slid down the wall; his head slumping forward. Nari held her hands tightly over her ears; she hadn't realised just how deafening the AK47 look alike would be at this close range.

After reaching the basement safely, the pair exited through the huge door and onto the street. They were both relieved to hear no sound except for the cool air of the night whistling around the air ventilators.

Doc realised how warm it had been inside, with the air conditioners not running.

"We need to get back to the marina and warn Dick about the *Warrnambool*."

They made it back to Doc's house by 0300.

"You'd better get some clothes together love, and whatever else you want to take with you; but keep it light. I'll go down to *Footy* and warn Dick."

"What about your clothes Doc?"

Doc pointed towards *Footy*.

"I have some on board, all ready to go. I keep them there for emergencies."

Nari was silent for a minute. She stood before the aging Doctor and kissed him gently, asking, "Do you really want me to come with you?"

Nari had tears in her eyes. She'd just remembered that she was Korean, and that this might not go down too well with Doc's new found friends. Doc had never thought of her as 'being Korean,' all that mattered to him was that he loved her.

"What? Don't say another word! Of course you are coming with me! What else would you do? Stay here, and do what, get shot? Or worse? And besides that, I want you to come!"

He held her reassuringly, telling her over and over that it would be all right.

Leaving the relieved triage nurse to collect her things, Doc went back down to *Footy*, then rang Dick's number.

Brrr ... Brrr ... Brrr ...

Dick picked up immediately.

"You rang Doc?"

"Dick we've got the supplies; it was a bit hairy, but we made it. I must warn you that the Alliance have another F-Boat. It's the 204 ex-*Warrnambool*; only now it's manned by Indonesians."

"Thanks mate! Where is she now?"

"I'm not sure. It's not at Queens Pier, although they could have gone to refuel."

"No problems. Where are you now? Are you ready to hit the frog and toad?"

"I'm on *Footy*; Nari is getting packed up in the house. Dick, there's something I need to tell you before we board."

"Yeah mate! Shoot."

"Nari is South Korean ... and my girlfriend."

Dick felt a bit stunned at hearing Doc's news. Vince had shown him how to plug the phone in on the Bridge; and he was now standing there with it switched on to speaker phone. As he looked around the room, he could see the shocked expressions on everyone's faces.

Doc spoke again.

"Dick, did you get that mate?"

"Yeah, sure did. We see no problems with that."

Dick turned the phone off speaker before continuing.

"We're abeam of the casino mate; just hanging!"

Nari joined Doc as he was grabbing his gear; he'd always kept an emergency bag of his own, packed with socks, jocks, a couple of changes of clothes, bathroom stuff and drugs.

She jumped on him from the jetty, almost knocking him overboard in her enthusiasm.

"Steady girl! I'm an old man you know!"

Excitedly, she whispered as she kissed him passionately, "I love you Doc."

Doc could feel movement at the station again.

"We don't have time right now my love; we have to get all this gear to the outside marina finger."

Nari looked around.

"Would one of those trolleys be okay my man?"

"You're a gem Nari. I never thought of that."

After quickly sourcing two trolleys, they loaded one up with Nari's case and the two emergency bags. The second carried Doc's black medical bag, his sea bag full of clothes, the brick phone, and a clear plastic sack full of pantry items.

Listening carefully, they could hear the muffled underwater exhaust of the FCPB. Realising they were close; Doc shone a small torch to direct them in. Dick bought her alongside with one fender hanging over the side, just nudging the port bow to the marina finger. He put her in neutral, and then slow ahead; on and off while keeping a light positive pressure on the walkway.

Vince, Jack and Laurel were on hand to grab the gear as Nari, and Doc passed it up to them. Laurel grabbed Nari's arm and yanked her up onto the forecastle, while Vince helped the old doctor on board, saluting smartly as he did so.

"Welcome aboard Sir!"

Chapter 10
Raiders North

I was enjoying all the female attention and was in my element; I really enjoyed keeping the women under my wing. If it hadn't been for the fact that the other two women were Patch and April, I knew Annie would have been extremely jealous.

"You're lucky they aren't 20-year-olds Sarge!"

"Oh Annie, I wouldn't do it to you."

"Yes, but I know what you used to get up to with all the other guides."

"That was ages ago."

Patch had finished helping April back from the toilet; by now she could manage quite well with only one other person to assist. After breakfast, we talked about what might be happening with the run into Kings Town; all of us were wondering how it was going.

"They should be there by now. Let's hope they can find Doc quickly before he heads off to work."

For April's sake, Patch was trying to stay optimistic.

"What's on the agenda today boss?"

I smiled.

"Day off! You can go for a swim or sling a line if you want. I'll even take the RHIB out into the middle of the bay and show you how to use it. Whatever you like."

As I was talking, we noticed the horses becoming more and more restless by the minute. Annie was looking at Bob and Zen, who in turn were looking north up to where the track became visible.

BOOM!

"Shit! That's the Claymore!"

I grabbed my SLR and made a run for the track. Patch and Annie had rehearsed this scenario more than once, and together they picked up April and took her to the huge rocks they'd hidden behind when the Alliance Patrol Boat first arrived. They made sure that the French woman had water and a weapon, and that she was as comfortable as possible.

I was already at the scene. The blast had swaged a path through the intruder's body from their knees to their neck. All that remained was a head and partial upper torso. Looking around, I realised our problems were about to get bigger.

"Annie!"

"Yes Sarge?"

"Get two horses out. Looks like we've got one on the loose; we're going to have to run them down."

Patch and Annie hastily saddled up Tom and Zen. Patch looked at Annie.

"Sarge might as well ride Zen Annie."

"Thanks Patch, I know he will really appreciate it."

Annie grabbed the F1 from Patch and before I was back down, she was ready, with a set of wither bags strapped on, containing snacks, water and ammo, and coats tied on the back of each saddle. She handed the reins to me as I approached. I kissed her, quickly reporting,

"It looks like they were hiking. One's dead, and the other one's obviously wounded; we just need to kill him or her before they get too far. They have seen the campsite.

"Patch, you're in charge. The shotgun and cartridges are over there, and the SLR and ammo here. There's plenty of other weapons if you need them. Are you right with operating them?"

Even though Patch nodded, she didn't look all that confident, so I gave her a quick reminder about the safety and magazine removal.

"Remember ladies, if it's Broken Arrow, get in the RHIB; I've shown you how to start it. Then get the hell out to sea."

From Dick's stories told around the campfire, they all knew that Broken Arrow was a Military term used to describe the situation when an enemy has overrun the Base.

By the time I'd finished and mounted, Annie was already halfway up the track; the powerful showjumper literally bounding up the narrow animal trail. Zen didn't waste any time in catching the seventeen-hand Tom.

"Don't look Annie," I yelled out, but it was too late. The perky twenty-eight-year-old had already arrived at the blast scene and was horrified by what she saw. I reached her just as she negotiated around the huge rocks which were our doorway out into forestry.

"Looks like they're only kids Annie, probably out hiking. Couldn't be much more than teenagers. Well, what's left of that one anyway!"

"That's a bloody awful weapon Sarge! So, they use that a lot in the Army?"

"Afraid so love."

Looking down at the track they could see a trail of blood.

"Looks like they're injured badly enough to favour one leg," reported the ex-Sapper.

"Yeah, I noticed that Sarge."

Although they hadn't expected it would take too long to catch up with the run-away, twenty minutes later they were still in hot pursuit. I pointed out the obvious.

"Shit! The bugger is legging it!"

Annie, who realised she would be doing the same thing if the shoe had been on the other foot, retorted, "We'll catch him Sarge! Our lives depend on it!"

As we followed the trail of blood, I thought about the possible ramifications if this teenager were to make it all the way back to Willy Town. Annie was right. If he or she managed to alert the Alliance troops, they would definitely invade our hiding place.

What we would have to do then would be to kill all the inhabitants of Willy Town; something that we were simply not prepared for. We could hold them off for a while, maybe even until the *Fremantle* returned; but it would be extremely difficult and was a confrontation I would rather avoid.

Back at camp, Patch boiled the billy, while April sat in a camp chair, feeling reasonably comfortable, with Jack's .243 across her lap. The weary French woman shook her head in disbelief.

"It's all go here Patch!"

"Yes! Never a dull moment."

Although the pair laughed, they were both fully alert and ready for whatever might come next.

"Can't hear any gun shots April. They must have got further away than Sarge expected."

"Well Patch, if it was me, and I stumbled across this camp and watched my mate get blown in half, I'd be piss bolting it too, quick fast!"

"Too true my friend. How about I get some water heating up so that you can have a good hot wash with no one else around.

I might go for a swim; do you reckon you can manage on your own?"

April looked up at the fifty-four-year-old with a grin.

"Trop a' droite!"

Patch set the French woman up with a basin, towels, and hot water, as well as a bar of soap and some clean underwear. Leaving April to enjoy her hot wash, she went down on to the beach and stripped off, thinking to herself, 'There's no one else around; won't wear the togs today.'

Plunging into the sea, Patch flinched for a moment as she felt the sting of the salt water hitting her body, then started lathering herself with a cake of saltwater soap Dick had found on the *Fremantle*. The slight chill made her nipples stand up and she thought of Dick, wondering where he was, and whether he was all right.

Back on the chase, Annie on Tom was still following the intermittent blood trail. We had been gone over two hours now, and were both convinced that by now we must have been closing in. Under normal circumstances it would have been almost impossible for the runner to keep up at a horse's pace.

I whispered to Annie, "Running scared can make a person achieve superhuman things!"

Without warning, Tom took a sidestep, and I thought a branch must have knocked Annie out of the saddle. I wasn't really sure what had happened at first, thinking Annie must have fallen off, but then, as logic took over, I realised that was pretty well impossible!

Out of the corner of my eye I caught sight of the perpetrator wielding the log that had dismounted my girl. Annie, recovering quickly, jumped up and attacked the other girl, throwing her to the ground. Her attacker must have been stronger than she looked because Annie suddenly found herself flying through the air yet again; landing on her back took the wind right out of her.

Acting instinctively, she pulled the 9mm out of its holster, but then hesitated; possibly because the person she saw in front of her was just a girl!

There was no time to think, it was obvious the girl was about to lay open Annie's skull. So, I shot her, placing two rounds in her chest. The blast threw her back a couple of feet.

Annie blurted out in shock.

"But Sarge! She was only a girl!"

I quietly reminded her, "But she was about to kill you, Annie."

Annie sadly looked at the body of the NK National.

"She was probably only thirteen or fourteen years old Sarge."

"You would be surprised love. It's hard to tell. They all look younger than they really are."

Back on the beach, Patch picked up the towel and dried herself off. Feeling great, and definitely reinvigorated, she dressed before re-joining April, who was just finishing getting dressed.

"Do you feel better Patch?"

"I sure do April! What about you?"

"Like a new woman! Well, one with a hole in her."

At least her friend was able to laugh about it.

"1200. Might make us some lunch April. What do you feel like?"

"Damper my dear. Do you know how to make it?"

"Sort of April, it's been a while. I can do it in the coals or in the camp oven. What would you prefer?"

"Let's be traditional, in the coals Patch. I've never eaten it that way before."

"You're in for a treat then."

April watched as Patch mixed about six cups of flour, along with salt and sugar, together in the camp bowl, then added the milk slowly, forming a soft dough. After kneading it lightly on a floured board, she shaped it into a round loaf before flattening it out to a couple of inches thick. The last thing to do was to brush some milk over the loaf and cut a cross in the top.

"Wow Patch! That's a work of art!"

Patch, who wasn't so sure about her cooking ability, adding, "Maybe you'd better wait till you've tasted it!"

After waiting an hour for the dough to rise, Patch scraped the coals off the fire; spread some ash on the bottom, then placed the Damper on top of the ash, then more ash and then coals. Patch was hoping the temperatures were about right.

"Glad the fire wasn't too hot!"

"How long does it take to cook?"

"From memory, usually about 40 minutes."

Sarge and Annie had travelled further than they would have liked. Annie looked around, trying to work out where they were.

"What do you reckon Sarge? Do we keep going and scrounge some fresh vegies from Willy Town?"

I looked at my watch, quickly calculating we had around 6 hours of daylight left.

"If we give the horses a run we could be there in an hour."

Annie didn't need any encouragement; she was off! Much to my shock, Zen overtook the big thoroughbred 300 metres down the track; the acceleration was phenomenal, although it was short lived. As Tom stretched out, he easily passed Zen again, who, by now, was coming back to more of a sedate lope. I now understood why Zen was a quarter horse, literally the fastest horse in the world, but only over a quarter mile.

Annie and I enjoyed the exhilaration of the race, although I made sure not to thrash Zen too much. I knew Patch might not be impressed if I wore out her mount.

Annie had been thinking.

"I'm pretty sure the shack opposite the track into forestry had a great garden Sarge."

I looked at her.

"How can you remember that love?"

She laughed.

"You know me Sarge! I love my veggies!"

Back at the camp, Patch scraped the ash from the now cooked damper.

"You have got to flick it like this April," she said, tapping the loaf with her fingernail. Patch smiled at the hollow sound she'd been hoping to hear.

"That means it's cooked!"

After brushing the ash off with a sprig of gum, she placed the damper on the board and cut off a slice, revealing a perfectly cooked interior.

"Name your poison April."

"Butter and jam please. I've got some of my homemade jam in the tent."

As she dished up the jam laden slice to April, Patch declared, "Hope you're not offended, but I can't go past Vegemite!"

"Knock yourself out Patch!"

April was giggling as the melted butter and jam dribbled down her chin.

"Now that's a sight!"

"You're a wicked woman Patch!"

"I don't know what you mean April!"

They were both laughing now.

After crossing the Oxford to Bronze Road, Annie and I dismounted behind a small cluster of trees. We tied up Tom and Zen, who by now were relishing the rest.

Annie checked out our surroundings before reporting.

"There's two NK Nationals in the backyard Sarge."

I was more interested in finding out whether any of them were armed.

"The question is, where is the guard?"

Annie turned to me and declared aggressively, "Let's kill the fuckers Sarge!"

"God you're turning out to be a bloodthirsty woman love!"

"Can't help myself Sarge. I hate them so much!"

Annie watched as I approached the first NK National, who was working in the garden. After sneaking up behind him, I placed my left hand over the man's mouth while I sunk my pig sticker into his back up between his ribs and into his heart. Without blinking I moved on to the next victim; a woman in her late 20's. She was the same age as Annie. She turned but saw me too late, as I buried the knife into her ribs, striking upwards under her ribcage and into the heart. She was dead in less than three seconds.

Patch and April sat enjoying the afternoon sun, they both felt full from all the damper they'd eaten.

Patch looked at April.

"A bit heavy, but very satisfying. What did you think of your first coal-cooked damper April?"

"Not bad Patch! Once we get this hole in my shoulder fixed, I'll have a go myself, you know, and surprise the troops."

April had a snooze while Patch went off to groom the horses, finding Bob, Cowboy, Fannie and Socks having a little doze in the warm sun themselves. It felt like the temperature must have been somewhere around 22 degrees. As she worked, Patch thought about possibly going for another quick swim before collecting some more firewood and then kicking the fire up, ready for the night's meal.

She wondered how Sarge, and Annie were going. They'd been gone a long time, and she was hoping they were all right.

Because of the lateness of the hour, she elected to wear bathers this time; she didn't want to give the others a fright if they returned while she was still in the water.

Once we'd got to Willy Town, Annie set about collecting some fresh vegetables while I inspected the house. My ex-Sapper skills came flooding back as I entered the back door, with the 9mm Browning drawn and at the ready. I'd found this was a bit easier to handle at close quarters than the more cumbersome SLR.

The back room was clear. There was a short hallway leading to the front door, with a kitchen and lounge on the right, and a bathroom containing the toilet and two bedrooms on the left. I could detect noises coming from the bathroom.

Noticing the door was ajar; I was wondering whether it would be better to kill whoever was in the toilet, or whether I should check the bedrooms first. I figured the sounds I could hear were probably the guard doing his business. I could hear the familiar sound of toilet paper being dispensed off the roll; looked like the decision had been made for me. It was a matter of seconds now before I would be confronting whoever was in there.

I kicked the door open to discover a startled Alliance trooper in the act of pulling up his trousers. His Type 68 was leaning against the wall, but he had no hope of reaching it in time. A single shot to his head left the wall newly decorated with blood and brain matter.

Patch enjoyed her swim, thinking she might like to try snorkelling some time. Maybe when Dick had time, she could get him to teach her. The only other time she'd tried it before had been while on holiday in Fiji, but this was quite a few years ago now.

She looked at the position of the sun, figuring that by now it must be around 4 o'clock. Time to get that fire going. After gathering an armful of firewood, she was surprised to find April still asleep. The older French woman must have been extra tired from the morning's excitement.

Deciding to let her be, Patch went about her duties, building up the fire and thinking about what to prepare for the evening meal. She sifted through the tent for vegetables, then investigated what was in the sealed plastic bags suspended in the cold stream at the end of the beach, wanting to use the oldest meat first, and deciding in the end that the best choice was a large, already cooked chunk of corned beef.

A 'Chuckinski' was what her mother had called the dish, and it was just as it sounded, everything got chucked into the pot together; veggies, herbs, spices, diced corn beef, a couple of tins of tomatoes and some curry. Patch's mouth was watering already! She went to check on how April was doing.

"Shit!"

She found her friend slumped over; from the position of her head, it was clear that she was definitely not sleeping!

Back at Willie Town, I jumped as I heard someone yell out from the front of the shack.

'Bugger! Looks like I'm not finished yet!'

As I cleared the first bedroom I was met by a very surprised girl, who was as naked as a Jaybird. Judging by the look of her body, this girl couldn't have been much older than thirteen or fourteen. I could see massage oil and condoms on the bedside table, and putting two and two together, I realised that the young guard had probably been dipping his wick into the young girl when a call of nature had beckoned. She'd yelled out for him after hearing the weapon going off and was coming to look for him.

Startled at the sight of me brandishing the 9mm pistol, she turned and tried to climb out of the window. I grabbed her around the neck in a sleeper position. Although she was kicking, with her arms flailing everywhere, she couldn't scream because of the pressure on her larynx. I heard her neck snap and placed her body on the bed. As I covered it up, I marvelled at the sight of the young firm body, it brought back vivid memories of earlier days while trying to get into the pants of every guide working for Dick and Patch!

At Hell's Beach Patch dumped the bag of corned beef on the table, yelling out,

"April, are you awake!"

Getting no response, she shook the woman hard. Still nothing, Patch managed to move her down on to the ground, and placed her in a coma position, thinking, 'Shit! What a time for this to happen!'

Patch was well aware that she was not the best person to administer first aid; it had never been one of her strong points. She breathed a sigh of relief as she detected a pulse.

'Thank you, Lord! At least she's not dead!'

Wringing a face towel out in cold water she washed April's face. After what seemed like an eternity, the French woman stirred and opened her eyes.

"Well thank goodness for that April! You had me fucking ... oops, sorry ... scared! How do you feel?"

April took a while to answer, replying in a weak voice, "I feel really drowsy, and all washed out."

"You just rest there while I go and get the rolled up single swag."

Once April was propped up against the swag Patch put the billy on.

After a quick search, I found Annie engrossed in the task of collecting veggies and fruit. It looked like the place had a good selection of plum and apricot trees.

Annie looked up as I approached.

"Heard the shot! Who was it?"

"Guard on the shitter."

"Was there anyone else inside?"

"Just a girl in the bedroom."

I thought it best to leave out some of the details. She didn't need to know everything. I suggested it was time to get going.

"We'd better mount up; they'll be wondering where we've got to."

"How long will it take us to ride back do you reckon Sarge?"

"It's 1600 now, so I figure we should be there before dark, but only if we up the pace."

Annie quickly filled my saddlebag with the booty before mounting up, crying out, "Race you!"

Grinning widely, she was off like a cut cat.

As we crossed the main road in a blur, I once again caught the big thoroughbred up, thinking that this was going to be one hell of a ride!

Patch and April heard Bob and the other horses calling out. Patch laughed.

"Can't get past that lot!"

April agreed.

"Better than a watchdog Patch!"

Patch had dinner simmering slowly and just ready to eat by the time she saw Annie and I appear.

"Well timed you two!"

While she helped us de-tack, Patch told me about April's turn for the worse.

"Can you have a look at her please Sarge?"

I wasn't sure what I could do, but I could see that my mate's wife was obviously worried about April, and I agreed to have a look. That is, at least, if the French woman would let me; she was a bit funny about that sort of thing.

April was feeling much better, but she did let me take her pulse and have a quick look at the wounds. The one in her thigh was still kind of messy and needed a good clean up, but the shoulder was definitely looking worse, and was still weeping blood. With the ongoing loss of blood, it was no wonder she'd gone through a bout of secondary shock. The pain must be immense and all they had to give her was Panamax.

Chapter 11
Jun Lee Sung

General Jun Lee Sung was born in August 1954; the son of General Wan Zu Sun and Hee-Young Sun.

Military institutes, including the Pyongyang Academy, which became No. 2 KPA Officers School in January 1949, and the Central Constabulary Academy, which became the KPA Military Academy in December 1948, soon followed. These institutions were considered essential for the education of political and military officers for the new armed forces. Jun Lee's father had been one of their star pupils, graduating in 1950, just before the Korean War, before working his way up the promotional ladder to the rank of General in 1987, at the age of 58.

During the opening phases of the Korean War in 1950, the Korean People's Army, or KPA, quickly drove the South Korean forces south and captured Seoul. Jun Lee's father played an instrumental role during this phase, leading his men to victory. By the time Jun Lee had come on the scene, his father was stationed at Pyongyang as a Captain, instructing at the Academy. By now, the war had left his father scarred; something that he himself came to acknowledge later in his own military career.

As a child, Jun Lee was raised with a huge heart, after mainly being brought up by his mother while his father was away. He and his siblings, brother, Wun Too, and sister, Ven Loo, were fascinated by all things American, and loved to play baseball, albeit with a stick and a handmade ball. Jun Lee also would watch the sailing boats with awe, swearing that one day he would learn to sail. He loved the way they moved gracefully through the water, with nothing propelling them except the wind.

Like most army children, young Jun Lee grew up within the military system, and although his heart was elsewhere, his honour was to follow his father. He joined the army at the age of 16; electing to join the Infantry, and worked his way up the ranks, attaining the rank of Sergeant Major in 1982.

He attended the Central Constabulary Academy, then later that same year, re-joined XI Corps, staying with them until transferring to the Korean People's Army Special Operation Force (KPASOF). This was an asymmetric force, with a total troop size of 200,000. Since the Korean War, which was widely known as the Korean War of Liberation, it has continued to play a role of concentrating infiltration of troops into the territory of the Republic of South Korea and conducting sabotage missions. This was something that Jun Lee became very good at.

XI Corps saw combat during the Libyan–Egyptian War in 1977, followed by the Angolan Civil War until 2002. Around 2004, as an instructor, Major General Jun Lee Sung trained Hezbollah fighters in guerrilla warfare tactics, prior to the Second Lebanon War in 2006. President Gin Jum Kim, having designed the Alliance, now needed a well-respected leader to lead the ground forces in Taswegia. At 54 years of age, Major General Jun Lee Sung was promoted to the position of General in 2010, bettering his father's record by four years.

He celebrated his 60th birthday during a visit to Taswegia, where he was accompanied by Raj Sumatro from Indonesia, Captain Li Chun and other officers from the invasion forces; all pretending to be senior citizens on holiday.

He returned to North Korea in late August 2014, to sort out the military side of the invasion, as well as to oversee the finalisation of the construction of the Super Tankers. By now this was grossly behind schedule, and with world events ramping up, the ball had started to roll; something that neither President Gin Jum Kim nor Jun Lee had any control over.

In 1974, he had married his childhood sweetheart, Chae-Yeong, who gave him two sons and a daughter, his eldest son being born 10 years later, followed by his daughter and youngest son, born 2 years apart. His eldest son became a teacher of Agriculture, specialising in the milling of flour, and was chosen to join the first convoy because of his skills in this area. As the General's son, he was automatically given a berth; but he still felt proud for achieving this under his own merit.

The draw of berths was controlled by the President, with places on the first Convoy strictly adhered to. Because of this, Jun Lee's family was allotted a berth on the 4th Convoy. His wife, Chae-Yeong, was on the *Julia Maersk*; this was supposed to set sail just after the 3rd Convoy, around 20th November. Unfortunately, the departure of the 4th Convoy was delayed; mainly due to the Super Tankers not being ready on time, along with other contributory factors such as political unrest, and people fighting over who should be allowed to go. It didn't sail till much later, on 10th December.

Jun Lee's daughter and youngest son were on the *Elizabeth Maersk;* like the *Julia Maersk*, this Super Tanker sailed on the 10th December. Included in this Convoy was the Presidential staff. Their escort vessels, which were considered to be of suitable size for the job, were two Najin Class Light Frigates which had been built in North Korea and refitted in early 2014 for the trip, four North Korean built Sariwon Class Corvettes, and two brand new Nampo Class Light Frigates. Unfortunately for all those on board, they only made it 840 nautical miles before they were all destroyed by the Nuclear Blast.

Chapter 12
Sabotage

0345 Saturday 17ᵗʰ January 2015 ... FCPB Fremantle, Chook Point Marina

"Doc, this is Jack, Chief Engineer. Laurel is on signals, and Vince on electronics and comms. Crew, this is Captain Johns, and ...?"

Dick left his introduction hanging, deciding to leave Doc to fill in the gap.

"Thanks Dick. This is Nari, triage nurse, and now my girlfriend. And what about you Dick? What do you do? Are you the skipper?"

"Used to be," grinned Dick. "Not any more mate; she's all yours. I'll just work the bang stick on the bow and torpedoes, do tricks on the wheel and pretty much whatever you want me to do."

Dick had already gone astern from the marina and was heading up the river towards the Bridge.

Doc asked,

"So, what's the plan Dick?"

Doc was still trying to work out how on earth his old mate had acquired the 203. Even more amazing was that he was now skipper!

As Laurel took Nari below, she yelled out to Dick, "Are Doc and Nari in the Skippers cabin?"

"Of course they are Laurel."

After showing the triage nurse where the showers and heads were, she gave her a quick look around the Galley and the Mess.

Dick continued.

"My plan Doc was to take the 203 to Fels Point, where we can refuel and re-water. It's all courtesy of the Alliance, but now that we think the 204 is up there as well, things are even better! We'll be able to do a soft berthing alongside of her.

"Vince, Jack and I will despatch the crew; shouldn't be too many remaining on board. Then, if we can get everyone to help hook up the refuelling hoses, we can refuel. If there are spare drums, we'll take those as well; the more the merrier.

"Once we have done that, the plan is to clean out the *Warrnambool* of all her ammo, weapons and as much food as we can get our hands on. Hell! If I thought we could unload their torpedoes I'd do it!"

Doc had been looking around the Bridge.

"Looks like they've ditched the push button throttles in favour of Morse Controls; they're probably less of a hassle."

Dick had handed the helm to the new skipper. Doc was now on his final approach to the *Warrnambool*, so Dick and Vince deployed the fenders. They were coming in on their port side, which meant they would berth on the 204's starboard side.

Dick whispered,

"With a bit of luck, the re-fuelling hose will still be on 204's deck. All we'll have to do is extend it."

Vince, Jack and Dick had armed themselves with their 9mm pistols, and Dick also had the silenced .22. Once the boys were clear and on board the 204, the girls would tie up. Laurel and Nari were busy getting lines ready as Dick left the Bridge. He gave Doc a grin.

"Mate! She's a stunner!"

Doc blushed.

"Thanks mate. You don't know how much that means to me."

Out on deck, there was a distinct chill to the early morning air, as well as the unmistakable scent of diesel mixed with oil.

Laurel had found Nari a jacket and the pair had taken up positions fore and aft, ready to secure the boat. The boys double checked their weapons, and each with one leg over the guard rail, waited until they touched. Doc skilfully glided the 137-footer alongside and with a short burst astern, brought her to a stop.

Wasting no time, the three were quickly aboard, and entered through the starboard hatch into the annex. They could hear the hum of one generator supplying power to the craft. As Vince made his way towards the Bridge, just along the passageway and up the stairs, Dick opened the XO's cabin door and shot the sleeping occupant with his .22. He checked the Captain's Cabin but found it empty.

Vince returned.

"All clear," he whispered.

After descending to the mess deck level, they made their way forward to the Junior Sailors' Mess. It was pitch dark down there, and there was a strong, but unmistakeable smell of stale body odour, mixed with the aromas of food and alcohol.

Stepping back outside for a moment, Dick motioned to the others that they would go on 'three', before silently signalling the count with his fingers. He turned the light switch to the 'up' position, revealing six sleeping beauties. Jack shot three, and Dick buried his knife into one sailor's chest, while Vince did the same with another. To their amazement the last one continued to snore away, oblivious to the danger he was in.

"Fuck! He'd be no good on watch!"

Even Vince's exclamation didn't wake him. The ex-petty officer technician quickly broke his neck.

Dick thought over the layout of the vessel.

"Better check the Senior Sailors' Mess next."

As he ascended the stairs, Jack softly called back, "I've got it Dick."

"Right Jack. Can you go with him Vince, and check out the Comms Centre on the way please?"

Dick made sure that all the junior sailors were dead, then checked every little nook and cranny, thinking to himself, 'We don't want any nasty little surprises now, do we!'

Meanwhile, Jack had finished in the Senior Sailors' Mess and reported.

"There were three more in there. I'm checking the Engine Room as well; they were only running one generator, but it's possible someone might be doing rounds."

Satisfied they had covered all bases; Dick went to report the all clear to Doc.

Working as a tight knit team, they all started hooking up the fuel hose and water line.

Puffing a bit as he went, Jack reported, "You were right Dick! Looks like the lazy bastards had finished but had neglected to put the hose back in its stowage. Makes things easier for us!"

Dick and Vince started unloading all the ammo and weapons. More good news; it seemed that she was as well stocked as the *Fremantle* had been.

Down in sick bay, Laurel and Nari went through the supplies. Nari knew exactly what she wanted. Laurel, who had been quietly observing the young South Korean girl since they had first met, suddenly blurted out, "I like you Nari!"

The younger girl had been worried that the others would not accept her and was taken by surprise at the older woman's comment.

Blushing she said, "I like you too Laurel."

Once they'd moved all the medical supplies to the 203, they started on the fridges and freezers. These had obviously been resupplied that day and were well stocked for their up and coming mission.

Jack was monitoring the refuelling progress, while Doc was on the Bridge, cleaning out anything of value he could find. Dick and Vince finished unloading the weapons and ammo then went to give the girls a hand with the food.

Dick looked around and announced with satisfaction, "Pantry is fucking full as!"

"You bet Dick!" said Laurel, "but you should have seen the freezers!"

Dick laughed; he loved his food.

"That's great! It means we can eat well for a while"

Satisfied that they wouldn't be going hungry, Dick turned to Jack.

"Do you reckon we can get our Hiab to reach their RHIB?"

Jack looked at his mate before replying, "Dick, I'm with you. You're a crafty old bastard!"

Doc, who'd been listening to the conversation, added with a grin,

"Are you thinking what I think you are thinking?"

He was too late; Jack was already on to it. After unhooking and extending the small crane as far as it would go, he turned to Dick, saying, "It won't reach Dick!"

The ex-CD, who'd seen the issue coming, was already tying a line to the 204's RHIB. Then, with a bowline tied in the end, he dropped it over the crane's hook.

"Give her some height Jack!"

It didn't take much effort; in no time at all the 204's RHIB was over on the *Fremantle's* deck. Then, after shortening up, he hoisted the RHIB into the cradle.

Doc was amazed.

"You're a smart bastard Dick! Well done. That will certainly come in handy back at Hells Beach."

They assembled on the Bridge of the *Fremantle*. Doc looked at Dick.

"What do you reckon we should do now with the 204?"

Dick gave him a wide grin.

"It's a shame, but I reckon we should blow her up; make it look like an accident. Jack, did Sarge give you the dynamite?"

"He sure did Dick!"

"Bloody hell Dick!" exclaimed Doc in amazement. "You've thought of everything! How much weaponry have we got?"

Jack stepped forward, giving Doc one of those cheeky grins from under his cowboy hat.

"I can answer that Doc. Shit loads!"

They replaced the re-fuelling hose where they had found it. Jack had managed to find six 200 litre drums and had filled them to the brim. They sprayed the diesel fuel around a little for effect, letting it run down inside the cowling, down the Engine Room hatch and along the main passageway.

Just as Vince and Dick were lashing the drums, a figure appeared, and started making his way down the long jetty. The ex-navy CD whispered, "Looks like it could be one of the crew coming back on board."

Jack quickly picked up Dick's .22, but then stated with dismay, "Shit! It's out of ammo!"

"No problems!"

Dick hopped the guard rail and waited. The man proved no match for the ex-Clearance Diver; quietly collapsing on the jetty as the end of Dick's twenty-centimetre knife blade entered his ribcage and pierced his heart.

After dragging the body on board and dumping it inside, Dick gave the thumbs up.

Doc whispered, "Slip all lines."

Laurel and Nari took the turns off the bollards while Dick hopped back on board, leaving Vince to light the cluster of dynamite, and heave it down the Engine Room hatch of the 204 before vaulting back on board as Doc eased out astern.

As they headed back down the river at slow ahead, the new Skipper enquired, "How did we go gents?"

Dick answered, "Well Doc, we were just able to add to the whiteboard I put in the armoury as we loaded, giving us a weapons status at a glance ..."

He was interrupted by the sound of the 204 exploding in a ball of flame. As they looked back the crew could see she was gently settling on the bottom.

Dick continued what he'd been about to say.

"... And it reads like this:

- 70 boxes of 50 calibre
- Six 50 calibre machine guns pedestal mounted
- 80 boxes of 7.62mm
- 56 boxes of 40-60 (5 clips in a box giving 1120 rounds)
- 20 old SLR's
- 30 Pindad SS2 Assault rifles
- 5000 rounds of 5.56mm

- Two F1 sub machine guns
- Two Armalites
- Six 9mm Browning Pistols left once I issue you and Nari one each
- 16,000 rounds of 9mm ammo
- A special SLR with Sniper sight and muzzle suppressor
- One hundred 80mm mortar bombs
- Six flare pistols and 60 flares
- Four Ultimax 100 light machine guns.

"All the ready use lockers are full of 40-60 shells, the gun is loaded and ready for action, and three 50 Cal's are ready. There's one on each Bridge wing and one on the quarterdeck."

Not to be outdone, Laurel looked at the skipper, adding.

"Freezers are full. We've got almost four whole lambs, a shit load of small goods, over two dozen chickens, beef roasts, and full back straps, full rumps, and sirloin. Then there's 150 kilos of potatoes, 50 kilos of carrots, 100 kilos of rice, 10 cabbages, 50 kilos of onions, 15 large cans of tinned tomatoes, 6 large cans of coffee, 4 boxes of tea, 5 cartons of UHT milk, numerous tins of herbs and spices, 12 cartons of soft drink and also about 50kg of Dim Sims. Oh! And then there's the grog."

Dick nodded.

"We're still waiting for the final count on the grog. Plus, we've now got a countless supply of sanitary items Doc."

Doc was impressed.

"Well done crew! And a great job in destroying the only threat to us on the water. 0610. Time to get out of here before Kings Town wakes up!"

Doc eased the throttles forward to half ahead.

"Make revolutions for 15 knots Chief."

"Roger that Skipper."

Jack grinned as he took over the throttles; he was taking a shine to his new captain.

Doc was fully aware that, up until that point, Dick had been in charge, and he certainly didn't want to take anything away from his old mate. God knows, he certainly deserved the accolade; just to be able to organise and pull off what the group had done under his leadership was phenomenal!

"Dick, what do you reckon? Stand down and alternate sleep for everyone? Looks like we could all do with it."

The ex-CD agreed.

"Sounds good to me Doc. You, Nari, Laurel and Vince take first break. Jack and I will keep the morning watch. Is that all right with you Jack?"

The ex-navy Sniper grinned.

"No problems Dick. We can make it happen, as long as you make the brews!"

Everyone left the Bridge and retired to their cabins. Doc and Nari had the Captain's Cabin, while Vince and Laurel had the whole Senior Sailors' Mess to themselves.

"Hot showers all round!" yelled Laurel, playfully grabbing Vince on the arse cheek.

"Jack, steer course *one eight zero*. I'll make the brews."

As they headed out of Kings River, Dick enjoyed his coffee. Jack re-emerged from his rounds, reporting,

"All good mate! She's purring like a pussycat."

Dick asked his mate's opinion.

"What's your take on today's events Jack?"

The slightly younger CD thought about it for a minute or two.

"Mate, for an aging bunch of ex-Pussers, I reckon we kicked arse!"

He was smiling under the hat that had become his trademark.

Dick concurred.

"I agree Jack, but do you think we have what it takes to wipe out the Alliance?"

Jack paused for a moment to think about that before replying.

"I'll be honest here Dick. If you had asked me that question a few days ago, the answer would have been a big fat, NO. But now, with the crew you are assembling and this boat, I believe we have!"

Dick added, "I think, with this vessel, and if we can find some more pockets of resistance, and, with our expertise, train them into a fighting force; unless the Alliance arrives in a destroyer or two, we do have a chance."

Doc and Nari cuddled up on the king single bunk in the Skipper's Cabin. The hot shower had done wonders for them both.

"I like your friends Doc," she whispered.

"They are your friends now love."

Nari smiled and put her head on his chest.

"I am happy now."

Although he didn't show it, Doc was feeling a bit overwhelmed with the events of the night. He was extremely grateful to Dick and the rest of the 203's crew for saving their lives; he only hoped that he and Nari could save Jack's wife.

In the Senior Sailors' Mess, Vince and Laurel were having a similar conversation.

"You like our new skipper, Vince?"

The ex-navy Electronic Technician replied, "Time will tell, but he seems to know what he is doing. I don't think Dick would let just anyone take over."

Laurel nodded.

"What about Nari?"

"She seems to be a good person. I bet the pigs gave her a really hard time; especially being South Korean."

Vince was secretly wondering why Nari had been allowed to live, when so many Taswegians had died.

By 0950 they were out in Thunda Bay proper, steering *one three zero*; the weather was on the nose, blowing in from the southeast. Dick pulled the throttles back to 10 knots, trying to take the thumping out of it.

"You take the wheel Jack, while I give them all a shake. Just keep her on that heading for a while."

Dick tapped on the skipper's door saying, "Time mate."

To his surprise, a voice yelled, "Come in Dick."

He entered to find Doc and Nari sitting up in bed, a bit like lord and lady muck! Doc started, "Dick, Nari has something to say."

As Dick took a seat at the desk, he looked at the pretty Asian girl, realising she'd probably been to hell and back. Nari, who was dressed in one of Doc's tee-shirts, spoke up shyly.

"Dick, I would like to say thank you for saving our lives. I am deeply in your debt. I know you and Doc go a long way back; I am lucky to be part of your lives now."

She put her hands together in front of her face and bowed, then got out of bed and gave Dick a big hug, blushing slightly as she did so. As she climbed back into the skipper's bunk, Dick realised that the girl had no underwear on.

"It's my pleasure," was all he could think of to say in reply. He turned to go, and then stopped at the door and finished his report.

"In Thunda Bay, off Red Beach; punching into a light swell, force 4."

After first knocking on the door to the Senior Sailors' Mess, he woke Vince and Laurel from one of the best sleeps the pair had enjoyed for what seemed like forever.

Jack yelled from the Bridge, "Here we go again Dick; on the UHF!"

Dick made it to the Bridge just in time to hear the last of the signal through the repeater …

"Bravo Zulu. Bravo Zulu. This is Bravo Echo. Do you receive? Over."

Jack, who already had the microphone, handed it to Dick with a 'here we go again' look.

"Bravo Echo. Bravo Echo. This is Bravo Zulu. Go ahead. Over."

There was silence.

"The signal is weak mate, see if Vince can make it stronger."

With that, Jack shot down to the Senior Sailors' Mess to ask Vince to have a look at it.

"Bravo Zulu. Things are not so good here. Indo Alliance has set up HQ. Fear cannot hide much longer." Shhhhhhhh …

Vince appeared on the Bridge. He realised the problem straight away.

"I'll see what I can do."

He disappeared into the Comms Centre just as Doc surfaced. Dick quickly filled the skipper in.

Vince gave a yell from the Comms Centre.

"Give that a go Dick!"

"Bravo Echo. Bravo Echo. This is Bravo Zulu. Go ahead. Over."

"Bravo Zulu receiving 20/20. Cannot rely on hiding place much longer. Are you able to assist? Over."

Dick locked at Doc.

"What do you reckon Skipper?"

"We will operate on April first, then go and find these people."
He turned to Jack.

"What's our fuel status Chief?"

"Full tank when we left the 204 four hours ago. Plenty of fuel Skipper."

"Right. We will work out the logistics later. For now, the most important thing is to get Jack's wife on the up and up. Tell them we'll be a few days, and can they hang on till, say, Tuesday?"

After pressing the talk button Dick transmitted.

"Bravo Echo. Bravo Echo. This is Bravo Zulu. That's an affirmative! Repeat. That's an affirmative! Can you wait till Tuesday? Over."

"Bravo Zulu. Thank you. Thank you. We will be here. Be careful! The roads are treacherous! Over."

Doc looked at Dick.

"I've got an idea. Ask them if anyone there has a brick phone. The NK Nationals won't know what that is if they are listening. If they've got one, give them the number."

"Bravo Echo. Bravo Echo. This is Bravo Zulu. Don't suppose anyone has access to a brick phone? If you can get to one, dial 0189991236. Repeat 0189991236 at sparrow's fart Tuesday. Out."

"Station calling on UHF repeater channel 1, do you copy? Over."

Dick looked at the UHF set.

"What the fuck! Who was that?"

"Unknown Station Delta Echo. Repeat Delta Echo. Bravo Zulu reading you faint. Go ahead. Over."

We all knew Delta Echo was the international code to use when a signal is hard to read. The Bridge was silent, with everyone wondering who the other station was. Was it the Alliance trying to catch us out?

"This is Fortescue. Repeat Fortescue. 0184721651. Over."

"What was all that about?" asked Vince, looking at the others. The 203 punched into another wave head on, sending a shudder through the boat and the bow wave spraying out each side.

"Beats me," said Jack, shaking his head. "I know what it is. It's a bloody brick phone number! But who the hell is Fortescue?"

Dick replaced the microphone before he accidentally pulled the cord out of its socket in the constant moving of the boat.

"That I can answer! That, my friends, was Johnny Badman calling from Strong Fort Bay."

Dick and Jack left them on the Bridge. Jack had filled Vince in with Engine Room rounds and told him to give him a shake if anything was out of place.

Jack showered in the junior sailors' heads; he had the whole Junior Sailors' Mess to himself. Choosing a fore and aft bunk with a good fence, he was soon fast asleep.

Dick showered in the officers' heads and retired to the XO's Cabin. He was wondering about Patch and the team back at Hells Beach; he couldn't wait to be with her again.

Nari had found the sea conditions not to her liking at all, so Doc suggested she stay lying down in their cabin. Vince, Laurel and Doc got to know each other as they did alternate tricks on the wheel.

Laurel appeared back on the Bridge.

"It's too bloody rough to go up on the Flying Bridge!"

Doc agreed.

"You got that right Laurel!"

Laurel was feeling a little off herself, and opted to go back to bed, leaving Vince and the Doc to look after the Bridge.

By 1300 the FCPB was off Cape Ray.

"Vince," said Doc, "can you get Dick and Jack up please mate?"

The forty-seven-year-old had a bit of a smirk on his face.

"Gee! Manners! That's a first for a skipper."

Although Vince was smiling, Doc wasn't sure what to think of the ex-Pussers Communication Technician.

He turned to port, steering *zero nine five*. The weather just seemed to drop off; the sea state was .5, and the swell non-existent.

Doc pondered over the charts as he worked out a course to Benowa. The distance from Hells Beach was about ninety nautical miles; six hours steaming at fifteen knots. If they got away bright and early Tuesday morning, say 0300, they should arrive at the Gulch by 0900. He certainly knew the area well enough; he'd been there many times in *Footy*, and in the old *FCPB 211 HMAS Bendigo* as well.

Dick appeared from below, asking, "What do you guys feel like for scran?"

Dick realised he hadn't eaten since last night; he was starving! After rounding up some Dim Sims from the freezer, he soon had them steaming. announcing half an hour later.

"Scran is served! Hot steamed Dim Sims with soy sauce accompanied by fresh bread ... well, as fresh as we're going to get it anyway ... thawed and heated in the oven. Help yourselves!"

After devouring a Dim Sim or two, he took over the wheel from Doc.

"I'm sure glad they retro fitted the wheel back and got rid of the bloody joystick Doc!"

Vince did his handover to Jack and grabbed a bowl of food on the way aft to Laurel in the Senior Sailors' Mess.

Doc ran the figures past Dick and explained his plan to get the people out of Benowa.

"The Alliance was expecting the *Fremantle,* so let's show up and re-fuel. I know the layout at the Gulch. If we can get the survivors to wait in the bush adjacent to the Gulch until we give the signal, then we might be able to pull it off.

"If we are challenged, Nari can speak a little Indonesian, and if all else fails, we'll have to shoot it out."

The ex-navy CD was smiling.

"Sounds like it could work Doc, although there's one problem I've just thought of."

Doc looked at Dick, wondering what he'd missed.

"What's that mate?"

"Well, Hells Beach is not that big. The introduction of another dozen people will fill her to bursting point. I'm thinking we should take them to John at Strong Fort Bay instead.

"They will have better facilities there than what we have at Hells Beach. We could even help train them to fight. Do you want me to ring John now on the old brick phone?"

Doc agreed.

"Sounds like a plan Dick. Give him a call, but don't tell him we are going past the door. There's a deadline we have to meet first; April's surgery."

Dick picked up the brick phone handset and dialled the number John had given them.

018472165 ... *Brrr ... Brrr ... Brrr ... Brrr...*

"Hello?"

The voice on the other end sounded hesitant.

"Yeah mate," responded Dick. "Is John there?"

"Speaking. Who's this?"

Dick gave John a real quick run-down on the events so far and asked him about facilities and numbers.

John explained their situation.

"We are holed up in the old camp; we've felled a huge tree across the access road and have it guarded day and night. So far the Alliance haven't got through, although I don't know how long we can hold them off if they manage to cut the tree up.

"Oh, and we have twenty-nine residents: eight couples, one single and twelve children. Can you assist?"

Dick explained to John that they were trying to save some people from Benowa and would try to get them to Strong Fort Bay by sea.

Doc whispered to his mate, "I see Dick that you didn't actually tell them what sort of vessel we're in."

"You know Doc, what they don't know won't hurt them!"

After a buzzing sound from the brick phone, there was silence. Dick listened for a minute before stating, "I think the prick's hung up!"

Doc was wondering how Nari was feeling.

"I'd better see how she is mate; see if she wants something to eat. Well done on the scran."

Jack came up from below, with his bowl crammed full of the tasty Dim Sims.

Dick asked, "Mate, are you a bit hungry?"

The fifty-one-year-old replied, "I'm bloody starving Dick! I've had nothing to eat since last night."

"Yeah! Funny about that."

"Was that the phone again just now Dick?"

As Dick filled the ex-CD in on the basics of what was happening, they throttled up to fifteen knots, and then headed towards Mans Island.

Brrr ... Brrr ... Brrr ...

Dick looked at the caller ID, picking it up as he realised it was John calling back. John told him that the phone had cut out because of low battery; he'd fixed the problem by plugging it into the solar charger. He thought the idea of taking the people from Benowa was a good idea, but wanted to know how they were going to do it, and whether their yacht was big enough to carry everyone.

Dick didn't let on; just told him not to worry about the details. When they got close, they would call on the UHF channel twenty-seven.

John asked, "Do you have any weapons? Or is there anyone there who's capable of training us to fight back? I know you told me you are ex-navy."

Dick answered with a grin, "I'll get back to you on that mate."

Doc found Nari sound asleep. After eating his Dim Sims, he stripped off and climbed in alongside the little triage nurse. She was naked and woke with a smile after Doc started caressing her smooth body.

"I'm hungry Doc."

"I thought you might be."

Doc handed her the bowl of steamed Dim Sims, before dressing and heading off to get more to eat. He returned to find Nari sitting up in the bunk finishing her lunch. After sharing a soft drink, she snuggled back down below the covers, leaving just her eyes showing.

"What time you go back to work my man?"

The sixty-five-year-old replied, "Got about three hours. Why do you ask?"

Nari gave him a cheeky grin.

"Let's make love."

Vince found Laurel looking better, and ready for some lunch.

"It seems a lot calmer now Vince."

"Almost like a mill pond Laurel!"

The pair quickly dozed off together.

1600, and they were coming up on Mans Island. After easing her rounc to port, and steering course *zero zero five,* Dick announced, "We're heading home Jack!"

TRF vessel FCPB Fremantle in Thunda bay
Photograph compliments of LS/POETP Gary Haigh

Chapter 13
Laurel Bradley

aurel Bennett was born in 1970 to her parents, Ian and Moira Bennett. She was raised in Victoria in a little town near the Navy training establishment, *HMAS Cerberus*.

Her father was a civilian contractor who worked at the depot as a catering contractor, dealing with the requirements of all the messes on board. Her mother worked as a teller in the local Commonwealth Bank at Frankston. Laurel had a brother, Tony, who was two years her senior.

With Ian working at *HMAS Cerberus*, she came into constant contact with junior sailors, senior sailors and Wardroom staff, and with navy life in general. It came as no surprise to anyone when young Laurel announced her intention of joining the Royal Australian Navy at the dinner table one night.

She was 17 by then and was accepted into the RAN as an adult recruit in October 1987. Her early childhood had been pretty normal for a girl living in a middle-class family. She had the usual boring friends, did horse riding at school, hated her brother, and didn't get on all that well with her parents.

They spent more time trying to manage her brother's life. He was constantly getting into trouble with the law; either for doing drugs or for breaking and entering. Tony had a rap sheet as long as your arm by the time he was 16 years old.

There's nothing much to tell in the way of the boyfriends who came along as she was growing up; there was the odd pimple-faced kid who tried to get into her pants, but who got nowhere with the strong-minded girl, who stuck firmly to her morals.

She loved her dog Smooch, a golden retriever, and would spend hours with him, even showing the dog at local shows from time to time. Laurel felt more strongly about Smooch than she did about her family and told them so on many an occasion.

Poor Smooch came to an untimely end when he was run over by a passing car after Ian accidentally left the gate open; Laurel was 17 at the time, and this was the catalyst for her to decide to enlist.

After joining *HMAS Cerberus* and completing recruit training in December 1987, she signed up for the Communications branch, completing her comms training at *HMAS Watson* in Sydney in April 1988.

Laurel served at numerous bases around the country, eventually meeting Vince Bradley in Darwin in 1989, whilst he was on shore leave from the Guided Missile Destroyer (DDG), *HMAS Hobart*.

Her relationship with the then Petty Officer Electronic Technical Communications sailor was on and off over the course of the next year, but they stayed together long enough for Vince to finally ask Able Seaman Bennett to marry him in December 1990.

Married life worked well with their Navy careers and suited them both. They eventually paid off in 2006, and, after looking for somewhere to settle, they decided to move to Taswegia.

Chapter 14
Radar Contact

I t was 1645. Jack was doing a trick on the wheel, just for something to keep his mind active. Dick was consulting the charts as the *Fremantle* cut through the frothy sea like a spoon through the froth on a cappuccino. The pair of old warhorses were chewing the fat about all sorts of things, their time in Pussers, shooting, cars, and also Jack's new found interest in boats again after their little jolly in the CJ.

As always, on the agenda was the inevitable question of whether or not they were going to survive the war. They could both see that this was what it was all ending up as now, a bloody war.

The sixty-one-year-old leaned over to look into the radar screen's tunnel. Jack jumped as Dick exclaimed, "Holy shit Jack! We have a contact!"

Jack took a look at the large blip bearing green *zero eight five* on the 916 Radar screen, adding, "It's stationary Dick. After the E1, it might just be a dead-in-the-water freighter or something."

Dick waited for three minutes before taking another fix on the vessel.

"No, she's making way. Better get the Doc."

Jack moved to the stairs, saying, "I'll go mate!"

Doc and Nari surfaced on the Bridge five minutes later. After taking a look for himself, Doc agreed.

"You're right Dick. She's making way; she's moving slow but is definitely making way."

Doc looked at Dick, who was already going for the ship's broadcast microphone. Dick pressed the transmit button.

"All hands to the Bridge! All hands to the Bridge!"

They all gathered and listened to the findings; contact twenty miles to sea, off Hippolyte Rocks.

Doc spoke first.

"The way I see it we have two options. The first is to do nothing and just keep going to Hells Beach so that we can get on with the long-awaited operation needed by Jack's wife, April.

"Our second option is to alter course and investigate the contact. If my hunch is correct, we have an NK tanker in our sights. This will be one of the long-overdue convoys and is probably the one with the replacement doctors and nurses on board."

The silence was deafening. Vince enquired, "How many people are on this tanker Doc?"

Nari was quicker, and answered Vince.

"If it's like the first one, there will be 200,000 NK Nationals and 75,000 Alliance troops, 44 jeeps and 100 trucks!"

Vince looked at Doc.

"And these are the ones that will make your colleagues obsolete Doc?"

Doc, who had a slight tear in his eye, looked at Vince.

"I guess that's one way of putting it!"

It was a difficult decision to make. Doc turned to Jack.

"Hey Chief, you have the most at stake here. What would you do?"

They all knew that Doc was talking about April. Her pending operation had already been delayed long enough. Should he delay it a little longer, or was that too big a risk?

The ex-CD sniper didn't hesitate.

"Starboard thirty. All ahead full Dick. Let's sink that sucker!"

Dick got the nod from Doc. Looking around the room, he knew the decision was unanimous.

"Starboard thirty steer *zero eight five*, distance to run twenty miles."

Doc looked at Jack, who was near the throttles, saying, "Jack, all ahead full. Increase revs to make twenty-five knots."

The Patrol Boat leapt forward like a surfer catching a six-foot wave. With the turn of speed, the bow lifted, and the stern dug in, creating a stern sheet six metres high. Between them they worked out a plan.

As they approached the tanker, Nari, Laurel and Doc, dressed in some of the Indonesian uniforms that had been stored on board, would be on the Flying Bridge. It would be a bit of a squeeze to get into them, but it should work from a distance. Dick would be on the 40-60 Bofors, with Vince loading for him, and Doc would be on the wheel. Nari and Laurel would operate the .50 calibre machine guns, if necessary, with Jack playing torpedo man.

Vince looked at the others.

"Who knows how these bloody torpedos work anyway!"

Jack butted in.

"Dick's our weapons man."

The sixty-one-year-old ex-CD Specialist smiled before launching into his explanation.

"Thanks Jack. This will be boring to some, but you asked for a run down. Well, here it is.

"The twenty-one-inch diameter Bliss Leavitt secretly designed MK 48 torpedo was developed post World War II. The Mk 48 was the U.S. Navy's first 21-inch by the shorter 18-foot torpedo. Speed was 48 knots and the maximum range 36,000 yards ... that's 33,230 metres, or 3.3 kilometres.

"Weight is 2600 pounds, or 1100 kilos. They feature an electric motor propelled acoustically guided with 466 pounds of plastic-bonded explosive in the warhead, and they're ten times more deadly than the original MK 8 torpedoes. They were designed to be tube-launched off Patrol Boats by compressed air and have an internal battery-driven electric motor to drive the torpedo. The direct-action warhead explodes when it hits something. It's simple but effective. These puppies are guided by the noise of the ship's engine and screws; you set the depth before they are fired.

"They were originally launched by a small explosive charge, but they found the grease used to lubricate the torpedo in the tubes used to catch fire, which left a smoke trail and alerted the enemy to its origin. I can say that we have four MK 48s on board. It's a simple sighting system; the torpedo man, who in this case will be Jack, will use the primitive sight on the launch tube to sight the target. Using local comms, he will recommend a course alteration to the Bridge until he gets a firing solution.

"When the Bridge tells him that we are at firing range, he will hit the plunger to release the compressed air, and ultimately the torpedo. Once the fish is in the water the electric motor will drive the fish at forty-eight knots towards the target. The in-built homing device uses sounds from the target to acquire a signal, and then homes in on it."

Following Dick's history lesson, each of the crew had very different thoughts on the matter. Doc, while peering into the 916 radar at the blip on the screen, was deep in thought about his compatriots back at the Kings Town hospital. More the question, what was going to happen when the Super Tanker berthed? He knew that Li Chun, under the direct orders of General Chun Lee, would simply execute all the doctors one morning at muster. As much as he loathed the Alliance, he had been thankful knowing that, as long as they didn't have their own medical staff, the Taswegian staff would be relatively safe. Doc wondered what would happen when the General realised that he and Nari were missing. He'd left no clues about how they'd left. He was fairly sure that the General knew nothing about *Footy*, but even if he did, she was still moored in the marina. Maybe he would come to the conclusion that they were both dead.

Nari was sitting on the chart table alongside Doc. She couldn't help thinking of all the times she'd been raped and beaten by the Alliance officers, who'd treated her like a dog. 'No!', she thought, feeling full of hatred towards them, 'Worse than they'd treat a dog!' She thought about the 200,000 NK Nationals who were about to die; they had no knowledge of what the Alliance was doing here in Taswegia. As far as they were concerned, they were merely coming to a new place, where they could begin their lives again, although it would be extremely naive of them to think that the Taswegian population would just let them have it!

As he did his machinery rounds in the Engine Room, Jack was thinking of those members of the Alliance that he had directly come into contact with already. To him it was simple; they were the enemy, and you had to kill them before they killed you. He refused to let the numbers of unarmed civilians who would die on the Super Tanker weigh heavily on his mind, he was quite certain that if the shoe was on the other foot, they would have no compunction about killing him, or any other Taswegian. The thought of April, the love of his life, with an Alliance bullet in her shoulder, close to vital arteries, sent shivers up his spine. He knew he was doing the right thing.

Vince, who was sitting in the port lookout's chair, felt quite impartial about the decision. Although he and Laurel had seen with their own eyes the extent of the Alliance's cruelty and sadistic killing, it wouldn't have worried him if they simply went home. He had not been part of what had happened to the Doc and Nari, but in a way he could sympathise with them. Being a Sailor meant that he was used to killing people in a ship-to-ship battle, both in theory and in real life; to him this was no different.

Laurel, who'd taken a seat in the starboard lookout's chair, hated the Alliance with every part of her being, witnessing the death and destruction of the last ten days or so had made her re-think how she felt about the whole idea of what is right and what is wrong. Having to take part in killing some of the troopers herself had made it easier for her to understand and recognise how trained killers dealt with the same thing. However, she knew it was going to take her a long time to get over the things she had seen.

Dick was on the wheel, watching the horizon for signs of the contact while monitoring the compass repeater to make sure he stayed on course *zero eight five*. He was not even thinking about the 200,000 NK Nationals; to him they were just the enemy. Like any trained killer, Dick was just doing what he had been trained to do, with no emotion; it was a simple 'them or us' scenario. He had seen enough of the Nationals to know they would have killed him in the blink of an eye if given half a chance. In Vietnam he had been put in the position of having to kill what some people would have seen as civilians, but he had been well trained to look beyond the façade and into the political world of the Khmer

Rouge; where through communism, they had turned 50,000 peasants into fighters. Every one of them would have died for the King!

By 1800 Nari, Laurel and Doc, dressed as Indonesian naval personnel, were up on the Flying Bridge. Dick and Vince had each managed to find a camo shirt which almost fit their bulky frames, and were waiting on the Bridge with Jack, who, with his smaller build, fitted quite well into a shirt he'd found. It had four gold stripes, the rank befitting a Master Chief Petty Officer.

"What's the range Dick?"

"Range five miles Doc."

After peering through the binoculars at the Super Tanker, Laurel reported.

"They're signalling us Doc, although it obviously makes no sense to me!"

After taking a look through the glasses himself, Doc said to the ex-Communicator, "Read it out as they signal, please, Laurel."

"*Di … di … di … di…di da da…di … da…da … da … di…di di…da di…* translates to 'hwag-in'."

Nari knew what it meant, and quickly explained that it was the North Korean term for 'Identify'.

"Here we go!" said Doc, then continued, "Nari, can you please translate this for Laurel to send on the signal lamp."

Nari gave him a nod as he continued.

"Indonesian Navy PB203 English please!"

The triage nurse thought for a second, then wrote the message down in the North Korean language.

"Indonesia-eo haegun PB203 yeong-eo hasibsio."

Laurel worked out the Morse before turning on the Aldis Lamp and sending the reply.

Di di…da di…da di di…da da da…da di di… di di di…di di…di da… di…da da da…. sending the whole message in Morse.

Dick reported, "Range three miles Doc!"

"Roger that Dick! Laurel, get ready to lower the Indonesian flag please; we might as well go in with no colours at all."

Dick overheard Doc's order and yelled, "I can fix that Doc."

A few moments later Dick stuck his head up on the Flying Bridge and handed Laurel the small white ensign he had carried in his Pusser's grip.

Doc smiled.

"Bloody beautiful Dick! When I give the order, run that up the tree Laurel."

As the ex-communicator clipped the tattered ensign to the flag halyard, she said to Dick, "Looks like it's off one of those A-Boats you were on Dick!"

Dick laughed, admitting she was right.

"Well, it's like this Laurel, I had to get a little souvenir for my services."

Laurel reported, "They're sending again, this time in English Doc."

She scribed the message as she translated the Morse code.

"*Super Tanker Kim Maersk out of Haeju North Korea bound for Kings Town as part of the Alliance requesting engineer's assistance main engine only operating at 5% acknowledge over.*"

Doc and Nari looked at each other.

"This would explain why they are so late arriving. Ask them where the other vessel is in their convoy Laurel."

Laurel flashed off the message.

"*Report whereabouts other tanker in your convoy over.*"

The return was swift.

"*Separated by bad weather a week ago, somewhere astern of us?*"

As he thought through what laid ahead Doc asked, "What's our range Dick?"

Dick checked the 916 Radar screen before answering. He could see the Super Tanker was now appearing as a very large blip.

"Range two miles Doc!"

"Roger that Dick."

Grabbing the ships broadcast microphone and hitting the Claxton at the same time, Doc broadcast to his Crew.

"Action stations! Action stations! Close up torpedoes and the 40-60! Laurel run up that ensign!"

He pushed the throttles all the way forward, bringing the FCPB to its maximum speed of thirty knots. The bow lifted in response to the two 3,200 HP MTUs, it's stern sheet spraying like a peacock's tail and the bow cutting through the waves like a hot knife through butter.

Jack manned the forward torpedo tube on the port side, finding it better to sit astride the tube in the *Fremantle's* motion. Sighting at the Super Tanker, he realised he was off target by ten degrees at least. He could be seen from the Bridge, but used the portable UHF radio to request, "Alter course ten degrees to port Doc."

Doc turned to port.

"Steering *zero seven five.*"

"Spot on Doc. What's our range?"

"One mile Jack. Fire when ready!"

Jack opened the locking plate on the accumulator tank firing button, then, after checking one more time to make sure he could see the ship in his sights and on course, he pushed the plunger.

"Fish away!"

The eighteen-foot torpedo was ejected from the tube. A sudden rush of compressed air pushed the twenty-one-inch cylinder out into the ocean, hence triggering the electric motor gyro and acoustic homing mechanism to come to life. The single four blade propeller drove the Mk 48 torpedo towards its target at an astonishing forty-eight knots. They were well within its 3.3-kilometre maximum range, and it was pre-set at a depth of four metres. The firing solution looked good; taking it just seventy-five seconds to reach the *Kim Maersk.*

Doc reported, "Torpedo track looks good people."

The explosion was huge! Doc quickly turned the 203 to starboard and throttled back to fifteen knots as the Super Tanker was hit just forward of the superstructure, which was the presumed position of its fuel tanks. Everyone on board felt the shockwave.

"Small arms fire coming from the tanker!"

Laurel and Nari ducked below the Flying Bridge cowling to try and avoid being hit. Doc spoke into the ship's broadcast system again; they could hear the anxious flutter in his voice.

"Engage 40-60 in your own time! Target that fire!"

Dick, in the operator's chair, and Vince, standing on the loading platform, had already closed up on the 40-60 Bofors gun. They had previously taken ammo out of the ready use lockers and loaded the racks on the platform, which meant that all Vince had to do was to take them out of the rack and sink them into the loader on top of the gun. Dick lifted the locking bolt, and fired up the hydraulic motor, turning the mounting to port and sighting the trouble area.

Vince pulled back on the cocking lever, lowering the breech, then pushed it forward to load a round. Dick immediately pulled the trigger attached to its new cable, which in turn depressed the firing plunger on the gun near the breach assembly, allowing the firing pin to come forward and fire the gun. The recoil of the gun ejected the brass casing on the back stroke, spewing it out on to the deck, and then picked up the next round, pushing it into the breach. This would continue all the time Dick kept depressing the trigger, and for as long as Vince kept ramming the four round clips into the top of the gun.

One round in four had a red tip, meaning it was a tracer; the white phosphorous would leave a smoky trail to aid sighting. It didn't take too many clips to silence the small arms fire coming from the bow section of the tanker.

Laurel reported,

"Light machine gun fire coming from the second deck of the superstructure Doc!"

By then the *Fremantle* was past the bow of the tanker and turning hard to port. As Doc brought her down the port side of the ship, the 7.62mm rounds from the light machine gun came thick and fast. He had to duck away from the incoming fire saying

"I'm going below to helm her from the Bridge!"

Dodging a hail of bullets, Nari followed the aging Doctor below as Dick opened up with the 40-60 again. Three clips were enough to silence the machine gun.

The *Kim Maersk* was settling by the stern. Her bow was well clear of the water as Dick continued to sink round after round into the tanker, aiming at the waterline and annihilating the lifeboats.

Doc declared in frustration, "This is taking too long! I'm bringing her around for another torpedo run. Are you right Jack?"

The ex-CD-come-engineer was ready, quickly moving over to the starboard side.

"Starboard number one tube ready Doc!"

After turning a figure of eight, Doc bought the 203 back on line approaching the port side of the tanker.

"When you're ready Jack."

Jack took aim, lining the tube sights with the tanker amidships, just forward of the superstructure.

"Port five degrees Doc."

As they turned to port Nari reported, "Half a mile Doc!"

"Fire Chief!"

Doc continued to port, ending up off the bow of the tanker, as the fish dropped into the ocean. Some thirty-seven seconds later, an explosion ripped into the *Kim Maersk*, right under the superstructure; followed moments later by a huge explosion. Dick ceased firing, then turned to Vince with a broad grin, saying.

"Looks like that was the fuel tanks."

Doc announced, "Finished with the 40-60."

Vince and Dick reported to the Bridge. The *Kim Maersk* was not in good shape; she had started to list to port, and as they watched, some of the containers on deck began to slide overboard.

Laurel, who was glued to the binoculars, reported from the Flying Bridge.

"Still can't see any sign of people," before adding, "Negative! Looks like troops on the Bridge wing with an RPG. Yep! Incoming!"

Doc turned to starboard and pushed the throttles forward. The 203 surged up to thirty knots as a rocket propelled grenade grazed the flag deck and then exploded as it ricocheted off the steel guardrail stanchions on either side of the communications aerial.

Dick climbed up onto the Flying Bridge wing and pulled the starboard .50 Calibre machinegun around to bear on the trouble. As the Patrol Boat came about, he wedged both feet hard against the cowling to steady himself in the violent movement. As they headed down the starboard side of the tanker he engaged, sending a box of half-inch rounds into the Super Tanker's Bridge wing.

Vince manned the port .50 Calibre as Doc swung the 203 about, bringing the port gun to bear. Vince opened up, almost frightening Nari out of her wits! She had never heard anything like it before and was shocked at the noise. Even Laurel was a little shocked at how fast it had all happened.

After bringing the FCPB to a dead stop Doc asked for a status report.

Dick was feeling the thrill of the action and was in his element. He reported, "40-60 fully loaded and ready! .50 Cal's reloaded and ready!"

Jack reported, "Engine Room ready Doc!"

Jack, Vince, Laurel and Dick joined Nari and Doc on the Bridge. In solemn silence, they watched the tanker slide gently under astern. Dick spoke first.

"Well team, I am extremely proud of all of you! For those of you who have never been in action before, you outdid yourselves. I know you will agree Doc?"

The aging doctor was feeling more than a little bit stunned. With his twenty-five-year-old girlfriend hanging on to his arm like grim death, he found it hard to speak. He realised that, as Skipper, it was his job to do what Dick had just done, but it was his first time in action, and he was speechless and trembling terribly. All he could manage was.

"Top job on the 40-60 guys!"

Jack spoke up, quickly realising that out of everyone in the room, it was only he and Dick who had any prior combat experience.

"And Doc, you handled the old girl like a pro!"

Doc looked at Jack and Dick with a slight tear in his eyes, admitting, "You two! I couldn't have done it without you two! Hell! I couldn't have done it without all of you!"

Laurel went white. As she started to slide down the bulkhead, Vince caught her and cradled her in his arms, stating, "A bit much for my girl I think!"

Doc hugged Nari a bit closer, adding, "And mine Vince! And mine!"

He smiled at Nari and gave the triage nurse a kiss.

"Come on you two," laughed Dick. "Get a room!"

Jack looked at the tanker.

"She's just about gone!"

The *Kim Maersk* was in her last throws. As they watched, she gently slid under, leaving only a small oil slick and a bit of flotsam as evidence that she had ever been there. Even the couple of containers that had fallen overboard had sunk to the bottom.

Vince exclaimed, "I can't believe that they didn't try to abandon ship!"

"1900! Shit! Is that the time? What's for scran?"

That broke the tension in the room. They all laughed.

"Is that all you think of Dick?"

"Nope. But that's because Patch isn't here!"

Jack took the wheel, steering *three three zero*, while Dick rustled up some grub. While Doc and Nari retreated to their cabin, Vince and Laurel sat in the Junior Sailors' Mess and watched Dick at work in the Galley.

After putting on a huge pot of train smash, fresh new potatoes and cold corned beef, he served Vince and Laurel's meal before finishing his own scran, then tapped on Doc's door on his way to the Bridge.

"Come in."

As Dick entered, he found Doc sitting on the bunk with Nari.

"Scran's ready! Permission to splice the mainbrace Skipper!"

Coming out of his daze, Doc replied, "Yes of course Dick. And mate, once again, thank you for everything."

Dick relieved Jack on the Bridge, informing him of the skipper's decision, and giving him a chance to eat. A bit later they all pulled up a pew and toasted the success of the 203; Jack with a mug of Johnny Walker black and coke, and Vince and Laurel with a cold beer; while Doc, Nari and Dick enjoyed a mug of Shiraz.

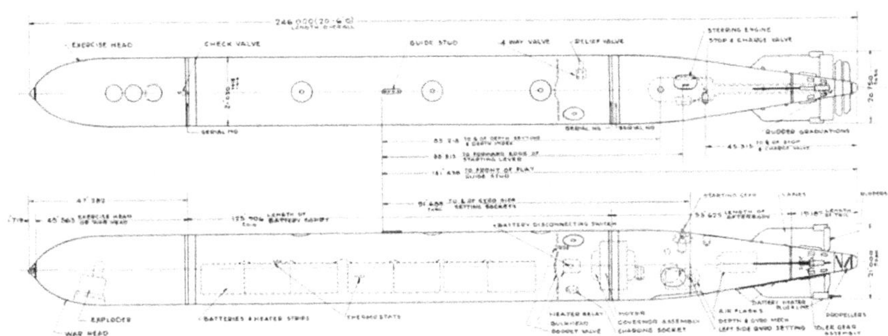

Mk 18 Torpedo

Chapter 15
Indo Maersk

On board the *Indo Maersk*, Admiral Adi Atmadja was sitting at his desk in his day cabin, pondering over his meeting with the Alliance General the day before. He was not happy!

Conditions on board were far worse than he'd wanted the General to know, and on top of that, the unloading had got off to a slow start. The kill and clean-up squads had to go out first, which was slowing up progress considerably.

The Admiral had called an emergency meeting with his top three officers. The first was Captain Raja Atmadja, who was the Admiral's nephew and the son of his brother and was also in charge of transport. Major Huje Samira was in charge of logistics, while Lieutenant Colonel Raj Sumatro was in charge of placements.

"Good morning gentlemen. Thank you for coming. As you know, we now have a major problem. Because the Alliance does not have sufficient vehicles and manpower, we are restricted in transport, as well as in the availability of the homes.

"I have allowed for 10,000 of our troops to assist the NK Alliance in making sure this problem is rectified quickly. It seems that some of the back-road properties have been missed. Captain Atmadja can you update us please?"

The younger Captain stood and consulted his notebook before speaking.

"Admiral, we are able to put together the following: 100 Alliance trucks, 135 of our own M35A3 trucks, and 50 jeeps.

"With a total of 235 trucks, each carrying fifty personnel, we can move 11,750 at once. If we reduce the number of troops in the jeeps, we will be able to carry another 200 in them, so, a total of 11,950 in one convoy."

"Very good Captain. Now tell me about logistics Major Samira?"

Huje Samira was a veteran soldier with thirty years' experience.

"Admiral Atmadja, I suggest that we try and move two convoys each day at first, and then, as the distances become longer, drop back to one per day. I know this will put a strain on our drivers and troops, but far better that, than to have more deaths on board."

The Logistics Major was referring to the many deaths that had occurred due to the accommodation decks below them being so crowded. Although the ship had been designed to carry 200,000 Nationals and 75,000 troops, they all knew that the reality was greatly different to what had been intended. Some two weeks into the voyage, it had come to the Admiral's attention that, instead of the planned 200,000, they were actually carrying 250,000 Nationals on board. The main cause of this overload had been because of greed, and also the inability of those in charge to control the loading situation. Lack of extra food, dysentery, disease, and unsanitary conditions had all taken their toll.

There had been 900 deaths so far, and if they couldn't unload quickly, it was obvious that there would soon be a lot more.

"Estimated time to disembark all the cargo Major?"

Huje, who was secretly hoping for some kind of miracle, advised, "Ten days Admiral."

The Admiral turned and looked at Lieutenant Colonel Raj Sumatro.

"And tell me, are we going to have enough homes available to place all these people into?"

The Lieutenant Colonel replied, "Based on original investigations, we should be able to house whole family groups in these very spacious Taswegian farmhouses, so I do not anticipate any problem with numbers, Sir."

The Admiral looked at his three officers.

"This is great news gentlemen, and as promised, you and your families will be rewarded with the pick of the properties on route. What is the turn around to the first lot of properties Captain Atmadja?"

The young officer had anticipated the question and had already done the sums.

"Barracouta is around 100 kilometres away; convoy travelling time there is two hours. It will take them approximately one hour to disperse the occupants along the way, meaning the estimated time of a return journey is five hours. As we get closer to Benowa this time will double."

Major Samira stood up.

"I have a proposition Admiral. Perhaps we should just concentrate in getting everyone off. When we get as far as Benowa, we can look for suitable buildings in which to house them temporarily, then distribute them further up the coast later."

Adi thought on this matter.

"Do you think this will work Major?"

"Yes Sir. Half the trucks can be utilised to run backwards and forwards to Benowa around the clock, while we use the other half to distribute the people up the coast."

The Admiral nodded in approval. With a satisfied smile, he dismissed the three officers.

"Let the games begin!"

Loading was already taking place, with family groups travelling together in one truck where possible, and with each truck departing the minute it was fully loaded.

A troop jeep led the way; they figured that, by the time the drivers had completed their first or second trip they would know the route backwards.

The Indonesian M35A3 variant was introduced as part of the military's main transport vehicle fleet in 1994. They had Caterpillar 3116 diesel engines and a lot had their manual transmissions replaced with automatic. Built by AM General in the USA, the original version was 6.98 metres long, but it had to be cut down to fit into a 6-metre container. The first one off the assembly line was built in 1950 and had a petrol 127HP motor. This 6x6 2· ton, triple-axle cargo truck, with its now diesel engine, was perfect for the work that had to be done in Taswegia.

The original CAT 3116 engine had been refitted at the time the inner Alliance was formed; the seating capacity was normally twenty, but with a centre seat running down the middle they could now squeeze fifty into it.

Captain Atmadja would travel in the lead jeep and supervise the first convoy. He considered this to be a smart move, because he had his eyes firmly fixed on a property just out of Barracouta!

"Let's hope the Alliance jug-eum-ui-bundae death squads and bundae leul jeongli clean up squads have done their job!"

Raja still intended to send a single jeep with every five trucks to provide protection. He was also well aware that the Admiral wished for two troopers to be assigned to each farm as protection, rather than one trooper, as was the case with the NK Alliance; however, he was well aware that this would stretch their troop numbers very thin.

As they headed out of town, he could already see Taswegian homes which were now occupied by NK Nationals. Very soon it would be his turn. After driving through East Kings Town towards Soothe, they passed the former Kings Town Airport, which was now more like a ghost town. They then turned left at the Soothe junction and headed up into the more 'bush-like' areas. He had fallen in love with these whilst travelling in Taswegia on their reconnaissance trip the year before.

His own family was in the truck travelling behind him. There was just himself, his wife, her parents, and their four children; his was considered one of the smaller families.

Major Huje Samira, who was travelling a bit further back in the convoy, was also pleased to be out of the town. With 20 or so trucks in front of them they were creating quite a stir with the NK Nationals. Indeed, Huje was quite certain that many of them were not even aware that the Indonesians were part of the Alliance.

He had also been on the trip last year and had his eye on the perfect property for his large family. Not only were both his and his wife's parents still alive; he also had 12 children. He carried quite a tribe and felt that the property he had found at Rocky Bay, overlooking Scallop Bay, would be perfect for their needs.

He had fallen in love with the vineyard at Devils Beach, but unfortunately the Admiral had chosen it first. As they passed through the seaside town of Oxford, he knew that by now the first trucks would be unloading, just north of Barracouta.

Lieutenant Colonel Raj Sumatro travelled in the last jeep of the first convoy; his job was to make sure that everyone had taken their allotted homes, and to iron out any squabbles that came up along the way.

He had also been earmarked to run the Benowa headquarters. The amount of planning that had gone into mapping every home, property, shack, and business from the outskirts of Barracouta, right up to St Anne, had been phenomenal. His team of placement staff had then offered a ballot for each family group to take. In other words, if a family wanted to run a farm, they applied for the ballot on farms. Raj's staff also took into consideration the size of the farm and the size of the family, the livestock it carried, and also the social status that would come with it.

The ballots were divided into different groups: vineyards, cattle, sheep, vegetables, fishing, accommodation houses, hotels, motels, takeaway shops and restaurants. These categories were for the more affluent families, with the general farm and other hands ending up with the shacks and smaller homes.

Raj's family consisted of his wife and their three children, along with their respective parents and his grandfather.

He was to remain in the military and be stationed at Benowa and had taken a shine to a large house built right on the beach. It was quite a new dwelling and was certainly well beyond his status back home. But here in Taswegia, as Colonel in Charge of Placements, he had a very good chance of acquiring it.

Captain Raja Atmadja's jeep pulled up at the property known as 'Billroger'; a 10,000-acre property, which carried cattle, sheep and deer. It came with a six-bedroom brick house that overlooked the valley.

He supervised the unloading of his family, and told them he would be back later, before moving up the road a few kilometres and stopping to unload the next family. And so it went on for the next twenty-four farms. As each truck emptied its load, it returned to Governors Wharf; with the lighter load, the return journey didn't take anywhere near as long to complete.

As the second convoy for the day reloaded, Raja reported to the Admiral that all was going well. A constant stream of trucks was now travelling up and down the coast, and his transport staff was doing a marvellous job. His Master Sergeant in particular was doing such a good job that he decided to recommend him for a property he had seen today.

Huje Samira unloaded his family at Rocky Bay. This property was huge, and although it had mainly been used to run cattle, it had an oyster farm attached as well. His father and mother had worked on an oyster farm back in their hometown of Tanjung Ringgit, on Lombok Island.

He knew he was going to love it here, and that his father and the rest of the family would be at home running this 5,000-acre property. It came equipped with two houses and a granny flat, as well as numerous out buildings, including an oyster handling shed. Although there was no power, they soon had outside fireplaces operating, and with plenty of fresh vegetables out in the garden, he felt he was truly in heaven. He couldn't wait to spend time with his family in his new home.

He would be able to do this soon enough; his time in the military would be complete once all the Nationals had been placed in their new permanent homes.

Although Lieutenant Colonel Raj Sumatro had unloaded his five trucks, he was still a long way from Benowa. He would have to wait a couple of days before being able to unload his family at the seaside town. After returning to the *Indo Maersk* to pick up the next convoy, he was handed a communiqué by the Admiral.

"Colonel Raj. Benowa now has been cleared of Taswegians, except for the two doctors we have spared for now. Well, not quite so; one has been executed for insubordination. However, we have news of one or two pockets of resistance that may be gather'ng at Benowa. They were last heard on the UHF channel One.

"As of Friday, the ninth of January, it seems there were twelve of them, and there also appears to be a smaller pocket somewhere north of Benowa. Their whereabouts is unknown at the moment. Your mission, once you are settled in at Benowa, is to find them and kill them all!"

Chapter 16
Look what the Cat Dragged In

Saturday 17ᵗʰ January 2015 … FCPB Fremantle, Hells Beach.
Through Doc's eyes …

By 2200 the FCPB 203 was carefully navigating the entrance to Hells Beach. I grabbed the microphone and piped, "Hands to anchor stations!"

Then, after positioning the Patrol Boat in the middle of the bay.

"Let go!"

With the anchor chain rattling down the hawse pipe, the pick quickly settled on the bottom. I went astern, setting the anchor in the sand, some eight metres below, then throttled ahead and stopped.

After Vince had applied the brake to the windless, I yelled out to Jack,

"Finished with main engines Chief."

I turned to Dick and Nari.

"How do you see this happening with April mate?"

Dick could hear Jack climbing up out of the Engine Room and waited until the ex-CD was on the Bridge before answering.

"I've been thinking about that. Out of the two choices we have for where to carry out the operation, it makes more sense to do it here in the sickbay. It's cleaner, and everything is fixed at a far better height. But you two are the experts, it's your call. What do you want to do?"

Nari and I looked at each other.

"Sickbay? I didn't think these old girls had a sickbay!"

"Too true Skipper. I guess I should fill you in about all the modifications our esteemed Indonesian friends have done.

"Well, the sickbay was once what you knew as the ship's office. They did a pretty good job of converting it, with an operating table, a second prep table, a huge settee and plenty of storage for medical supplies.

"You already know about the torpedos and the RHIB. This twenty-two-foot inflatable is a black one and was used for covert operations by their *Korps Marinir*. The twin 150HP Mercury Veradas will push it along at nearly fifty knots. Mind you, they are pretty banged up, you can see where they've been patched and repaired a few times. They're also smaller than our twenty-six-foot Hamilton Jet versions; only seating six in front and four behind the centre console.

"Because of the overhang, they did away with the rocket launcher on the quarterdeck, and of course they had to fit a large older style Hiab to lift it on and off. There's lots of other little changes, but you'll be able to check these out for yourselves."

I was rather in awe of all the changes; looking at Nari, I could see that she was too.

"We agree Dick. We'll do it at 0900 tomorrow morning in our sickbay. Can you arrange for April to be transported out to the ship?"

Dick nodded. He was watching the navigation lights from the RHIB as it approached from the starboard side.

"Looks like Sarge is on time. Doc and Nari, for tonight at least, are you right to bunk down on board? It's probably a bit kinder than staying in the camp right now, especially as we don't have anything in place for you."

Sarge appeared on the Bridge and was introduced to the pair. Jack reported, "Running on the port generator only."

"Right. See you two at 0900."

Sarge butted in.

"Dick, we had a raid planned tomorrow, just Annie and I. But now you're here, do you think you will be up for it? I Thought Jack and Patch might like to stay behind and assist the Doc, and Nari of course, with the operation."

Dick mulled it over, saying, "Well, if everyone can do without me, I'll come and assist. Where did you have in mind?"

Sarge explained.

"We're off to Bronze mate. Thought we would come in from the other direction and cause some havoc, as well as collect a few more weapons and ammo. And, most importantly, we're planning on bringing back some chooks for April to play with once she's recuperated enough. Patch says it's okay for me to ride Zen again."

Jack, Vince, and Laurel boarded the RHIB, leaving Nari and I to enjoy a night alone together. Patch and Annie were waiting on the beach, and came forward to give Dick a hug, while Jack made a beeline to where April was propped up in bed.

"I really missed you Chook, and you too Annie. Oh, and you of course Sarge."

As they dragged the RHIB up the beach, Dick added, "I could go a cold one Sarge."

The ex-Sapper looked at his illuminated watch, saying that, although it was well past bar hours, this time he would make an exception; then wandered off in the direction of the stream refrigerator yelling, "Anyone else while I'm there?"

Patch yelled out, "I'll have a wine darling!"

Vince and Laurel answered together, saying, "A beer would be great. We'll give you a hand Sarge."

Sarge was smiling to himself as the pair joined him.

Later, as they relaxed in the camp chairs around the fire, Dick recapped the events of the last few days. By then Jack had appeared with his half bottle of Johnny Walker, reporting that April was finally asleep.

"She's pretty tired. I told her about the transfer to the 203, but she didn't seem too worried; I think she just wants it over and done with."

Annie gave him a hug.

"She's a pretty tough old bird Jack!"

Sarge was interested in hearing about how it had gone with the raid. He listened attentively as Dick and Jack told the others about the sabotage of the other Patrol Boat, as well as the tanker and especially the weapons and ammo they had acquired.

The ex-Sapper asked curiously, "How's Doc, Dick? And tell me all about his girlfriend. How did Millie die?"

Dick filled in all the spaces.

"She's a pretty good kid. Apparently, she's also a great triage nurse, but I reckon you'll get to witness that tomorrow. Speaking of which, what time did you want to get away Sarge?"

Annie answered for him.

"We reckon Bronze will be about four to five hours away, depending on our speed, so we should leave here at 0600. This will give us around three hours' trouble time when we get there."

Dick directed his next question at Sarge.

"You think the backpacker's accommodation up behind the café is where the Alliance troops hang out?"

The forty-five-year-old nodded in agreement.

"Based on what Vince and Laurel reported, that seems to be the only place they could use as a headquarters mate. If we get in and kill whoever is there, as well as take all the weapons and ammo we can get our hands on, it will assist us with the next part of the plan you were telling us about."

Sarge was referring to the training he had been asked to deliver at Strong Fort Bay. Annie went on to tell the group about her plan to bring back a couple of chooks for April to play with.

"As she gets better, she's going to need something to do that's not too hard on her body, so I thought having some chooks around would be a great idea. I saw a pen full at the old fellow's place; you know the one that had the porker."

Everyone agreed it was a good idea, and that April would really appreciate the opportunity to get more into the sustainable way of living that she liked.

Dick summed things up.

"So, the plan is for Annie, Sarge and I to go on the raid. Vince, Jack, Patch and Laurel will transfer April into the RHIB and on board the 203 so that Doc and Nari can start the operation by 0900. That is unless you want to come along with us Vince; keeping in mind that you would have to spend twelve hours in the saddle on either Cowboy or Fannie."

Vince pulled a face as he thought about it.

"Thanks for the offer Dick, but I think I'll pass. I thought Laurel and I could load up the excess weapons and ammo on to the RHIB and transport it to the Freo if that's all right?"

Dick smiled to himself as he answered.

"That's great mate. Don't forget to leave the personal weapons, as well as a good amount of ammo, just in case. Sarge can use most of it when we train John's mob."

"How well do you know John, Sarge?" asked Patch.

"From memory, Dick and I have met the man maybe three times. Oh, and Vince, you should leave a couple of Claymores here for reserve; just in case we get anymore unwanted visitors!"

"What unwanted visitors?"

Sarge had forgotten that he hadn't told Dick and the others about what had happened in their absence.

"We had some drama while you were away."

Sarge and Annie went on to describe the events that had unfolded; how they'd had to track the kid, about the ride to Willy Town, and all about the four that Sarge had to kill while they were there.

"I brought the trooper's weapon back, along with a hundred rounds."

Patch then told them about the turn April had taken for the worse, and how she had been worried about how long Sarge and Annie had been away for.

Yawning, Sarge looked at his watch.

"It's after midnight! We've all got a big day tomorrow. Time for bed I think."

Dick and Patch peeled off and crawled into their swag. As the rest of the camp quietly dispersed, Dick whispered, "Are you right helping the Doc and Nari tomorrow, Chook?"

Patch snuggled up to the man she loved.

"I sure am Love, and you make sure you take things carefully at Bronze."

Dick had been thinking about April.

"Just how bad was April, Chook?"

Patch explained how she had found April slumped over after she'd returned from her swim, and about what Sarge had said after he and Annie returned.

"April seemed to come right after that, although, I don't think she's 100% right Love."

Dick could hear the concern in her voice.

"Let's hope Doc can get that bullet out! I'm sure in a few days she will be feeling a lot better."

Laurel and Vince liked their new sleeping arrangements; now that the two single swags had been zipped together, they were actually larger than a conventional double swag. They also liked the privacy provided by the canvas screens set up around them.

Laurel sleepily whispered, "Good of Dick to invite you along Vince."

Vince, who knew that he would never have lasted twelve hours in the saddle, said, "Yeah. I must admit that I would have liked the action. I'm sort of wishing I had seen more while I was in the Puss."

"Who do you reckon will go to Benowa, Love?"

Vince thought over the options.

"I reckon you and I should stay here and guard the fort. Annie might stay as well, although, I reckon if Sarge is going to do the training, she will want to go with him."

Laurel smiled as she remembered the way she had felt while they were on the Patrol Boat.

"Good idea Love. We could clean up, do a bit of skinny dipping, and maybe you could even get some fishing in off the *Cecil Jane*. Should be able to catch something from where she is moored in the Gulch."

Vince gave his wife a cuddle.

"It sounds good to me."

Annie and Sarge were discussing the impending raid.

"I'm glad the big fellow agreed to come with us Annie; we could sure use his expertise."

Annie was well aware that Dick would be a great asset. It would really be Dick and Sarge doing all the fighting, she would just assist where possible. Being in a fight scared her a bit; she was still reeling from the time when she'd had to jump Tom over the gate with the Alliance troops hot on her tail. Sure, she liked the adrenalin rush it had given her at the time, but it had still scared the crap out of her.

Even when she'd pulled the trigger at Buckle Peak, she knew this had been more of a reflex action. What she had been too embarrassed to tell the others was that the sudden noise of the weapon had made her slightly lose control of her bladder. It hadn't been enough for the others to notice but had been embarrassing none the less!

"What weapon do you want me to use tomorrow, Hon?"

Sarge replied, "How did you like the pump action 12 gauge?"

"It's a bit loud, and I couldn't hold it properly when it went off. I really don't think I'd be able to aim it properly. Do you think I could have a go with the one Patch had?"

Annie was referring to the F1 sub machinegun.

"Perfect Doll; I'll take an SLR. Don't forget to strap on your 9 mm Browning as well; you'll also need at least three clips for the Browning and four for the F1. That's because, when you squeeze the trigger, the bullets keep coming out until you let go, which means ammo tends to get used up fast."

Annie snuggled closer, "I love you Sarge!"

"I love you too Annie!"

Jack crawled into bed alongside April, being super conscious not to move her or bump her shoulder. He lay there watching her breathe, and thinking about the operation tomorrow. He knew Doc and Nari were her only hope. He was secretly glad that Dick hadn't asked him in front of the others to go on the raid.

They'd discussed it in private and both agreed that he would be better off staying and assisting where possible, instead of spending the time worrying about what was happening with April. He could boil water and fetch whatever was needed, as well as assist Patch with feeding the group for lunch.

Jack's thoughts wandered to the Benowa trip; he really liked being back in the Engine Room, although he really wanted to train some of the others to help. He went over the fuel consumption in his head; they'd used a bit more than expected when they'd torpedoed the Super Tanker, although they still had shit loads left.

He realised they would have to re-fuel whenever they could, and that it was possible that one day they might not be able to. They would simply run out. They still had the drums on deck, but he'd already decided to save these until the absolute last minute.

On board the FCPB, the gentle hum of the port generator was barely distinguishable from the Captain's Cabin. Nari and I had both enjoyed a hot shower, in fact, she had started to get a little frisky while we were under the water. I was well aware of the water restrictions and was already feeling a bit guilty about having a shower, knowing the rest of the gang wouldn't have had one, so I persuaded her to wait until we went to bed. Nari didn't bother getting dressed; she pretty well dragged me by my old fellow over to the king single Captain's bunk, before wrapping her arms tightly around my neck, causing us both to collapse on to the mattress. To say that Nari took a commanding role in this frolic would be an understatement! It was good to be alone at last.

Later, sitting up in bed, I made a note on my pad to remind me to get Jack to give me a status report on the fresh water on board. They might have to re-water at Benowa at the same time they re-fuelled.

Nari prodded me under the ribs.

"Are you worried about the operation tomorrow, Doc?"

I looked at her, mesmerised by the way the sweat made her breasts glisten in the twenty-four-volt lighting; she looked so beautiful, with the afterglow of our love-making still lighting up her face.

"Are you worried my Love?"

She laughed.

"Not when I am with you! You are the best Doctor, and you are my man!"

I ran through the procedure in my head, hoping that we would have all the right instruments. I was pretty certain that, between us, Nari and I would have acquired whatever was needed. We would be right. The plan was to sedate April, then, with no x-ray facilities available, to just go in and get the round out; fixing any problems that we encountered along the way. The biggest risk I could think of was the possibility of a major bleed; and we would be ready for that.

"I'll cook you eggs and bacon for breakfast my man?"

She was already sliding on top of me again. Was it possible that the colt from old regret could rise again? It looked like the answer was "Yes!"

Chapter 17
Bronze Raid

Sunday 18th January 2015... Hells Beach Campsite

0515. Sarge looked at his watch then nudged Annie, realising that at some stage in the night, they had removed their underwear. Sarge, who couldn't remember doing it thought to himself that he must be getting old. He grinned to himself, 'I better not tell Annie that!'

"I'll shake Dick and get the billy on Doll."

Annie dressed quickly as she replied, "Love it when you call me that! I'll go and saddle up."

Dick was well and truly in the land of nod when Sarge slipped his arm in through his side of the canvas screen. They'd both agreed that this was the best way to wake each other up without disturbing their respective partners. He gave the big fellow a shake.

Dick yawned.

"Thanks mate. What time is it?"

Sarge showed him the illuminated dial of his watch; 0524.

Trying to exit a swag without waking the other person sharing it was an art all on its own, and one that Dick thought he was good at. But not today!

Patch grabbed the ex-Clearance Diver and hugged him tightly; he thought he could discern a tear in her eye but wasn't sure. In the pre-dawn light, he could have been wrong.

As he collapsed into a camp chair Sarge handed him a cup of coffee.

"I've put the lemon in Dick, along with a dash of cold water; just the way you like it!"

The ex-CD was still only half awake.

"Gee Sarge, I've trained you well. I needed that. Where's your missus?"

After giving Dick that 'what the fuck' look, Sarge nodded in the direction of the horse enclosure.

"Oh! I see," laughed Dick, "How silly of me to ask!"

After leaning forward and turning the bacon, Dick cracked another egg on to the steel plate, which by now had heated up nicely. He could see Sarge had some of Patch's left-over damper toasting on the side.

Annie quietly crept up behind the big fellow and put her hands around his neck; Dick reacted instinctively. With a speed that almost scared the petite twenty-eight-year-old out of her socks; he yanked her over on to his lap, keeping her in a tight headlock.

Sarge shook his head as he looked at Annie.

"I've told you not to sneak up on the old fellow like that! You're likely to get hurt."

Dick kissed her, apologising for scaring her.

Annie gave him a hug.

"It's all right Dick. It was my fault. Sorry."

After they'd finished eating, Sarge and Dick went over to the tent to select the weapons they'd need. Sarge picked up the F1, along with four spare magazines.

"Annie wants to try the F1 mate."

"Should suit her down to a tee Sarge. It's definitely better than that old scatter gun!"

Once Annie had strapped on her 9 mm Browning semi-automatic pistol, Sarge handed her the three spare mags to go with it. Then Dick and Sarge followed, also adding their SLR bayonet scabbards. On top of that, the two men chose the old faithful SLR's; first checking that the mags were full, then picking up a spare magazine each as well as six speedy clips. They stowed all these into the wither bags, along with a couple of grenades apiece.

By the time they'd finished, Annie had all three horses tacked up, and had cleaned their hooves and made sure the emergency saddlebag was full and strapped to the near side of her saddle. The two canvas rifle buckets were strapped to Bob's and Zen's offside rear saddle dees. She also tied on the large canvas double bags they planned to use to carry the weapons they were hoping to collect. These, of course, would also carry the chooks. They knew Bob would appreciate any weight-saving that they could pass on to him.

Dick went to answer a call of nature, before going back to the swag to give Patch a big kiss.

"See you tonight, Chook. Hope all goes well with the op."

"You be careful Dick!"

There is something about the smell of freshly cleaned saddlery; it was obvious that Annie had taken the liberty of cleaning all the gear, including Dick's saddle and bridle. Dick untied Bob before wrapping his lead rope around the sixteen-hand Waler's neck and tying the traditional cavalryman's knot. This was an efficient way of keeping the lead rope out of the way while riding, but still easy to get to in a hurry if needed. As he watched Annie and Sarge do the same to Tom and Zen, the big fellow felt pretty bloody proud of them both.

He looked at Sarge and pointed to his wrist.

"0556 mate."

After leading the horses through the sleeping camp, they got to the bottom of the track that led up out of the beach. Annie was already in her lead rider position; patiently waiting until Sarge and Dick had mounted. She had been taught that the lead guide always mounted last; just in case there was a problem they had to attend to.

As Dick watched Sarge mount Zen, he realised he'd fallen into the old habit without thinking about it. 'Yes,' he thought to himself, 'I'm not the guide today.'

After swinging his left foot up into the near side oxbow, he grabbed a handful of mane with his left hand, and whilst still holding onto the reins, reached over and held the off side knee pad. He mounted with ease, not moving the saddle at all, then gently eased into the seat of his eighteen-inch Australian stock saddle; being careful not to bounce on his aging mount.

Dick loved the feel of the 16mm rope reins in his hands as he held them comfortably in the middle. Some riders thought his reins were too short, but he'd always loved them that way, with no excess to get in the way. The only disadvantage was when Bob wanted a drink; at those times Dick had to go with him, leaning forward to allow the big bay brown to quench his thirst.

He remembered using a pair of traditional five-foot webbing and leather reins back in the beginning. They hadn't lasted long. One day, when he'd been cantering Bob on an exercise ride, the buckle end of the reins had landed on the seat of the saddle just as he'd come back down onto the seat. He'd never forgotten the excruciating pain!

After mounting, Annie turned in the saddle, "Are you two old fart's all right?"

In the dawn light Dick thought he could detect a nervous smile.

Annie led the trio up the steep path that ended at the top of the sand dunes, overlooking Hells Beach. From his place at the rear, and with the F1 slung over her back, Dick thought she looked more like a Greek Partisan than a Taswegian horseback trekking guide.

As she rode over the top, she came across the small log which had been placed across the track. Just in time she remembered to stop. Sarge, who had already caught up to her, handed the reins to Dick as he dismounted Zen. After walking the extra twenty metres the ex-Sapper knelt and disconnected the trigger wire to the Claymore Mine.

"Right, you two."

Annie and Dick proceeded through the trap, with Dick leading Zen.

Sarge completed the re-wire before mounting again; then the three set off at a walk.

Dick turned in the saddle.

"Mate, I think that was a great idea of yours to place the Claymores where you did; especially now that we've already had one incident which justified their reason for being there. By the way, was it much of a mess to clean up?"

Sarge moved Zen up closer to his mate, trying not to speak too loudly. He didn't really want Annie to hear. He was thankful that, by now, she was a good forty metres in front.

"Mate, I didn't let Annie see the god-awful mess. You know Claymores. There was absolutely nothing recognisable from the waist down; just blood and bits of flesh all over the foliage. I managed to drag the upper torso away and throw it over the cliff, although I couldn't do much about the red stains everywhere."

Annie turned, asking, "What are you two whispering about?"

Dick and Sarge had been heavily engrossed in conversation and hadn't noticed the twenty-eight-year-old guide slow down.

Thinking quickly, Dick pretended, "Just admiring your arse, Annie!"

This had been a favourite saying of his from his guiding years. People would often ask why he liked leading from the rear, not realising that his real reason was so that he could observe their riding ability.

"You bastard, Dick!"

Although Annie was feeling a bit embarrassed, she was still smiling as she added, "I know you two are up to something!"

Sarge looked at Dick.

"Not us Doll!"

Moving forward, Sarge caught up with Annie and gave her a cuddle as he whispered a few words of encouragement. Then, after slowing Zen down a bit, he waited for Bob to settle alongside.

Dick looked at Sarge, asking, "Is she a bit nervous mate?"

The ex-Sapper nodded. This trip was different to the first one; it wasn't a spontaneous act like before. This time they were riding to Bronze for the main purpose of killing as many Alliance troops as they could.

No wonder Annie was feeling nervous; to be frank, Sarge really hadn't expected her to want to come along. Sure, they'd talked about getting some chooks for April, but then one thing had led to another, and before they knew it, they'd found themselves discussing the raid on Bronze. Collecting more weapons had become of paramount importance once they'd heard about Dick's conversation with Johnny Badman.

Dick had always found that, once a track became familiar, it never took as long to travel it as it had the first time. This was certainly the case here. They could see John's old farm now; just becoming visible through the plantation. Although they were still a couple of clicks away, they could make out NK Nationals working in the fields.

They turned right, then continued through the plantation, heading west towards Bronze. Sarge was wondering whether Vince's bike was still where he'd left it.

"Good question Sarge; let's hope no-one has found it."

The scenery was a far cry from how it had been the last time the pair of ex-military riders came through. Sarge was telling Annie about all the mist that had been around that morning.

"But today is brilliant! Not a cloud in the sky."

Dick was thinking that it was a great day for killing but decided not to say that out loud. He and Sarge had both wondered whether Annie would pick up the location of Vince's bike as they came to it; they were both happy when she rode right by it without seeing it. They didn't tell her until sometime later.

"I don't believe you two!"

Sarge laughed.

"Believe me, it's true! I'll show you on the way back, Doll."

They were approaching the old couple's farm on their left; they could see smoke coming out of the chimney. For now, Annie just wanted to make sure that the chooks were still there. After stopping the horses at the same place Dick and Sarge had tied them up last time, Sarge whispered, "I'll go and do a reccy Doll."

He smiled at the twenty-eight-year-old and gave her a wink as he grabbed the SLR out of the bucket and disappeared towards the farm. It was a couple of hundred metres to the first shed; by the looks of it, it was an old dairy. A lot of these old farms still had these remnants of the days when you used to milk your own couple of house cows.

The old two-stand dairy still showed signs of its former glory, with the old vacuum pump still in place in the little room alongside of it. The hoses were still coming through the wall, although they were perished and useless by now, and their suction cups were long gone.

Right next door to the dairy was the chook shed. Sure enough, there were still a good number of chickens in there, happily scratching away, totally oblivious to what had happened in the rest of the world. Coming closer, Sarge counted ten chooks and also a couple of roosters. He smiled as he went back to join the others, thinking to himself, 'Annie will be pleased.'

Even before he had climbed back under the fence Annie asked, "How many chooks Sarge?"

She was full of excitement; just like a kid who wanted to please her mum.

"I reckon there's a dozen Doll; ten chooks and two roosters."

Annie handed Sarge his reins.

"How many do you reckon we should relieve them of?"

Sarge re-mounted Zen and the trio started walking off in the direction of Bronze.

"I'm thinking three chooks and a rooster should be a good starting pen's worth."

As they approached the outskirts of Bronze the time was nearing 1030. As Dick moved up to the front, Sarge said to his mate.

"Looks like we made good time, Dick."

"Time coes fly when you're having fun mate."

Before crossing the Julia Bay Road, they waited for a moment to make sure it was clear; then, once they were all safely across, moved into the bush behind a couple of homes. After turning right, they could see the old café, come service station, behind the houses.

Vince had told them that the backpacker's accommodation behind the café was now the troopers' base. From what they could make out from their cover, the place looked like it was alive with troops. The trio stayed hidden, observing all the activity for around twenty minutes, and trying to identify exactly what was happening.

Sarge thought he was beginning to make sense of their routines.

"I reckon they must come back from a job and then go in for a coffee break. As you can see, the truck comes in and unloads about twenty of them, and then leaves again fifteen minutes later."

Dick nodded in agreement.

"Sarge, I reckon you've got it almost right, although it's not the same group leaving. I reckon they must change over crews each time. I suggest we wait until the next truck leaves and then we go in. We have no idea how many are inside, although, given the size of the café, there couldn't be any more than a truck load's worth left. With staff and a few dead heads, maybe thirty troops tops!"

Annie clutched Sarge's arm.

"Isn't that too many Hon?"

The ex-Sapper looked at the woman he loved.

"It'll be fine Doll. You stay and look after the horses, although I wouldn't tie them up, just in case we have to leave in a hurry."

Dick gently put his hand on Annie's shoulder.

"Remember Love. If anyone comes this way don't hesitate to shoot first!"

Sarge grinned as he added,

"Unless it's us, Doll!"

The pair made sure that both of the twenty-round SLR magazines were full. They had taped the second magazine upside down to the one that was already in the weapon; this would make it quicker to change magazines once the first was empty. They each had a couple of extra clips in their cargo pockets; adjusting their trouser bottoms, they both checked that the rubber bands were set right.

"Ready when you are Sarge!"

The ex-Sapper nodded, before leaning over with a smile to give Annie a kiss.

"We shouldn't be too long Doll."

The nervous ex-trekking guide wrapped her arms around Sarge's neck and whispered, "You'd better not be! I love you Sarge."

Crouched down by a large industrial wheelie bin, Sarge and Dick quietly looked at each other as they fixed bayonets, knowing that from there on in they wouldn't need to talk unless there was an emergency. Once they were both ready, they sat waiting for the old KM 450 truck to leave, watching as the troops poured out of the café and climbed into the back of the truck. A fresh driver and off-sider mounted up front, then they heard the aging cat diesel engine turn over and fire, followed by the crunch of the truck's tyres on the gravel as it headed off. After reaching the main road, it turned left towards Sand Alley; passing the next truck as it came in to unload. It didn't take long for its occupants to exit the truck and make their way into the café.

After a thumbs up from Dick, they were off, reaching the nearest door into the café in ten strides. This was the back door come staff entrance and led directly into the kitchen. Sarge entered first, with Dick covering. Two staff were inside; the first had his back to the pair, while the second was getting something out of the gas oven. Sarge targeted the NK National who was bending over; and, with the butt of the SLR delivering a well-aimed crack to the skull, the man dropped like a stone.

Dick did the same with the one with his back to them. A quick lunge of Dick's bayonet, saw the eight inches of steel embedded deeply intc his chest. Sarge followed suit, running the NK National through the back, before placing his foot on the cook's back and withdrawing the bayonet.

The café itself sounded pretty noisy. Dick took a look through the little glass window in the middle of the door, before turning to Sarge and flashing his hand five times. Sarge understood this to mean that there were twenty-five troops inside. As they looked around the kitchen, they realised the pair they had just despatched had been about to dish up a feed.

Sarge took a quick look, acquainting himself with the layout of the café. Most of its occupants were sitting at various tables and enjoying a cup of something hot, while their weapons were all leaning against the end wall. Tapping Dick on the shoulder, he pointed to his weapon and leant it up against the wall, before pointing to the end of the café. Dick nodded, before holding three fingers up, then two, then one, to signify the count down.

Sarge moved forward first, stepping in through the swinging kitchen door, then quickly moving left towards the side door and the weapons. Dick went right and towards the back of the café, which was where most of them were sitting. Sarge was cool and calm as he fired his first eight shots as was Dick. Simultaneously and systematically, they made their shots, carefully aiming for the head and upper body areas. In the enclosed space the noise was deafening!

The NK troopers were taken completely by surprise; some of them just sat there, as if they were in a dream. For some of them it would have been their first time in battle; they would have been mesmerised at seeing the two aging warhorses kitted out for killing.

Sarge and Dick were able to despatch sixteen troopers before the others realised what was going on. It was absolute bedlam! Finally waking up to the danger they were in, the remaining troopers sprang to their feet in a desperate rush to get to their weapons. Unfortunately for them, their way was blocked by Sarge, who continued to fire, quickly bringing down another four and then finishing off another couple, who were lying on the floor, with his 9mm.

Dick reloaded, then shot another two against the other wall before being attacked by one of the troopers in a frenzied last-ditch lunge. The ex-CD ran his bayonet into the man's stomach, twisting it as he withdrew, and then hitting another would be attacker with the butt and finishing him the same way as they had the kitchen staff.

It was all over inside two minutes!

Sarge quipped with a laugh,

"Think they were faking it mate!"

Dick double checked the bodies for signs of life while Sarge kept a lookout outside; they were both surprised that no-one had come running towards the café. From the outside it must have sounded like World War Three was going on!

Dick emptied all the ammo out of the troopers' pockets while Sarge collected the weapons, then whistled to Annie from the back door. Keeping a wary eye out for trouble she bought the horses over for the lads to load up. They secured the Type 68 assault rifles in the deep canvas bags; these were a good size, meaning they could easily fit eight into each side, as well as store the loose ammo in the bottom of the bags.

After filling four bags Dick disappeared back inside, telling the others to meet him in the bushes.

Annie, who just wanted to get out of there asked, "Where's he going Sarge?"

Sarge mounted Zen and took Bob on the lead.

"Don't know. He'll have his own reasons."

Annie mounted and followed Sarge.

Back inside Dick soon found what he had come for. He'd noticed there were four officers amongst the men; they were all armed with pistols as well as assault rifles. After securing the four Type 54 semi-automatic pistols and eight spare magazines with webbing, he emerged from the back of the café and headed over to where the others were waiting. He was only halfway there when a shot rang out, hitting the dirt just in front of him.

He only had a split second in which to decide whether to turn and fight or simply keep running. It had sounded like a pistol shot; definitely not the AK47 knock-off that the troopers were using.

Dick turned to face his attacker whilst still on the run. With the additional four pistols and the heavy SLR he was carrying, this was no easy thing to do, and Dick ended up tripping over a mound of dirt. The one thought in his mind as he flew forward was 'Don't drop anything!' Ridiculous of course; the best option would have been for him to drop the lot! But no! Dick ended up head-butting the gravel in the car park.

It only took a split second for the sixty-one-year-old to realise that he had made a big mistake, and, depending on the accuracy of his assailant, one that could easily cost him his life!

He braced himself, holding his breath as he waited for what he knew would come next; thinking, 'That's it then!'

Then came the rattle of an automatic!

From where Annie was standing, she saw Dick clear the back door, and had just turned to Sarge to acknowledge this when she heard the shot. With no time to think, she levelled the Australian manufactured F1 on her shoulder, pushed the safety forward and pulled the trigger.

The F1 spewed forth half a dozen rounds in the direction of Dick's assailant at a rate of over 600 per minute; wounding him enough to bring him down.

Quickly moving into the open on Zen, Sarge fired the fatal shot, hitting the young officer in the chest. He leaned down towards the ex-navy CD.

"Are you all right mate?"

Dick scrambled to his feet. Although he was out of breath, and couldn't speak for a minute, he gave Sarge the thumbs up, with the pistols and SLR still in his hand, before depositing the booty in his wither bags. After dragging his sorry arse up on to Bob, he finally managed to speak.

"Thanks Annie! You're a legend."

The youngster smiled before turning Tom and starting to head back the way they'd come.

As the trio waited to cross the Julia Bay Road, they realised that they had most certainly stirred up a hornet's nest. Another truck had arrived on the scene, along with a jeep.

Sarge was watching the mass of troops pouring out of the back of the truck. Turning to Dick, he asked, "What do you want to do Dick?"

Dick rubbed his gravel-rashed face as he answered his mate.

"We haven't got a hope of getting across the road with all that going on; and we certainly can't stay here."

Dick could think of only one solution: a decoy!

"Annie, you stay here, while Sarge and I go back to the café and finish the job. That will bring them all down on top of us. When you hear the commotion, get across the road fast; we'll meet you at the back of the old fellow's farm. That's about eight kilometres away."

Annie nodded, although she wasn't really happy about the plan.

Sarge and Dick turned around and followed the path back. As they came around the bend, they ran down two troopers who happened to be coming their way. After knocking the pair unconscious, Dick dismounted quickly and finished them off with his bayonet. After struggling a bit to re-mount, they set off again, stopping in the bush area that overlooked the car park at the back of the café.

They could see the officer in charge giving instructions. After tying up Bob and Zen the pair emerged into the open, and with a new clip in place and the other reloaded, they fired on the group.

Sarge counted fifteen bodies.

Dick made his way in through the back door again, while Sarge went in the side door, just as a trooper was running out. The kid didn't have time to stop, impaling himself on Sarge's bayonet and then sliding to the ground. Sarge heard Dick's SLR engage again, sending another two to their maker.

As they met in the middle, they could see a few civilians outside, nosing around. Sarge emerged out of the front door, yelling, "Bad mistake Gook!" as he shot the three inquisitive NK Nationals at close range. Dick took aim at the others he could see moving towards them, killing two of them before they had a chance to run away.

Over the other side of the Julia Bay Road, and to the left of where they were standing, Sarge caught sight of a large group who were just about to enter the old Bronze museum.

After loading another twelve rifles and ammo into Dick's saddlebags, Sarge quickly mounted Zen, pulling a grenade out of his wither bag as he did so. Getting his drift, the ex-CD mounted his aging horse, as Sarge said, "I'm guessing you're thinking what I'm thinking Mate!"

As Dick nodded, they trotted over the road, and right up to the museum. After pulling the pins on the grenades, they threw them into the building, and then turned and cantered down the Julia Bay Road, with Dick shooting another NK National as he was emerging from his house, just before the blast hit them.

At the noise of the explosion, both horses shied, moving sideways at lightning speed. The pair nearly came off but managed to hold on to the reins.

Dick instantly gave the big bay brown a rub on the neck, reassuring his trusty steed.

"It's all right Bob."

As they approached the spot where they would turn off into forestry, a trooper, who'd emerged from the entrance to the closest farm, managed to get off a shot. Sarge was hit in the thigh, but only after the bullet had been slowed down by the assault rifle in the back bag. Although it was clear Zen would have preferred to just keep going, much to his disgust Sarge managed to haul him around to the left; and return fire.

The trooper, although wounded, was still able to fight, and quickly crouched down behind the fence. Preoccupied with Sarge, he didn't see the sixteen hand Waler, with Dick atop, come in from the side as he drew the 9mm. Dick's bullet hit him in the face, shattering his cheekbone and exploding out of the back of his skull.

Meanwhile, Sarge, who'd spotted someone through a window, rode Zen through the front door; shooting a woman in the back as she ran down the hallway.

Dick followed him in. The pair found themselves in the kitchen, facing a frightened old lady and a small child. Even though they were still mounted, with the high ceilings there was plenty of room; without thinking too much about it, he shot the pair where they stood, before reaching down and opening the back door.

After coming out into the backyard they could hear screaming coming from the direction of the museum.

Sarge looked at Dick.

"Had enough mate?"

Dick grinned back at him.

"Yep! Let's get the hell out of here!"

After exiting the property through the back gate, they decided to turn left instead of right; the plan was to lay down some tracks going in the wrong direction.

A short distance away they could see another farm, with another NK National stickybeaking over the fence.

"Look at this dickhead mate!" declared Sarge, shooting him through the chest, before adding, "I'm out Dick!"

His mate tossed him the last clip, and he pushed the five rounds into the magazine. They rode along for another kilometre or so, before dropping into a stream and heading right.

Dick turned in the saddle, saying, "We'll follow this for as long as we can, then get back to the plantation track. Annie will be wondering where we are by now!"

"Roger that Dick."

Back at the old fellow's place, Annie was starting to worry. After hearing the explosion, and waiting for half an hour, she was thinking that the boys should have been there by now.

What to do? Should she go back and look for them?

No! She decided to stay put and follow her instructions. What she could do while she was waiting though, was to go and pick up those chooks.

After tying Tom to a tree, she crept towards the chook pen, armed with her 9mm in one hand and a hessian sack in the other. She knew this was going to be noisy, but until she tried to grab one of the chooks, she didn't realise just how noisy! Grabbing one chook would have been bad enough, but four! It's lucky she was not very tall.

Annie made it back to Tom, wondering the whole time how she'd managed to get to that point without anyone coming to investigate all the commotion. After tying the top of the bag with twine, she strung it alongside the assault rifles they'd picked up at the café. By now Tom had quite a collection hanging off his saddle!

Annie glanced at her watch, realising that it was almost 1400, and thinking that the pair should have been back well before now. Where were they!

She jumped at a sudden sound coming from somewhere behind her, and quickly unshouldered the F1 as she hid behind a tree.

Carefully peering around the trunk, she was relieved to see Sarge and Dick, trotting down the track towards her; with their over-filled sacks containing the collected weapons, the ammo and the occasional pistol, rattling as they rode. They didn't expect to see a perky woman brandishing a sub machine gun, and she gave them quite a scare as she stepped out from behind the tree.

"Sorry we're late Annie," said Sarge. "We had to put them off the scent by making some false tracks heading off in the opposite direction."

Annie looked at the pair.

"I must admit you had me worried!"

Sarge dismounted.

"I'd better get the chooks then."

Annie informed them with a proud smile,

"You're too late; I've already got them!"

As they rode back through the plantation, the two men gave Annie a blow-by-blow description of the afternoon's events. Having acquired forty-nine Type 68 assault rifles, as well as four pistols, they were more than happy with their haul.

Annie asked curiously, "How many Alliance troops do you think we killed Dick?"

The tired ex-CD looked at Annie. He couldn't help feeling proud of her achievements.

"I don't know Annie. Forty or fifty maybe, as well as a couple of dozen NK Nationals. I guess I lost count!"

He did know one thing though; he was aching all over! He moved around in the saddle a bit, thinking to himself.

'Might have to go out to the *Fremantle* and secure a hot shower when we get back!'

Chapter 18
The Operation

Doc and Nari were out on the quarterdeck at 0900, ready to greet the RHIB. They had been up since 0700 and had enjoyed a hearty breakfast of eggs and bacon cooked by Nari, before scrubbing the sickbay table and surrounds clean. This was something that hadn't been done for quite a while! As Doc commented to Nari, he wasn't impressed by the cleanliness standards of the Indonesian Navy.

He remembered the days when he'd served on *HMAS Bendigo*, and how clean everything was kept. This was the one trait that the Australian Navy had inherited from the Royal Navy.

Nari had flashed up the autoclave and sterilised all the instruments they would be using that day. She had even found a clean sheet and mattress cover for the table.

Jack and Vince managed to half-carry and half-lift the French woman up on to the 203's deck. As she followed them to the sick bay, Patch carried April's overnight bag. After making sure that they were all right, Vince excused himself, explaining to Doc that he and Laurel would be busy transporting weapons aboard, ready for the next voyage. Leaving Patch, Doc, Jack and Nari standing around April, who was lying on the sickbay table, Vince took the RHIB back to the beach.

Doc was thinking about the impending operation.

"Jack, can you get me a status on the fuel and freshwater levels mate, and Patch, can you boil up some water, just in case we need it."

Patch was thinking to herself that she might as well have a coffee at the same time and asked whether anyone else wanted one.

Nari and Doc shook their heads.

"No, we're right Patch. We should probably just get on with it."

Doc discussed the procedure he would follow with Nari, pointing out that, for a patient with a gunshot wound to the neck or upper chest, the classic teaching was to rule out major vascular and aero digestive injury by using a combination of CT imaging or angiography and bronchoscope/endoscopy.

"Identification of such injuries would have taken us down relatively well-established care pathways, which normally lead to either the operating room or endovascular suite. The real question is, what to do when we do not have the luxury of these machines."

Doc signed before adding, "I guess we'll just have to go in and find the bullet and be prepared for the worst!"

Nari handed Doc a syringe containing a mixture of Benzodiazepines and Propofol. It was all that they had been able to secure from the Kings Town hospital's supply room. After first removing April's upper clothing, Nari sanitised the area around the injury. Doc took his time inspecting the entry wound; it was still quite open and was starting to show signs of infection. He shook his head.

"We don't want to wait any longer love! You'd better wipe the thigh wound area as well; I'll have a look at that in a minute."

Doc injected April's forearm and they watched as the French woman drifted off into a state of unconsciousness.

By now Patch had returned with the boiling water. Nari dropped the cloths she'd be using into the water after adding some Dettol. With April well under the influence of the anaesthetic, Doc chose a medium probe, and then, after working out the bullet's trajectory, inserted it into the wound; then followed it until he hit the round.

After withdrawing the probe, he selected the long forceps, then followed the same pathway. It took a fair bit of manoeuvring before he was finally able to withdraw the forceps, while keeping a firm clasp on the 7.62mm round.

Nari gave an urgent nod to Doc as he dropped the bullet into the stainless tray.

"We've got problems Doc!"

"Shit Love! It must have been keeping the damaged artery blocked. When I pulled it out, she started to bleed. We've got to move fast!"

He reached for the scalpel, and quickly opened up the area, revealing a damaged artery which was spurting a fountain of arterial blood. Nari had already placed a tray holding the suture equipment on the table beside him. After quickly clamping the end, he proceeded to suture the artery wall with the tiny, curved needle and thread.

"I can't leave the clamp on too long because that would restrict blood to the brain, which means she will die anyway!"

Patch watched on in amazement, this type of thing was not normally her cup of tea. She didn't really like seeing blood, and usually tried to avoid putting herself into a situation where she had to see it. She would always do whatever was necessary of course; especially if one of the kids had hurt themselves, or if Dick needed medical attention, although she usually had to find a quiet place to be on her own afterwards, while she tried to control the nausea which typically followed once the situation had been dealt with.

This was different. This time she was relieved to find that there was no sign of nausea, which meant she was able to watch on as Doc worked frantically to save April's life.

"Swab please, Nari."

Doc was having trouble seeing, The young triage nurse was kept busy, constantly wiping Doc's brow, as well as swabbing the sweat which kept running down into his eyes and blurring his vision.

Within three minutes he had finished. After releasing the clamp and allowing the blood to flow again, he waited for a minute before announcing,

"Looks good people! We will close her up now."

Once the wound had been sutured up, Nari applied a non-stick pad to the area, then added a dressing over the top before finally bandaging the whole shoulder firmly.

"Good job Nari. Now let's have a look at that thigh."

Patch had forgotten all about the other wound and was thankful that Doc was keeping his mind on the job. Nari cleaned the area thoroughly before Doc sutured up the entry and exit wounds. Once finished, he stood back and surveyed his handywork with satisfaction.

"I'm certainly happy with that! Could you dress that for me please Nari."

He checked April's breathing, then turned to Patch.

"Thanks for your help, Patch."

She looked at the pair.

"Gee guys, I didn't do anything. You two did all the work!"

"Ah yes, but you were here if we'd needed you."

Doc came out of the sickbay, and went to find Jack, who was waiting out in the mess.

"How's she doing, Doc?"

Doc decided that Jack didn't need to know how close things had been to a real emergency.

"Fine Chief, she's doing fine."

Patch looked at the clock on the wall.

"Shit! It's almost 1300, Who wants a feed?"

Jack reported the freshwater status to the skipper.

"85% Doc, that's 5,100 litres left."

"And the fuel Chief?"

Jack had been so relieved at finding out that April was going to be okay, that he'd totally forgotten to mention the fuel figures.

"Sorry Skipper! We're down to 72%, or 7,100 litres, plus the 1,200 litres we're holding in drums on deck."

"Thanks Chief! We will try and re-water and re-fuel at Benowa."

After dropping April's blood-stained clothing into the ship's washing machine, Patch served cold corned dog rolls with dead horse. She smiled, this had always been a favourite with the boys.

During the morning they'd heard the RHIB come and go a few times, and it wasn't long before Laurel and Vince arrived in the mess.

"Just in time guys. Scran's on!"

Nari went to check on April. Jack, who was desperate to see his wife, asked if he could go with her.

"Of course, Jack. That would be lovely."

As Vince tucked into a roll, he asked, "How did it go Doc?"

Doc looked around the group with a serious look on his face, glad that Jack wasn't there.

"Seriously, it was touch and go for a while; but I'm pleased to report she'll live. She's pretty tough for her age, especially when you take into consideration all that she's been through lately."

Smiling, he added, "Not that you heard that from me, about her age I mean. But what about you? How did you two go?"

Vince had his mouth full of corned dog, so Laurel answered for the pair.

"Good. We got all the weapons and ammo on board, except for the personal 9mm Browning's, a couple of Claymores, two 303's and the shotguns. Oh, and of course the ammo to suit."

Patch had just poured Doc, Laurel and Vince a cuppa, and sat down on the lounge to enjoy her own, when Jack flew through the hatch, yelling, "Doc! Come quick!"

April was awake; she was still a bit drowsy from the anaesthetic, but her mind was clear enough about what she wanted to say.

As Doc entered the room, half expecting the wound to be gushing blood or something even worse, the French woman, who was obviously extremely angry, exclaimed, "Who gave you permission to fucking undress me you bastard!"

Doc let out a relieved laugh, thinking to himself that she was meaner than a Taswegian Devil defending its food.

"Well! Glad you are all right April."

"I fucking mean it Doc! When I'm able to get up out of this bed I'll …"

Her voice faded away as she slumped back onto the bed. Doc stood over the weakened sixty-one-year-old, shaking his head.

"Well, you're a mean old bitch, April. I save your life and all you fucking care about is whether or not we have seen your fanny!"

Doc left, leaving Nari and Jack to sooth the savage beast.

"He didn't mean it April."

April just glared at him. Jack looked helplessly at Nari with a 'back me up' look clearly showing on his face.

Nari gave him a reassuring smile as she did her best to make sure the French woman was comfortable.

"Are you warm enough April?"

April was embarrassed to have spoken to Doc like that. Deep down, she knew he would have had to undress her in order to operate, but she still had trouble dealing with knowing this, and hadn't been able to stop the feeling of rage and anger that still built up in her at times when she felt she had no control over what was happening. After all, the abuse she had been subjected to during her marriage to Jacque, she was still extremely reluctant to let anybody, except Jack, see her naked, and even though she knew Doc was a medical professional, this made no difference to how she felt.

Vince and Laurel finished storing the weapons and ammunition in the armoury. As they worked, they marked them down on the status whiteboard on the bulkhead just inside the hatch. He looked at Laurel.

"Great job Love!"

Laurel blushed. She realised how much she liked working alongside Vince; unfortunately, this was something that rarely happened at home.

After fronting up in the main mess, the ex-navy Technician asked, "Do you want anything done back at camp, Patch? Laurel and I thought we might go back and have a swim. It will also double as a good wash."

Patch thought about the evening meal, she had planned a big celebration dinner, but was not all that confident about cooking with a camp oven. Looking at the oven in the Galley she had an idea.

"Can you please get the fire revved up, and just heat up the camp ovens later on in the afternoon."

She decided to cook the large lamb roasts in the ship's oven, along with roasted spuds and fresh vegetables; and then transport them to the beach later, ready to serve for dinner tonight.

Vince said they would be back to pick everyone up around 1730, after Dick and the others arrived back in camp.

Patch looked in on April, who seemed to be doing a lot better. Nari had given her something for the pain, and had moved her from the operating table, propping her up on the sickbay bed.

April blurted out in frustration, "It's ridiculous Patch; they've told me I have to stay here for a whole week!"

She was obviously upset at the thought of not being able to return to the camp with the others. Patch could see her point but tended to agree with Doc and Nari.

"You know April, I reckon that really is for the best. Besides, I reckon Jack will probably stay on board as well."

April hadn't thought about that; the possibility really lifted her spirits. She looked at her friend with a hopeful look in her eyes.

"You reckon he will be allowed to Patch?"

Patch laughed.

"Who's going to stop him Love?"

While April settled down for a snooze, Patch went back to the Galley to get the roast lamb started. She found Doc and Nari there, enjoying a well-earned brew. Realising how long it had been since she'd had a good wash, she asked, "Is there enough water for a tubs Doc?"

The aging Doctor looked at his mate's wife, who was obviously hanging out for a proper hot shower.

"Sure Patch. Plenty of water. Do you want a hand preparing for dinner?"

"If you really wanted to, you could peel some spuds for me."

As she left the Galley she added, "Same heads Doc?"

Jack, who'd just finished Engine Room rounds again, joined Doc and Nari in the Galley and poured himself a cuppa.

"I just wanted to say thanks for all you've done for my girl."

To Nari's surprise, he was looking more at her than Doc. She blushed as she responded.

"Why thank you Jack. I really appreciate the sentiment, but it was Doc who saved her life."

Nari suddenly remembered that Jack had no idea of the drama they'd faced during the operation and thought to herself, 'Shit! I shouldn't have said it like that!'

Jack looked confused and a little bit frightened.

"What do you mean Nari? Doc! What went wrong?"

The aging Doctor told Jack all about the trouble they'd had with the damaged artery; something they couldn't have anticipated until he removed the bullet.

"Geez Doc. I had no idea. I owe you big time. Does April know?"

Nari stood and put her arm around the ex-CD's shoulders.

"No Jack, she doesn't know; and it would probably be better if we don't tell her. Well, not at least until she gets stronger."

Jack could feel the tears welling up in his eyes.

"How long before she can be moved, Doc?"

Doc thought carefully before he answered. He wasn't happy about her having to be on board for the Benowa trip.

"She'll have to stay here for at least a week Chief. You are most welcome to stay on board to be with her tonight, and from tomorrow onwards we will all be on board; except for Vince and Laurel of course."

After excusing themselves, Doc and Nari went off to have a shower. Patch reappeared in the Galley, feeling refreshed and definitely much cleaner after her shower. She put on the roast veggies, while Jack disappeared into the Junior Sailors' Mess to enjoy a shower himself.

She couldn't help wondering about how Dick, Sarge and Annie were going with the raid, and whether they were all right? She missed him so much whenever they were apart. She also missed being part of the action and had assumed she would miss out on the trip to Benowa and Strong Fort Bay; thinking she would be permanently relegated to stay in camp. She'd felt more relieved than she'd let on when Dick told her she was going with them.

"Of course, you'll be coming Chook; you'll bunk down with me in the XO's Cabin."

Patch wanted to go and have a look at where they would be sleeping. Jack, who had returned from his shower, sniffed the aromas in the Galley with appreciation. His mouth was starting to water. Patch had just finished putting the veggies on and was happy that the roast was going well.

"I might go and have a look at the XO's Cabin, Jack," she said to the ex-Sniper, "although I have no idea where it is."

"It's up the stairs Patch, the way you came in, on the right. It's next to the Skipper's Cabin."

It was easy to find, most of the doors had brass nameplates on them. After opening the polished timber door, she entered the cabin and looked around. She could see a desk and a chair to her left, just inside the door, and next to them was a huge wardrobe, with a king single bunk running fore and aft. Opposite this was a day couch, with drawers fitted below the mattress.

There were more drawers under the bunk. 'At least there's plenty of storage,' she thought to herself. The cabin was finished in polished timber panelling; there was a photo of the Patrol Boat screwed to one bulkhead, while the other sported a photograph of Joko Widodo, Indonesia's President.

Patch sat on the chair, wondering what it would be like to be sleeping at sea in the bunk with Dick. Would there be enough room for them both? After all they were both tall, and Dick wasn't a small man!

The noises she could hear coming from the adjoining cabin had her puzzled for a while, although it didn't take her long to work out what it was. Patch stifled a laugh as she realised the sounds must have been coming from Nari and Doc, who were obviously enjoying some rather robust sex together!

At 1740, Vince tied up the RHIB alongside, before carrying the two large camp ovens, both wrapped in towels, on board. He made his way to the Galley.

"You're just in time Vince. I'll tell Jack we're leaving, and that his and April's dinner is in the oven. Can you please bang on the Skipper's Cabin door and tell them as well?"

Patch made her way to the sickbay, where she found the ex-CD fast asleep in the chair alongside of April. The French woman was wide awake.

"Look Patch," she laughed. "He's sleeping like a baby! Are you off ashore?"

Patch covered Jack with a blanket.

"Yes, we're off. Are you two going to be all right tonight?"

April replied, "Sure Patch. I dare say Nari and Doc will look in on us when they come back on board."

Vince placed the night's feast in the bow of the twenty-two-foot RHIB, and, once Doc, Nari and Patch were on board, they hurtled back to the beach. Laurel met them at the water's edge.

"There's still no sign of the trio Patch; but they shouldn't be too long now."

This was Nari and Doc's first real look at the camp; after being given the grand tour they all sat and enjoyed a drink while they waited for the others. Patch had already chilled the wine, and after making sure Vince and Laurel had their customary beers, she placed the camp ovens alongside the fire to keep them warm, before starting to make the gravy.

"Nice fire Vince!"

He smiled back at her.

"Thanks."

At 1810 they all heard Fannie give a loud whinny; this was the tell-tale sign that another horse was approaching the camp. Cowboy was next to let them know; by now all eyes were fixed on the top of the dunes. Sure enough, there was Tom with Annie, and Bob with Dick, with Sarge bringing up the rear on Zen.

"They look really loaded up guys!"

Doc was amazed at just how many weapons they'd managed to cram into the saddle bags.

After greeting the weary riders, Vince and Laurel de-tacked the horses, before leading them into the horse enclosure. Annie didn't want any special treatment, and personally made sure that the three of them were groomed and fed before she plonked herself down alongside of Sarge.

Doc spoke first.

"Bloody well done you three. I'm impressed with what you have achieved! f I know the Alliance, it wouldn't have been a walk in the park either. What an effort! These extra weapons are going to be a huge help in arming our newfound friends."

Patch didn't say anything, she was just relieved to see Dick back safe and sound. She gave him a hug and a big kiss, asking him, "Ready to eat, Love?"

Both Sarge and Dick answered in unison.

"Too bloody right! We're starving!"

As he washed down his roast lamb, gravy, baked spuds, carrots, onions, and peas with a mug of Sav Blanc, Dick felt he was in heaven. Well, almost; all that was missing was a hot shower. Ah well, that would have to wait until tomorrow.

At 2100 Doc and Nari said goodnight to the others and headed back to the RHIB. Patch yelled out to the pair,

"Doc, can you please make sure Jack sleeps in a proper bunk tonight. He's going to suffer tomorrow if he doesn't!"

The sixty-five-year-old replied, "I sure will Patch. Oh, and Sarge, I'll have a good look at that leg of yours in the morning."

TRF FCPB Fremantle at anchor at Hells Beach
Photograph compliments of LS/POETP Gary Haigh

Chapter 19
Strong Fort Bay

Monday 12ᵗʰ January 2015 ... Badman Farm, Julia Bay

By the time John Badman made it to the back door, he was so much out of breath that his wife Helen, couldn't understand a word he was trying to spit out!

"Calm cown John! You'll give yourself a heart attack! Now what are you trying to tell me?"

Although John was still finding it hard to breathe, he knew what he had to say was as important as life or death. Collapsing on to a kitchen chair, he managed to gasp out, "Pad and pen Helen!"

His heart was thumping madly in his chest, but his writing hand was calm as he meticulously wrote down what he wanted to tell her.

Monday 12ᵗʰ January 2015

"Just hoping the right people find this note!

I rode the treddly up to visit my cousin Sid in Bronze last night. As I got there, I could see some kind of foreign troops. They were killing everyone in the house! Looked like they might have been Chinese or something. From where I was standing, I could see some of the other houses ... looked like the same thing had happened there.

Luckily, they didn't see me!

I got back here pronto. I've packed up the family (baker's dozen less five) ... we're heading to canal ... dinghy across the channel twenty-seven and making way to (Fortescue) being cryptic I know, will gather as many people as I can with weapons ... J."

Helen watched as her husband of twenty years wrote the note. Although she could read the words, her brain was having trouble coming to terms with what he actually meant by them.

'Is this some kind of joke?' she thought.

A voice screeched out from the lounge room.

"Mum, I'm hungry!"

"Not now Billy! Your father and I are busy."

After placing the pen down on the table, John looked up at Helen's face.

"Do you understand what I am saying?"

She shook her head as she gave a grim smile.

"Well John, I hope you think this is funny. Because I certainly don't!"

John stood up, grabbed his wife, and shook her ... hard!

"This is no fucking joke, Helen!"

By now Trish and Billy were at the door, watching with their mouths open.

"Dad! What's going on? Why are you hurting mum?"

He looked at his daughter, who was starting to cry.

"Trish! Billy! Come here please."

John explained to them what he had written in the note.

"Our only course of action is to leave immediately."

"Why are they doing it John? Can't we just talk to their superior or something? Maybe those people did something wrong."

John shook his head.

"I'm only going to say this once! We are wasting time! I don't know why they are killing people; I didn't feel like asking them at the time. And NO, we will not be talking to their superior! Pack only what you can carry in a backpack … Now!"

He went to the gun safe and extracted the .22 rifle that had been his since he was a boy, along with all the ammunition he had, and the 12-gauge shotgun with whatever cartridges were left in the belt.

Helen was sobbing; frozen with fear, she simply could not move. John could hear Billy and Trish in their rooms, packing their backpacks. He placed a comforting arm around his wife's shoulders,

"Come on Helen, please go and pack. Otherwise, I'll have to do it for you, and you certainly won't be happy with what I'd pack!"

This was the catalyst needed to break her fear.

"Oh no you won't! I'll pack my own bag thank you!"

After lifting the top sheet of the pad, he wrote on the next page … *To Whom*

It May Concern, we have mail to deliver.

After folding the top note, he ran out the front door to the mailbox at the end of the front path. As he placed the folded note inside the box, he thought to himself, 'I sure hope this gets to someone that knows what to do with it!"

Billy was first back in the kitchen; his face lit up with excitement.

"What next, Dad?"

The exuberant twelve-year-old probably thought it was a bit of an adventure.

"Mate, go and get some food to take with us. Try to make it light if you can; we have enough to carry already!"

John went to their bedroom to see how his wife was going. He found her carefully folding her clothes before laying them out on the bed; like she would if she was packing for a trip to Paris! Not that they had ever been to Paris.

As a matter of fact, he had been born on this very farm, and had spent his whole life here. The furthest he had travelled was to Millburn once on a school trip; and that was back when he was a teenager!

Realising his wife appeared to be in a daze again, he yelled at her, making her jump.

"Helen! STOP! You're not thinking straight! You won't need that bloody dress where we are going! Just pack sensible clothes."

She looked at him, still sobbing.

"And just where are we going? Why do we have to leave our home? What's going on?"

John realised he hadn't thought too much about the direction they were going, only that it would definitely be in the opposite direction to Bronze.

"We'll hike to the canal and grab the yacht, warning as many people as we can along the way. I'll work out the details as we go along. Now, get a bloody move on! The bastards could be here any minute!"

Quickly packing his regular camping clothes, he suggested to Helen that she should do the same. Once done, he yelled the same thing out to Trish before topping up his backpack with firelighters, matches, some camping cookware, and water bottles.

"How did you go with the food Billy."

The twelve-year-old had set out an assortment of different things on the large table in the middle of the kitchen; he'd gathered dried pasta, peas, beans, a slab of bacon, some corned beef and as many dehydrated camping meals as he could find.

"Great job, Billy!"

John was proud of the boy, he'd obviously inherited his logic from his dad!

Once all four of them were back in the kitchen, John divided the food evenly between their backpacks, and loaded the ammunition into his and Billy's packs.

"We each need to take a waterproof jacket; put them on so you don't have to try and squeeze them into your packs. You'll also need bathers and boat shoes, because we're going to the yacht.

"But that's miles away dad!"

"Stop grizzling Trish! You'll have to put up with it! Think about it; you could be far worse off."

The prissy thirteen-year-old looked at her father with all the contempt she could muster.

"Oh yeah? Like what?"

John pulled no punches, informing his daughter, "You could be DEAD!"

He handed the .22 rifle to Billy.

"This is your responsibility now son!"

The boy was excited; he'd always known this would be handed down to him sooner or later. Looks like the time had finally come!

After slinging the shotgun over his shoulder, John placed the second note on the table, making sure it was hidden amongst the debris they had left. At the front door he paused for a minute, then went out to the shed.

"What row John! Why do you want to bring that old thing?"

Helen was clearly frustrated at the whole ordeal.

"Just in case Helen. Just in case. You never know when the old brick phone might come in handy!"

The time was 8.10pm. There was still an hour of daylight left, and at least twelve homes to walk past on the way to the canal. The first two homes were shacks and had been vacant since the E1 hit. The owners would have had no way of getting to them. If he remembered rightly, John thought that one was from North Kings Town, while the other lived at Soothe.

The third house was also a shack, although this time the owners happened to be in residence at the time the E1 had destroyed all the vehicles. With no way to get back home they'd found themselves stranded at Julia Bay.

After knocking on the door of number thirty-two, John was greeted by an elderly English woman. He knew her only as Mrs Smythe.

"Hello Mrs Smythe. Is Mr Smythe in?"

The elderly woman knew John and his family.

"Hello John, won't you come in?"

She looked at the others, who were standing by the front gate, loaded up with their packs.

"Going camping John?"

She showed John into the parlour, where Mr Smythe was enjoying a glass of port.

He gestured to John to help himself if he would like to.

"Thanks, but no thanks. However, I do have something very important to say to you both."

John went on the describe the events of the last four hours. He couldn't believe everything had happened so fast! They listened intently, without interrupting. When John finally finished speaking, Mr Smythe looked at him, saying, "I think it's time you started to call me James." Turning to his wife, he added, "And this is Miriam. Now! If everything you say is true, what would you suggest we do?"

John explained that he thought their best escape would be to travel due south to the canal, and from there to Strong Fort Bay. He had no idea why that particular place had come to mind, but it was better than nothing.

"Miriam, better pack some things!"

John asked James whether he had any weapons.

"Sadly, no, my friend, although I think the neighbour does."

John suggested that he and James should go to see the neighbours next door and try to convince them they also needed to leave. James was happy to leave his wife to the packing, and agreed that was a good idea, so he and John headed off to the next house.

After knocking twice, James called out, "Only me!", then, without waiting for an answer, opened the back door of number thirty-four and went inside. He'd obviously done this before and was quite comfortable inviting himself in without waiting for an invitation.

They found the occupants sitting around the kitchen table and playing a game of cards. Robert and Gina Crawfield were a couple in their late sixties and were living there with their children and grandchildren. They listened wide-eyed to what John and James had to tell them; it seemed like something right out of a science fiction movie!

"We can use our boat, John, we've got a twenty-six-footer at the canal."

He thanked them, suggesting to the elderly gentleman that he should come with them to alert the next home, while the rest of his family packed for the trip. By now Helen and the kids had joined Miriam and were helping her sort out some of the more essential items that would be needed, including extra food and camping equipment. Robert and Gina's son, Sid, decided to join John and James, leaving his father, mother and wife, Ellen, to pack, with the assistance of their two kids, Helen and Craig.

Next, they came across the Jones family at number thirty-six; this extended family had all been caught at Julia Bay after the E1 had hit. There were six of them, as well as a friend; they also had a yacht.

By now it was 9.40pm. It was well and truly dark outside, so they decided to take up where they'd left off at first light. They all agreed there were possibly another eight occupied homes in the street that would need to be checked out in the shortest time possible. From there it would only be a short 200 metre walk to the tiny bend in the canal, where most residents pulled their boats up.

Robert and Gina suggested that the Badman family should stay at their place for the night, along with James and Miriam and the residents of number thirty-six. Although it was crowded, somehow, they all managed to cram in together. They all agreed there was safety in numbers.

Robert's old .22 rifle, along with a box of ammo, was now firmly in the hands of his son Sid.

John sighed. This was going to be a very long night!

Tuesday 13th January 2015 ... Crawfield Residence, Julia Bay

After taking it in turns during the night to keep a lookout, they mustered the group at 0730. There was a fair bit of disgruntled mumbling from some of the teenagers, who considered this to be far too early to have to get out of bed!

John suggested the main part of the group should head straight for the boats, while James, Sid and himself went from house to house, and tried to talk the occupants into coming with them.

The pair in number thirty-eight refused to come. They thought the lot were bonkers and slammed the door in their face.

Number forty belonged to the Frank family: a young couple and their four kids. It only took them a minute to decide to join the group on their way to the boats.

The elderly couple in number forty-two, were the Oglios, who were only too pleased to join them, and were soon on their way.

Next was number forty-four, which was occupied by Cedric, who was nearly eighty years old, but still very with it, and his wife Aileen. Although she was a lot younger than her husband, it was obvious she was not in good health.

John thought to himself, 'I wonder what's wrong there.' She seemed to him to be quite poorly.

As John helped Cedric to gather a few tools from his shed, he spotted a set of bolt cutters.

"By all means John. Take whatever you think we will need."

The other homes in the road turned out to be unoccupied.

Down by the boats, John found the group chatting amongst themselves and getting to know each other better. He decided to push his boat into the water, as well as Sid's boat and the one belonging to the Jones family. Then, after leaving his son Billy to keep watch, John proceeded to cut the chains from the other three yachts which were chained to the posts.

"I say old chap! Isn't that stealing?"

John grinned at the old fellow, who he now knew as Cedric Bilton.

"Well Sir, they are not here. If they were, I am quite sure we would be using their boats as well."

He looked around the group.

"Now, who can sail?"

Craig Crawfield was the first person to step forward.

"Can you skipper your own boat? What's she called ... *Zanadoo*? It looks like she's a twenty-six-footer. How many do you think you can comfortably carry?"

Craig's father, Sid, spoke up after thinking it through for a while

"I reckon about six John; although it depends on how far we are going."

The next boat was John's eighteen-footer, *Badman II*.

"I'll skipper that; there's only enough room for my family!"

Robert, Sid's father, came forward.

"I can sail John."

"Great Robert! You can skipper this yacht, the *Silicon*. By the looks of it, it's also about a twenty-six-footer. You can work out who you want to crew her, but she'll need to carry at least six."

Sloth belonged to the Jones family. She was a twenty-two-footer that both Mick and Sarah Jones were able to sail.

Next to *Sloth* was an old whaler. *Moby* was a heavy open twenty-eight-foot-long timber boat; although she was a bit long in the tooth, John thought she would be worth bringing along.

"Mick, are you right to skipper her?"

"No problems John. I'll take Roger and Shelly with me, as well as anyone else who needs a ride."

After walking along the shore, John came to the last yacht. He'd found plenty of motorboats along the way, but all were useless now. There in front of him was *Siren*; a twenty-foot skiff that was a pure racing boat. Whoever decided to travel on this was going to get very wet! Josh Frank was as keen as; he had sailed skiffs before for his school and couldn't wait to get going on this one. He decided to take his twin sister Jill along with him.

Once they'd sorted out who would go on which boat, they started loading the gear aboard. John took stock of their fleet.

"It looks like four of the boats; *Badman II, Zanadoo, Silicon* and *Sloth,* all have UHF. We'll keep them switched on so that we can communicate. The other two will just have to keep in touch by sailing close.

He turned as young Billy came running along the track. Although he was puffing badly, he managed to blurt out,

"I think they're coming Dad!"

John and Sid carefully made their way back to the road. From where they stood, hidden behind some bushes, they could see the Alliance troops, systematically entering every home. It didn't take them long to check out numbers thirty-two, thirty-four, and thirty-six. After that came number thirty-eight.

The screaming came first, closely followed by the sound of automatic rifle fire. They knew that the screams had come from the young woman who'd so rudely answered the door to them, and then slammed it in their face. She bolted out of the back door; only to be chased down by a rather exuberant young trooper, who bayonetted her in the back as she fled, then stabbed her repeatedly once she'd hit the ground. He must have thrust the bayonet into her torso at least twenty times.

Craig was first to react.

"Mate this is madness! You were right John to alert us! Let's get out of here! Hopefully the wind is blowing the right way."

John wasn't about to say no!

Back in the canal, *Silicon, Sloth, Moby* and *Siren* were well under-way. They were mid-stream in the channel and heading towards the Julia Bay narrows. With plenty of helpers, John was soon afloat in *Badman II,* with Sid not far behind him on *Zanadoo.*

"Keep a sharp eye out Billy; let me know if you see anyone!"

The boy kept a keen watch over the stern of the eighteen-foot fibreglass yacht. By 1338 they too had reached the narrows.

"Lucky the tide's running with us. Did you see anyone watching us Billy?"

The boy shook his head.

"Couldn't see anyone, Dad."

Sid's yacht, *Zanadoo*; a well-rigged and much faster yacht, was a-beam of them now. John gave him the thumbs up, yelling, "I'll see you at the rendezvous at South Bay!"

South Bay was the place they'd all agreed to head to ... once safely there they would get together and come up with a plan.

As he cut across the bottom corner of Julia Bay, John could see the little flotilla strewn out in front of him. It looked like the *Siren* was out in front, closely followed by *Silicon*, *Sloth*, *Zanadoo*, and *Moby*, and with them bringing up the rear.

By the time John's boat finally rounded the point it was 1700; as he drew closer, he could make out the rest of them sitting there, all tied together and swinging off *Zanadoo's* anchor. After Pulling *Badman II* up outside of *Moby*, Billy helped him to secure the boat, before climbing over the other yachts with his father and going aboard *Zanadoo* to discuss the next leg.

It was decided to spend the night where they were, then for the flotilla to head off the next day to Deep Roger Bay. Although it was only a distance of fifteen nautical miles, because of the different yacht styles and sailing abilities, they all agreed it would be better to stick together.

The group shared a mixed dinner. With the vessels better equipped now, they appreciated the hot drinks and a hearty meal. Miriam's casserole went down a treat with everyone.

Thankfully there were enough vessels with a cabin for everyone to find a place where they could sleep out of the weather. A little rain mist had started to drift in from the east; if they'd had to sleep outside, it would have been a very damp night for them all!

Zanadoo and *Silicon* both had reasonable cabins, with similar layouts; four berths up forward and the table, which dropped to become a double berth if required. They rigged a tarp over the boom on *Moby*, creating a space large enough to lay out swags for those who had brought them along. John, Helen, Billy and Trish all stretched out in the small, but adequate cabin on *Badman II*. It was not the most comfortable place to be, but it kept them dry enough!

Wednesday 14th January 2015 ... South Bay

John woke to the sound of the wind whistling through the rigging of the flotilla; miraculously they hadn't dragged the anchor. The wind would be on the port quarter today, which meant that the conditions would not be all that great for the slower boats.

He checked the chart with the twins, Josh and Jill, making sure they knew when to stop. It was obvious that they would beat everyone else there by a country mile.

John realised that his distraught wife wasn't coping too well with all that was happening. She was feeling cold and miserable.

"Are you all right, Helen?"

He held her close and tried to warm her up; the kids had already gone aboard *Silicon* and bought back hot coffee for their mum and dad.

"Thanks kids. We really appreciate it."

At 0900 the next morning, they slipped all lines and hoisted their sails. As suspected, the twenty-foot skiff catapulted out of the bay, really liking the conditions, which were almost on the nose. John remembered a sailing nut he'd once known from years ago. His favourite saying had been, 'You know the way you tell a well-made yacht is to sail her into the wind.'

They had a long day ahead and did their best to try and make the time go smoothly, making sure that everyone had a go on the helm. But no matter how much they tried, they couldn't get much more speed out of the old trailer-sailor.

Zanadoo, the twenty-six-foot Adams fibreglass cruising yacht, was being skippered by Sid Crawfield, who was an ex-railway worker as well as an avid sailor. His wife Ellen, their children, Helen and Craig, along with Tony and Mary Oglio, had all joined him on the yacht. Craig was very happy crewing for his dad, and Helen felt the same. Unfortunately, Ellen was not a very good sailor, and spent most of the day feeling sick.

Tony and Mary were no stoushes at sailing. In their younger days, back home in Italy, they had lived at a seaside town, and had enjoyed sailing on a regular basis. Tony, who was now sixty-eight years of age, was happy on the whole to leave it up to the younger sailors amongst them, although every now and then he didn't mind taking the lead. Mary was quite happy to assist Helen and Ellen with the meals.

Once they were clear of the point, Sid looked at Tony.

"Want to take her, Tony?"

The old Italian was grinning from ear to ear.

"Yeah, too right! Thanks Sid."

With Helen, Craig and Tony eager to assist as helmsmen, Sid was satisfied that things would run smoothly.

John was pretty happy with the sailing ability of those in control of the various yachts. He'd been bought up in the area; his father's only past times, apart from farming, had been sailing, and fishing on Julia Bay. Of course, John hadn't had any choice in the matter; something he really appreciated now, wishing he had pushed his own two kids into being involved. All they'd seemed to do was watch TV and play computer games!

If there was anything good about the E1 catastrophe as far as he was concerned, it was that there were no longer any electronic distractions for his kids anymore. This had really bought Billy out of his shell, and recently he'd taken a more active interest in the farm and outdoor life.

The twelve-year-old broke the silence, asking, "Why were those soldiers killing everyone, Dad?"

John knew that Billy had most likely been watching as the troopers had killed the occupants of number thirty-eight.

"I suspect it has something to do with the Nuclear Holocaust son."

Upon hearing his words, Helen went into meltdown again, sobbing uncontrollably. She was definitely not coping with what was happening. On the other hand, to John's bewilderment, his daughter Trish seemed to be bearing up unexpectedly well under the immense strain of it all. He decided to change the subject.

"I know kids! Let's drag a fishing line and see what we can catch for dinner."

John dragged out the old fishing gear and found some bacon to bait the hooks with. Then, after setting up a salmon lure and a couta jig, he streamed them off the stern.

Sarah Jones, the reluctant skipper of the twenty-two-foot steel cruising yacht, *Sloth*, had a crew consisting of her children, Roger, Jimmy, Shelley and Michael, as well as Graham, who was a friend of her husband Mick. Her reluctance came from not only having to skipper when she didn't really want the job, but also because she was away from Mick. Despite this, she was quite competent with handling the *Sloth*, which had been aptly named because of her slow speed.

Sarah gave Graham a lesson on steering.

"A little more to port mate. No, the other way. Left. That's it! Just look up and keep the sail full."

Their youngest, who loved the boat, asked, "Mum, what's to eat?"

The thirty-eight-year-old smiled.

"Shelley, can you please find something for Michael to eat."

Roger and Jimmy stood up from where they'd been sitting on the side cushions.

"We'll go Mum!"

Sarah knew damn well why they would volunteer.

"Yes, all right. You can get something as well."

Graham was looking a tad green.

"Better take the wheel Sarah, I don't feel that well!"

Sarah looked around at her crew, thinking 'A fine lot I have here!'

"Graham! Graham! Mate, if you're going to be sick, you'd better do it on the other side of the boat!"

Billy was the first to get a strike.

"Got something Dad!"

John helped his son pull in the line, realising at that moment that he had not taught his son how to fish, or in actual fact, taken any of his family fishing. The last time was with his father some fifteen years ago, before the kids were born.

Trish was excited, urging Billy and John to pull it in.

"What is it, Dad?"

John landed the three-foot Barracouta, which started shedding its scales as soon as it hit the deck. After a sharp tap with the paddle, it was all over.

"Well done, Billy, that's dinner right there!"

Trish was so distracted that she didn't realise that she also had a bite.

"Let me do it on my own Dad!"

John stepped back to allow his over-confident teenager to pull in the line. Billy was leaning over the stern.

"I can see it! It's sort of silver in colour."

Trish was really starting to get into the spirit of the moment, when, just as the fish cleared the water, *whoosh*! A flash of silver-blue came out of nowhere and swallowed the fish, along with the trace, and a foot of line as well, leaving Trish holding only a piece of line.

"What the f ... was that, Dad?"

Looking at his daughter John laughed.

"That, my dear, was a very hungry Barracouta."

By 1800, Deep Roger Bay was visible from the starboard side. As they drew closer, they could see the others waiting; same scenario as before, with all of them swinging off *Zanadoo's* anchor. Sid and Robert were the first to greet them.

"Glad you could make it John. We're having a BBQ; would you like to join us?"

Everyone joined in with the feed. After dinner Sid and John pondered over the chart as they planned the next day's destination.

"Rain Bay looks good Sid. The next part could be interesting though. We'll have to sail across Plunder Bay; and that could be populated with the heathens!"

Thursday 15ᵗʰ January 2015 ... Deep Roger Bay

Robert reported, "0600. The wind has swung around to the west; it's coming straight over the cliffs."

John was wondering whether or not the statement from Robert was a warning.

"Yes," he responded. "We should have no problems until we start to turn into Rain Bay. There's not much shelter there, and with the wind directly on the nose, some of us will have to do a fair bit of tacking. It might take a while to get in."

John thought it best to call a meeting before they set sail.

"This next part, for those of you who are not familiar with it, will take us right across the tourist section of Plunder Bay, and the town of Falcons Neck. Let's hope the heathens have not got that far. Unfortunately, we won't be able to go inshore to try and warn others of what could be about to happen. That's simply because we can't be certain that they're not already there."

As he looked around the group, John could see that the conditions were taking their toll on the older members. All he could think of was to say,

"See you at Rain Bay people."

It was a bit like the start to a disunited sailing race; they all let go and were soon filling their sails with the on-shore breeze. After turning right at the entrance to the bay, they headed due south; this course would get them clear, and then after a couple of hours they would turn to starboard and head in closer to Plunder Bay.

The twenty-foot Skiff shot off and was well clear of the point before *Badman II* was even halfway there. John looked up from the compass.

"Looks like the Frank twins are enjoying themselves!"

Although John was just trying to make conversation, unfortunately his wife seemed to have been in another world since Monday. He hadn't been able to draw her into any conversation at all; most of the time she just stared out at the horizon, her brain unable to digest what had happened.

Her upbringing had been just like a lot of farmer's daughters; first a sheltered childhood, and then on to private boarding school where she'd really let her hair down. Later she'd mixed in all the 'right circles' in an effort to find the 'most desirable' husband. Typically, they had met at a Bachelor's and Spinster's Ball held at Bronze. These events were more commonly known as B&S Balls.

Realising that Billy had been on the helm for a while, John suggested, "Why don't you take a spell mate and go and help your sister make some lunch; I'll relieve you for a while."

Trish was already hacking into the fresh bread they had baked on Sunday and had the gas stove on for a drink.

Billy shook his mother, "Do you want a cuppa, Mum?"

The boy received no response from Helen.

"Just make it tea mate!" yelled John.

Life on board *Moby* was a lot rougher than it was for the rest. With no shelter from the elements, Mick Jones had only a tiller steer; this was basically a wooden lever on the end of the rudder. His crew, who consisted of Bentley, Barbara, Blyth and Anna Frank, were extremely happy to help with anything that would keep the twenty-eight-foot aging whaling dinghy, with her single large mainsail and primitive rigging going. Mick was gaining a new appreciation of how tough things used to be for the whalers.

"Take over will you Ben, while I try and get that main up a bit further."

With no winch to pull the halyard tight, it was muscle power only.

Barbara was more than happy to make the lunch and just keep the youngsters out of the way.

Bentley, or Ben, as he liked his friends to call him, had no sailing experience at all. Despite this, he was kind of getting the hang of it. The ex-law firm accountant had come to Julia Bay for a holiday, just as they did each year for Christmas; it was a great place for the kids, safe and there was plenty to do.

'Safe! That's a joke now,' he thought, as he remembered the gun shots and the screams. 'How awful!'

Ben called out to his wife.

"Want to come and help me, Barbara?"

Barbara, with young Anna firmly clutching her leg, sat alongside her husband. As she held the tiller with one hand, and his hand with the other, she wondered what would become of them.

After a starboard tack all day, this did not change when John turned slightly to port and started to head to Rain Bay. From their position at the rear of the flotilla, he could see the others spread out in front. The closest to him was *Moby*.

'Poor bastards will be getting wet in that slop,' he thought to himself.

There was no sign of much activity at Falcons Neck, and he wondered whether the Asians had made it that far yet. Having never had any real interest in anything of a military nature, he had no idea who they were; he assumed they were army, and of Asian background, but that was all.

Later in the afternoon the breeze swung around to the Northwest, giving the *Badman II* a real push. After clearing the point into Rain Bay at 1645, they found the group as before; the only difference this time was that they had a few fishing lines out.

The Olios and the Biltons were sitting back with Robert and Gina Crawfield on *Silicon*, enjoying the afternoon sun.

Billy helped to tie up before going on board *Zanadoo* with his father. As he made his way across *Moby*, he could already see a good selection of fish; definitely worthy of making their way onto the plates that night.

John spoke up in a voice loud enough for everyone to hear him, as he described the situation at Strong Fort Bay.

"It's a very secluded bay, with a Ranger Station and backpackers' accommodation, which houses up to sixty people. From memory,

I think there are both women's and men's ablution blocks. The Ranger Station also has a three-bedroom house attached.

The bay is twenty-two kilometres off the main road; this should be our only threat. If the Asians come in, we're pretty well stuffed!"

"What are you proposing we do John?"

"Well James, I'm hoping the rangers have a working chainsaw, although it would have to be an old one because of the E1. I'm thinking that, if we can cut a tree down close to the main road, we'll be able to drop it across the track. I have an area in mind that might work. The tree will have to be large enough to mean that they won't be able to tow it out of the way without a bulldozer."

He paused as Robert started to ask a question.

"Yep, I'll answer questions when I'm finished Robert! Once the tree is down, we'll have to keep a guard station above where it's lying; this is where we can monitor their movements, so that we'll know immediately if they start trying to move the tree."

He paused and looked at Robert.

"You had a question, Robert?"

After taking down his arm, the sixty-eight-year-old retired dentist commented, "We don't have much of an arsenal, John. I think all we have is two .22 rifles and your 12-gauge shotgun, and there's not much ammo for either!"

John nodded, acknowledging that the man was correct. However, there wasn't much they could do about it, so he continued explaining his plan.

"If they manage to move the tree, or come in on foot, I suggest that the watch keepers let off a flare to warn us and then engage the troops as best they can. Some of us will need to go and give them a hand. I know it all sounds a bit airy fairy, but at the moment, unless someone else has an idea, that's all we have. Now, is there anyone with any kind of military service amongst us?"

There was silence.

'Damn,' he thought, hoping desperately that maybe help would come from some other direction. 'Who knows, maybe there will be others already there.'

There wasn't much they could do for now except to enjoy fried flathead and Barracouta for tea, followed by the rest of Helen's fresh bread and jam.

Friday 16th January 2015 ... Rain Bay

By 0620 the skippers gathered on *Zanadoo* and enjoyed a hot cup of coffee while having a last look at Sid's chart.

"Looks like the wind's dropped right off Sid."

Sid looked at his father in agreement.

"Yes. It might take us longer than we thought!"

Bentley asked whether the twins were still happy to sail the skiff.

"Sure Dad, we're having a ball."

As he gazed up at the huge cliffs towering above them, John wondered what the convicts had thought of the place. It would have been the same rugged coastline the sailing ships had passed some two hundred or so years ago on their way to the New England penal colony.

On *Silicon*, they had trouble getting the main halyard winch to work. This was an issue most shack-based boats caused their owners. Because she had been sitting unused for quite a while, everything had seized up.

Zanadoo had a well-equipped tool kit on board and came to their aid with some CRC lubricant. After undoing the winch housing and taking the salt and corrosion encrusted cogs out, they cleaned the whole thing up with CRC and soon had it put back together.

Although Skipper Robert Crawfield would rather have been on his own boat, he was willing to do anything to help. Crewing for him was Gina, his wife of forty years, with the help of the aging

James and Miriam Smythe and Cedric and Aileen Bilton. By the time they were finally under way they were trailing the group; even *Badman II* was in front of them!

With the likes of a retired dentist, his receptionist, a retired schoolteacher, plus an architect, a shipping agent and a self-employed hairdresser on board, the conversation was always stimulating. The subject never waned far from the same topic; who, what and why? Of course, they were referring to their unwanted Asian visitors.

"What's your theory Cedric?"

The retired shipping agent looked at Robert.

"World domination I suspect mate! Somehow, they escaped the Holocaust, or possibly, God forbid, they started it; and now want a piece of our little bit of heaven."

Miriam waded in on the conversation.

"But I can't understand all the killing! Why don't they just take everyone prisoner?"

Her husband James quantified the problem, asking a simple question.

"And where exactly would you keep 600,000 Taswegians?"

The penny dropped as the retired teacher finally got what he was saying.

"Oh! I see! Yes. If that's the case, I suppose they will have to look after us as well."

On *Badman II,* John handed over the helm to Billy, before going over to sit alongside his unresponsive wife.

"Just steer *one nine zero* mate."

He looked at Helen, his wife of twenty years, figuring that this was the only thing that had ever rattled her cage. It was even worse than when her parents had died, or during the drought years, when they'd had to put down hundreds of what should have been good stock.

He whispered, "I love you darling!"

The words seemingly just floated around in her brain; she heard them all right but didn't seem to know how to process the information.

As she looked at John; a smile slowly crept into her face.

"I'm sorry John, were you talking to me?"

John gave her a hug.

"Doesn't matter darling. We're nearly at Rain Bay."

He could see the entrance to their evening stop.

"Bring her round to starboard Billy, and then head for the point."

For once *Badman II* was not the last vessel in. So, this time, it got to moor alongside of *Zanadoo*, which was already swinging at anchor in Rain Bay. This was a desolate moon-shaped bay and was mid-way between Plunder Bay and Strong Fort Bay.

As they approached the flotilla, John was shocked to see that *Silicon* appeared to be on fire; flames and smoke were clearly emerging out of the twenty-six-foot cruising yacht. Apparently, a gas stove had been left on after coffee was served, and the roll of the vessel had taken the curtain too close to the flames.

Sloth quickly went to *Silicon's* aid; thankfully it didn't take long for a well-aimed fire extinguisher to put the fire out. Shaken but not deterred, the elderly crew took it on the chin, with plenty of belly laughs all round; and blaming dementia as being the cause of the fire.

Saturday 17th January 2015 ... Rain Bay, East Coast Taswegia

Setting sail at 0600, the flotilla left Rain Bay. It was a beautiful morning as far as weather went; there was only a light breeze, but it would be enough to keep them moving along at a reasonable speed. They were hoping the short journey to Strong Fort Bay would be swift; with only four nautical miles to travel, they had planned to arrive at 0700.

The twenty-foot skiff was first to enter the bay, followed by *Zanadoo, Sloth, Silicon, Moby* and then *Badman II.*

The bay looked peaceful enough; there was only one other vessel, a forty-foot cruiser, which looked like it had been there since the E1 hit. By the time John arrived, the group had successful y done a reccy after landing on the beach.

"Looks l ke our luck is with us John. Sid found a chainsaw in the Ranger Station, and it works."

It had been agreed that John and his family should have the house, with Graham bunking in the Ranger's Station. Leaving his wife and kids to unload the boat into the Ranger's house, John and a few volunteers travelled the eight kilometres to the area where he had visualised cutting the tree down.

"I'll cut the tree down. Who wants to go first at guard duty?"

Graham and Bentley agreed to go first. After a quick lesson on the weapons, they decided to use both .22 Rifles.

Selecting the tree was easy; the biggest one there was perfect. John made short work of the 110-metre giant Swamp Gum, although, with a girth of three feet, it was a bit of a challenge for him to get the 064 Stihl, with its twenty-four-inch bar, through the beast.

After accurately placing it well and truly across the road, he left the pair to guard the way in, and made the trek back to the beach. By the time he found himself wading through the surf to *Badman II,* it was nearing 1030.

'Doing well,' he thought to himself.

John went about gathering up his belongings and handing them to Billy. They both jumped as the UHF suddenly crackled into life.

"Bravo Zulu. Bravo Zulu. This is Bravo Echo. Do you receive? Over."

"Bravo Echo. Bravo Echo. This is Bravo Zulu. Go ahead. Over."

"Bravo Zulu, things are not so good here. Indo Alliance has set up HQ. Fear cannot hide much longer." Shhhhhhhh ...

"Bravo Echo. Bravo Echo. This is Bravo Zulu. Go ahead. Over."

"Bravo Zulu receiving 20/20. Cannot rely on hiding place much longer. Are you able to assist? Over."

"Bravo Echo. Bravo Echo. This is Bravo Zulu. That's an affirmative! Repeat. That's an affirmative! Can you wait till Tuesday? Over."

"Bravo Zulu. Thank you. Thank you. We will be here. Be careful! The roads are treacherous! Over."

"Bravo Echo. Bravo Echo. This is Bravo Zulu. Don't suppose anyone has access to a brick phone? If you can get to one dial 0189991236. Repeat 0189991236 at sparrow's fart Tuesday. Over."

John and Billy couldn't believe their ears! He could see by the commotion that others had heard the UHF as well. Grabbing the microphone, he quickly hit the transmit button.

"Station calling on UHF repeater channel One. Do you copy? Over."

"Unknown Station Delta Echo. Repeat Delta Echo. Bravo Echo reading you faint. Go ahead. Over."

John yelled to Billy, "Son, get that bag I've got stowed on the shelf up forward."

Once Billy passed him the canvas bag containing the brick phone, he pulled it out and lifted the lid to reveal his old number.

"This is Fortescue. Repeat Fortescue. 0184721651. Over."

Nothing but static! Sid, Robert and James came rushing over. Sid spoke first.

"John, who do you reckon that was?"

John shrugged as he plugged the brick phone into the little solar panel on the deck head of *Badman II*. No response from the phone. Only silence.

As he continued to unpack the contents of his yacht, Helen and Trish made themselves at home in the old Ranger's house. At 1300 Billy and Trish bought him a round of sandwiches.

"Brrr... Brrr ... Brrr ... Brrr ..."

John nearly shit himself; the bloody phone was ringing! Sid and James, with their boats moored alongside of John's, were on hand to hear it as well.

"Hello?"

"Yeah Mate, is John there?"

"Speaking, who's this?"

"Dick Mann. You may remember me but that's not important right now."

Dick gave John a real quick run-down on the events so far, then filled him in about who his team was, before asking about facilities and numbers.

"Held up in the old camp and Ranger Station. We have felled a huge tree across the access road and have it guarded. So far, the Alliance, as you call them, can't get through, but I don't know how long we can hold them off if they do manage to cut the tree up. We don't have any weapons. Oh, and we have twenty-nine residents: eight couples, one single and twelve children. Can you assist?"

Dick explained to John they were trying to save some people from Benowa and would try to get them to Strong Fort Bay by sea.

"Holy shit! Better get the rest of them together so I can let them know what's happening."

John sent Billy to round up the rest of the group. *Badman II* was anchored in the shallows of the bay, only some ten yards off the beach. By now the surf was diminishing, and everyone in the group had made the trek out to the yacht, wading out in the near pristine conditions.

"Thank you for coming. I have just had a phone call on the old brick phone from Dick Mann and his team of ex-military weapons experts. Looks like they are willing to come and assist us with the fight to get our state back. I need to charge the phone and get more information, but it looks like it will all be happening early next week."

For the first time in a few days, there was a buzz of excitement in the air. They finally had some answers, and also some hope for the future.

Dick had told John all about the invasion, the Alliance troops, the killings, and the mass genocide that was happening around the state; not only down south but up north as well.

John explained that the brick phone hadn't been used in over twenty years and would need twenty-four hours to charge properly.

After hearing about the call from Dick, the whole camp was in a better frame of mind and went about getting set up in their new quarters with enthusiasm. The backpackers' accommodation was divided up into six bunk rooms, along with some twin and some double rooms.

The kids shared the six bunk rooms, with boys and girls in separate rooms. The twin and the double rooms were issued to the elderly couples first, and then to the other married couples. In the end, most people were happy with their billets.

John and his family shared the Ranger's house, while Graham, the only single male in the group, slept in the Ranger's Station on the day bed. Rosters were drawn up to take food to the watch keepers, with a regular change of watch to take place each day.

All food supplies had been pooled together, and communal cooking took place in the kitchen of the backpackers' quarters. This kitchen was large enough to cater for sixty people, so had no problems catering for the twenty-nine in this party. The group had found a reasonably stocked pantry at the backpackers. It was mostly dry and tinned food, but this would fit in well with what they had brought with them.

One of the first items of business was to investigate the motor cruiser which was anchored in the bay. The plan was to strip her of all usable products, including food, fishing gear, ropes, and flares; basically, anything they could use.

Their first night in their new home was a mixed affair; some thought of it as an adventure, whereas some, like John's wife Helen, thought of it as hell! She had sunk to a new low, and just spent all her time sobbing in the bedroom. Nothing that John, Trish or Billy said would change her mind. They left her and ate with the group before taking back a plate, but she refused to eat.

The activity of the past three days had taken its toll on both Billy and Trish; worn out they were asleep in minutes.

John slid under the covers and held his wife. He found himself shivering; not because he was cold, but through fear of what could be ahead. Slowly he drifted off to sleep.

Sunday 18th January 2015 … Strong Fort Bay

Life in the backpackers came alive around 0600, with the excited children running around, just doing what children do. Miriam, Gina, Sarah, Aileen, Barbara, Jill and Mary were up and busy in the kitchen just after 0730.

They sorted out cereals for the children and then put together a selection for breakfast for everyone else. The replacement watch keepers would eat first, and then go and relieve the others; allowing them to come back and eat. It was a simple but effective system.

"What are you cooking girls?"

A nosey James stuck his head around the corner, only to be met by Miriam playfully flicking him with the tea towel.

"Baked beans on toast."

John, Billy and Trish arrived at 0745. Sarah, who was quite concerned about Helen, looked at John.

"Is she still the same?"

John looked at the group of women; they were all in the same boat as his wife but seemed to be coping well enough. He sighed as he answered, "Afraid so Sarah."

Barbara suggested, "Maybe we should go and see her after breakfast. You know; try and cheer her up. What do you reckon girls?"

There were nods all round.

Sid and Mick had drawn the next guard duty, and after devouring a hearty feed of baked beans, proceeded down the road to the tree. John talked to the others about the cruiser, calling for volunteers to come with him to investigate. They decided to take the cruiser's dinghy; a twelve-foot alloy which was still on the beach where the owners had left it. Josh, Tony and Billy accompanied John and together they rowed out to the anchored boat.

The *Billow* looked to be in great shape as she rode at anchor.

'What a waste,' thought John.

At just over forty foot, the steel cruiser looked well set up for coastal cruising. The dinghy drew alongside, and Josh tied her off to the swim platform at the stern. As they made their way on to the quarterdeck, they could see she was well decked out, with cushioned bench seats on three sides.

The main cabin come wheelhouse, opened up into a well laid out Galley, with seating for ten around the table; she had a great helm position with good instruments and a single screw, and was decked out with sat nav, radar and UHF and VHF radios.

John instinctively turned on the UHF, while the boys disappeared below to the cabins. Tony and John cleaned out the Galley supplies, finding safety equipment, mops, brooms, buckets, crockery and cutlery; all things that were a little light on back at the camp. Having found two doubles and a twin bunk, they reported back to John about the cabins.

"There's not much in them John," reported Josh.

"Any toilet paper Josh?"

Tony was thinking outside the square.

"Sorry Tony, didn't think of that."

Billy went off to check, returning soon after with six rolls of paper.

"Now listen boys, never overlook this stuff; it could become quite rare in the weeks or months to come. Hopefully, a lesson learned!"

Down in the Engine Room they found a huge white donk; the 210 Cummins diesel.

"Shame about the E1 Tony. Otherwise, this would have been a great fird! As it is now though, it's useless; the motor is totally destroyed."

"Mate! If the E1 hadn't hit, the bloody thing wouldn't be here!"

John felt embarrassed.

"Yes, I suppose you are right."

Billy yelled out from the quarterdeck.

"Found the fishing gear, Dad!"

Josh added, "More on this side John."

Upon lifting the tops to the bench seats, they had found a great selection of fishing gear; four rods, half a dozen handlines, and boxes of various sinkers, hooks, swivels and traces. Tony lifted the stern seat to reveal coils of rope, along with a small rubbish bin containing a grab all net.

"Guys, this is a real bonus!"

"We might set this later on, out off the point; it might supplement our food."

John, who had never done any net fishing, asked, "Do you know how to use this, Tony?"

The sixty-eight-year-old Italian replied with a laugh,

"Sure John! I was bought up fishing this way in Italy. We can easily do it out of the dinghy. It's a two-man job; one to row, while the other one works the net."

The task of loading all the booty into the dinghy was a bit of a delicate job.

"Lucky it is twelve-foot-long, and not eight foot, like some of those tenders you see John."

"Yes, and with no davits it must have been towed behind the boat."

After dragging the dinghy up the beach, John suggested, "We'd better not bring her up too far if we are going to set the net later on today."

They unloaded and started transferring the gear to the camp, storing most of it in the huge storeroom that was attached to the kitchen.

Once Miriam, Gina, Sarah, Aileen, Barbara, Jill and Mary had finished with the breakfast dishes, Miriam said, "Who wants to come and try to cheer up Helen?"

They all agreed to go with her. Sarah yelled out to Roger, "Watch your brothers and sister while I go to the ranger's house."

Barbara added, "Can you help entertain the kids Jill?"

There was a quiet response from Jill.

"Yes Mum."

Trish added, "I'll help too Mrs Frank."

They found Helen Badman curled up in the foetal position on the unmade bed, still dressed in her pyjamas. The group were a bit like a tornado; working together quickly, they soon got things sorted, making the bed and cleaning up in the kitchen while Miriam helped the forty-two-year-old get dressed.

Once they were done, they all sat around the kitchen table, just talking. They were careful not to talk AT her, just around her; about nothing in particular. Just normal stuff, like the weather, the camp facilities, the kids, and what a great job John and the other men were doing.

It took almost an hour, but finally Helen spoke, asking, "What are your rooms like?"

This was all they needed. Miriam looked at Aileen and Mary with a wink, acknowledging that they were winning the battle. Even though Helen had not seen a lot with her own eyes, just the thought of what was going on had sent her world spiralling down into depression. If there had been some way to get her some professional help, they suspected she might have been suffering from some sort of Post-Traumatic Stress Disorder.

"The girls must be with Helen?"

John could see that all the women were missing; although the older kids had the youngsters occupied outside with games. Billy asked his sister, "Where did you find all the games stuff, sis?"

Trish answered, "It was all in the storeroom. There was a whole load of balls, cricket sets, a table tennis table, a volleyball net and a lot of other stuff that I don't recognise."

At 1130, John made up a couple of lunches.

"I'm going to take these to the men at the tree, Tony. Can you let the ladies know that they don't have to make lunch up for them please? I should be back in an hour."

Tony looked at John.

"Geez mate, you're going to have to run! It must be twelve kilometres there and another twelve kilometres back."

John laughed.

"No Mate, I found a bike. I'm going to ride."

Sid and Mick had arrived at the tree around 0900, relieving Graham and Bentley who were quick to report no activity so far. After handing over the weapons, they left to head back to camp.

"I'm bloody starving Graham."

"Me too Ben!"

From their vantage point, they were about twenty metres above the tree, and had good vision all the way to the main road, which was about a kilometre away.

One end of the tree had ended up landing in the water, while the other end was in dense bush; there was no way anyone could get a vehicle around it. At three-foot-thick, it would take some chain-sawing to cut through it.

The previous night's watch had rigged up the canvas tarp they'd brought with them to run over the two swags which had been donated by John's family for the job.

"How much ammo you got, Mick?"

Mick carefully counted what was in the box.

"Forty-seven rounds mate, and the magazine holds ten. What about you?"

Sid did the same with his lot.

"Twenty-nine, plus five in the magazine. The old man's weapon is pretty ancient."

Hearing a noise coming from behind them, Sid and Mick turned around to see John peddling down the hill towards them.

"Holy shit mate! Where did you find that?"

Puffing a bit as he dismounted, the forty-seven-year-old farmer grinned.

"It was in the shed behind the ranger's house; there must be twenty of them. I'll go through the lot and find some more that are in going order; this will make it easier for the watch keepers to get to and from work."

"Anything that will make it faster to get here could be a great advantage, especially if the shit hits the fan!" said Mick.

Chapter 20
A Black Day

0800 Thursday 8th January 2015... Benowa, East Coast Taswegia

For George Black, the day started just like any other normal day. Well, as normal as it could be since the Nuclear Holocaust and the subsequent destroying of the E1 satellite.

George was a schoolteacher based at Benowa; a small fishing village and tourist town on Taswegia's East Coast. His wife, Wendy, was a nursing sister who was attached to the Benowa Medical Centre. George and Wendy had two children, Kelly, aged twelve, and Rob, who was one year younger.

On this particular morning, both kids had stayed home from school because they were sick. As George walked his wife to work, and then continued on to the school, he felt uneasy. He couldn't explain why, he just sensed that something wasn't quite right! He looked around, all he could see was the normal foot traffic, with plenty of kids heading into the school grounds. It was a beautiful summer's day, so nothing to do with the weather! No matter how much he tried, he just couldn't put his finger on what was wrong.

As he crossed the main road, he caught sight of someone riding a pushbike from the south; he realised that the rider, who didn't look well at all, was trying to yell out something to anyone who would listen. The rider caught sight of George and headed straight for him, dropping the bike as he reached the forty-two-year-old schoolteacher and thrusting an audio tape into George's hands before collapsing on to the ground. George could see blood running down the man's back. After putting the tape into his jacket pocket, he picked up the injured man and manoeuvred him into the fireman's lift position before carrying him the twenty or so steps back to the medical centre.

Wendy and one of the other nurses helped George to place him on to a trolley, and then whisked him into the little triage room. Two minutes later the doctor and Wendy emerged, shaking their heads as they told George that they hadn't been able to save the man. He'd been shot twice in the back. The doctor said he couldn't understand how he'd been able to make it anywhere at all, let alone ride a bike.

George explained the little he knew, and then remembered the tape which was still in his pocket. He pulled it out and gave it to the GP, who inserted it into the battery powered boom box in the reception area. As they listened to the recorded message from 2nd January, which had been made on the UHF repeater channel 1, other staff members joined them; all trying to make sense of what they were hearing.

It sounded a bit like some kind of radio drama, and even though they'd seen for themselves the injured and bleeding bike rider, none of them really understood at first that what they were hearing was real.

They soon changed their minds once they started to hear distant gunshots, and the sound of heavy trucks coming up the road.

It was George who worked it out first.

"This doesn't look too good, the old fellow must have been shot by the Alliance!"

He glanced out the front window as he heard a truck pulling up outside. He could also see more trucks heading down pretty well every street. There was no time to discuss things; he simply grabbed Wendy's arm and ran out the back through the fire escape, and into the trees.

"Don't look back, Love!"

As they ran through the bush towards their house, they could hear the sounds of gunshots and people screaming. The death squads were already at the bottom of their street, bursting into the houses, one by one, and systematically executing everyone they found.

Wendy came to a dead stop!

"What about the other kids at school?"

There was no time to think. George dragged Kelly and Rob away from their books and told Wendy to pack a few things for the kids and herself while he grabbed his rucksack and loaded a few clothes in it. It already contained the necessary cooking equipment they would need if they had to hide in the bush for a while, as well as some ready to eat meals.

'Lucky we were planning another bushwalk!' he thought to himself as he extracted some more dry provisions and four water containers from the pantry, before heading for the back door, where his family were waiting.

George could hear the truck getting closer by the minute; the gunshots were quite loud by now and sent shivers down their spines.

Kelly cried, "What's happening Dad?"

There was no time to explain.

"You've got to trust me, Kelly! We'll tell you everything once we are safe. Right now, we've just got to get out of here; then head to Jack and Joan's place up on Lookout Hill."

They escaped out the back gate and into the bush. George was thankful they'd bought a property that bordered state forest. The plan was to move as quickly as they could and avoid civilisation as much as possible. There was only one street to cross; then it was back into the relative safety of the bush.

Looking over some of the fences into the back yards they passed as the four made their way south, George realised that the trucks must have been there before them. Everywhere he looked there were dead bodies lying where they'd been killed while trying to run away from their pursuers.

They found Jack Davis in his shed, completely oblivious to the horror that was about to unfold.

"Jack, can you flash up your UHF mate, and while you're doing that, you'd better listen to this!"

George handed Jack the tape, while Wendy went inside to warn Joan. The retired fisherman listened and then whistled through his teeth.

"Is this for real son? Or is it some kind of sick joke?"

George grimly beckoned Jack over to the doorway of the shed, which overlooked the town of Benowa. Jack watched on as the death squads in their trucks stopped at each street.

People were running in all directions, screaming as they went, but were executed without mercy. He saw an attractive woman, with a child; she was down on her knees and begging for her life. A trooper shot her in the head at close range, before bayonetting the child; most likely to save wasting ammunition.

The reality of the danger they were all in finally dawned on him as George exclaimed, "Jack! Look at the carnage! They are systematically executing everyone in the town! That's everyone! Men, women, kids, babies, the sick; everyone!"

"How long do you reckon we've got George?"

"Mate, I reckon we've only got minutes before they get here!"

Jack went to the radio set.

"It's warmed up George, what do you want to do?"

Just as George grabbed the microphone, he heard a truck approaching.

"It might be a waste of time, but then again, it might not."

The truck changed gears, sounding like it was starting to slow down.

"Shit! There's not enough time! Jack, can you dismantle this so we can take it with us?"

"Sure can!"

With that, Jack packed up the set, along with the battery pack and tape recorder.

"Where are we off to George?"

Wendy had found Joan washing up the breakfast dishes.

"Hello dear, what brings you here on a workday?"

She filled Joan in about what had transpired in the last couple of hours. The retired schoolteacher listened intently; she could hear the passion and fear in Wendy's voice and didn't need to question the validity of her story. She knew the Nursing Sister was telling the truth.

The two women packed an overnight bag with the essentials.

"Well, my dear! It's a good thing that we replenished our medications yesterday!"

After inspecting the pantry, Wendy selected an assortment of food items to take with them. As the two women went back outside, they met Jack, George, Kelly and Rob, who were coming out of Jack's shed.

Jack had a sudden thought.

"I've got an old .22 rifle here that I can bring if that's any use to us son."

George nodded in agreement.

"Mate, you'd better bring all the ammo you've got as well!"

They left the property and ducked back into the bush just in time. Looking back, they could see the death squad truck pulling up at the end of the street.

"We should warn the neighbours George!"

The younger man grabbed Jack's sleeve, just as he was about to head in the other direction.

"There's no time mate, they will be on us in minutes! But we will try and warn some of the others on the other side of the hill, if they are still alive when we get to them."

Fifteen minutes later they were overlooking the Blowhole.

"Jack, you go that way, and I will try these two homes. Remember, at the first sign of a truck you need to get out of there. If whoever is home doesn't believe you first time, you'll just have to leave them! Wendy and Joan, you'd better stay here in the bush where it's safer."

Looking at his two children, George added, "And that goes for you two as well!"

Jack entered the yard at the back of an old shack. He wasn't sure who lived here, or even whether it was a local resident. It might even be a shack belonging to someone from Kings Town. After approaching the back door, he opened it carefully; ready to run for his life if he needed to.

It wasn't clear who got the bigger shock, Jack or the inhabitants of the shack! Mick and Peter had been sitting at the kitchen table, enjoying a coffee, when they were suddenly confronted with the sight of Jack standing in the open doorway, and brancishing his rusty rifle. He must have looked a sight!

Recovering quickly, Mick blurted out, "What the fuck! Who are you and what do you want?"

Mick Swab was fifty-five, and was a barman at the local pub. Since the E1 had hit, he was not usually required to start work until teatime. Sixty-year-old Peter Howe was once a fisherman but was now unemployed.

It took Jack exactly three minutes to tell his story.

Neither man needed to hear it twice! It only took them a short while to put together a couple of knapsacks full of gear; and then they were ready to go.

Jack quickly told them where Joan and Wendy were hiding, before heading off to the next house.

After crossing a vacant block, George entered the back door of a beautifully appointed home. He could hear voices coming from the front of the home, and upon entering the lounge room he found the Smith family: Brian, Yvonne, and Hilary.

He'd met Yvonne before; she worked with Wendy at the Surgery and had been rostered on to start at lunchtime. Brian, who used to work at the service station, was now out of a job, and, of course, he knew young Hilary from school.

Ignoring the startled looks on their faces, he blurted out, "Sorry for the intrusion! We have a big problem!"

George went on to explain to them what had happened and encouraged the trio to pack quickly. As he helped Hilary sort out her bag, he could see that the six-year-old was visibly upset. He comforted her by telling her that Kelly and Rob were going to be with them.

The next house Jack checked out was empty, and obviously had not been used for a couple of months. 'Definitely a shack,' he thought to himself as he made his way back to the group behind the fence. Mick, Peter, Brian, Yvonne, and Hilary were making themselves known. Jack realised George was nowhere to be seen.

"Where's George?"

Brian told him that George was checking out the last two homes in the street.

George listened intently to the sound of the truck, realising that it was in the next street down. He thought he probably had just enough time to search this house. Running to the back door, he found it unlocked, and went inside, only to find himself smack bang in the middle of a hairdressing salon.

The salon belonged to Eleanor Fame, who ran a small hairdressing business from home. Since the E1 she had been working on a bartering system instead of for money, although this was fine, and suited both her and her customers well. Sitting in the chair was Clinton Ramon; an invalid pensioner who had his hair trimmed once a month by Eleanor.

Eleanor's partner was David Numa. Before the E1 he'd worked in a motel; unfortunately, there was not really much need for his services these days!

As George told his story; the distant gunshots they could hear quickly had the trio convinced and ready to go.

Clinton asked anxiously, "Have I got time to go home and get a few things?"

After finding out where the pensioner lived, George convinced him this was not a good idea!

"No mate! It's too dangerous! They have already been down your street."

The group wasted no time, moving quickly into denser bushland, where it would be easier to hide. Once he thought it was safe to stop for a while, George allowed them to take a break while he explained his plan.

"We'll make our way east towards the Gulch, staying hidden in the bush. This deep ocean ravine in-between the craggy rocks of little Governor Island and the Benowa shoreline, is where the town's fishing fleet used to shelter from the Taswegian Sea swells.

"Later tonight we will transmit on the old UHF radio and hopefully make contact with others who may have escaped the Alliance. I don't know how long we'll have to stay hidden, but what I do know is that if we are caught, we die!"

The group was silent while they thought about what he'd told them. Old Jack was the first to speak.

"Do we go and raid for food George? I'm thinking the stuff we have here won't last us for too long."

"That seems like the only option for us right now Jack. Maybe if we can scavenge from the empty homes we find along the way, we'll find enough to keep us alive."

They found a secluded spot overlooking the Gulch. Peter could see that the fishing boat he'd used to work on was still alongside and suggested he should go and empty the larder. George pointed out that, being this close to Benowa, they would not be able to light any fires, and that all cooking would need to be done on the little gas burners. Unfortunately, they only had ten spare cylinders for these.

The evening meal was a combination of different types of packet pasta. It wasn't flash, but it filled their empty stomachs.

Around midnight, Peter returned from his raid, bringing with him what looked to be the entire contents of the boat's pantry. Feeling rather pleased with himself, he added it all to the group's supplies.

0030 Friday 9ᵗʰ January 2015 ... The Gulch, Benowa

"Let's set that UHF up Jack. Oh, and can you please pass me the recorder?"

Those who were still awake watched as George set up the tape recorcer, then hit the play button while holding down the microphone switch.

Beep ... Beep ... Beep...

"Here is the news for Friday 2nd January 2015, Alex Brand reporting.

As I speak, we have reports that forces, calling themselves, 'The New Alliance,' have landed at all major ports in Taswegia.

In Kings Town, Commander of the invasion force, General Jun Lee Sung, has summoned all the members of the Taswegian Parliament on to the lawns in front of parliament to discuss our surrender details!

This is crazy, who do these people think they are. Surrender? Why? And to who?

Wait. I have more reports coming in. They're systematically executing everyone. Oh no! They have beheaded the Premier! People are running for their lives. People are being shot down by the Alliance force, which is at least fifteen hundred strong. Some return fire now by local police but this seems insignificant. What a mess!

More news ... in his statement, the General reiterated the only personnel safe from this slaughter are the doctors attached to hospitals.

This is madness! I can't believe that this is happening!

Wait! I have more reports coming in from our man on the ground, Bill Green on portable ..."

"Thanks Alex," said Bill Green as his voice took over the commentary. *"The city is in chaos. More troops are arriving from what looks like two old tankers docking at Macquarie Street Wharf. This looks like something out of the Second World War, with old trucks and jeeps disembarking more troops."*

"Thanks Bill ..." Alex Brand's voice returned, *"What? Oh no! We'll have to shut down this broadcast. Troops are approaching the building! Stay tuned f ... Shit! They're coming up the stairs! If we can get another ..."*

Bang, Bang ... Schhhhhhhhhhh ... Only static ...

"This is Bravo Zulu, Bravo Zulu. I have a copy."

"Bingo! We have a hit; thank the Lord for that!"

With tears streaming down his face, George started transmitting.

"Bravo Zulu on Channel 1. Glad to hear your voice. Where are you?"

"Station calling Bravo Zulu, negative position, who are you?"

By now, everyone in the group was listening intently. George transmitted again.

"Bravo Zulu, we are survivors situated Benowa East Coast Taswegia. Following the Holocaust Taswegia has been invaded by troops, possibly from North Korea. They call themselves the Alliance. They are systematically killing everyone except for medical staff. Can you help? Over."

"Station at Benowa East Coast Taswegia this is Bravo Zulu. Over."

"Bravo Zulu this is Benowa receiving 20/20."

"Benowa, we have also survived. Nice touch to replay the broadcast. It's too dangerous to give place names; you never know whether the bad guys are listening. Suggest you use Bravo Echo. How many in your party? Over."

"Bravo Zulu, this is Bravo Echo. There are twelve of us, made up of five families. How many of you?"

"Bravo Echo there are six of us. Over."

"BREAKER BREAKER! DO NOT TRANSMIT! THEY ARE LISTENING!"

"Bravo Zulu how far are you away from us? Over."

"Bravo Echo too far! Repeat too far! Will try to keep in contact. Out!"

Jack stopped recording the transmission and replayed the last section …

"Bravo Echo there are six of us. Over."

"BREAKER BREAKER! DO NOT TRANSMIT! THEY ARE LISTENING!"

"Bravo Zulu how far are you away from us? Over."

"Bravo Echo too far! Repeat too far! Will try to keep in contact. Out!"

"Did you hear that, George! There was another station coming in with a breaker; they sounded like they were trying to warn us someone was listening?"

"Well at least we know now that we are not alone."

Brian moved up closer to the radio, asking, "How come you said there were only twelve of us George? You know there are fourteen!"

"It won't hurt to keep a few cards close to our chest, Brian."

Every night, once it was dark, Peter, George, Brian, David or Mick went off on a scrounging tour. Sometimes they were lucky, but other times they were not.

As they discovered more about what was happening in the town, they reported back to the others. They watched on as the clean-up squads steadily worked their way through the now-empty houses, and then saw the introduction of Alliance Nationals to the town as they moved in.

Their diet consisted mainly of pasta and vegetables, occasionally supplemented with a dozen eggs. One-night Mick was excited to come across a side of lamb which was hanging up in someone's back shed; it had obviously been slaughtered in preparation for the new inhabitants.

Great discussion was held by the group as to whether or not he should have taken it; some were worried that the missing lamb would cause suspicion, and whether it would bring the Alliance down on top of them if they started looking for the culprits.

At one stage George had a brief talk with the local doctor. Dr Margaret Bones GP had been spared by the Alliance, who needed her to run the medical centre. She was exhausted and looked a mess. It seemed that the other doctor; Dr Ronald Bygraves, had refused to do anything to help the Alliance. He'd been shot on the spot, leaving only Margaret to keep the place going on her own; although there was some talk that another doctor might be joining her soon.

She had told George that she'd heard of more survivors living somewhere out near the old wildlife park, which was just out of Benowa. She had overheard some soldiers talking about their orders, which were to find them and kill them all.

George asked her if she had heard anything about their own group; he was relieved to hear that the answer to this question was "No."

Saturday 17ᵗʰ January 2015 ... The Gulch, Benowa

After a brief group discussion, they all agreed they should try and make contact with the other station, Bravo Zulu. They would be taking the risk of the Alliance listening in, but by now they were becoming desperate. The town was filling up with Indonesians, and it was getting more and more difficult to move around without being seen.

Jack set the UHF and recorder up and then handed the microphone to George.

"*Bravo Zulu. Bravo Zulu. This is Bravo Echo. Do you receive? Over.*"

"Bravo Echo. Bravo Echo. This is Bravo Zulu. Go ahead. Over."

"Can't hear them, Jack! Maybe try and move the aerial around a bit."

George tried again.

"Bravo Zulu, things are not so good here. Indo Alliance has set up HQ. Fear cannot hide much longer." Shhhhhhhh ...

"Bravo Echo. Bravo Echo. This is Bravo Zulu. Go ahead. Over."

"Bravo Zulu receiving 20/20. Cannot rely on hiding place much longer. Are you able to assist? Over."

As they listened, everyone in the group held their breath as they waited for the reply.

"Bravo Echo. Bravo Echo. This is Bravo Zulu. That's an affirmative! Repeat. That's an affirmative! Can you wait till Tuesday? Over."

"Bravo Zulu. Thank you! Thank you! We will be here. Be careful! The roads are treacherous! Over."

"Bravo Echo. Bravo Echo. This is Bravo Zulu. Don't suppose anyone has access to a brick phone? If you can get to one dial 0189991236 Repeat 0189991236 at sparrow's fart Tuesday. Over."

Brian and Yvonne blurted out in unison, "What the bloody hell is a brick phone?"

The old ex-fisherman smiled, as did the other older members of the party.

"The question is not what is a brick phone but where are we going to find one?"

Clinton piped up, "I know where I can find one; well, at least it was there a few years ago. I used to volunteer in the little museum; you know, the one just down the road from the hardware."

Yvonne added, "Yes, I remember it. I once looked at the vacant shop next door; wanted to run the hairdressing from it. Unfortunately, it ended up being too expensive."

George asked, "What happened to it Clinton?"

"I think it just shut down. As far as I know, the stuff is still inside."

George gave a wide grin.

"Well, we shall see tonight. Clinton, you and me will take a look see; of course, that's if you're up for it?"

"Too right mate! I'm going stir crazy just sitting around here!"

0130 Sunday 18th January 2015 ... the old Museum, Benowa

The streets were deserted. It hadn't taken long for Clinton and George to make it safely to the back of the group of three shops.

"The Museum is the middle one George."

After using his coat to muffle the window, Clinton stuck his elbow through the glass pane alongside the back door.

"You look like you might have done that before mate?"

Clinton looked at the schoolteacher.

"I haven't always been a pensioner you know!"

Inside the building everything was covered in a thick layer of dust. Despite this it didn't take them long to find what they had come for; in a glass cabinet was a brick phone and a 12V charger, as well as a carry case.

"Perfect!"

George suddenly grabbed Clinton's arm, pointing towards the front of the shop. It seemed an Alliance trooper had been working security; he'd obviously been drawn to investigate the light from the torch the pair were using.

Before George had a chance to make his way around the stuff in the shop, the door opened, and the trooper, with his rifle shouldered, stood in the open doorway, using his powerful light to scan the room. It was obvious he was ready for trouble.

George crouched behind an old Lightburn washing machine, trying not to move a muscle. He could feel his heart thumping heavily in his chest.

'Shit! he thought, is this the end?'

The blinding light from the torch swept the wall right above him. As he watched it move down towards where he was hiding, he shut his eyes, waiting for the bang.

Thump!

The trooper went down like a bag of spuds. When George picked up the torch, he saw Clinton, grinning like a Cheshire cat! He shone the light on the trooper's head, realising that it had been smashed in so badly on one side that it looked like there was only half a head left intact!

"Christ mate! What did you hit him with?"

"This!"

Clinton was holding an antique cast iron frying pan.

"What are we going to do with the body?"

"Well mate, I reckon we just hide him in here, then take his rifle and ammo. We'll have to find something to cover the broken glass pane, and then lock the door when we leave."

The pair stripped the body of ammo before dragging it behind the Lightburn, and then looking around for something to cover the glass pane. They couldn't believe their luck; among the other treasures in the museum there was a small stained-glass panel, the same size as the broken one. They made sure it looked as if it was meant to be there, and then locked the door securely behind them.

They decided to head back a different way, which took them right past the school. It turned out not to be the best decision they'd ever made. As they drew level with the entrance to the school car park, they were distracted by a horrible stench coming from the direction of the school buildings. After a quick investigation, the pair were horrified to find the bodies of the kids, along with those of a few teachers. There were about thirty bodies in the quadrangle behind the first classroom. George recognised two teachers, or what was left of them anyway. He'd known the mother and daughter duo well.

The body of the older Mrs Smith looked like a pin cushion; with lots of holes from the bayonets that had stabbed her to death. She'd obviously been trying to shield some of the children, and was still huddled in the corner, with the kids behind her.

Although she must have died a horrible death, her twenty-four-year-old daughter, had suffered far more. George had heard that she'd been considered the most eligible of the single teachers, and that she'd had all of the single males, as well as most of the married ones, drooling over her body.

The term, 'always dressed to kill,' certainly applied now! George looked in disgust at what they'd done to her half naked body. Her dress had been shoved up over her head, and her underwear was nowhere to be seen. There was plenty of evidence that she had been pack raped.

Every one of them had been bayonetted; George suspected they'd been trying to save ammunition.

They discussed what they'd seen as they made their way back to camp; agreeing it was probably better not to tell the others about the trooper, or about what they'd seen at the school. They'd all been through enough trauma already!

The following day they plugged the brick phone in to the 12V solar Panel and waited for the old relic to come to life.

"From memory George, they take a bloody long time to charge!"

"No problems there, Jack! We've got until Tuesday morning."

Over what was left of Sunday, and all through Monday, they witnessed the unloading of what appeared to be more Indonesian Nationals as they settled into the local homes. The body clean-ups continued. By the look of the smoke coming from the direction of the local tip, they figured this was probably where the bodies were being disposed of.

They talked about whether or not to move camp closer to the highway into Benowa; wondering whether this would make it easier for their saviours to extract them by road when they arrived.

Mick disagreed, shaking his head.

"But what if they come by sea?"

The general consensus was that this was not likely, seeing as the E1 had killed all the engines. The possibility of simply escaping on a sailing boat didn't even cross their minds.

Tuesday 20th January 2015 … The Gulch, Benowa.

Camp life had been tough for those who weren't used to it. The essential but mundane task of latrine duty, which meant digging a hole, then filling it in after each use, was a constant challenge. Scrounging fresh water for a group of this size was hard enough; and then there was the need to constantly prepare meals for fourteen hungry people, as well as having to maintain constant guard duty.

From their vantage point they had good vision of the Gulch, and also the main fishing wharf, which was their main source of fresh water. To replenish supplies they had to sneak onto the wharf, and then fill the drums from the main line which had previously been used to fill boats.

By 0530 that morning the group were all wide awake and enjoying a breakfast of tinned food. There was spaghetti, baked beans, sausages and ravioli; pretty well whatever they had left.

"I think we have done well to use the food up. Great work everyone! I know things haven't been easy for you all. Time to dial that number! All of our hopes are resting on this antiquated old phone!"

George turned on the brick phone and dialled 0189991236.

Brrr ... Brrr ... Brrr ... Click.

"Hello, is that Benowa UHF Bravo Echo?"

George was so excited that he nearly forgot to speak!

"Yes! This is George from Benowa."

"Great George! My name is Dick. Now listen very carefully. We are about two hours away and will be coming in by sea. So, you'll all need to make your way to the Gulch. From memory there is good cover in the bush area overlooking it.

"When our vessel arrives, we will give you a signal by light; three short bursts. Then we will cover you all as you come aboard. You'll need to move as fast as you possibly can. We would prefer to only be alongside for thirty minutes at the most.

"Can you get to the Gulch on time?"

"No problems Dick; we're already there! Oh, and how will we recognise your boat?"

On the other end they could hear Dick laughing.

"Well George, given the E1 situation, I shouldn't think there will be any other boats coming into the Gulch this morning. But just in case, I will give you a hint. You'll be looking at a navy Patrol Boat."

George's mouth went dry; he was having trouble getting the words out.

"Sounds fantastic Dick! But I have to tell you that we have identified another problem we'll need some help with"

Chapter 21
Benowa

I opened my eyes and instinctively looked at my watch.

"Holy fuck! It's 0947. What a sleep!"

Annie was stirring alongside of me. Hearing me swear she asked sleepily, "What's wrong Sarge?"

I looked around the camp. There was no movement from anyone.

"It's fucking nearly 10 o'clock!"

The fire was almost out, with just a few embers still glowing. As I pulled on my trousers I winced; my leg was really sore. By the time Dick appeared I had gathered some wood and was stirring the fire back to life.

"Morning Sarge, Annie. How's the leg?"

"It's a bit sore mate. But I'll live."

By 1045 the whole camp was up. As we sat around the fire after breakfast Dick admitted, "Well, we all must have needed the sleep! It's not every day that all of us sleep in."

Basically, there was a lot of yawning going on, and not much inclination from anyone to do much at all.

I could hear the RHIB approaching the beach. Doc and Nari soon appeared, with Doc saying, "Morning all! You lot look like you've only just got up."

Patch asked, "How's the patient Doc?"

"She's fighting fit! And I mean that in the nicest possible way."

He grinned as he went on to tell the group that Jack had slept in the chair in the sickbay all night. They'd found him in the Galley after April had sent him off to get a feed and a cup of coffee.

"How's the leg Sarge? I'd better have a good look at it."

Doc was pointing to the area where Annie and I slept, so I hobbled over and stripped off my trousers while Nari opened Doc's bag. Doc cleaned the wound before jabbing a needle into my thigh, saying, "I'd better put a stitch in this."

With Nari's assistance, the whole thing was over in ten minutes.

"There you go son! Good as new."

As I pulled my trousers back on, I admired the really neat bandaging job he'd done on my leg.

"Thanks Doc and Nari, it feels better already."

Dick handed Doc and Nari a coffee.

"We need to go over the plan for tomorrow, Doc. Do you want to do it now?"

The sixty-five-year-old Doctor smiled as he took his first sip of the hot brew.

"Might as well Dick. As per our discussions a couple of days ago, we should all sleep on the *Freo* tonight; with the exception of Vince and Laurel, who have volunteered to stay behind and guard the fort so to speak.

"Wakey, wakey at 0230, main engines at 0250, then get under way at 0300. We should be approaching the Gulch by around 0900.

"We will go over the plan for that on the way."

Doc looked at Dick.

"Does that sound all right to you mate?"

"It sure does Skipper! Now how about I run through everyone's place on the crew for this run. Obviously, Doc will be Skipper and Nav Officer. I'll go as Mate, comms and backup Nav Officer, as well as do tricks on the wheel when needed.

"Annie, we thought you might like to help Jack in the Engine Room. Are you up for that?"

Annie was excited at the thought of finally being part of the crew.

"Sure thing, Dick! I can't wait."

Dick continued.

"Nari, you'll be looking after our patient in the sickbay, and Patch, you can be lookout and maybe do a trick or two on the wheel. Sarge will be coming along as armourer, as well as checking weapons and manning the .50 Calibre if need be."

Most people, including me, nodded their approval. I looked at Vince.

"Vince, if you like I'll give you a run down on how the Claymores work; you know ... just in case."

Vince replied, "That would be great Sarge. Laurel and I are planning to do some fishing, re-stock the wood supply and finish the chook pen; that's if we don't do it today."

Doc said to Vince, "Mate, we've now got two RHIBs; one will stay here for you to use, and of course you have the use of the CJ herself if you find yourselves overrun."

Vince asked Dick to give him a run around on how the CJ worked.

I hobbled over to the fire and tossed out the dregs in my cup, saying, "Let's build a chook pen."

Dick grabbed my arm.

"Mate, I think you'd better sit this one out. I think we have enough bodies to handle the job; it's time you took it easy. Well, at least for the rest of the day. After all you have a few busy days coming up."

Annie looked at me and smiled.

"He's right love; we can do it."

Vince and Laurel had already collected a range of driftwood suitable for doing the job, while Jack had found a roll of chicken wire in the Engine Room of the CJ. This is what had given him the idea in the first place.

I just sat back and relaxed, and watched Annie pour me another coffee.

Later in the afternoon, after packing their overnight bags, the group made their way to the RHIB. Jack, who had brought her back in earlier, had packed for both April and himself.

Dick had showed Vince and Laurel the ins and outs of the CJ.

"Remember you two, no heroics! If the Alliance comes over the hill, just get the fuck out of here!"

He explained that all they had to do was get to the CJ, taking what weapons they had with them, then drop all lines, hit the battery isolator, hit the starter, then jam her ahead and go.

"Remember they can't follow you. Laurel, you'll have to man the RHIB and then meet Vince once he clears the Gulch. If it all happens too fast just take the RHIB; but be prepared for them to work out how to use the CJ and follow you."

Vince thought for a minute.

"Mate, we could piss off in the RHIB, and then double back and get the CJ going. I don't think they would see the CJ from the beach."

Dick nodded.

"I like it mate."

"Is that what I think it is Dick?"

I was pointing to the bag of what looked like crayfish.

"Right Sarge! I thought I would do curried crayfish for scran, served with rice."

Patch licked her lips.

"Yummo, Love!"

Once the group was on board the Patrol Boat, Jack operated the Hiab crane, securing the RHIB and lifting it back into its cradle. Annie and I went to visit April and Jack.

"You look better April."

"Why thank you Sarge! I feel much better. I really want to get up, but the Doc says I have to stay another day in this damn bed!"

After leaving the sickbay, I showed Annie to our bunks down the bottom of the stairs on two deck port side in the senior sailors' cabin. We decided to squeeze into one of the king single bunks.

As she made up the bunk Annie said, "I'm very excited to be working with Jack in the Engine Room! I've never done anything like that before."

After scran, Vince and Laurel took the other RHIB back to the beach; leaving us to relax over a drink.

Tuesday 20ᵗʰ January 2015 … FCPB Fremantle, Hells Beach. hrough Sarge's eyes …

Dick stirred when he heard me tapping on the door.

"0230 Dick, Patch."

Sitting up, he replied, "Thanks mate."

Dick kissed his wife, who was now wide awake.

"You know love, I'm excited about all this. I hope I make a good sailor."

Dick looked at his naked wife.

"Chook, you'll do just fine. Although, you'd better put some clothes on, or we'll never get out of here!"

The Galley was a buzz of activity. After downing a quick brew, people disappeared off to their part of ship. Jack took Annie down to the Engine Room, issuing her a pair of earmuffs before showing her around. With port already running, they started the starboard generator, with Jack going through the procedure of paralleling them. He had to yell over the noise.

"Remember Annie, we need all the power we can get to weigh anchor."

They opened the fuel lines to the huge MTU main engines and turned the port over until she fired. The adrenalin which was rising in Annie's body showed in the way her eyes were sparkling. She carefully copied Jack and started starboard. Leaning close to the ex-CD Sniper she smiled, "It's kind of sensual, isn't it Jack?"

The ex-stoker just grinned.

"After all these years my dear, it still does it for me! Now let's go and report."

Dick showed Patch the chart table and flashed up the ship's radar. After taking her up to the lookout positions on the Flying Bridge, he gave her a set of binoculars.

Doc and Nari were on the Bridge, discussing whether it would be safer for April to stay in the sickbay, or whether she would be better off in the forward mess, strapped into a bigger bunk.

"Let's decide in an hour or so, Love, once we've cleared Mary Island. We'll see how rough it gets."

Nari agreed.

Appearing on the Bridge, Annie piped up, "On two generators and main engines ready, Skipper."

She giggled as she tried to emulate the Chief. Jack smiled to himself as Doc replied, winking at the Chief.

"Roger that Chief."

As Dick and I went forward to man the windlass, Doc reached for the ship's intercom, and piped, "Weigh anchor!"

Patch was sitting in the lookout chair on the Flying Bridge. Doc, along with almost everyone else on board, joined her there, appreciating the stillness of the night air. Dick pointed straight ahead, and Doc gave the throttles a touch ahead. The Anchor cable rattled into the locker and Dick gave the straight up and down signal.

Leaning towards Patch, Doc explained what was happening.

"Okay Patch. The first signal from Dick told me the direction of the anchor. I went ahead to take the strain off the windlass, then Dick gave the second signal, which meant that the anchor had left the bottom."

Doc pushed the throttles to slow ahead, Dick and I completed the task, applying the brake and retaining links.

As we eased out of the bay, Doc asked for an update from Dick on the radar.

"All clear Skipper."

After disappearing to the armoury, I'd bought back a couple of .50 Calibre machine guns. I secured them into their port and starboard cradles, and then attached the ammunition boxes.

Dick joined Patch on the Flying Bridge. She was amazed at how far she could see in the moonlight.

"I didn't think it would look this clear Dick!"

"It's not like this every night Chook. You should make the most of the moon."

Jack showed Annie how to do a set of rounds in the Engine Room, what to look for, and how to take the fuel readings and enter them into the log in the tiny control room. She also needed to make sure that the ready use fuel tanks were kept full by transferring fuel from one of the main tanks; this also assisted in the boat's trim.

"You don't have to stay down here all the time do you, Jack?"

Annie was quite sensitive to the movement of the boat and wasn't too sure about how she'd go staying down there with the smells.

"No Annie. You've just got to do rounds about once an hour. Having said that, now that there are two of us, you'll be able to miss one now and again."

"Nope, I want to do everything you do Jack."

The ex-CD could see the determination in her eyes.

Throttling up to fifteen knots, the Patrol Boat pushed a good bow wave; the sea state was calm with only a slight swell rolling in from the Northeast.

As he gave the helm to Dick, Doc said, "Steer *zero three five* mate. We'll go check on the patient."

"Roger that Skipper. Steering *zero three five*. Do you want to take the wheel, Chook?"

Dick showed Patch how to read the compass repeat.

"It's a bit confusing Dick. I only expected the needle to move, not the whole thing."

"Gets everyone the first-time love! The needle stays permanent. The best way to get your head around it is to think of the boat being the needle, with the background being the compass."

After leaving his wife on her own for a moment he checked on me. I was on the Bridge wing, checking that the .50 Cal ammunition boxes were secured properly to their mounts.

"There's one box on each pedestal Dick, and two more in the ready use lockers."

Dick looked at me with admiration. I was clearly adapting to the life of a sailor quite well, as a matter of fact we both were. It appeared that Annie was loving life in the Engine Room.

Doc and Nari paused in the passageway outside the sickbay as they tried to assess whether the boat was pitching too much for April to stay there.

"What do you reckon Nari?"

The triage nurse smiled as she looked at her lover.

"Let's let April decide."

They opened the door to discover a very grumpy French woman who was trying to get dressed.

Doc barked, "And what do you think you're doing!"

Nari hid a smile as April looked at Doc in fury. The look on her face scared him for a minute.

"Doc! You've got to get me out of here! I'm fed up with being cooped up all the time. I want some fresh air!"

Doc explained that, although, in his opinion, she wasn't ready for that much moving, he would allow her to make the choice of whether to stay in the sickbay or move to the forward mess. Whichever way she decided, she would still be confined to her bunk.

Stubborn as always, April just extended her middle finger in defiance.

"Screw you, Doc!"

Doc sighed heavily and looked at Nari, who was desperately trying not to laugh.

"All right April. We will let you go up to the Flying Bridge for an hour or so; but after that it's back to bed!"

Back on the Bridge, Dick asked, "How's it going on the wheel, Chook?"

Patch looked back towards the Flying Bridge to where Dick and I were sitting and smiled.

"I think we're going in the right direction."

Jack and Annie appeared from the Engine Room about the same time that Doc and Nari manoeuvred April through the Bridge. Jack moved over to April, helping his wife with the last couple of steps.

"You sure you're right to be up here, Love?"

She just gave him, 'the look'.

Nari grinned.

"Don't argue with her Jack! She's a mean woman!"

After helping April into the helmsman's chair and making sure she was strapped in and comfortable, Doc inspected her wounds to make sure there was no bleeding.

"Look after her Jack."

Dick took a reading off the radar to plot the course and recommended an alteration in direction.

"Recommend we steer *zero three zero.*"

He'd already showed Patch how to change course. She proudly yelled back, "Steering *zero three zero,* Skipper."

Brrr ... Brrr ... Brrr ...

I picked up the receiver.

"Dick, it's for you."

It was 0700, and they were abeam of Beer Bay, ETA the Gulch at this speed being 0845. Doc was pleased with the results; especially now that he'd been able to persuade April to retire to a nice comfortable amidships bunk in the forward mess. He piped all hands to a crew meeting in the wheelhouse.

"Dick and I have come up with the following plan. Feel free to change it if you can think of something better."

Doc went on to describe what he saw happening over the next few hours.

"The tide's right to enter the Gulch from the north; we should get there at 0845. Annie, Jack, Patch and Nari will be dressed in Indonesian uniforms. You too Sarge, that's if you can get close to fitting into a shirt. You'll all need hats on please to help disguise your faces.

"Nari and Patch will be on the Flying Bridge pretending to helm the boat, while Annie and Jack will handle the refuelling when alongside. Sarge will man the .50 calibre on the Flying Bridge. Dick will bring the boat alongside from the enclosed Bridge, while I man the Aldis lamp, which I'll use to flash the bush area opposite the wharf.

"Hopefully, the group will be on their toes and ready to board. I'll get them below as fast as I can; from what George Black tells us there are thirteen altogether.

"Jack, one mooring line amidships only; once the fuel and water lines are fixed, I'll need you to man the .50-calibre sniper rifle on the Bridge wing. Meanwhile, Annie will monitor the water tanks and turn the valve off when we're full.

"Nari can speak a little Indonesian and will use the ship's broadcast to disguise her voice if need be.

"My thoughts are that these people will probably not challenge us because they are Indonesian as well. If anything, they should be friendly.

"Dick will have the silenced .22 and be ready to move stealthily ashore and dispose of anyone who gets, 'too friendly'. We also have the backup from Jack with his silenced sniper's rifle. How long to refuel Chief?"

Doc looked at Jack, who was going over his figures with Annie.

"Twenty minutes if it's a decent sized hose, Skipper."

"Any questions or suggestions?"

There was silence until Dick spoke.

"I think you have it covered Doc. So, it's in and out inside 30 minutes. Speed is of the essence!"

Tuesday 20th January 2015 ... FCPB Fremantle, The Gulch, Benowa

It was 0830 as they entered the Gulch at Benowa, East Coast Taswegia.

"Slow ahead. Port twenty Dick."

"Roger that Doc."

Dick brought the *Fremantle* round to port and gingerly entered the Gulch, making sure he missed the few sunken fishing boats which served as a grim reminder of the E1.

"Amidships, half astern, take off all way. Dick, can you spin her and go in astern to the refuelling jetty; just in case we have to exit the area fast."

"Roger that Doc."

Dick, with the wheel amidships, took control of the boat on engines only, moving half ahead port and half astern starboard the *Fremantle* turned in her own length. Throttling both astern, Dick manoeuvred her portside alongside the jetty.

"Leave main engines running Doc?"

"Roger that Dick."

Patch and Nari, dressed in Indonesian uniforms, were already on the Bridge; their slim frames easily fitted the mottled camouflage fatigues. The pants were cargo, with plenty of pockets, and the tunic top extended to mid-hip, with breast pockets and epaulettes. Annie and Jack were on deck securing a mooring line amidships; once they'd finished, they proceeded to run the fuel and water lines on board. Sarge had been carefully scanning the area with the binoculars.

"All clear ashore."

Doc was manning the Addis lamp. After pointing it up into the bush overlooking the wharf area, he gave the short three flash signals.

Nari appeared on the Bridge after checking on April.

"You'd better go and have a talk to your wife Jack. She's threatening to get out of bed again!"

Jack disappeared down below and found April trying to get dressed.

"You've got to get back into bed Love; you know it hasn't been long enough! You might open up those stitches if you don't."

April looked at her husband with frustration.

"I'm bored! Not only that, but I'm missing out on all the fun! Just let me get up and sit in the mess; I can help by talking to the new arrivals once they get here."

The ex-CD gave in and helped his wife dress. After making her comfortable in the Junior Sailors' Mess he gave her a cuppa and made her promise to stay put unless she had to use the heads.

Sarge had been keeping a watch for any movement.

"There's people approaching the jetty Skipper!"

Dick and Doc were on deck ready to escort them aboard. The women and children went first, followed by the men; with the last one they presumed being George Black.

"Boy, are we glad to see you guys! Nice boat!"

"Ten minutes!" warned Annie.

"Water tanks full Doc!"

George turned to Dick.

"What do you reckon about the other problem?"

Dick looked at Doc.

"It's your call mate."

The aging doctor looked at the team. Jack and Sarge were on the Flying Bridge with Nari and Patch, while Annie, Dick and Doc were just below in the Bridge.

"Dick, Sarge and George. You'll need to find a vehicle in the next five minutes, then commandeer it and get to the wildlife park and then back to the medical centre; all within, say 25 minutes if that's possible. It's your choice; I can't make you do it."

"I'm in," said Sarge, "and I think I've just found us a jeep!"

Approaching the jetty was a jeep. They could see four troopers sitting in the back and two in the front.

"You'd better get to them before they get out of the jeep, Dick. Nari, you go with Dick and say 'hello' or something that might convince them we're okay. You follow them Sarge, with George. George, you'll need to put on a uniform shirt and hat first."

Dick shoved the .22 down the back of his trousers before making a beeline with Nari towards the jeep, which was starting to slow to a stop.

"Selamat pagi," yelled Nari, trying to make her voice as deep as possible.

Dick waved his hand in a friendly manner. Keeping his head down to hide his Western appearance, he held out his left hand as if in preparation for a handshake, while drawing the .22 with his right, and then shot all six in the head at point blank range.

"Where are we going to hide the bodies, Dick?"

The ex-navy CD pointed to a container sitting on the jetty. It had obviously been used as a ready-use store. Dick soon smashed the padlock from its hasp and staple, then helped Nari as she started to drag the bodies from the jeep.

"We'd better take off their jackets first; there is a distinct colour difference between the uniforms of the Indonesian Navy and their Army. We would stand out like sore thumbs driving around in their Navy fatigues!"

George and Sarge joined in, helping with the last four troopers. Once the area was cleared of bodies, Dick gazed in Doc's direction, giving him the thumbs up.

The skipper yelled, It's 0910. If you're not back by 0940 we go without you!"

Dick grinned.

"Make it 1000 and it's a deal!"

As the others donned their new army coats, Nari went back to the Patrol Boat. Sarge gave Dick the SLR and jumped behind the wheel. Dick was alongside, with George in the back.

"I reckon they were looking for us!" exclaimed George.

"Well, I guess they found you! Now, which way George?" smiled Sarge.

"Are you right to shut down main engines Annie? Might as well save a bit of fuel if we have to wait another 40 minutes?"

Annie was already disappearing down the Engine Room hatch yelling, "Can do Skipper!"

Patch left her post on the .50 Calibre machine gun and went off to find April, who was busy getting to know the new additions to the crew. With a few eager volunteers to assist, Patch rustled up some sangers.

"You kids must be hungry!"

While Jack monitored the final bit of refuelling, the rest of the newcomers settled into the forward and Senior Sailors' Messes. Meanwhile, Doc was scanning the shoreline; feeling sure that any minute the whole Indonesian Army would turn up on the wharf.

Within minutes Mick, Brian, Peter, Jack, David, and Clinton were all in the Bridge in front of Doc. Old Jack spoke up for all of them.

"Doc we are so much in your debt; what can we do to help?"

Doc looked at the rather motley crew in front of him.

"Can any of you use a weapon? And is there anyone with any military experience?"

Mick spoke up first.

"I'm not a bad shot with a deer rifle."

"Great!" said Doc, handing him one of the SLR's, and then showing him how to load and cock the weapon.

Old Jack added, "I've shot plenty of bunnies in my time Doc!"

Armed with SLR's, old Jack and Mick soon found themselves on the Flying Bridge keeping watch.

"Mick, Brian and Peter, you'd better grab some jackets so you can assist Jack with the refuelling please!"

With the *Fremantle's* fuel hoses stowed, Jack reported to Doc.

"I've found some more 200 litre drums. I reckon we should fill some of them and get them on board as spares. What do you reckon Skipper?"

Doc came down on deck.

"Go for it. Fill as many as you can. These three will help you roll them on board."

Jack assembled the team and proceeded to fill the drums.

"Make sure the lids are screwed on tight. We'll stow them amidships on the quarterdeck. Don't forget to leave room for the RHIB overhang."

Once Patch and Nari had resumed their positions on the Flying Bridge, they scanned the area. Looking at his watch, Doc saw it was 0920. He couldn't help wondering how long their luck was going to hold. He'd felt sure that the noise, although muffled, would draw attention to them and attract unwanted visitors. With the main engines stopped the noise was back to almost nothing apart from the small hum of the generator.

The skipper warned, "Remember! Keep your eyes peeled and yell out at the first sign of activity ashore! Your life may well depend on it!"

Sarge drove the Indonesian built Mercedes copy 4 x 4 jeep into the heart of Benowa, passing the school and the new

Alliance headquarters on the way. There were not too many people about; and even those who were didn't pay particular attention to them.

"So far so good," Dick muttered as they approached the medical centre.

"Swing around the back Sarge and leave the motor running. I'll go and warn the docs if I can."

George jumped out of the back and ran along to the various windows, peering into each one in turn. At times he had to duck down fast to avoid being seen by the Indonesian troops inside.

Eventually he spotted a doctor in a room on his own. Although, he didn't recognise the man, he was aware the Indonesians had been planning to bring in another doctor to assist the one already in residence. He quickly tapped on the window and exchanged a few words with the doctor once he'd opened it to investigate what was happening.

Once George had made it safely back to the jeep, Sarge drove out of town towards the old Benowa Wildlife Park. More than once, they had to dodge some of the E1 fallout vehicles that had been pushed out of the way by the Alliance trucks. As they drove, George filled them in about what he'd learned from the doctor he'd spoken to.

"Doc Simpson tells me they are actually in the park; and I reckon I know where they'll be. There is an isolated area which was used as quarantine for sick animals; it's got underground burrows for the wombats. We will have a look there first, but if that's no good, maybe we can get back to the medical centre and pick up the two doctors. Same as before, we'll need to head round the back and try to get their attention."

0928. They passed a truck coming towards them, and saw a few waves from those inside, but apart from that the journey was uneventful. As Dick turned around to watch the truck disappear, he commented, "That was the clean-up truck picking up bodies."

This was something George had not come across before, he found the thought of it quite gross.

Doc checked the time, 0940. Although they had now reached the first deadline; he knew deep down that he wouldn't be leaving without his mates.

"Damn! I hope they get back by 1000."

Patch looked up at his words.

"Do you think they have a chance Doc?"

The skipper looked at his mate's wife, stating confidently,

"If anyone can make it, Dick will. And the more I learn about Sarge, they would be a formidable team! They will come back; that I know for sure. But as to who they have with them, well that's in someone else's hands."

Patch was thankful for the reassurance.

"Yes, Sarge is a good man! It's so quiet Doc with no one around, it's kind of spooky!"

Doc stuck his head back out on deck to see Jack's team busily loading fuel drums.

"Main engines required at 0955 Chief!"

As he started on the next drum, Jack yelled back, "Roger that Skipper!"

'I hope those boys are all right,' he thought to himself. 'I don't want to think about what could happen if they don't make it back in time!'

George opened the gate to the back road into the Wildlife Park, and then directed the group to the area he'd described earlier. After he'd let out a cooee, they waited to see if there was any response.

0935.

"Shit! There's not much time George! It's going to take us 10 minutes to get back to the medical centre."

Seeing a head appear from out of the wombat hole, George called the man over. William Green, one of the attendants from the park, was smartly dressed in his Wildlife Park uniform. He was tall and muscular, with short, cropped hair and an infectious smile. He was closely followed by Helga Sven, a six-foot Nordic blonde athletic type who was always up for a piece of adventure. Well, she had to be! She was an exchange student from Sweden, who'd travelled halfway across the world to work in a Wildlife Park on Taswegia's East Coast. She'd been working there for the past 12 months.

"Get in quickly!" yelled Dick. Sarge accelerated back to the main road as soon as they were on board. He glanced at Dick, pointing as he saw a jeep pulled up on the side of the road. It was obviously a hunting party looking for the pair they'd just picked up; the good thing was that most of the troops were off searching in the bush.

The officer stepped out in front of Sarge, holding up his hand for them to stop; as the jeep got closer, he spotted the pair in the back and quickly went for his service pistol.

"Don't stop Sarge!" Dick yelled, holding on tight as Sarge ran the officer down before continuing on towards Benowa. Dick took a glance behind them.

"Doesn't look like there's anyone coming after us yet Sarge."

It was bang on 0950 when Jack filled the last drum and closed the bung, leaving Brian and Peter to roll it on board.

"Drag those bodies out of the container guys!"

Back on the *Fremantle* he went down to the Engine Room to join Annie, who was obviously concerned about what was happening with Sarge and Dick.

"The bastards are cutting it a bit fine, Jack!"

Although the ex-CD could see tears welling up in the corner of Annie's eyes, there was nothing he could say. He gave her a hug instead; to his surprise she took it! That was a turn up for the books!

As the time approached 0955, they proceeded with the pre-start up checks, trying not to think about what could happen next.

Mick Swab had joined his fellow renegades; helping them to lash the drums into place. Kelly, Rob, and Hilary were sitting with their mothers, Wendy and Yvonne, in the Junior Sailors' Mess. Pretty much everyone else was up on the Bridge with their eyes firmly staring in the direction the jeep had disappeared.

Doc picked up the intercom microphone and cleared his throat, ordering, "*Herr* ... Start main engines."

By the time they got back to the medical centre it was 0947. George didn't even wait for the jeep to stop; jumping clear as it was still moving and making a dash to the window where he'd spoken to the doc earlier. He soon got Dr Simpson's attention and then ran back to the jeep. Less than thirty seconds later, Dr Rob Simpson and Dr Margaret Bones emerged from the building through the back door. They'd almost reached the jeep when they were spotted by a trooper who'd followed them out, but thankfully he was unarmed, and turned to go back inside.

Sarge was faster than Dick, and drew his 9mm Browning, shooting the man in the back. As the jeep lurched forward another trooper appeared from the same doorway; this time Dick disposed of him with the SLR. Sarge gunned the engine and hit the main road at forty kilometres per hour as three more troopers emerged from the front door, firing their Type 68 Assault rifles as they ran.

"Hang on boys and girls! This could get a bit hairy!" yelled Dick.

He and Sarge kept their weapons ready as Sarge headed for the wharf.

0955. As they turned left into the street where George and Clinton had raided the old museum, they found that troops were already there; busy removing the body they left inside. They turned when they heard the jeep and did a double take, quickly realising something was wrong.

Dick yelled to the others in the back to get down as he opened up with the SLR, but not before one of the troopers got off a couple of rounds. After making short work of the two that were out on the street, Dick commented, "This could be a hot extraction!"

The four passengers slouched in the back of the old jeep looked scared out of their wits. Helga vomited over William's arm as he tried to console her.

After turning right into the little street alongside the school, they went left into the street to the Gulch; almost running down two more troopers. Sarge clipped one and Dick shot the other. As Sarge drove the jeep straight up onto the old timber jetty they could hear the roar of another vehicle, not too far behind them. He would have liked to have driven straight on board, but there was no room to fit the jeep past the container, so he pulled up just before it, yelling, "Run!"

Sarge and Dick covered the others as they headed for the Patrol Boat. George had been hit and was limping. By now they could see the jeep, which, although still a fair distance away, was coming up fast behind them. The injured trooper Sarge had hit had obviously made it to his feet and joined the others; there were five of them in hot pursuit. Suddenly Dick heard the unmistakable *Boof* of the .50 calibre sniper rifle.

"Jack's back!"

The head of the jeep's driver exploded, and the vehicle turned violently to the right before rolling over onto its side and spewing its occupants headfirst on to the track.

Sarge and Dick made it safely back to the *Fremantle*, although Sarge had to hobble rather than run. They slipped the single mooring line as they boarded.

Boof! Boof!

Two more troopers went down, leaving a couple still crouched behind the upturned jeep. It sounded like one of them had started yelling something at them.

After making it up onto the Flying Bridge, Sarge grabbed the .50 Calibre and placed a burst into the jeep yelling, "Finally! They're all dead!"

Doc's voice came over the intercom as Dick took over the wheel.

"Half ahead both!"

Surprisingly, there was no other movement to be seen on the shore as the FCPB *Fremantle* snuck out in the same way as she'd come in some ninety minutes earlier.

The sixty-five-year-old Skipper ordered, "Starboard twenty. Steer *zero seven zero* all ahead full and bring her up to twenty knots!"

There were hugs all round for Dick and Sarge, as well as for George, who was sporting a graze to the right thigh. Dr Rob got one hell of a shock to find his old workmates were alive and kicking.

"Doc and Nari! What a sight for sore eyes!"

Nari gave Dr Rob a hug, while Doc shook his hand, saying, "Mate, there'll be plenty to catch up on around the dinner table tonight. Better get George down to sickbay. Rob, can you and Margaret look after George please?"

After twenty minutes, Doc put out a call over the ship's broadcast.

"Starboard ten, steer *one nine five*. Make for fifteen knots. I would like to officially welcome our new guests on board. There will be a full briefing in the mess after lunch."

Dick and Patch had already defrosted a heap of sausages and were happily cutting up potatoes ready to make into chips. Things were busy all round, with bunks being allocated, people being shown around the Patrol Boat, and the first of the Benowa refugees taking a hot shower.

Wendy said to Patch, "That was the best shower ever! I can put up with camping for quite a while, but I do miss a real shower."

Dick came up from below to find Doc pondering over the navigation table. The Skipper brought his mate up to speed.

"Just plotting a course to Strong Fort Bay, Dick. We should be there by late tonight."

"No problems Doc. Now, how do you want to run the briefing, and how much do you want to tell them?"

Doc looked at his old mate, concerned that he'd been looking a fair bit older over the past few days. He could see the toll everything was taking on the ex-CD Specialist.

"Well mate, I thought you might like to lead off. After all, it was you who started this whole thing!"

1300. Jack was on the helm, and the FCPB was on course *one nine five*, making fifteen knots. Patch, Wendy and Nari were cleaning up after lunch, while everyone else was sitting in the Junior Sailors' Mess.

Dick looked around the room; the original crew had worked hard to make the newcomers feel welcome. The sea state was calm so there wasn't much movement right now. The girls finished and came to join the others; Nari on Doc's lap, Wendy with George, and Patch sitting alongside of Dick. Dick got to his feet.

"Welcome everyone. I hope by now you've all had time to settle in, and at least have a bunk and bedding and know where all the facilities are. Make yourself known to the crew and feel free to come and ask myself or Doc anything at any time.

"We are currently heading down the coast, approximately 10 miles to seaward of Rifle Island; our destination is Strong Fort Bay. This is where we'll be dropping you off and leaving you in the capable hands of Johnny Badman and his group."

Dick went on to spell out all the events as he knew them since the first broadcast over the UHF channel on Friday 2nd January, adding with a sigh, "That was only 18 days ago! It seems like a lifetime doesn't it!"

The Benowa group sat there in total amazement; a lot of them were only just starting to believe they were safe, and that it was this motley group of ex-servicemen and their partners who were the ones that had saved their lives.

Even though he realised some of the kids would find it a bit gruesome, Dick had decided not to pull any punches. He wanted to shock everyone, including the kids, into realising that this was the real deal. It was life or death, with nothing in between; not only for them, but the rest of the Taswegian population. Who knew how many of them would be left alive by now?

First up, he ran through the strengths and military qualifications of each member of the original group, as well as those with a non-military background who had proven themselves already in fire fights. He paused and looked around at the group, pleased to see they were taking what he was saying seriously.

"I'll now lay out our five-step master plan, well, it's the one we have at the moment. The plan is ...

1. To train as many people as possible at Strong Fort Bay; forming a fighting force to fight back and re-take the Peninsular. This group will be armed with what weapons

they had on board and added to that will be whatever they can take off the Alliance. Sarge will head up the training, along with myself. The aim is to turn those civilians into soldiers.

2. To find the original engines that the fishermen were supposed to destroy back in 2000. There's probably a heap of these still sitting in their sheds. We're hoping the fishing boats will still be around. The plan is to extract the engines and steal the boats, then re-power these to form a fleet of fighting vessels. As far as we know, at the moment the Alliance has no power on the water; and from what we've learned lately, it looks like there is no likelihood of any more reinforcements turning up.

3. Try and make contact with anyone else around the State who might have managed to survive the invasion. We'll be using the UHF system and any of the old analogue brick phones we can find to do this.

4. Next step will be to take the *Fremantle* to these areas of resistance, and then train these people to do the same as we are doing at Strong Fort Bay. The ultimate aim of course is to gradually take back our homes.

5. Because we have been able to contact people over the brick phones, we know that we can get line-of-sight with the satellite and get a signal. Our ex-navy Communication Technician, Vince, has explained that all Royal Australian Navy ships still had analogue transmitting gear locked away in their Comms Centres onboard. If we can set up some sort of distress signal and send it out, hopefully one of our warships is still intact and avoided being wiped out during the Holocaust. We can't know for sure, but it's worth a try."

It was time to give Doc the floor.

"I'll let our Skipper continue with anything else. For those who don't know him, he is Doctor Roger Johns, better known as Doc to his friends. Doc is also an ex-Captain RANR."

As Doc made his way to the Galley servery, Dick stepped aside and sat down beside Patch.

"Thanks Dick. I think you've already covered most of it. Before I begin, I would personally like to take this time to thank the core members of the group for acquiring this wonderful piece of naval history. Without it our job would be pretty well impossible; not only that, but without the expertise of our Chief Engineer Jack, we would be really stuffed. She's an old lady and deserves constant TLC, but I am confident that we can keep her going long enough to finish the job we've started.

"At the moment we are just a thorn in General Jun Lee Sung's side, but if the plan that Dick has laid out comes off, we will become more like a bayonet in his side and cause him some real pain!

"Our ETA at Strong Fort Bay is around 2200 tonight, so make yourselves at home. If you start to feel queasy, I'd suggest you go and lie down; if you put something under the small of your back, this will stop the contents of your stomach moving about. A rolled-up towel will do the trick. The weather doesn't look too bad, and I'm sure that the crew will rustle up something great for the evening meal.

"As Dick has already said, if you have any questions don't hesitate to ask."

A hand shot up.

"Jack Davis here Doc. What do you really think our chances are?"

"Well Jack, given what we have achieved so far, along with what Dick, Jack, Sarge and the team have pulled off, I think we have a really good chance. As stated already, the Alliance doesn't know our strength or our capabilities, and with a lot of luck they don't even know that we have the *Fremantle*."

Another hand.

"Brian Smith here Doc. Are there other children at the place where we're going?

"Yes, I believe there are other children at Strong Fort Bay."

"George Black here Doc. What are the living arrangements at Strong Fort Bay? Are we going to be able to stay together in our family units?"

"George, that will be a question for Johnny Badman to answer, although I am sure he will do his best, with whatever facilities he has at his disposal, to make everyone as comfortable as possible."

"Wendy Black here Doc. What do you expect the women to do?"

"Well Wendy, given the seriousness of what's been happening, I would expect every woman that is capable, to fight alongside the men."

Jack yelled down from the Bridge.

"Skipper sorry to break up the meeting. We have a radar contact."

Doc and Dick got up to leave, along with Sarge, Patch and Annie. Back on the Bridge, Dick took a look at the radar screen.

"Bearing *one two zero*, range forty miles. Nice work Jack."

Dick relieved Jack at the helm while Doc took a look at the screen before turning to the crew.

"What do you reckon?"

Dick spoke first.

"I reckon we can't take the risk of it being another Super Tanker, or worse an Alliance naval ship; even though it looks a smaller blip on the screen."

Sarge and Nari were the first to agree, closely followed by the others.

"Port ten steer *one two zero*. Increase revs to make twenty knots."

As he pushed the throttles forward, Dick replied, "Roger that. Steering *one two zero*, making revs for twenty knots."

Doc took another look at the screen, then consulted the chart and plotted the unknown ship's position. He grabbed the ship's broadcast microphone.

"We have altered course to investigate the radar contact. ETA 1600. Lookouts to the Bridge."

Dick said, "Doc, I might take this time to ring Johnny Badman on the brick phone; I'll let him know who is coming and how many. That will give him time to sort out their living arrangements."

Doc agreed, asking Sarge to take a trick at the wheel.

Dick turned on the phone as well as the aerial booster and dialled 018472165.

Brrr ... Brrr ... Brrr ... Brrr...

"Hello Dick, how are things with you?"

"Not bad Johnny. More to the point, how are things with you? Have you had any trouble from the Alliance?"

"We had an Alliance truck try and come up the road into us a couple of days ago. The sentries reported that a truck with four troopers in it arrived at the tree. Apparently, they looked around for a few minutes and then left. We're thinking they probably had nothing with them they could use to move the tree or cut it up. How's it all going Dick? How did the recovery mission go?"

"John, that's why I've rung. I thought I would give you the details of your new members and give you some time to work out the accommodation for them. If you have a pen and paper, I'll read them out. There's a few more than expected, but that should work in our favour in the long run."

"Ready when you are, Dick."

"Right John, the list goes like this …

"George Black, aged 42, Wendy Black (44), Kelly Black (12), and Rob Black (11). Then there's Mick Swab (55), Peter Howe (60), Clinton Ramon (60), and Jack and Joan Davis (70 and 72 years old respectively).

"Next we've got the Smith family; Brian and Yvonne (both 28), and their daughter Hilary (6 years old)."

Dick paused to look at his notes, then continued.

"Okay, there's also Eleanor Fame (29), and her partner David Numa (38), as well as William Green (34), Helga Sven (29), and last but not least, two doctors; 55-year-old Dr Robert Simpson, Gynaecologist, and Dr Margaret Bones, GP, who's 51 years old.

"That makes eighteen altogether, including the three children and the two doctors."

"Thanks for that Dick. Are any of the singles a couple? Apart from David and Eleanor of course."

"I don't think so mate. I'm pretty sure that William and Helga just worked together at the wildlife park; although I haven't asked them."

"What about the two doctors Dick? Are they a couple?"

"No mate. Margaret was the GP here at Benowa, and Rob was bought in from Soothe, although apparently he previously worked in Kings Town with Doc."

"Right then. I'll get the team together and sort out where to house them all. I'm hoping we've got enough rooms at the backpackers' hostel to make into family rooms. What time are you arriving?"

"Well, it was going to be 2200, but we're now on our way to investigate a radar contact, so that could change. It could be well after midnight."

"All right Dick. You all take care and don't wake us when you arrive. See you in the morning."

Once Dick had reported the conversation to Doc and the rest of the crew, Doc suggested that Nari and Margaret go and take a look at their patient. He was thinking that April might appreciate the female attention instead of having to put up with Doc checking her out. Jack, who'd been thinking it was probably time for April to go back to bed anyway, said he would go with them.

They found April already talking to Margaret. Nari tactfully suggested they head to the sickbay to take a look at the dressing.

With the exception of the lookouts, the remaining survivors were asleep in their bunks. Mick was absolutely loving being back at sea again, and old Jack was not faring too badly himself.

After making Jack promise to get her up around 1900 for scran, the grumpy French woman agreed to go back to bed once she'd visited the heads with his help.

Patch, who wasn't really a rough weather sailor, was enjoying her time on the Flying Bridge; she definitely preferred to be outdoors, rather than being below decks.

"Do you want a trick on the wheel Chook?"

"Love to Dick. It might give me something to do as well as take my mind off the constant motion of the boat. I'll do it from here if that's okay."

Patch took over from Sarge, who then went off to relieve old Jack Davis from lookout duty.

"You might as well get some rest mate; we'll call you if things get hairy."

"Thanks, Sarge; it will be good to keep Joan company for a while."

"How are you travelling Mick? Do you need a break?"

The old fisherman looked at Patch, Dick and Sarge on the Flying Bridge.

"Christ no! I'm loving it!"

It was 1545.

"Ease to starboard, steer *one two five*. Lookouts … anything yet?"

"Not yet Skipper," replied Mick.

Doc came up onto the Flying Bridge.

"Should be dead ahead, range four miles."

Sarge and Dick saw it at the same time.

"Small vessel. Estimate around 90 feet; definitely not a Super Tanker!"

Sarge added, "Or an Alliance warship!"

Doc had a look.

"What do you reckon Dick?"

"Well Skipper, my guess is it's a fishing boat. She's not under way; probably been out here since the E1. What do you reckon Mick? Do you recognise it?"

The *Fremantle* Class Patrol Boat was now within two miles of the other boat.

"Slow ahead. Make revs for 10 knots."

The old fisherman squinted as he strained through the binoculars.

"Looks like a squid boat; you can tell by the black ink stains all over the sides of her. She's probably out of Barracouta."

After taking over the wheel from Patch, Dick brought the *Fremantle* around to port, making a slow circle around the squid boat.

"No sign of life Skipper."

Doc took another look.

"It's been 43 days since the E1 hit. Dinghy is still in the cradle; they must have thought it was too far to row."

Dick bought the boat to a stop.

"I reckon in this sea we'll be able to get alongside of her Skipper."

"I agree Dick."

Doc broadcast over the ship's intercom.

"Jack, Sarge and Mick, can you get the fenders out of the forward lockers and strap them to the starboard side. Use all the ones we have; we'll try and get alongside."

Once the six huge cane fenders had been strapped down the starboard side, Doc manoeuvred the FCPB alongside the black squid boat. Sarge, Dick and Mick quickly jumped aboard and secured two mooring lines forward and aft.

Dick expressed his disgust at the terrible pong that the squid ink left inside the nostrils.

"Geez, what a stink! How can anyone work in this stench?"

As he and Sarge entered the wheelhouse, Jack and Mick went aft. Sarge descended down the ladder to the mess deck.

"Shit Dick! We've got two bodies here!"

Dick stuck his head back out on deck and yelled out to Patch.

"Chook, you'd better go and get Doctor Rob and Doctor Margaret; we might need their services!"

The doctors made their way down into the little space forward of the wheelhouse where the four bunks were; there were two top and bottom, right up in the bow.

Dick exclaimed,

"I think this one still has a pulse!"

By now it was getting pretty dark, and the small space made it difficult to avoid working in each other's light.

Margaret declared one deceased, suggesting, "Maybe we should try and move him up into the wheelhouse."

Jack and Mick entered the wheelhouse at the same time.

"Got another one down in the Engine Room; looks pretty bad."

Doctor Rob followed the two to investigate. Margaret checked the squid sailor out, finding him very weak, and extremely dehydrated but still alive.

"Do you think we can get him to sickbay?"

"Sure thing. I'll get the stretcher."

And with that Sarge was off, quickly returning with the stretcher, as well as Brian and George.

Doctor Rob found the sailor in the Engine Room; it was the same situation, with not enough light to assess him properly. They laid him down on the hold cover; Doctor Rob's diagnosis was the same as Margaret's had been.

They eventually managed to get both the squid sailors to the sickbay, where Rob and Margaret, assisted by Nari, got on with the job of caring for them.

Dick asked Doc what he wanted to do with the vessel.

"Is it going to be of any use if we tow it back to Strong Fort Bay Dick?"

"Well with a bit of a clean-up, it could be. It has four bunks up forward, two in the wheelhouse and another four bunks down aft. It also has a fully functional Galley. There are over 8000 litres of fuel left in its tanks, and it has reasonable sized water tanks, although these are empty at the moment.

"Yes, I think it could be of use; but how much extra time will it add to our trip? What speed can we make if we have to tow her?"

Doc consulted the chart.

"We've got approximately 80 miles to go; so, at 8 knots, that's 10 hours steaming, with an ETA of 0300 tomorrow."

Dick looked at Doc and pointed to the ship's intercom. After getting a nod from Doc he grabbed the microphone and broadcast, "We have two survivors in the sickbay. A third person with them is deceased. We will be taking the *Black Ink* with us under tow. We feel she will be an asset to us at Strong Fort Bay; but it will mean our new ETA will be 0300 tomorrow morning. For most of you this will not make any difference because you will be asleep; although, we might call on some of you to keep watch."

Doctor Rob and Brian had the job of disposing of the *Black Ink's* third crew member.

Sarge, Mick and Dick extracted the 200-metre tow line from the aft locker; first paying it out onto the quarterdeck, then connecting the end to the tow bollard. Mick ran the end out through the fairlead on the stern and over onto the *Black Ink,* then passed it through its bow ring and onto her anchor bollard.

Once they'd let go of the fore and aft mooring lines, Doc moved the *Fremantle* away, gradually paying out the tow line until it took up the slack. With the weight on the tow, Doc eased the *Fremantle* up to eight knots, while Dick inspected the line, giving the skipper the thumbs up.

Back on the Bridge, with Dick on the wheel, Doc gave the order.

"Port twenty steer *two two five.*"

"Roger that Skipper steering *two two five.*"

Doc checked the radar again, going over his calculations on the chart, before telling Dick, "I'm going below to check on the patients."

Patch was happy to take over the wheel on the Flying Bridge; Sarge and Mick were lookouts, and Jack was seeing to April. Annie had just completed Engine Room rounds when Dick declared, "I'm going to put scran on. Are you all right on the wheel Chook for half an hour or so?"

Annie smiled.

"I'll give you a hand Dick."

Sarge said he would take over from Patch when she got tired.

Life below decks was abuzz, with the sickbay full of medical personnel working on the two fishermen. Wendy and Yvonne were sitting on the lounge enjoying a cup of tea.

Annie and Dick found four whole chickens in the freezer and set about defrosting them in the microwaves. The two girls came into the Galley to offer their help just as Annie was selecting a bag of spuds, onions and some carrots.

Annie took Wendy with her to the pantry to get some tinned vegies, leaving Yvonne peeling spuds. The birds were already stuffed and in the oven; it didn't take long before the rest of the vegies were on as well.

"Crikey! Let's hope everyone is hungry," said Yvonne.

The advantage of taking the *Black Ink* in tow was that it acted as a huge sea anchor, meaning that the motion mellowed out considerably.

Leaving the women to it, Dick stuck his head in the sickbay to check on progress there. The fishermen had been hooked up to saline drips in an effort to try and replace the fluids they'd lost. Doctor Margaret explained that there could possibly be some brain damage as well, because of the time they'd been dehydrated.

"That's not good! I'll leave them in your capable hands."

Dick returned to the Flying Bridge and found his wife and best mate handling things very well. Mick piped up.

"Your missus is a natural, Dick!"

Patch was grinning as Sarge asked, "What's for chow mate?"

The roll up for scran at 1930 was pretty reasonable. The kids didn't make it, nor did Joan or Helga.

Jack, Mick, William and Brian, who had eaten earlier, were on watch; Jack and Mick were taking it in turns for tricks on the wheel, with William and Brian acting as lookouts. Jack had taught both William and Brian how to read the radar, and they were quite happy sitting up on the Flying Bridge in the lookout chairs.

Mick and Brian would go out and check on the tow line every hour or so. The sea state was starting to get reasonably lumpy, and the breeze had stiffened as well; meaning it could very likely get quite dangerous in the dark. It would be easy to lose your footing and end up over the side, which is why two people went together.

Dick and Patch had the midnight until 0400 guts watch, so after a shower they both collapsed into bed. Sarge and Annie retired to the senior sailors' cabin.

As Doc and Nari finally left the sickbay, Nari dragged him off to bed, ignoring him as he grumbled that he really needed a shower. She simply grabbed him between the legs and said, "Officers' showers are being used by the doctors; that means we have time to use this first!"

Doctors Rob and Margaret had been told to use the officers' showers; as the only other people using these were Dick, Patch, Doc and Nari. The plan was for Doctor Rob to bunk down in the Wardroom, while Doctor Margaret would use the Comms Centre bunk.

Margaret made it to the showers first, while Rob set up his bed in the Wardroom. Once he'd finished and thinking enough time had gone by for her to be done, he towelled up and made a dash next door.

After entering the steam-filled room and dropping his towel, he literally bumped into the completely naked Margaret as she exited the shower cubical. As she grabbed the handrail to try and steady herself, she blurted out to the now embarrassed Rob that the ship's motion was making it hard to wash.

It was then that the *Fremantle* pitched sideways, putting Margaret completely off balance, and knocking Rob over. They ended up on the floor, with the fifty-one-year-old GP sitting astride the fifty-five-year-old Gynaecologist. Later, neither of them could work out whether it was simply the pent-up emotion from all that had happened in the last three weeks, or whether the obvious hardness in Rob's loins had anything to do with it, but somehow they ended up embracing passionately as his tongue found its way into her mouth.

While still on the hard deck he entered her from below; literally exploding within seconds. She kissed him again saying, "We will have to rectify that problem, Doctor!"

After grabbing the mattress from the bunk in the Comms Centre they made a cosy bed on the floor of the Wardroom, where they made love again, only slower, and much more passionately this time. Synchronising the movement of their bodies with the power of the FCPB's thrust each time she came out of a trough only made the experience all the more exciting.

Afterwards, they lay there contentedly for a while, just relaxing in each other's arms. Rob went to fetch a couple of glasses and a decanter of port from behind the fiddle rail; mimicking the accent of a Scottish officer as he asked, "Would ye care to partake in a wee drop M'am?"

2345. Jack knocked lightly on Dick's and the Skipper's doors. Both couples had enjoyed amorous evenings and were feeling exceptionally well. Dick was first on the Bridge; after checking the radar he did a fix and marked it against the chart.

"All good Jack. You might as well go see how that missus of yours is going."

"Not yet mate. I'll just do one more set of rounds down the hole."

Patch surfaced, shivering in the cool breeze.

"It's colder than I expected hon, might stay down here for a while if that's okay."

Doc and Nari emerged. After checking the chart and the radar, Doc asked, "Anyone want a brew?"

The reply from all three was a resounding, "Yes!"

"I'll give you a hand," laughed Nari.

Life on the Bridge at night was very different to what it was like in daylight hours. The red night lights took some getting used to, but once your eyes had adjusted, the night sky was fantastic. Even on a cloudy night there was always the glimpse of a star or two in between the clouds. Tonight's sky was an absolute pearler, with a million stars to behold, and not a single cloud in sight.

"There is a coat on the bulkhead behind you, Chook. You can use that when you go up top for lookout."

Patch snuggled up into Dick's arm and kissed him on the cheek.

"Get a room you two!"

Doc was grinning as he and Nari returned with the brews.

"Glad to see everyone happy! How about we leave these two lovebirds alone Nari and go up top."

0235 Wednesday 21ˢᵗ January 2015 ... FCPB Fremantle, Strong Fort Bay

Having relieved Doc and Nari half an hour earlier, Dick was back on the wheel. Doc watched the radar as they approached the entrance to Strong Fort Bay.

"Right on time, Dick!"

Dick looked at the dark outline of his long-time mate.

"Well, if we can't keep schedule on a night like this, we never will!"

Doc grabbed Nari around the waist and gave her a kiss, saying, "Better wake Sarge and Annie, as well as Jack and maybe Mick. We could need some assistance dropping anchor before securing the *Black Ink* alongside for the night. We don't know the fishing boat's anchor system, and we don't really want to be learning it in the dark!

"Oh, and better wake Dr Margaret and get her to have a look at our patients."

In the dark, Nari playfully grabbed Doc between the legs and pushed her tongue down his throat before saying, "No problems my man, but where will I find Mick and the Doctor?"

Dick smiled, suddenly realising that not everyone knew where they all slept.

"Nari, you'll find Mick in the forward mess, second bottom bunk on the port side. That's the left side looking to the front. The good Doctor is in the Comms room."

The ex-South Korean triage nurse stuck her tongue out at Dick.

Doc had forgotten that there were already eight vessels in the bay; and had to be careful to decide the right place to anchor, especially given the swing that the FCPB would have. He knew well that, when you stop a tow boat, the main thing you have to be aware of is that the vessel being towed does not stop!

Nari ascended back onto the Bridge sounding confused.

"I found everyone except Doctor Margaret."

Dick winked at Patch as he suggested, "I reckon you could try the Wardroom Nari. No, on second thoughts, just leave it till the morning."

Quickly pulling in the tow line proved to be of paramount importance when it came to positioning the *Fremantle* alongside the *Black Ink*. The same with tying off before dropping anchor and letting enough cable out.

Once Dick and Sarge had applied the brake and secured the cable Doc yelled, "Finished with main engines, Chief!"

Sarge, Annie and Mick had drawn the morning watch. Happily leaving them to keep a watchful eye out for any sign of trouble, the rest turned in.

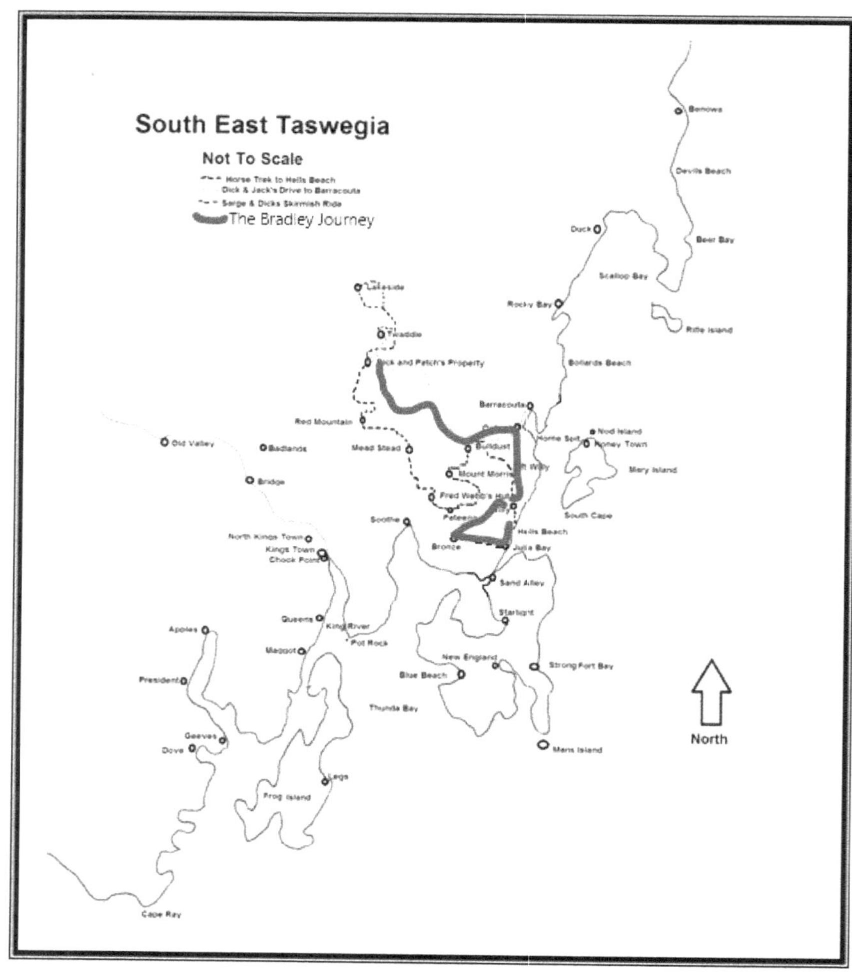
South East Taswegia
Not To Scale
Horse Trek to Hells Beach
Dick & Jack's Drive to Barracouta
Serge & Dicks Skirmish Ride
The Bradley Journey
Benowa
Devils Beach
Beer Bay
Duck
Scallop Bay
Lakeside
Rocky Bay
Rifle Island
Twaddle
Dick and Petch's Property
Bollards Beach
Barracouta
Red Mountain
Nod Island
Old Valley
Bulldust
Morris Split
Honey Town
Badlands
Mead Stead
Mery Island
Bridge
Mount Morris
Bit Willy
Fred Webb's Hut
Petees
South Cape
Soothe
Hells Beach
North Kings Town
Bronze
Julia Bay
Kings Town
Chock Point
Sand Alley
Starlight
Queens
King River
Apples
Pot Rock
Maggot
New England
Strong Fort Bay
President
Blue Beach
Thunda Bay
Geeves
Dove
Mans Island
Legs
Frog Island
Cape Ray
North

Chapter 22
Raj Sumatro

Lieutenant Colonel Raj Sumatro was honoured to be promoted to the position of Commander of the Ground Invasion Forces on the East Coast of Taswegia. Coming directly under the authority of Supreme Commander Admiral Adi Atmadja, Raj was given the task of supervising the placement of the 200,000 Indonesian nationals.

He had been born in Labuhan, on the western side of Indonesia in 1980. Village life for young Raj was simple, but he'd loved every minute of it. His mother Amanda and father Agung were different to many Indonesians; electing not to carry their surnames. Unlike their parents, and most others they knew, they chose to keep the surname 'Sumatro'.

Their village housed the port for ferries and boats heading to Sumbawa. The town centre of Labuhan, Lombok, was only 1.8 miles, or 3 km west of the ferry terminal, and according to the tourist information available at the time, was rather a scruffy place to visit.

It was a great surprise to everyone when 18-year-old Raj decided to join the army. Given his intense interest in all things to do with the sea, his parents had assumed that, if anything, he would have joined the navy. Basic training took place just outside Jakarta, and Raj quickly found military life to be to his liking.

His Grandfather was ex-army, his father suspected that his many stories of his adventures were probably the catalyst for Raj choosing to follow in his footsteps.

At the age of 28, Warrant Officer Raj Sumatro made the leap from enlisted man to officer training at the Indonesian Army Officer Candidate School at Bandung, West Java. In the Indonesian language, this establishment was known by the grand sounding title of 'Sekolah Calon Perwira Angkatan Darat, Secapaad'.

Within its walls, potential commissioned officers or in other words, officer candidates, were trained assessed and evaluated ready for taking up service in the Indonesian Army. During this training period they were known as senior NCOs, or Warrant Officers.

Completing the Secapaad course was one of the few routes available to those who wished to become a commissioned officer in the Army. It was a rigorous 20-week, 5 to 6-month course which was designed to equip officers to achieve the rank of Second Lieutenant within the Army. When compared to other officer training programs, it was the shortest route to becoming a commissioned officer and was only open to senior enlisted personnel and warrant officers.

By the time Raj had been commissioned as a Second Lieutenant, he had married Adina. The Sumatro household was becoming cramped to say the least. When Adina came into his life, she'd brought her mother Ambar with her. The two of them joined Raj, his father Kevin, his mother Indah and his grandfather Wayan to make one rather large household. Before too long Raj's life was blessed with three children. They all lived together in their home in the fishing village of Sadatau on the south coast.

Promotion came fast for the extremely intelligent Raj. Early in 2014 he made it to Lieutenant Colonel, and one day found himself in front of the Supreme Commander of the Indonesian Forces, who encouraged him to see the President.

This was when he learned about the plan of the Alliance and the impending War on Terror. He was chosen to take part in a reconnaissance mission to Taswegia and accompanied the North Korean Alliance contingent. It wasn't until they were on the East Coast of Taswegia that Raj was told by General Jun Lee Sung of the complete invasion plan.

Knowing that he would be in charge of the ground forces occupying everything above Barracouta, and all the way through to St Anne, seemed to be just a little bit surreal! He'd had many questions, mainly around his family, whether they could come, and where they would live. He soon found out that a senior Admiral would be the Supreme Commander of the Indonesian invasion force.

Unlike Jun Lee, Raj had no control over the fitting out of the Super Tarker. All he knew was that one day in mid-September the *Indo Maresk* arrived in Jakarta. He simply went about his usual routine until ordered to board in early November.

Being an officer, his cabin was more luxurious than those of the Indonesian Nationals; even with all his family squeezed in it was no more cramped than it had been in their little village hut in Sadatau!

Chapter 23
Indonesian HQ

Monday 19th January 2015 ... Sumatro Residence, Benowa, East Coast

The day had finally arrived for Lieutenant Colonel Raj Sumatro to move into his new base at Benowa. Along the way, he had picked up a Doctor Rob Simpson from Soothe. Dr Simpson was required to help run the two-doctor medical centre at Benowa.

Unloading had been going well over the last three days, with more than 70,500 Indonesian Nationals now housed in approximately 6,000 homes. Raj was to lead his team from his new headquarters in the seaside town of Benowa; his first priority was to find suitable premises for these headquarters.

Raj was thinking that the old Three Sands Resort in the middle of town would make excellent headquarters. The accommodation there would be used for troopers, while his married staff would occupy nearby homes. His mother and mother-in-law would teach at the soon to be opened school once the clean-up squad had been through it; just another job he had to organise.

Raj's father was to be the maintenance man at the Alliance HQ, even his grandfather would be kept busy as one of the cleaners.

The four other motels in the town were to be used as temporary accommodation for the Indonesian Nationals awaiting placement in properties further up the coast.

Out of the 75,000 troops that had landed in Kings Town, he had been assigned a garrison of just 15,000 troops to cover the area from Barracouta through to Benowa and all the way up to St Anne.

There would be a further 5,000 stationed at St Anne, with 5,000 more at St Mona. Regarding the rest of the now supplemented Indonesian Nationals, some 230,000 would be dispersed into homes all the way up the East Coast. The plan had been to allocate the troopers at a rate of two per household; with the remaining 50,000 troops covering the 25,000 homes. However, as is often the case with many good plans, this was simply not possible. The restrictions with the number of available vehicles was only part of the problem, making things hard to manage.

His family's new home on the beach was waiting for them. The residence he had chosen was situated just along the main road, and off a little street that led down to the beach. There were enough rooms to house his entire family, with space left over!

The house itself was made of huge sandstone blocks, and boasted six bedrooms, as well as a large rumpus room which he was planning to use as a meeting place.

The kitchen was enormous; his wife couldn't get over the size of everything. Back in their hometown, homes had been very small, with most of the children sharing the one bedroom. Here in their new home, they would each have the luxury of a room to themselves; this was something they'd never dared to dream of until now.

The manicured lawns out the front were absolutely perfect, and ran right down to the sand dunes, while at the rear of the house there was a huge shed and a four-car garage.

Such opulence! Raj smiled to himself, thinking, 'I have hit the big time now!'

At the bottom of the road were some public toilets, although he felt that these were far enough away from his new residence to avoid any issues happening.

With the placement of Indonesian Nationals in the first 6,000 homes, he was well aware he was losing two troopers to every home for its protection. By the end of this round of placements he would have lost a total of around 44,000 troops to protection duties.

This was an increase to the NK Alliance ratio for troopers. However, given the reports he had to hand, and the fact that there appeared to be more Taswegian insurgents than originally expected, he was not taking any chances.

At the present time, in order to make it all happen, Captain Raja Atmadja was running around 600 transport drivers in a two-shift arrangement.

To bring himself and his officers up to date with where they were with all that was happening, Lieutenant Colonel Raj Sumatro called a 1300 meeting with Major Huje Samira, head of Logistics, as well as Captain Raja Atmadja, who was in charge of Transport.

Also present were the members of Raj's staff, made up of four Lieutenants, three Warrant Officers, six Sergeants and two non-military Clerks. He had asked for the Lieutenant in charge of the 100 *Korps Marinir* to be present as well; it had taken a fair bit of persuasion, but in the end the Admiral had reluctantly agreed to assign a portion of the elite marine corps for his use. One of the many challenges currently faced by the young Colonel Sumatro was to try and put together a series of special squads, for the sole purpose of dealing with insurgent eradication. These would be made up of 500 elite *Korps Marinir.*

"Hello everyone and welcome to our new headquarters here at Benowa. I have called the meeting today in order to bring us all up to date with where we are as far as placements go. Are we keeping up with our promise to the Admiral? Captain Atmadja, how is the transport going?"

The Admiral's young nephew looked around in awe at the well experienced military officers who were present.

"Well gentleman, I am proud to announce that we have transported 150,000 Nationals so far. These have been distributed to 14,000 homes. Apart from a few outlying properties, we have now filled all of the homes between Barracoute and Benowa.

"Out of the 150,000, we currently have 7,600 waiting here in Benowa. These will be transported north very shortly."

"Thank you, Captain Atmadja. I can also add that we have not filled all the homes in Benowa as yet. Some of the smaller residences are still available and will be filled by troops and resident workers over the next few days.

"Major Samira, do you have anything to add?"

The aging Major, who was looking forward to his impending retirement, stood and paced around the room; something that was a well-established habit of his.

"Ah! Yes! Logistics! Where do I start Colonel? We still have 90,000 Nationals on board the *Indo Maersk*, although, with your drivers now working around the clock, we will have dispersed them all by Friday night. Finding temporary housing here in Benowa has been somewhat of a problem, but we have been able to use all the motels in the district.

"The staff required to feed the group is being supplied by our troops' catering division. As we continue to place personnel at large properties we have been confiscating the beef cattle we find with the intention of slaughtering these in order to feed the population. In addition to the beef, the 4,000 tons of rice that we were storing in the Super Tanker's hold is finally finding its way up the line to Benowa."

The Indonesian Alliance had made provision for every household to receive approximately 250 kilos of rice; this would be issued over a twelve-month timeframe. The balance was to be held here at Benowa in one of the wool stores.

Raj moved on to the next item on his agenda.

"Now we come to the problem we are facing with these resistance pockets!"

By this time Raj was pacing up and down the room; his voice rose excitedly as he reported on the progress being made in this area.

"We already have a party searching the area north of Benowa; apparently one of our troopers saw someone around four kilometres north. Starting tomorrow morning, we will start to send search parties into all of the bush areas around Benowa, as well as conduct intensive house-to-house searches of all unoccupied dwellings."

Raj waited until all had left before heading home for the day and then, relaxing on the couch which sat in front of the huge, double-glazed windows overlooking Waubs Bay. Once his wife had made a pot of hot tea, she joined him on the comfortable couch.

"Raj, I cannot believe that we are finally here, and all this is ours! The Admiral was so generous to gift us this wonderful home."

Raj looked fondly at his wife.

"Yes, my dear, we have certainly earned our place. I am honoured that the Admiral has trusted me to control the whole of the East Coast."

Raj could detect a tear in his wife's eyes.

"What's the matter dear?"

"I feel sad for all the people who used to live here. I wish it was not necessary to kill them Raj."

The Indonesian Colonel felt for her, not wanting to admit that he too had those thoughts at times, especially whilst on the reconnaissance mission last year. What could he say!

Tuesday 20th January 2015 ... Alliance Headquarters, Benowa, East Coast

At 0800, Lieutenant Colonel Raj Sumatro assembled four teams in jeeps and gave them his instructions.

"Two teams will search north, and one will search towards the entrance to the town. The fourth team will search above the town, and over to the blowhole side. I must have these resistance scum dealt with by tonight!"

The first jeep started searching north of the town, in the state forest above Benowa. The second, who were to assist them, moved further north towards the old wildlife park.

Meanwhile, at the other end of town, team three got on with the job of searching the bushlands surrounding the refuse site where they were burning all the bodies, while team four searched the blowhole area.

By 0900, team three had finished their sector and had made their way around the road past the Gulch. As they approached the wharf the senior trooper exclaimed, "Good! Our navy brothers are with us!"

Surveying the massive navy Patrol Boat with awe, the four troopers chatted excitedly amongst themselves as they watched two of the navy sailors approaching the jeep. One of them called out a greeting as they approached. As he extended his hand to accept the other sailor's handshake the driver was dazzled by the flash of the silenced .22. Everything went black. It was the last thing he would ever see!

At 0940, team two decided to head towards the Benowa Wildlife Park and start to search the sides of the road in that area. The team headed off into the bush, leaving only the Lieutenant, along with one of the other troopers, to stay with the vehicle.

Another jeep approached theirs, moving fast enough to arouse their suspicions. Trooper Nui watched Lieutenant Soo exit the vehicle and stand in front of the oncoming jeep. He put up his hand to stop them, but they didn't make any efforts to slow down, simply running over the young officer like a dog.

Trooper Nui was gobsmacked! He froze in place as he watched the Alliance jeep drive off, thinking to himself, 'Someone is going to get in big trouble over this.'

Hearing the commotion, the rest of his team returned, first searching the area around the jeep before moving on into the park.

Finding no-one around, they returned and helped Trooper Nui to load the dead body of Lieutenant Soo into the back of the jeep, before speeding back to Alliance HQ.

"What do you mean it just kept driving!" Colonel Raj Sumatra was furious. "Who was driving this jeep?"

The young Trooper Nui could only shrug his shoulders.

It was obvious he would get no sense out of the troopers. The Colonel ordered them to make their way around to the area team four was searching and find out whether it was their jeep that had done such a horrible deed.

After picking up another two team members, the jeep sped off towards the Gulch.

"Stop here! We will search the bushes alongside of the road."

The two who had just come on board continued on foot, searching the brushy verge, while the jeep disappeared down a side road.

Without warning another jeep flew around the corner, clipping one of the troopers searching the verge, before shooting the other at close range with a heavy calibre rifle. The man's chest virtually exploded!

The other trooper set chase on foot, stumbling along on his injured leg until the other jeep returned and picked him up. Once they'd heard his story, they took off after the other jeep. By the time they caught sight of it they were almost at the wharf.

Boom! Boof!

The head of the jeep driver exploded! The now-driverless vehicle rolled, and the injured trooper found himself caught up in a fire fight with what looked to be one of their own navy vessels. He yelled to his fellow troopers, who were pinned down behind the overturned jeep.

"Why are they shooting at us!"

As they peered cautiously over the wreck, they could see the other jeep up on the wharf. None of it made sense!

Boof ... Boof...

The injured trooper stood up and threw his hands in the air as he yelled at the big grey boat.

"We are on your side!"

There was no mistaking the sound of heavy machine gun fire as it let loose.

Boom ... Boom ... Boom ... Boom...!

Eventually, team three started driving back around to the back of the Gulch on their way to HQ. They were stopped in their tracks by the carnage that confronted them. Most of these soldiers had not seen any action apart from the occasional farmer shooting at them; all they were used to was shooting innocent unarmed civilians.

They could see one jeep on the jetty, and another flipped over on its side with eleven dead bodies scattered around it. At the unexpected sight of the bloody mess in front of them, one of them vomited violently!

Team three's Corporal Nui stood with the rest of the troopers in front of the Colonel's table; trying to explain what they had seen. Rather stupidly, they had already moved the bodies and had taken them to the disposal ground; thinking that this act would please the Colonel.

"You idiots! How am I meant to work out what happened if you tamper with the evidence? You are dismissed!"

Raj was not certain what it was that he was dealing with. Could it be a rogue team? Not only had they run down Lieutenant Soo, and then injured Trooper Woo; but they had then gone on to have a firefight with team four. It made no sense at all!

"I shall have to investigate the incident myself!"

As Colonel Raj stormed off, he was confronted by the sight of the troopers pulling the body out of the old museum. One stood to attention as he reported,

"It looks like his head has been bashed in, Sir."

Early model mobile or 'Brick Phone'

Chapter 24
High Head, 'The Gathering'

Saturday 10ᵗʰ January 2015 ... High Head Tunnels

The group had successfully carried out another raid last night, mainly around the East Beach area. Although group three had tried to cover their elected area, they'd found the distances to be a bit too far on foot. Group two had made it into Gary Town before being scared off by the increased numbers of Alliance troops on the streets.

Once they'd gathered for their daily meeting, Gaz started things off.

"I reckon we're going to need a vehicle if we're going to cover all this ground. At the moment it's taking us way too long to get where we are going; if we had some sort of transport, we could start a bit ater in the night."

By the look of the nods all round, they all agreed with Gaz. Ernie had a suggestion.

"Perhaps we could commandeer one of their jeeps. We'd have to despatch the current users first, but I haven't got a problem with that. The thing we have to think about is where on earth we are going to hide it until we're ready to do the next raid?

A few people came up with various ideas for hiding places, but all of them were too close to home so to speak; none of them were really suitable. The Alliance would eventually find the vehicle and possibly set an ambush. Worse still, they might find their tunnel system.

Nic had been thinking.

"What about the old bomb shelters I was talking about, they would be big enough to hold a car or two. Not only that, but they're far enough away from here not to bring a world of hurt down on top of us."

"Good idea, Mum," agreed Boz. "I reckon it would only take about forty-five minutes by treddly to get to the shelters. They're definitely secluded enough to hide our comings and goings and I think they'd be big enough to hide three jeeps."

Kylie gave a snigger.

"You mean we're going to steal three of them?"

Charlotte piped up, "That's a bit ballsy isn't it?"

The sixty-four-year-old Ernie replied, "I don't see why we can't. Well, maybe not all of them on the same night. On the plus side, if we had three vehicles, each group would have a vehicle to use. All we'd have to do is to find one parked outside a home, then kill the occupants and get the keys. Voila!"

Claudia wasn't too keen.

"Can't we just steal the jeeps without all the killing?"

Smokey was obviously annoyed that the question had even been asked.

"Well, it's like this. First, we need the keys, Love, and second, well it's them or us!"

After tossing ideas around for a bit longer they agreed on the plan for that night. With the aim of stealing a jeep, or maybe even three, they would concentrate on the Gary Town area. Some members of the group had come across a few jeeps while out on previous sorties, and all were keen to be more mobile.

The idea was this … Smokey, Nic, Baz and Bill would make their way to the old airstrip and investigate what needed to be done to get the bunkers ready for a jeep or two. Ernie reminded them to try and make sure that the entrance to the bunker was the side facing away from the road.

"It's most important that we try and avoid anything that looks like it could be being used."

They all nodded as Ernie continued.

"We'll try and lift a vehicle as soon as possible and get it to the bunker. We'll need to take fuel and engine oil into consideration of course. There's a few old service stations around; we might have to see if we can break into one of them."

Boz shook his head.

"That won't work Pop! There's no power. We're going to have to try and find an overhead fuel tank somewhere."

The sixty-four-year-old felt a bit silly for not thinking about that himself.

"Of course. I just wasn't thinking mate. But now that you mention it, I do know where there are a couple of overhead tanks. There's one at the Bull Bay crane yard where I worked; I think I might even still have a key here somewhere."

Ernie smiled, thinking to himself, 'As if it would still be locked!' He continued from where he'd left off.

"The other overhead tank is at the wreckers, somewhere inside the yard. Both tanks hold 1000 litres."

Smokey grinned at his father-in-Law.

"I'm a dickhead mate! I've just remembered we've got a fuel tank at the pilot station! It's not overhead, but I do know it holds 3000 litres, and right now it's full! There just might be enough gravity feed to top up a vehicle, and once it runs low we could probably try using a hand pump."

Everyone's mood lifted now that they had a plan. Gaz put a suggestion forward.

"How does everyone feel about riding a treddly to the airstrip? That way it won't take as long. All we'd have to do is acquire some bikes."

"Claudia and I have a couple in the shed at home." This suggestion came from Chris.

"Even better," said Smokey, "the house over the road has two of them still lying in the front yard where the kids left them before the invasion."

The raid was set for a midnight start. Group three were to head to the old airstrip, while groups one and two were to head to Gary Town. They were going to need as many bicycles as they could find.

Belle shook her head.

"This could get ugly guys; I haven't ridden a bike for about 30 years!"

Charlotte piped up.

"That's nothing Belle! I've never ridden one."

Belle was astounded.

"What, never?"

The thirty-nine-year-old ex-police officer explained, "Never. My parents were dead against them."

Sunday 11th January 2015 ... Outskirts of Gary Town

By 0015, groups one and two, working together, had managed to find four bikes on their way to Chris and Claudia's home. The two were pleased to find their bikes exactly where they'd left them. Smokey rode his own bike and dinked Charlotte on the back; Henry's bike wasn't robust enough to take two adults.

Boz and Kylie made it their business to keep Belle on the straight and narrow.

The team pulled up near the back fence of a home that appeared to have an Alliance jeep out front. Ernie carefully peered over the fence to check things out.

"Here's the plan. Henry, Boz, and I will go around the front and knock on the door. We'll take care of anyone who answers as quietly as we can.

"Belle and Kylie can you mind the bikes? I want the rest of you to hang about near the back door until we open it and call the all clear. If any gooks come out first, just shoot them.

"Once it's all clear, Belle and Kylie can move all the bikes to the front and stow them into the jeep, while we find the keys and gather up the trooper's weapons and ammo. Is everyone happy with that?"

Chris pointed out, "Could be a tad noisy Ernie. Maybe we should shoot through a pillow or something."

"Good suggestion, Chris. We'll keep it as quiet as we can, but you're all going to have to keep an eye out for the neighbours and shoot anyone who happens to wake up and stick their nose over the fence."

By 0130, everyone was in place. Henry and Boz were both kitted out with the new addition 9mm Glock's and the seventeen round magazines. Giving them the nod, sixty-four-year-old Ernie took a deep breath before tapping on the front door with the butt of his pistol.

They all froze, trying to avoid making a sound, as they listened for a response. After what seemed like an eternity, they heard noises from inside the house, and then a voice as somebody spoke. Ernie figured they were probably asking what the hell they wanted, or maybe even complaining of the late hour.

The door opened ever so slightly and a hesitant woman in her fifties peeped outside. In her sleepy state she'd forgotten to set the security door chain first.

This was all Henry needed, moving fast, he drove the 9mm Austrian designed Glock up into her abdomen and pulled the trigger. Surprisingly, there was only a slight *poof* sound, as the 9 9mm x 19mm Parabellum round exited her back and hit the ceiling with a dull thud.

Ernie supported the old girl as her dead body slid to the floor. As Boz and Henry moved around her towards the first bedroom, the sixty-four-year-old opened the second. He could hear loud snoring coming from the queen-sized bed. There was a uniform on the chair and a Type 68 assault rifle leaning against the wall; hopefully, this was where they would find the keys.

After picking up the old girl's pillow, Boz pushed it hard over the sleeping trooper's head and pulled the trigger. There was even less noise this time; although the punch of the round travelling at 375 metres per second sort of made the man's legs jump a little.

Henry gave Boz the thumbs up as he started looking for the keys.

Bang! Bang!

A couple of soft shots came from the second bedroom, which turned out to belong to the grandfather. Ernie had been holding the muzzle too far away from the old man's head; he was thankful it hadn't been louder than it was.

Boz realised he'd drawn the short straw. Upon entering the next room, he found it was a children's bedroom. There were three sleeping kids in there, ranging in age from ten to around fifteen. After placing a pillow over the face of the first one, he completed the act, just as the next kid woke up. The tears rolled down his face as he did what he had to do.

As Ernie entered the room he asked, "Are you ok son?"

The twenty-seven-year-old was still fighting back the tears; all he could do was nod.

"All clear," yelled Henry from the back door. This was the signal for Belle and Kylie to start carting the bikes around the front. Belle found out the hard way that you can't really carry any more than two bikes at a time; she wanted to get the job done as fast as possible, so decided to try and carry three at once. She only managed a couple of steps before one of them slipped from her overloaded grasp and hit the ground in front of her. She didn't have a chance to stop; next thing she knew her feet became tangled in the wheels, and she found herself flying through the air, headfirst into the concrete path. The expletives came thick and fast!

"Shit! Bugger! Poop! Bum!"

Charlotte, Chris and Claudia kept watch for signs of neighbourly activity. All was quiet as they gave Henry the thumbs up signal.

"Got them!"

Henry triumphantly held up the trooper's jeep keys, before starting to sort out the old Willy's knockoffs starting and gear arrangements.

Although, Belle had lost some bark off her nose, she ignored the pain, and helped Kylie to get all the bikes on to the back of the jeep before climbing on board with Kylie and joining Charlotte, Chris and Claudia under the canopy. That left Ernie, Boz and Henry to sit in the front once they'd worked out who would drive.

The ex-Crane Driver said, "I had one of these years ago Henry; I'm happy to drive if that's okay with you."

The ex-Gary Town Senior Constable was more than happy with this plan.

They first thought about trying to drive with no lights on; but quickly realised that, because they were in an Alliance jeep, using the lights would seem more normal to anyone watching, even at this late hour.

Henry made a suggestion.

"I agree we should be okay to use the lights at first, but I reckon we should douse them as we approach the airstrip, mate."

By 0230, they were at Gary Town airstrip, where group three had successfully cleared the entrance to the furthest bunker from the gate. Behind a couple of steel doors, they'd also found a concrete ramp that disappeared into what could only be described as a WWII bunker. There were seats fitted along the sides, and enough room in the middle to fit a couple of vehicles. There was also a sort of kitchen area at one end, well, what was left of it at least. Nic was ecstatic!

"It's just as I remembered. If we keep the bushes across the doors no one will ever know. We might have to tie them back out of the way when we come in and out, but I think it's perfect!"

Smokey gave his wife a hug as he suggested they leave the bushes tied back while they checked out the next bunker.

This was around 300 metres away. As they got closer to it they realised it was in a much worse condition. The steel doors were seized open, and it looked like a local animal contingent had moved in. The smell was bad; there was literally shit everywhere.

Nic looked at her husband.

"What are your thoughts, Love? Is it too far gone?"

The river pilot looked at the door thoughtfully before replying,

"I reckon we give it a good going over with CRC and then apply a bit of muscle. With enough bodies we might just be able to move it. Let's hope they don't come back with three jeeps tonight."

At 0300, the newly acquired jeep stopped outside the North Gary Town grocery shop. Ernie had caught sight of another Alliance jeep parked down the side of the building.

"You up for another one, Boz?"

Boz smiled to himself, knowing that one of his grandfather's favourite sayings was, 'You up for coffee mate?' He'd asked this question in the very same way!

"Yup, sure am."

The twenty-seven-year-old quickly told the others in the back of the jeep what they were about to do. The plan was to break into the shop and then quietly make their way through to the semi-detached residence at the back. This time Henry, Boz and Chris were to do the clearing, while Ernie stayed in the jeep, ready to shoot off out of there if there was an emergency.

Charlotte suggested, "How about I go instead Chris, while you stay and look after everyone else."

Without waiting for an answer, the ex-Gary Town Senior Constable cocked her Glock and pushed the safety catch forward.

Entry into the old IGA store proved to be easy; it was a simple matter to remove one of the boarded-up windows. As the trio entered the independent grocers' association store, they could see evidence that the new inhabitants had started to clean things up. It was obvious they were planning to run it as a store. Already there were a heap of bags of rice stacked on the swept area, along with other boxes of tinned food.

Henry suggested this could come in handy.

"Might relieve them of all that on the way back out, Love."

With the two Senior Constables up front, and Boz covering both sides, they approached the internal door to the residence.

"Great! It's not locked," whispered Henry as he slowly pushed it open. The aromas of Asian food cooking made his forty-two-year-old mouth water!

The first room was occupied by two children. Henry nudged his wife out of the way, giving her an 'I'll do this one' look. He didn't really want her to have to kill any children until she really had to. As he dealt with the teenagers by using a pillow to muffle the sound, he thought to himself, 'This is turning into a real battle!'

By the noises he could hear coming from the next room, he realised things weren't going quite as they'd planned.

Charlotte and Boz had opened the door to what appeared to be the master bedroom; Boz approached the female's side of the bed while the Senior Constable went to the side the male was sleeping on. Boz could see a Type 68 assault rifle leaned up against the wall in the corner of the room and realised that this was most likely where the keys would be.

Everything happened at once! The twenty-seven-year-old pillowed the woman's mouth while he jammed the Glock straight onto her sternum and pressed the trigger.

Boof!

The trooper was obviously high enough in rank to carry two weapons, and he had recently taken to sleeping with his Type 54 pistol next to him under the bed clothes. Quickly grabbing his pistol, he aimed it at Charlotte, who was approaching his side of the bed.

BANG!

At the exact second Charlotte's Glock spat out it's hot lead package, the trooper's 7.62mm x 25mm, 38 Calibre super round glanced off her Glock, hitting the thirty-nine-year-old in the upper-stomach and mid-chest area, and breaking the bottom two ribs as it entered. Her shot was true, hitting the man in the eye socket and killing him instantly.

Boz turned as Charlotte went down and ran to her aid.

"Shit! Shit! Shit!"

Henry, who'd cleared the rest of the house, came in to find Boz on the floor holding Charlotte in his arms.

"Fuck, Love! Are you alright?"

Charlotte had already drifted into unconsciousness. Boz answered for her.

"The bastard had a pistol in bed with him!"

The young twenty-seven-year-old was visibly upset, thinking something he had done must have been the reason for what had happened. The tears were streaming down his face.

Henry quickly applied a pressure bandage to the wound before checking Charlotte's back to see if there was an exit wound.

"Looks like the bullet's still in there mate! Give us a hand to get her out to the jeep."

After wrapping her in a sheet and tying a towel around her torso to try and stem the bleeding, the pair managed to carry her out the front, where Chris and Belle helped to lift her into the back of the jeep. They were all shocked at the sight of one of their own being injured.

Boz ran back inside to collect the weapons and the keys while Henry kept an eye on Charlotte. Boz and Chris started the other jeep and moved it up to the front of the shop as Ernie yelled, "We'll head to the tunnels and unload Charlotte there, then we'll meet you at the air strip."

His nephew nodded.

"Chris and I will load all this tucker first. There's no way we're letting them get away with this without suffering!"

0445. Ernie drove the eight kilometres to the dilapidated home near the pilot station, and then helped Henry to carry Charlotte into their base. Henry, Belle, Kylie and Claudia did what they could to clean up the wound and make Charlotte comfortable, while Ernie made the trip to the airstrip on his own.

As he turned into the strip road, he suddenly realised there was another set of jeep lights following him. This really shook him up for a while. At least until he realised that it was Boz and Chris who were behind him!

Chapter 25
Pirates

Tuesday 20th January 2015 ... Hells Beach

Vince and Laurel had made the most of having the camp to themselves. After an unusually passionate night they were both feeling relaxed and satisfied. They were not in a particular hurry to start the day and lingered in their comfortable double swag as they lazily planned the day ahead.

Vince couldn't help wondering how the *Fremantle* was going. He stretched as he checked the time.

"0700. By my reckoning they should be nearly there, Laurel."

Laurel looked at her husband.

"Do you wish you could have gone with them?"

He grinned back at her as he thought about the night they'd just enjoyed together.

"Well, it's kind of a 'Yes', but also a 'No' to that question my Love!"

After breakfast Vince headed off to gather the wood, as well as set some fishing lines off the Gulch. Laurel was planning to feed and groom all the horses, and then maybe enjoy a swim. The day was perfect, there was not a single cloud in the sky, and it felt like it was somewhere around twenty-five degrees. Maybe she'd be able to entice Vince to join her once he had finished over at the Gulch. Having said that, she knew well that, once he got involved with the IT and radio stuff he would be absorbed for hours.

Bob, Tom, Socks, Fanny, Cowboy and Zen were all glad to see her, the rest had done them the world of good. They'd been strip grazing the little paddock, which meant there was still plenty of grass once they'd been moved.

Vince set up four lines off the bow of the *Cecil Jane*, and two more off the rock wall, hoping to catch some flathead for dinner that night. He decided to have a look at the *Cecil Jane's* radio, and to monitor the UHF channel while he was there.

He'd had an idea, and this was the perfect time to have a bit of a play. He planned to strip the old high frequency radio of some of its valuable parts; thinking they could be of use in enhancing the brick phone's signal when trying to contact other people around the state.

As far as contacting others went, they had come up with a couple of scenarios. One was to find all the old phone numbers that Doc had in his little book and simply call them one by one. The other was to modify the phone to send a rogue signal to the satellite; this would trigger every phone to ring and meant they would be able to leave a message to call them back.

Vince was almost certain he could make it work with the few parts they had on board the *Fremantle*, along with whatever he could scrounge from the CJ. He was in his element and couldn't wait to get into it!

By 1000, Laurel had finished with the last horse. After collecting all the collapsible canvas feed buckets ready for the next feed, she prepared for her swim. Although she grabbed two towels in anticipation of Vince possibly joining her, she didn't count on that happening. Hell! She knew what he was like once he was immersed in radio parts.

With nobody else around, she decided to give the bathers a miss and headed out through the dunes to the beach, with the sun beating down on her head. 'Maybe I should have worn a cap,' she thought as she kept her head down, watching the sandy track for any sign of sharp shells.

Upon reaching the water she finally looked up at the bay; then almost fell over at the unexpected sight of a yacht. To see any unknown boat on the water was a total shock, especially after the holocaust and the Alliance invasion.

The first thing that came to her mind was whether or not they were Alliance troops? Had they come to invade and kill? Or were they survivors as well? Maybe they were part of the Strong Fort Bay mob?

She couldn't see any movement on the yacht. After glancing to her right in the direction of the Gulch, Laurel yelled out to Vince.

Because of the light breeze blowing in from the sea, the gunshot sounded louder than it really was. Thinking, 'What the fuck!' she looked to her left where she could see a small rubber boat pulled up about halfway along the beach, close to where they had pulled the RHIB up.

As the shot hit the sand just in front of her feet, Laurel could see the three occupants of the yacht running along the sand towards her; although they looked Caucasian, they didn't seem to be too friendly!

Without waiting to be fired upon again she ran for the camp; this was more challenging than she'd anticipated without her clothing. She finally realised why most female athletes wore sports bras!

As she ran, she tried to work out what she should do, and in what order. The first thing was to get to the flare pistol and raise the alarm. She hoped desperately that Vince would hear it, or at the very least see the smoke trail. Laurel wasted no time sending up a round. Her next stop was the tent where they stored the weapons.

She didn't quite make it! After tackling her to the ground, the heavily built Italian sat on her chest and slapped her hard around the face.

"How many are there?"

The first man had been joined by the other two. It was obvious that these were not nice people at all.

"She's not talking, Jake."

Jake was the obvious leader of this little band of cutthroats. He laughed as he stepped forward and fondled Laurel's breasts.

"Don't worry mate! By the time we have finished with her, she'll sing like a canary!"

Laurel knew that things were not going well for her, and managed to yell out in desperation, "Vince!"

The Italian punched her in the face hard and she momentarily lost consciousness.

As she started to come to, Laurel could feel someone's hand moving slowly up the inside of her leg. Thinking quickly, she gave a sudden kick, managing to smash the heel and part of the instep of her right foot into the man's face. The sudden pain in her foot told her she might have broken a bone, but it was worth trying.

Her efforts earned her another smack in the face; she could taste blood in her mouth. As she continued to thrash her legs around, they hit her again, and then carried her over to the timber frame they were using as a table. Two of them had her by the legs, while the other held her by her hair. She drifted in and out of consciousness as they tied her face down to the table. Her split lip and swollen face were really starting to throb painfully now.

From her lopsided position Laurel took a quick glance at the three of them, realising they were all now stripped naked from the waist down. Their anticipation at what they were about to do was obvious as she felt one of them start to invade her with their fingers.

As she helplessly fought against the well secured ropes that were holding her there, one of them snarled, "I'm going first!"

As the stocky little Italian approached her from behind and positioned his swollen member between her buttocks, she tensed in anticipation of the pain that was about to hit her. Out of the corner of her eye she caught sight of a sudden blur!

Whoosh!

At 1015 Vince had been listening to the UHF static. Smiling to himself he had listened closely as he tried to work out whether he could hear something or whether it was just his imagination. Heavily engrossed in the matter at hand, he was on the verge of cracking the problem.

The sound changed suddenly. 'What was that?' What he had heard was the unmistakable sound of a flare gun going off; although it took a few seconds for his brain to register that it was the emergency signal.

"Shit! Shit!"

Vince realised that he'd left his weapon sitting on the table after they'd had breakfast. It was the first time he'd forgotten to keep it with him.

He suddenly remembered seeing a spear gun sitting beside the scuba gear in the Engine Room; it didn't take him long to go and get it. The ex-navy Electronic Technician was soon cocking the twin rubber handmade gun as he made his way to the top of the track that overlooked the beach.

The thought that something might be seriously wrong didn't really sink in until he spotted the rubber dinghy. Even then, he was thinking that maybe it had just been Laurel wanting to get his attention to let him know they had visitors, without letting them know where he was.

Hearing Laurel scream out just as he made it to the beach was the clincher, although he figured it probably wasn't the Alliance troops; if it had been them, she'd already be dead. He moved stealthily through the opening in the dunes and into the camp; stopping suddenly as he surveyed the horrific scene in front of him.

The three-foot stainless-steel spear entered the Italian's back clean between the shoulder blades and came to a halt with the point of the spear halfway out of his chest. The thrust of the spear sent the would-be rapist sprawling forward on to Laurel's strapped down body, with the spear tip just nicking her left arm.

It seemed to Vince that everything seemed to move in slow motion after that. By the time Jake woke up to what was happening, Vince's heavy boot had connected with his scrotum with so much power that it split the sack of skin! Jake sank to his knees in agony, as he desperately tried to protect what was left of his manhood. Still reeling from Laurel's kick to the face, the other pirate tried to turn and run, but with his shorts down around his ankles he didn't get too far. It was just five steps to the breakfast table where Vince had left the SLR.

The man was busy trying to pull his shorts up as he ran for the cutting; although he didn't hear the cocking lever being drawn back, he most definitely felt the pain of the three 7.62mm rounds as they entered his back above the belt line and then exited through his stomach, taking his backbone and other organs with them.

After taking care of the screaming Jake, Vince dropped the SLR and ran over to Laurel, untying her before cradling her in his arms.

"I'm so sorry, Love!"

Still in shock, Laurel responded in a shaky voice, "What are you sorry for? You stopped them."

"Yes! But I shouldn't have taken so long!"

While Vince unscrewed the spear tip from the shaft before retrieving the spear, Laurel got dressed and then helped him to drag the bodies down onto the beach. Puffing a bit, he had a look at the yacht through the binoculars.

"Looks like she's about forty-five feet. Oh, and she's called *Hazard*."

They'd searched the men's pockets but had come up empty; all of them seemed to be between thirty and forty years old.

"Grab yourself another SLR, Love, and bring mine as well. I think we'll take a closer look at her" Once Laurel had returned with the two SLR's they made their way to the RHIB.

"Are you expecting trouble Vince?"

"Well Love, it's possible there might be another one on the yacht."

Dragging the Pusser's semi rigid inflatable down the beach was no easy task, especially at low tide! Once they finally had her in water deep enough for her to float, they jumped in over the stern. Laurel took up position at the bow while Vince lowered the twin Mercury Veradas two-stroke fuel-injected 150HP motors. He got them going and then pushed the throttles forward to full ahead. The RHIB jumped as if it was coming to attention; they were soon flying over the waves at close to fifty knots.

After coming alongside *Hazard* on the starboard side, Vince went hard astern until she stopped, then killed the twin engines and quickly tied her off amidships. Laurel covered him from the bow the whole time.

"Looks pretty quiet, Laurel."

Vince climbed up over the yacht's guard rails before starting to move below, with his weapon at the ready. Laurel was fast on his heels.

"You stay on deck Laurel, just in case someone pops up out of that forward hatch!"

"Roger that, Vince."

The layout was standard. There was a main saloon with a Galley and a fold-down table which could be converted to a double bed if needed. There were two bunks on the port side, with heads and shower on the starboard side. The bow had been fitted with a large double berth, with the sail locker right up forward. The Engine Room was back under the cockpit.

"All clear below," yelled Vince.

"Watch it Vince; you haven't checked the heads."

Vince felt like an idiot.

"Shit! How dumb am I!"

Still shaking his head, Vince opened the door to the heads; and then flinched as he felt the sting of an eight-inch carving knife being driven into his left shoulder. The intense shock drained the power from his body; and he could only watch helplessly as the young pirate pushed past him and disappeared up the stairs. The boy, who looked to be around twelve years of age, headed for the cockpit, but stopped in his tracks as he was confronted by the sight of Laurel standing directly in front of him.

By the time she had her SLR to bear, he was over the side and swimming to the beach.

"Shoot the fucker, Laurel!"

Laurel was more concerned about stopping the bleeding once Vince had yanked the long blade out of his shoulder. After quickly ripping a sheet into strips, she bandaged the area, and tied it off real tightly.

As they clambered aboard the RHIB, Laurel tried to get off a few shots at the boy.

"Oh! Give it here!"

Taking the SLR, Vince tried to take aim, only to find that the pain was so intense that he couldn't steady the weapon with his left arm. Laurel started the motors and untied the line and Vince turned the RHIB after the pirate.

"I'll get the little bastard!"

The twelve-year-old was a bloody good swimmer; by now he'd already made it halfway to the beach. Unfortunately for him he was not fast enough. The RHIB hit him at full noise, leaving him motionless in the water. After coming about, Vince rounded up on the body while Laurel leaned down with the boat hook. Catching him under one arm, she dragged him on board.

"Well he's definitely dead, Vince! He couldn't be much more than ten or eleven years old!"

Laurel moved his body over to where they'd left the others, and between them they managed to pull the RHIB a little higher up the beach before tying her off to a tree.

"We might have to come back down at high tide and pull her up some more."

By now, Vince had lost a lot of blood, and was in extreme pain. Getting him to the camp proved to be a real challenge, but she finally dic it. Once she'd applied clean pads on his wound and good bandages around his shoulder, she finally felt she could start to relax.

As Laurel kick-started the campfire it dawned on her that there was a real danger that Vince could possibly bleed to death if she couldn't stop the bleeding. Although, he was shivering violently, it looked like she had done enough to stop the flow of blood for now. To make sure, she added another set of pads and bandages to the others around the wound, and then pulled a blanket over him to try and warm him up.

"Warmer now, Vince?"

There was no response. He was delirious with pain, and although he kept muttering out loud, Laurel couldn't understand what he was saying.

She found the painkillers and made him take four of them; hoping this would help. As she collapsed beside her husband, she took stock of what had happened that day, as well as all the things that could have happened if things had gone as it had first seemed they would.

The thought of those dirty bastards touching her in that way made her feel sick as she realised how close they'd come to sodomising her. Laurel wasn't into that kind of thing at all; it was completely foreign to her line of thinking. How could people be so cruel! Sure, she was used to seeing the bloody aftermath which had followed the Alliance troops; but for behaviour like that to come from her own kind was something beyond her understanding.

Laurel sobbed herself to sleep; waking again some-time later she cuddled up to Vince, thankful that he seemed to be sleeping comfortably at last. Looking at his watch she realised it was 1930.

'Bloody hell! Where did the time go! I'd better get some more wood on the fire before it goes out!'

She felt her swollen face, realising she was sore down below as well; that must have been from what they'd been doing to her before Vince had got to them.

Laurel suddenly felt dirty, really dirty! Despite the change in the weather she ran down to the beach and stripped off her shorts and top, before plunging into the cleansing surf. The shock of the water hit her; the wind had come up and was blowing straight in off the sea. It was cold, very cold!

She looked at '*Hazard*' lying stern on to the beach, thinking,

'I sure hope the silly bastards set the anchor right!'

Her body was numb with cold, but she didn't care; wanting desperately to feel clean, she rubbed the freezing cold salt water into every crevice of her body. After heading back to the beach, she picked up the two towels she'd dropped earlier that day and rubbed herself dry.

Returning to the campfire, she found Vince was wide awake.

"How do you feel, Vince?"

He looked at his wife.

"I'm not too bad, although my arm is throbbing like hell! More to the point, how are you doing? You weren't here when I woke up. Where did you go?"

"Had to clean myself after those dirty bastards ... you know ... touched me; so, I went for a swim. It's blowing a gale now and it looks like it's about to pour down."

The pair moved in under cover; sitting on a couple of chairs sheltered by the awning above their swag. Laurel loaded up the fire as much as she could, admitting, "Don't know how long that fire will burn in this rain!"

As they cooked the last of the steaks, along with some potatoes and a salac, they realised they hadn't had anything to eat since breakfast.

After eating they enjoyed a couple of ports; the strong liquor seemed to take the edge off the pain they were both feeling.

Vince checked the time; 2200. "The *Freo* should be at Strong Fort Bay by now."

Laurel didn't want to say it, but it just slipped out.

"That's if they made it Vince! They could have been in a world of hurt at Benowa, who knows what might have been waiting in ambush!"

Vince looked at his wife. He didn't really want to believe that it could have happened like that, but there was no way of knowing for sure. And what if she was right; what then? What was their plan? Should they head for Strong Fort Bay?

Laurel tried to reassure him.

"They'll be all right Vince; you know nothing will stop Dick and the others."

As she watched her husband drift off to sleep, Laurel realised how anxious she was feeling. She was really worried about all of them. If things didn't improve, she would give the *Fremantle* a call in the morning!

Chapter 26
Weapons Training

Wednesday 21ˢᵗ January 2015 … FCPB Fremantle, Strong Fort Bay

At 0800, Annie and Mick did the rounds and rattled on everyone's door while Sarge prepared to lower the RHIB into the water. Dick and Patch had breakfast well under way by the time most people woke up.

"How are the patients, Dr Rob?" Doc was asking both Dr Rob and Dr Margaret.

"We checked on them this morning Doc; it looks like they will both make it."

Doc and Nari smiled, "You two seem to be getting on very well?"

Rob replied, "Mmmm! Yeah. Pretty well thanks Nari."

Sarge yelled out, "The first boat to shore will be leaving in five minutes."

Annie and Jack, who'd completed rounds in the Engine Room, as well as checking the fuel status, reported to Doc.

"Fuel report, Skipper. Fuel levels sitting at 80%, with both ready use tanks full. That's without counting the fifteen drums that have been stowed on the deck."

"Great Chief. Might get you to top up the tanks out of the drums; it always pays to have a full tank."

Brrr ... Brrr ... Brrr ...

Dick grabbed the brick phone, thinking it was probably Johnny wanting to know what was happening.

"Hey Johnny! What's happening mate?"

As he listened the colour drained from Dick's face.

"Right Laurel. Will pass it on." The ex-CD reported to the others.

"I just found out that Vince has been stabbed by pirates. They stabbed his left shoulder with a bloody eight-inch carving knife! Laurel thought she'd stopped the bleeding, but it's started again this morning."

The crew was silent as Dick filled them in with the brief details he knew.

Doc gave some thought as to what was the best thing to do.

"We'll stick to the plan. We will leave Sarge and Dick here to train the group in weapons, while we head back to Hells Beach to patch up Vince. We will be back in three days to help instigate the next part of the plan."

The unloading of survivors and equipment went on for most of the day, with many trips backwards and forwards in the RHIB as they deposited people, weapons and ammo for the training.

Jack secured the help of Mick, David and Clinton to assist with refuelling the *Fremantle's* main diesel tanks out of the drums stowed on deck. They used ten of the fifteen 200 litre drums on deck.

Leaving the boys to hose down any spillages, Jack made his way back to the Bridge, where Doc and Dick were having a meeting. Johnny had been invited aboard to discuss the ultimate plan.

"What do you want to do with the empties Skipper? Take them ashore or keep them on board?"

Doc thought about this for a minute, wondering whether they would be in the way if there was any more action.

"Are they in the way, Chief?"

"No, they'll be fine where we've planned to stow them. I'm hoping we'll get the chance to fill them again at some stage, although, it could be a long time between each refuel!"

"Right, that's settled! Stow them Chief."

"It's great to have some medical support, Dick; we could sure use it."

Doc was quick to respond to Johnny.

"Might have to use them for patching up gunshot wounds when things ramp up; it might get pretty ugly. Do you think your team has any idea about the consequences of what we are planning?"

Johnny thought about the question long and hard, realising that, until now, even he hadn't thought too much about it. The reality hit him hard.

'We are actually planning to go to war with the Alliance! Inevitably people will die!'

Sarge reported, "Everyone is ashore Doc; except for Dick and myself, along with Johnny."

Patch and Annie were on the quarterdeck to say goodbye to Sarge and Dick; even April was well enough to make it.

"See you in three days," yelled Doc. "Good luck with the locals!"

Sarge yelled back, "And good luck to you, with your nearly all female crew!"

Doc hadn't thought about that until then. Sarge was right. Apart from the Chief, he would have to make do with Patch, Nari, Annie and April; and she was still on light duties.

Jack took the RHIB back after leaving Sarge and Dick in Johnny's hands. The forty-seven-year-old farmer announced, "Come with me, guys. I'll show you to your accommodation."

Twenty minutes later they were sitting in the backpacker's lounge and enjoying a hot brew. Sarge looked out the window.

"*Freo's* leaving, Dick."

The pair watched as the *Fremantle* steamed out of the bay, turning around as Johnny asked, "So, how do you want to run this?"

"Well Dick's in charge," said Sarge. "What do you reckon mate?"

Dick thought about it for a second or two.

"I suggest we get everyone in for a chat, and then talk about the plan and the weapons they will be using."

He looked at Sarge's watch; realising it was already 1400.

"By the time we do that, I reckon that will be all we'll get done today."

Johnny asked Dick whether the kids would be involved as well.

"Mate, I reckon they are entitled to know what's going on. After all they could find themselves in the thick of it at any time."

Johnny disappeared to round everyone up; within twenty minutes the room was full. Even the two squid fishermen were pronounced fit enough to join the group. Johnny had given Dick the entire list of personnel now living at Strong Fort Bay; there were forty-nine people, along with Dick and Sarge. Two of these were keeping watch at the entrance.

There were nineteen men of fighting age, although, Josh Frank's mother, Barbara, was not too happy when Dick read out his name. Josh was only seventeen.

Sarge caused a bit of a commotion when he brought up the fact that there were also fourteen women of fighting age, including seventeen-year-old Jill Frank.

Someone yelled out, "You mean you expect women to shoot and kill people too!"

A strained silence came over the room while they waited for one of them to answer. Realising that these people weren't fully aware of the danger they were in, Dick simply replied.

"It's like this; you need to train to kill, or you'll be killed. If we mount an offensive and the Alliance break through your tree, what do you think they will do to you. They don't take prisoners, and they show no mercy to anyone! They'll simply kill every one of you!"

Clinton stood up at the back of the room. He told the others exactly what had happened the night he and George had gone to get the brick phone from the museum in Benowa. He pulled no punches, and for the first time since it had happened, he shared about what they'd seen when they'd checked out the school; with all the children and teachers bayonetted to death. Dick was right, there'd be no mercy!

As he sat down again, Dick looked around at the group. Shock was on all of their faces. Sure, they had heard all the tales from Sarge and Dick; but to hear it from one of their own was entirely different! There were no more protests.

The pair laid out the five-step master plan, just as they had on the way down the coast. Johnny's mob had not heard it before, and listened closely to the details ...

1. They would train as many members as possible at Strong Fort Bay to form a fighting force to fight back and re-take the Peninsular. The group would be armed with what weapons they had on board and with whatever they could take off the Alliance. Sarge would head up the training, and with the help of Dick and Jack, would turn these civilians into soldiers.

2. They would search for and find the original engines that the fishermen were supposed to destroy back in 2000;

these would probably still be sitting in their sheds. Once extracted, these would be used to re-power the fishing boats they were hoping would be still around, thus forming their own fleet of fighting vessels. This should give them an advantage over the Alliance, who were not likely to get any more reinforcements, and who, as far as they knew, had no power on the water.

3. They would try and make contact through the UHF system with anyone else around the state that had managed to survive the invasion.

4. They would take *Fremantle* to these areas of resistance and train these people to do the same as they were about to do at Strong Fort Bay; gradually taking back the homes.

5. Because they'd been able to contact people on the brick phones, they knew they could get line of sight with the satellite and get a signal. The injured ex-navy Communication Technician, Vince, had told them that all Royal Australian Navy ships still had analogue transmitting gear locked away in their Comms Centres. The plan was to try and set up some sort of distress signal, and send it out, hoping that one of their own warships had avoided getting wiped out during the Holocaust, and was still intact.

Dick spoke further about their first objective; taking back the Peninsular. All the time the enemy had no watercraft, the draw bridge at Sand Alley would act as a natural deterrent for the Alliance.

"Mick Jones here, Dick. How do we open the bridge? Surely you won't want to blow it up?"

"Good point Mick. Our plan is to get the *Fremantle* alongside at Sand Alley and use her generator power to open the bridge.

It's a bit gutsy but well worth the risk; they won't be expecting anything like this."

"Johnny here, Dick! Do they even know you have the Patrol Boat?"

"Another good question Johnny. The answer at the moment is that I don't think so. We're hoping to keep that little surprise up our sleeve for as long as possible. We'll be going in stealthily to do the deed; probably at 0200 in the morning. We'll have to reccy the place so that we can find out which side the electric motor is on."

"Jack Davis here, Dick. Wouldn't the motor have been knocked out by the E1?"

"We think it was probably too old to replace, which means the original would still be intact. If that's the case, the only issue is that we'll have no power; and that's something we hope we'll be able to rectify."

Most of the other questions were easily answered. The pair finished by saying that weapons training would start the next morning at 0800.

Thursday 22ⁿᵈ January 2015 ... Weapons Training, Strong Fort Bay

The next morning Sarge and Dick were up early; Johnny wanted to show them the entrance and ask the guys there if they could do another shift. They would change over the next morning and take part in the training then. Dick really liked the way the huge tree had made it virtually impossible to come through. Sarge agreed.

"They're going to need a huge saw if they want to cut this one up, and even if they tried, they would be sitting ducks!"

Dick was of the opinion that the troopers had probably thought the track would dwindle away to nothing; and was therefore not worth further investigation.

"Let's hope they continue to think that!"

Johnny asked how they were going to get past the tree so that they could carry out the raids.

Dick explained that most of them would be done from the sea at first anyway. He was planning on outlining the first raid at the conclusion of the weapons training. As they walked back to camp they all agreed that it was the perfect place from which to ambush any Alliance troops trying to enter Strong Fort Bay.

Dick surveyed the weapons they had available; these had been laid out on the table in front of them.

- Ten x 7.62mm Type 68 assault rifles (Alliance)
- 500 rounds of 7.62mm to suit the above
- Four x 7.62mm Type 54 pistols (Alliance)
- 200 rounds 7.62mm to suit the above
- Forty boxes of .50 Calibre rounds. They were mostly M2 Ball with M1 Tracers, but they did have some specials like armour piercing
- Three x .50 Calibre machine guns, pedestal mounted
- Twenty boxes of 7.62mm
- Twenty old SLR's
- Thirty Pindad SS2 assault rifles (Indonesian)
- 5000 rounds of 5.56mm rounds (Indonesian)
- Two x F1 sub-machine guns
- Two Armalites
- Six x 9mm browning pistols
- 5000 rounds of 9mm ammo
- One SLR with Sniper sight and silencer
- Four Ultimax 100 light machine guns 5.56mm 100 round drum magazines on tripods (Indonesian).

Dick wasn't mincing any matters!

"What you see here is the backbone of your weapons supply; along with this you must take every opportunity to relieve the Alliance troops of their weapons once you have killed them."

Sarge nodded as he added, "We will train you how to strip down, load and deal with minor problems; and you will all shoot some of the weapons. Now because ammunition is scarce, we will match you to a weapon at the end of the theory session. You will each fre five rounds from that weapon and then the 9mm pistols.

We can do this because we have a lot more 9mm ammo than anything else. Some of the weapons are Indonesian Alliance; some are North Korean Alliance, and some are ours."

Dick added, "It is imperative to take every opportunity to collect not only the weapons but, more importantly, the ammunition. We are controlled by what we have in stock and to win this war we will all need to think outside the box. Remember the Alliance is in the same boat so to speak; they have no manpower or ammunition reinforcements coming as far as we know."

The room was alive with chatter. Dick and Sarge spent the rest of the time up until morning tea running over each weapon, and explaining its faults, ammunition size and type, as well as whether they had adequate supplies or whether it was an Alliance weapon.

Sarge continued on this theme, "Each Alliance trooper will be carrying around 100 rounds of ammunition to suit their Type 68 assault rifles. Officers will be carrying the same to suit their Type 54 pistols; less of course what they have been shooting at us with.

"Now make sure you don't take unnecessary risks; only take the ammo after they are dead, and you have made sure you are not putting yourself or your comrades at risk."

Everyone had a turn at stripping down the various weapons as well as re-assembly and loading the magazines. There were numerous questions asked; mainly about stoppages and jamming, and how hard the weapons would kick when fired.

Some of the women joined in as well, asking whether they would be able to fire the weapons.

Dick let Sarge answer that one.

"As mentioned before, everyone except the smaller children will get to fire these weapons. Even the older children. Even if you don't go on a raid, you will still need to know how to use them. Assessment will be based on size and determination once we get to the range."

Dick, Sarge, Johnny and George sat down over lunch and looked at allocation of the weapons. Dick was hoping that Johnny and George would remain in their leadership positions, especially amongst their individual groups.

Benowa Originals	Age	Team	Weapon
George Black	42	1	Type 54 Pistol & F1
Wendy Black	44	Base	9mm Browning
Kelly Black	12	Base	
Rob Black	11	Base	
Mick Swab	55	1	Ultimax 100 LMG
Peter Howe	60	1	Type 68 Assault Rifle
Brian Smith	28	1	SLR
Yvonne Smith	28	Base	9mm Browning
Hilary Smith	6	Base	
Jack Davis	72	1	Type 68 Assault Rifle
Joan Davis	70	Medical	9mm Browning
David Numa	38	1	Ultimax 100 LMG
Eleanora Fame	29	1	Type 68 Assault Rifle
Clinton Ramon	60	1	Type 68 Assault Rifle

William Green	34	1	SLR Sniper/silencer
Helga Sven	29	1	Type 54 Pistol
Fishermen			
Harold Patmore	31	1	Armalite
Riley Patmore	20	1	Type 68 Assault Rifle
Strong Fort Bay Originals			
John Badman	47	2	Type 54 Pistol & F1
Helen Badman	42	Base	9mm Browning
Trish Badman	13	Base	
Billy Badman	12	Base	
James Smythe	75	2	Type 68 Assault Rifle
Miriam Smythe	75	Base	
Robert Crawfield	65	2	Type 68 Assault Rifle
Gina Crawfield	65	Base	
Sid Crawfield	40	2	Ultimax 100 LMG
Ellen Crawfield	37	2	Type 68 Assault Rifle
Helen Crawfield	15	Base	
Craig Crawfield	14	Base	
Cedric Bilton	80	2	SLR
Aileen Bilton	60	Base	
Mick Jones	38	2	Ultimax 100 LMG
Sarah Jones	38	Base	SLR
Roger Jones	12	Base	
Jimmy Jones	10	Base	
Shelly Jones	8	Base	
Michael Jones	6	Base	
Graham Walton	42	2	Type 68 Assault Rifle
Bentley Frank	48	2	Type 68 Assault Rifle
Barbara Frank	48	Base	SLR
Josh Frank	17	2	SLR

Jill Frank	17	2	Type 54 Pistol
Blyth Frank	10	Base	
Anna Frank	6	Base	
Tony Oglio	68	2	Armalite
Mary Oglio	72	Base	SLR
Medical			
Dr Rob Simpson	55	Medical	9mm Browning
Dr Margaret Bones	51	Medical	9mm Browning

After lunch, once Dick had read out the weapon assignments as per the list they'd put together, they all made their way to the range after collecting their assigned weapon. The pair had fashioned the makeshift range the night before. This consisted of a distance of twenty-five metres and forty metres, with a target at one end and a piece of cover at the other. For the purposes of this exercise, the cover consisted of a couple of old fuel drums and an old refrigerator.

Keeping everyone well back, Sarge called them forward two at a time, issued them with their five rounds each and let them load.

Dick watched their faces while the first five rounds were expelled: three at twenty-five metres and two at forty metres each.

Noticing quite a few people wearing earmuffs he yelled, "Take the ear muffs off! You won't be wearing them when we get in a fire fight. I want everyone to hear the sounds of the different weapons. Yes! Even the children!"

He could hear murmurings of disapproval coming from most of the mothers but ignored that as he continued with the training. They were about halfway through.

"Those of you who will be at the front line with us have Type 68 assault rifles. These are the weapons of choice for the Alliance semi-automatic, 7.62mm ammo, but are a different sized round to our SLR, so you'll need to get your ammo replenishments for these from the Alliance. It's a great weapon, modelled on the Russian built AK47; although it's slightly different.

"These rifles, along with the Type 54 pistol, are Alliance weapons. Whenever you come across any weapons and ammunition, your brief is to collect them both. We will need as many of them as we can find.

"The other essential items we are going to need plentiful supply of are sanitary items for the ladies. Whenever you have the chance, make sure you check the bathrooms and take all that you find. The ladies who are on the raids will need to educate any men who don't know what to look for.

"We will save the thirty Pindad SS2 assault rifles, along with 5000 rounds of 5.56mm ammunition, for when we go into Indonesian territory; as before, we will need to continue to supplement our ammunition supplies with whatever we can take from the Indo Alliance.

"Wherever possible, we are planning to fit the .50 Calibre machine guns to jeeps and trucks as we go along; the other LMG's can be used anywhere."

"All of you who will be staying back at base and have small children to look after have been allocated non-Alliance weapons. It is not expected that you will use as much ammunition as the raiding parties do. The best-case scenario would be if you don't use any at all!"

Dr Rob and Dr Margaret stepped forward to take their turns. After expending their allocated rounds, Rob asked, "Where are we to be stationed Dick?"

"Well Rob, I reckon one of you, accompanied by a nurse will be needed on board the *Fremantle,* while the other, along with a second nurse, will be stationed here. We were thinking that you and Nari will be best aboard ship, while Margaret with Wendy and retired Nurse Joan will remain here to handle whatever we bring back."

Both doctors concurred with Dick's suggestion.

Joan smiled as she commented,

"It's been a long-time young man! But I promise I'll do my best."

Sarge addressed the group.

"Is everyone happy with their weapon? From what I saw none of you had any problems with firing it. Some of you may need some directional training, but we really don't have time to turn you all into marksmen.

"Now, if you all step forward again in pairs, we'll give you a turn at firing the 9mm Browning or Type 54 pistol."

They lined up like school children, and then made their way to the cover provided. Dick and Sarge demonstrated the traditional stance, holding the weapon in the dominant hand and bracing with the other.

Dick called William Green forward. William had only been given the SLR for now because there were simply not enough Type 68's to go around. This was something they were hoping to rectify on the first raid.

"William, you must have shot before. You're not bad with the weapon!"

"Yes, I was in the cadets Dick. I used to love shooting with my old man."

Sarge handed William the special SLR Sniper rifle, fitted with scope and silencer. He set up a few more targets at the forty-metre range. After William made short work of these, they moved the range out to seventy-five metres. The longer distance made no difference; so, they next tried 125 metres. Even then he managed to hit three out of four.

"Well Will!" said Sarge, handing him the weapon. "It looks like you're now a Sniper!"

The rather embarrassed ex-Wildlife Attendant rubbed his stubbled growth as he studied the weapon in his hands. He was in awe of the thing; never before had he been this close to the Sniper special.

"Thanks guys! I don't know what to say!"

"You earned it!" laughed Sarge.

A quick lesson on explosives came next. The aim was simple; pierce the stick of dynamite and then insert the fuse. Times and measurements were important, but everything else was straightforward.

As they started to pack up, Dick asked if there were any questions. There were a few murmurs among the group when Roger Jones stepped forward, as did Helen and Craig Crawford. Helen acted as spokesperson.

"We were wondering if we could learn how to fire the guns please?"

That caused a stir. Dick and Sarge waited for a minute to see what would happen. Amongst the general mumbling from the crowd, a female voice rang out loud and clear.

"Oh no you don't!"

Ellen Crawford and Sarah Jones suddenly ran over and grabbed their children firmly by the arms, before trying to march them away.

"Come away children! This has nothing to do with you!"

Dick stepped forward.

"I beg to differ! Ellen, isn't it? Life is not like it was before. Don't you realise that your children may be put in a scenario where they will need to know how to fire a weapon. Would you rather they be killed or know how to defend themselves? It might even be your life they save if you're ambushed, and the enemy is about to finish you off!"

Ellen and Sarah were both close to tears. As mothers, giving permission went against every protective instinct in their bodies. However, Dick's words had hit home.

Sid came forward to console his wife. After a whispered discussion he nodded that they both agreed with Dick. Making the most of the change of heart, Sarge asked all the children to come forward; even the three young six-year-old kids. He first gave the older children a shot out of the SLR, and then let them all have a go with the 9mm Browning or Type 54.

Dick asked Sarge whether he was happy with the training, "Mate, they all did great! The parents of those kids should be proud. At least now, if push comes to shove, they will have had some experience at firing a 9mm."

Friday 23rd January 2015 ... Weapons Training, Strong Fort Bay

The next morning Sarge and Dick issued the replacement sentries with an SLR each, along with 200 rounds of ammunition between them.

"Take these with you and you will be able to keep them there for the sentries to use."

A bit later Bentley and Tony returned to camp after their double stint of guard duty.

"Ready for some weapons training guys?"

Dick and Sarge took them through the same procedure that they'd followed the day before. Halfway through the morning Dick looked up to find everyone had come back to recap on what they'd learned yesterday. Sarge laughed as he gave Dick a wink.

"This is great, mate!"

Because of Tony's familiarity with the weapons, he'd used back in the old country, they'd decided to issue him with the Armalite, or M16 as it was more commonly called.

"Never forget that once you push the lever forward this will have fully automatic capabilities; or you can leave it as semi auto if you prefer."

Bentley was issued with a Type 68 assault rifle. Both men had a good result at the range.

Sarge looked around at the watching group, then asked if there was anyone with a question. Seventeen-year-old Jill Frank came forward and asked, "Do you think I could have a go at the same gun as Josh?"

"You certainly can Jill!" smiled Sarge, knowing she was talking about the SLR. After passing her the weapon he watched her load the magazine with five rounds. Because this meant pushing the round against the resistance of the internal spring in the machine, she obviously found it difficult, but she didn't give up, and really looked the part as she shouldered the SLR and leant against the old fridge before firing off the rounds in quick succession.

Sarge didn't notice the small grouping at the target. He was too preoccupied with looking at the shapely seventeen-year-old; the sight of the trim young woman took him back to the times when he used to watch the trekking guides in the same way.

"Great shooting Jill!"

Dick came forward and took the weapon from her before giving Sarge a nudge. The ex-Sapper appeared to be mesmerised by the young girl.

"Stop looking at her tits mate!" he whispered.

Sarge realised he was still staring at the girl.

"Sorry mate!"

The girls did a fantastic job with the evening meal. With donations from the *Fremantle* and the *CJ*, they laid on a spread of porterhouse steak topped with crayfish tails and a great seafood sauce and accompanied by sides of vegies and chips. All of this was washed down with a selection of wine and beer.

Once the younger kids had been sent off to bed, Dick addressed the rest of the group.

"If you take a look at the list I've posted on the noticeboard, you will see where you are to be stationed. Some of you will remain at the base, which is here at the moment. The rest of you will either be part of team one or team two. The only exceptions are those in the medical section; I've sorted things out with them earlier.

"The first raid will be to New England and the second into Crayfish. We'll run over the logistics tomorrow when the *Fremantle* returns. I will leave it up to you to decide between yourselves which team should go into which raid."

Sarge and Dick left them to discuss the matter. By the sounds of it there was quite a lot of discussion going on; although they couldn't hear what was being said, some of the voices became quite elevated at times.

"How do you reckon they will go, Sarge? Have we turned them into soldiers yet?"

The ex-Sapper looked at his mate thinking he probably knew the answer already.

"Well mate, you know how it is. They will be a bit reluctant to shoot at first, but once they see some of their family members dying around them, they will start to harden up!"

"Yeah, I feel that we could lose a few, but I will do my best to keep that number to the minimum."

A voice called out from the other room.

"We're ready for you guys!"

By now the group was sitting silently and had obviously finished discussing the pros and cons of the matter. Johnny and George were standing up front.

George turned to Dick and Sarge and reported what they had decided.

"We have come up with a decision Dick; team one will do the raid at New England and team two at Crayfish. We realise that the *Fremantle* will have to deposit both groups at their locations. We have one question; are the raids going to be simultaneous, or will one follow the other?"

Dick looked at Sarge and said, "This is something we will need to go over with Doc and the rest of the *Fremantle* crew tomorrow. There will be a meeting on board with George and Johnny as soon as she gets back."

Saturday 24th January 2015 ... Strong Fort Bay

Sarge and Dick rose well before 0600; after a quick breakfast they headed off together towards the entrance to the bay. Their objective this morning was to find a way to get around the tree. Although, the time for this might be some time away yet, sorting it out now would assist the group with their efforts to take some form of control back once they started to acquire a few vehicles.

They didn't want to move the tree just yet. Instead, they felt sure there must be another track into the bay. The pair really enjoyed walking the eight kilometres, breathing deep as they inhaled the familiar forest smells, and appreciating the sounds of the native birds. They laughed as a startled wallaby hurriedly hopped off down the track in front of them.

"It all seems so normal, Sarge, It's hard to believe that we are in the middle of organising a reprisal with a bunch of civilians!"

Sarge agreed.

"I keep forgetting that only three weeks ago, none of this was happening. Since then, hundreds of thousands of Taswegians have been killed by these evil forces. It's a big responsibility knowing that their only chance of survival lies with us mate! If I was a betting man, I wouldn't take those odds."

"Well put Sarge!"

The pair arrived at the tree where Mick and Clinton were keeping watch. Mick joined them on their search to find an alternative track, leaving Clinton on his own to watch the road.

After climbing over the tree, the trio made their way down the road for a distance of around a kilometre. Once they'd crossed over Agnes Creek, they could see an old logging track running off to their right.

"I reckon this is what we are looking for Sarge!"

"Did you know there was one here Dick?"

"No Mick, although, from what I know about forestry, there had to be old logging roads here somewhere. I'm guessing if we follow this to the end to where it breaks up into drag tracks, we should find one heading Southeast. That track should eventually take us to the beach."

Sarge, who had disappeared back towards the creek, reappeared. By the looks of his satisfied grin, they could tell he'd come up with a plan.

"I reckon we have the perfect way to cover our tracks. If we drive into the creek, then continue downstream for a hundred yards before coming back out onto the track, there will be no tracks visible at the entrance to the logging road."

"Mate! That's an awesome idea!"

After 30 minutes hard work busting their way through the undergrowth on the old track they arrived at a clearing.

Sarge pointed out, "This is where they would have loaded the logs; you can see the old ramp where they pushed the logs onto the trucks with a bulldozer."

Dick consulted the compass, then led the way Southeast to search for a predominant drag track.

"Here's one," yelled Mick.

For the next three kilometres they continued to work their way through the old growth forest, with the occasional tree stump visible where they'd thinned it out fifty years earlier. With the overhead canopy there was plenty of leaf litter, as well as some pretty big wheel ruts in the ground. Although right now these were as hard as a brick, it wasn't difficult to imagine how muddy it must have become for the log skidders who worked the area during winter.

After climbing a small rise, the track suddenly ended.

"Bummer!" exclaimed Mick.

Dick and Sarge weren't ready to give up. They knew they were close; and, sure enough, a few hundred yards further on they found themselves on sand. From there it was only a short walk over the sand dune and onto the beach. They discovered they'd come out at the other end of the Strong Fort Bay beach and had almost reached the outcrop between the beach and Kayak Bay.

"Do you think we can get a truck or jeep through there Sarge?"

"No problems, Dick. We'll just have to disguise the tracks at the start of the old logging road."

The kids playing cricket on the beach looked up in surprise as the three men emerged from the bush before making their way back to the backpacker's complex.

"Have you got time for a cuppa Mick before you head back?"

Mick looked at his watch.

"No, better not. I'll have one with Clinton when I get there."

Sarge watched the ex-fisherman leave.

"There goes a good man, Dick!"

Dick nodded in agreement before pouring them both a coffee. Once they'd downed the steaming brew, they packed up the thirty Pindad SS2 assault rifles, and 5000 rounds of 5.56mm rounds which they'd planned to put away until it came time for the Indonesian part of the retaliation. Leaving the weapons and ammunition required there, they packed up the excess.

"We'll leave one of the .50 Cal's here, as well as some ammo for when we get a jeep in here to fit it to,"

"Sounds great, Sarge!" Dick took a look outside. "Hey, it looks like the *Freo* is back!"

1300. Jack picked up Dick, Sarge, George, and Johnny in the RHIB and took them out to the Patrol Boat, where they found the crew in the main mess ready for the briefing. Looking at the chart Doc had out on the table, Dick could see a pencilled course.

Doc took Dick and Sarge aside and filled them in about how Vince was and what was happening at Hells Beach. Vince had felt a lot better once Doc had him stitched up, while April had decided to stay behind to help Laurel.

"Vince has nearly finished the device he's putting together to enable us to contact all brick phones across Taswegia. It should be ready by the time we get back."

The three returned to the Junior Sailors' Mess, finding Jack, Patch, Nari, Annie, George, and Johnny already seated and waiting for them. Sarge gave Annie a huge cuddle as he sat down beside her, while Dick did the same with Patch. Doc grinned as the two girls spoke in unison.

"We didn't kill anyone; did we boys?"

Doc cleared his throat.

"It's time to get serious; we need to discuss the plan. We'll take both teams with us and move stealthily into Clan Bay New England, eta 2300, then transport team one ashore, led by Sarge.

"We then sail to Crayfish. 0130, team two led by Dick, will unload at the main wharf, where the *Fremantle* will refuel.

"The brief for both teams will be to enter as many homes as possible; operating in five teams of two and one team of three. Teams are to kill as many of the NK Nationals and Alliance troopers they come across as possible, not forgetting to collect their weapons and ammo.

"Whenever you find a jeep or truck you are to use that to move between homes to speed things up. By all accounts, and given that no one is expected to be awake, you should have at least four hours of uninterrupted killing time."

Doc acknowledged Johnny, who had his hand raised.

"What about small children and babies, Doc?"

Sarge answered on behalf of the others.

"It's unfortunate Johnny, but we have to kill everyone. Remember, they have spared no one except some of the medical staff; and that was only to cover up for their blunder."

The mood was sombre to say the least. Doc nodded and continued.

"The first jeep at Crayfish can be brought back to the wharf, where it will be fitted with the .50 Calibre. Based on the stats we have, there are about 250 homes in the immediate Crayfish area. We suspect there will also be a garrison of Alliance troops working out of there; most likely using the Crayfish Motor Lodge as a base.

"We will send two groups to attack them. Remember we have the advantage; it's the middle of the night, and some of you will have NVG's; so, where possible use bayonets in preference to pulling the trigger, or at least muffle the blast.

"There should be at least one trooper in each home, but we suspect their troops are pretty thin on the ground, so it's possible this rule may not have been followed.

"Clan Bay only has thirty shacks and shouldn't prove to be much trouble; but just up the road is the Bugle Hotel. By now this is quite possibly an Alliance base, who knows how many troopers you will find there. The good thing is that, apart from the three houses opposite it, and the one alongside that's all you'll have to deal with. From there it's a couple of kilometres to New England, so I'm hoping you can get some vehicles.

"Apart from the motel there and two homes it's pretty much just the Historic Site left. Your brief from there is to continue on towards Devil Bay, where you will find another forty shacks.

"After they are cleared, half of you will need to come across to Crayfish in a vehicle while the second half heads off to OH&S cove and another nine homes.

"The *Fremantle* will stay for as long as required at Crayfish, or until the first half of team one arrives. Along with half of team two, they will then head to Sand Alley.

"Hopefully the next night they will supply power to the bridge to open it, which will sever the Peninsular at that point. Any questions?"

There was silence for a few minutes while they all digested the plan.

George was first to speak up.

"Do we get picked up at the same points or do we need to make our way somewhere else?"

Doc could see that both men were feeling more than a little bit worried.

"With the other half mounted in vehicles to continue raiding, you will head back towards New England. This is where you will meet up with the remainder of team one; forming team four."

"This is where it gets tricky; whilst at Sand Alley the *Fremantle* will send the new team three to attack the Sand Alley Hotel that night, while the bridge is being opened. Four members of the team will stay and hold the bridge; these will be armed with sniper rifles, a light machine gun, and possibly a .50 Calibre machine gun.

"The rest of the team is to acquire vehicles, mount up and head towards Starlight, clearing all homes along the way. From memory there are only half a dozen shacks on the Peninsular side of the bridge, and the same between there and Starlight.

"It's at this point that you should all be able to see that the game plan is to meet in the middle. Both team three and four will have a brick phone, so they'll be able to keep us in the loop. If all goes well, we will all meet back here in around four days, where we will regroup, debrief and attend to any wounded.

"The main team will make its way back to Sand Alley to provide reinforcements, and then plan to finish mopping up all the side roads. Let's hope that we can flush some more survivors out while doing this."

A break was called for a brew top up. It was a lot to take in. The reality of George and Johnny taking on the responsibility of heading up a couple of the teams, was obviously now sinking in. Even though Sarge and Dick would be holding their hands initially, this was still going to be huge for both of them. As leaders, a big part of their job would be to keep the morale high and hold their teams together.

Johnny extended an invitation to all the crew to join them for dinner, and thanked Sarge and Dick for their efforts with the weapons training. They discussed the other track in.

"Let's hope we don't have to use it. By then we should have annihilated them all; if that's the case we can just cut a path through the tree and keep watch over it."

Dick was optimistic that this was how things would go. He was hoping that the Alliance was spread so thin that it would be a walk in the park for them all.

George had a question.

"Plan sounded a bit gory, what with the killing of people and babies with a bayonet; but the one question no one has asked, is when do you want to go?"

Doc looked at Dick and Sarge, who both nodded, "We go tonight! ETD 2100."

Chapter 27
Alliance HQ

Monday 19ᵗʰ January 2015 ... Alliance Headquarters, Kings Town

General Jun Lee Sung and Captain Li Chun were heavily in discussion about how everything was going.

"General, the Indonesians are going very well; in fact, they should have today set up their new headquarters in Benowa. Also, the unloading of the tanker *Indo Maersk* is ahead of schedule."

"Good Captain. Let us hope they can get rid of those resistance people. How is the monitoring of the UHF radio network going?"

Li Chun was a little uncomfortable with the question, knowing full well that the General would not like the answer.

"Well General, unfortunately, the radio monitoring team has had to be deployed elsewhere because of low numbers."

Although Jun Lee was not pleased with this, he too knew that because of the lack of reinforcements they were extremely thin on the ground. Messengers had made it through from the north of the state, with the reports showing that Lawn and Devonshire had been occupied successfully.

The General picked up the latest report detailing the dispersal numbers for the whole state.

'The 450,000 troops that arrived in convoys on the 2nd of January 2015 have now been dispersed across the entire state. As far as we are able to ascertain, the count is as follows:

- *250,000 troops deployed as house security.*
- *140,000 troops deployed to garrisons around the south of the state, averaging 100 in each.*
- *15,000 troops stationed in the immediate Kings Town area.*
- *5,000 troops stationed in the immediate Lawn area.*
- *5,000 troops stationed in the immediate Devonshire area.*
- *15,000 troops working as death and clean-up Crews.*
- *19,000 troops deceased.*
- *1,000 unaccounted for (possible deserters).'*

"How many troops do we have down the Peninsular, Captain?" Li Chun consulted his notebook.

"Of the troops that are either already in place or earmarked to go, we have 8,000 south of Sand Alley. These are made up of 3000 house security and 5000 fighting troops."

"That is far too many, Captain. Reduce that number to 3,000 plus security. If that paedophile, Colonel Ming Jun, can't manage to kill a few farmers with those numbers he is not worthy to be considered Alliance!"

The General pointed out to his Captain that the numbers from the second convoy would make an enormous difference to the statistics which had been detailed in the report.

"Our Southeast messenger reports that there was some trouble at Bronze yesterday, General. It seems that some locals raided the base there and caused quite a lot of damage."

"Did we catch these people, Captain?"

Although, Li Chun knew full well that they weren't certain about this, it was essential for him to convince the General to feel that they were in control.

"Eh … yes General. Four Taswegians were cornered and killed just north of Bronze."

"Very good! That will keep the troop Commanders on their toes. A little collateral damage every now and then does them good. So exactly how many troops did we lose?"

Li Chun nervously cleared his throat.

"Eh … eighty, General."

Jun Lee nearly choked upon hearing the number. He quickly changed the subject; not wanting the captain to see that he was worried.

"And how are things going at the hospital?"

Li Chun reported that everything was well; with the exception of a recent night raid, when a large amount of first aid supplies had been stolen. Apparently two guards had been killed.

"Did you find the perpetrator, Captain?"

"Not yet General, although, we believe we know who was responsible. Dr Roger and his whore Nari Kim have not been seen since!"

The General had been looking out of the window. Turning to Li Chun he asked, "And what of these two now, Captain?"

"We do not know their whereabouts General. We suspect that they may have escaped on the Doctor's yacht."

The General moved on to his next point of discussion.

"The third and fourth convoys should have been here over a week ago. One can only surmise that they were overcome by the nuclear fallout, along with our Navy and our President, Gin Gum Kim.

"This is a sad day for us Li Chun, as it means we are on our own. Be very careful not to get rid of any more of our doctors as we will need them now.

"Remember, it is essential that we keep the fear alive, and let them think the reinforcements are still coming. When morale is as low as it is now, our troops make too many mistakes."

Captain Li Chun smiled.

"General Jun Lee Sung, I have an idea that may increase morale. If we send out word that the third convoy has been sighted off the East Coast, this will reinstall faith into our troops and also in our Nationals."

The General paced up and down in front of the window. His office overlooked the port of Kings Town. He had grown fond of the place but felt saddened at now knowing that his family would not be joining him.

He felt torn in two directions; although he knew the young Captain had good intentions, he was not entirely in agreement that they should deceive their comrades.

"And what would be the end result Captain if they were to learn the truth? We would be accused of deception! No! I think we will find another way to boost morale."

Wednesday 21ˢᵗ January 2015 ... Kings Town Hospital

Dr Helen Smith arrived at work, just as she had on every other day since the Invasion. Thanks to Doc's intervention on that fateful day, she was somehow still alive, despite having to learn fast how to become, or at the very least appear to be, competent at her job as a doctor.

With no theatre cases booked for the day, and with triage having been under the pump for the last few days, she was thankful to have been assigned to work with Dr Ian Walters in triage.

It was a widely known fact that she was attracted to Ian. Before the invasion she had been part of a loving family of three. Thanks to the invasion force, her family was now non-existent; her husband and son were both gone. She suspected they had been killed by the heathens. Every night now she had to go home to an empty house.

She had toughened up a lot over the past weeks; she had Doc to thank for that. What a wonderful man he was. She couldn't help wondering what had happened to him. He and Nari had simply vanished one day; there was no way of knowing whether or not they were still alive.

As she thought about how much her life had changed, her thoughts drifted, as they often did, and she started daydreaming about Ian. Just as he was about to make passionate love to her on one of the triage beds, she heard a voice calling her name.

"Good morning, Helen."

Jerking quickly back into reality, she was embarrassed to find it was Ian who'd greeted her. She could feel her cheeks heat up as she blushed a crimson red colour.

"Good morning, Ian."

As she watched him tying the cord on his scrubs her desire for him grew until she could hold back no longer. She grabbed him and kissed him hard, letting her tongue slide between his lips.

Ian was smiling.

"Well, what's come over you?"

"I just wanted to do that now; before it's too late. You never know what's going to happen next in this shit hole!"

They were interrupted as the first batch of casualties was brought in from Bronze.

Genera Jun Lee had travelled to Fels Point with five of his most senior officers to inspect the sunken wreck of the *Warrnambool*.

The FCPB was still sitting at the bottom, with only the top of the radio mast visible above the water. The General shook his head in disbelief.

"This is very tragic! And we still don't know the cause of the explosion?"

One of his Lieutenants spoke up.

"No General, although it is widely believed that thieves may have attacked the boat and then blown it up to cover their tracks."

Their next stop was at the National Catamaran boat yard, where there were two vessels waiting for inspection. The *AKANE* was finished and was now awaiting delivery of its new engines.

It was most unfortunate that these had been coming on the third convoy. As Jun Lee looked at the huge, but now useless eighty-five metre wave piercing catamaran, he expressed his thoughts out loud,

"Another shame!"

The General was not having a good day!

Incat Hull # 068 AKANE, destined for the South Island of Japan
(Photo Compliments of Incat)

Chapter 28
Retaliation Begins!

Saturday 24th January 2015 ... Backpackers' Accommodation, Strong Fort Bay

1800. The backpacker's dining table was packed as they entertained the *Fremantle's* crew during the evening meal. After giving his glass a few taps with a spoon, Johnny stood and welcomed the crew, once again thanking Dick and Sarge for conducting their weapons training.

"As of tonight, we will be manning the tree position with those of you who are not on teams one or two. I have made a few suggestions as to a roster but will leave it up to you to sort it out amongst yourselves."

While some of the group could sense what was coming next, young Will Green pre-empted the next announcement.

"Does that mean we go tonight?"

There was a hush across the room, as they waited for Johnny to compose himself.

"Yes, we leave at nine o'clock. I realise this is not much notice, but timing is essential if we are to win back the Peninsular."

Ellen Crawfield broke down in tears and left the room. A few of the other women went after her; leaving the rest of the group in a sombre mood. A lot of the family groups excused themselves so that they could spend a bit of time together, as well as say their goodbyes in private. Before long the only people left in the room were the singles and the crew of the *Fremantle*.

Trying to make light of the events, Dick commented, "Well, that's poured cold water on the evening!"

Doc finished his drink.

"Let's get back to the boat and prepare for loading the troops."

2030. Sarge brought the first load of troops across in the RHIB. They had been told to travel light, carrying weapons and ammunition only. The less they had to carry, the more likely it was that they would survive.

After stowing their weapons below, they were made comfortable in the Mess where Dick addressed them.

"Make full use of the bunks if you wish and try and get some sleep until we get to Clan Bay. For those of you who are going on to Crayfish, well you will have a little more rack time!"

2250. Patch yelled up to the Bridge.

"Last load approaching now, Skipper."

"Roger that Patch. Start main engines Chief. All crew ready for leaving the harbour."

As Doc replaced the microphone on the hook, he could see Sarge and Dick lifting the RHIB aboard with the Hiab. With Nari and Patch standing by as lookouts, and Annie and Jack in their usual place down the hole, Dick and Sarge went aboard to operate the windlass.

Doc eased the FCPB slow ahead to take the pressure off the anchor. With the anchor stowed and clamped off, Sarge came up to the Flying Bridge. Doc piped, back to one generator, while Dick took the wheel as Doc ordered,

"Half ahead both, steer *zero nine zero*."

Dick swung the wheel to port as she came about; quick to respond as the two huge 2,400KW MTU diesels pushed her up and into the night, at a speed of nearly fifteen knots.

"Roger that. Steering *zero nine zero* and half ahead both Skipper, speed fifteen knots."

After consulting the radar, Doc waited to be clear of the entrance. Both Patch and Nari scanned the rocky outcrops on either side as they left the bay. By now Sarge, Annie and Jack were all on the Bridge. Doc checked his calculations on the chart against the radar screen before ordering.

"Starboard thirty steer *one six zero*, increase revs to give us twenty knots."

Dick knew he was running inside between the mainland and the Hippolyte Rocks. They were a fair way offshore, but at this speed there was no room for error.

"Roger that, steering *one six zero* making revolutions for twenty knots, Skipper."

The *Fremantle* punched into a light sou'wester as she came down the coast, with the swell running at about two metres. The motion of the grey warhorse was near poetic; the bow rising and falling gently as she punched into the waves. Coming from the southwest meant that the spray was running right to left. With the occasional fine misty spray finding its way to the Flying Bridge, you could quickly find yourself very wet if you were up there.

"I'll try and keep in close to the shoreline to get into the lee of this swell. Otherwise, the troops below might go on strike!"

Constantly peering at the radar screen, Doc made slight course changes to get the *Fremantle* in close to the shore. Rounding Mans Island just before 2350, they started their approach into New England.

Doc called out, "Steer *three four five*, Dick."

"Roger that Skipper, steering *three four five*."

Sunday 25th January 2015 ... FCPB Fremantle on approach to Clan Bay, Team 0025.

"Chief, I'm sure glad the exhausts are under water. We'll go in as silently as we can."

Doc had always admired the way the Fremantle Class Patrol Boats ran their exhaust outlets below the waterline. This had the effect of muffling the sound and allowing them better freedom of movement without detection.

With the boat operating as silently as they possibly could, she glided past the old convict town of New England. The skipper whispered, "Slow ahead, Port ten, steer *two eight zero*."

Dick bought her round to port.

"Roger that Skipper, steering *two eight zero*, slow ahead."

As they came astern to take the way off, Sarge read off the depths as she came closer to shore.

"Four metres, Skipper."

"All stop. Deploy the RHIB. Let's get team one ashore. Good luck Sarge; see you in four or five days."

As Annie kissed him, she whispered, "Don't be a hero my Love."

Dick jumped into the RHIB and stood behind the consul. After joining him there, Sarge watched on while the other twelve members of team one climbed down and took their positions up forward.

Sarge gave the orders in a whisper.

"Lock and load your weapons. From now on there is NO talking. Remember to use your bayonet if you can, rather than pulling the trigger, but whatever you do, don't take any risks."

He looked at his ex-CD mate and smiled; they both knew the risks that were about to unfold. Upon their shoulders rested the responsibility of bringing as many as possible back alive. Sarge had chosen to stick to his 9mm Browning, as well as the SLR bayonet for up-close and personal killing.

Dick manoeuvred the RHIB on to the beach alongside the boat ramp, touching the nose against the sand. Sarge gave the signal to get out; once everyone was clear he gave Dick the thumbs up. Neither of them had to say anything; they both knew well the consequences of what was about to start. After nodding once more to his mate he pushed the RHIB backwards.

After going astern, Dick swung the RHIB around before slowly making his way back to the boat. Looking back, he could faintly see Sarge and the team as they made their way to the last house on the beach.

Sarge had already made up the pairs; trying to match the different skills and ages as best he could, given that he hadn't had long to get to know them. It would have been worse with team one; at least he'd spent a bit more time with these guys from Benowa.

After directing the other five pairs to the next five homes, he entered the first home with his other teammate, Helga, who was packing the Type 54 Alliance pistol. The home was a small weatherboard shack, with two or possibly three bedrooms.

Sarge easily prised open the flyscreen door and found that the back door was not locked. Wearing his night vision goggles made things a whole lot easier for him as he negotiated the darkened home. Having made prior arrangements with Helga to stay in the main kitchen to cover his back, he entered the first bedroom. Two bunks, two children, and the smell of soap wafting in the air.

He covered the first child's head with a pillow and inserted the eight-inch SLR bayonet into the kid's heart. Although, the other child stirred, Sarge was quicker, completing the same task as before.

The next room was obviously the main bedroom; the smell of body sweat mixed with perfume filled the air and made him gag. After picking up a cushion off the chair in the corner he pushed it over the face of the male before pulling the trigger on the Browning; a split second later he did the same to the female. The 9mm's muzzle blast was well and truly muffled by the cushion.

After a quick search he located the last room. This was a small sunroom built into the original verandah. An Alliance trooper snored loudly as he slept on the single bed under the window.

Sarge stabbed the man through the ribs, with the blade entering his heart and killing him instantly. He returned to the kitchen to find Helga shaking uncontrollably. After slinging the Trooper's weapon and ammo webbing over his shoulder, he gave her a hug, whispering,

"It'll be ok. You stick with me."

Once Dick had stowed the RHIB, he made his way to where Patch and the rest of the crew were waiting on the Bridge. Doc moved slow ahead before asking his long-time friend, "You want to take her again, Dick?"

Dick turned to starboard to bring the head around to clear the bay, then they eased their way out into the main channel and past New England. Around one mile further down the opening Doc checked their heading.

"Half ahead, steer *one seven zero*. Make revs for twenty knots."

"Roger that, Skipper."

Johnny emerged from below. After acknowledging the ex-farmer, Doc asked how he was going.

"Can't sleep, Johnny?"

Johnny looked around at the men and women on the Bridge.

"Just thinking about what's to come. How do you guys do it!"

Dick passed the wheel to Jack.

"It's all in the training, Johnny."

The ex-farmer turned and looked at Annie, Nari and Patch, who were all sitting on the Flying Bridge. Pointing at the three women he asked, "Well, how do they do it? None of them have had any military training."

Doc replied, "It's simply a matter of necessity, as well as what you get used to. You know; kill or be killed!"

Dick felt for the man, hoping he would be able to hold it together for the sake of the team, and secretly wondering if he had made a bad choice with Johnny?

"Are you going to be all right, Johnny?"

"I'll be all right; although I'm not sure about some of the others Dick. I'll just think of it as something like having to put a heifer down!"

Sunday 25th January 2015 ... Clan Bay, Team One

Back at Clan Bay, George and Eleanora entered the second house at the same time as Sarge and Helga entered the first. Using his hand to block some of the light from the small torch he was carrying, George quickly found the trooper sleeping in the first bedroom. He knew it was a trooper because of the rifle and webbing which was standing against the wall.

He shook profusely as he used a pillow to try and muffle the blast. Unfortunately, he held his Type 54 pistol too far away from the pillow for it to completely block the sound, and there was a small *bang* as he fired the gun. The bullet entered the man's head through the side of his temple.

Hearing noises coming from the next bedroom, George quickly entered the door, finding the male occupant sitting up on the side of the bed. After swinging the F1 to his hip he squeezed the trigger; the five rounds hit the male twice, and the female alongside of him once.

The male was obviously dead, although, he wasn't so sure about the female. There was no time to think about it; after pulling his bayonet out of the webbing and steel sheath on his belt he stabbed her in the throat. Her eyes opened wide and then closed again as the blood oozing from the wound sapped her life away.

There were obviously other people in the house. Eleanora used her bayonet on an elderly man coming out of a bedroom; as she drove the blade into his stomach, the man, who was in his late seventies, dropped to his knees.

Out of the corner of her eye she saw a child of about twelve or thirteen years, as well as another younger child who was clinging to the older one's leg. She froze! This was a nightmare; when was it all going to end? They stared at each other for what seemed to her to be an eternity.

As George's F1 blasted away at them she snapped out of her daze. The older one was nearly cut in half by the burst, while the little one's head just turned into mash as the 9mm's soft lead blew the back of his skull off.

Sunday 25th January 2015 ... FCPB Fremantle, on route to Crayfish, Team Two

0200. "Starboard twenty, steer *zero six zero,* slow ahead make for ten knots."

Dick brought the boat around onto the new bearing. After carefully manoeuvring through the mixture of boats that were still on their moorings, they had passed the salmon farms on the port side and were now approaching the outer reaches of Crayfish.

"Slow ahead. Spin her round Dick and come in starboard side to. One mooring line amidships please."

Once Dick had brought the Patrol Boat to a stop alongside the main wharf at Crayfish, Annie and Patch secured the mooring line. Annie looked at her much-loved pseudo mother figure.

"Why does the Skipper only want one mooring line, Patch?"

"I think it is in case we have to leave in a hurry, Annie."

Back on the Bridge, Dick commented, "Full tide Doc. That works to our favour."

"Yes Dick; especially at Sand Alley."

Dick pulled Patch into their cabin to say their goodbyes. With tears in her eyes, Patch stayed below as the ex-CD gathered his team on the uppers for one last pep talk.

Sunday 25th January 2015 ... Clan Bay, Team One

Upon Jack and Riley entering the third house at Clan Bay, they found all the occupants in a drunken state. There were four adults in the lounge, every one of them in various stages of undress. It was obvious that a good time was being had by all.

The two women were naked from the waist down, while one man was completely naked and the other in his underpants.

It didn't take Jack or Riley long to dispatch them all with their bayonets. Both men were astonished at how easily the sharp bayonet attached to the ends of their Type 68 assault rifles achieved its deadly purpose. Most of the four weren't even aware they were there; except for one woman, who was briefly jerked back to sobriety as the blade entered her torso just under the sternum.

They inspected the rest of the building, but they found no one else, so after finding the trooper's weapon and ammo they left again.

Sunday 25th January 2015 ... Crayfish, Team Two

Once they'd reached Crayfish, Dick made sure that they all knew what they were likely to find once they left the ship. They would have to deal with whatever happened quickly and quietly if that was at all possible. He had a quick word with team two before they went ashore.

"Remember team, where possible, always use bayonets over triggers. You all know your first house; we will concentrate on the immediate area with about forty homes and the hotel. That's about eight each as per your list. Good luck to you all. Jill, you come with me."

Team Two split up and headed for the first six houses. Finding the front door unlocked, Dick and Jill entered and made their way down the hallway to the entrance of the lounge. As instructed, Jill was to watch Dick's back while he killed the occupants.

With night vision goggles and his trusty silenced .22 cut down rifle, he systematically entered each room and quickly shot each person in the head. After handing Jill the trooper's rifle and ammo they moved on to the next house.

Sunday 25th January 2015 ... Clan Bay, Team One

Mick and David made short work of the homes to which they'd been assigned to. Looking at his watch, Mick realised it was only 0100. He couldn't believe they had raided six homes and killed over thirty people so quickly. The only issue was that it was getting a little challenging to carry all the weapons and ammo they'd acquired.

Peter and Clinton were finished around the same time, as were William and Harold. All six team members had bloodied their hands, and not a loud shot had been fired.

William took the opportunity to try out his Sniper's rifle with the silencer. Because of the distances they had to travel, as well as having to go right up to the end of the beach, George and Eleanora, along with Sarge and Helga, were last to finish.

Helga froze as she came face to face with an older gentleman who was going to the toilet. He was probably the grandfather. Sarge came out of one bedroom to find them standing there looking at each other, he was obviously half asleep and was probably still wondering who she was when she plucked up the courage to run the bayonet into him. That house eventually yielded eight occupants; Helga bravely killed three of them.

George and Eleanora almost came unstuck when George found two people making love; the loudness of their sexual grunting drowned out any sounds the two raiders might have made as they went through the house. At first George couldn't work out how to kill both of them with his bayonet; he'd be able to deal with one with no problems, but as soon as he did that the other one would most likely retaliate. He ended up waving Eleanora in to despatch the female while he did the same with the male.

Sunday 25th January 2015 ... Crayfish, Team Two

0240. Back in Crayfish, Johnny and young Josh went well with their first house. Johnny stabbed the trooper in the chest, while Josh's first room was the kid's room. He didn't think too much about it; stabbing all three children and killing them quickly while Johnny dealt with the couple in the next room.

It wasn't until they got to their fourth house that Josh panicked; pulling the trigger on his SLR. The 7.62mm NATO round blew a hole in the man's chest after he had woken up to Josh approaching him. This sent Johnny into a spin, and he quickly had to use his pistol. Once they were safely back outside Josh apologised for his slip up and promised not to let it happen again. Apparently, he had knocked over a chair as he'd entered the room.

Sunday 25th January 2015 ... Clan Bay, Team One

Sarge gathered his team together, realising how proud he was of them all. There had been no casualties on their side, and no noise. They decided to leave the weapons and ammo in the middle of the road.

"We'll come back later once we've been able to commandeer a vehicle," whispered Sarge, as they made their way up the kilometre-long road to the Bugle Hotel. Stopping at the back entrance to the hotel, he sent George, Eleanora, Mick and David across the highway to deal with the three homes there, while the rest of them assaulted the hotel.

Sarge split them into two groups; each one was to cover one of the accommodation areas. One team, Peter, Jack, William and Clinton covered the outside block with its five rooms, while Sarge, Helga, Harold and Riley made their way to the top floor inside the hotel.

Inside the lighting was not all that great; their only source of light came from the battery driven exit signs illuminating the floors. Sarge asked Harold and Riley to watch the exits while he entered and shot the occupants, with Helga watching his back and keeping him in fresh magazines.

With each room, Helga would move into position in the doorway while Sarge, wearing his NVG's entered quietly and placed a pillow over each person's face before shooting them in the head. There were usually two troopers to a room; the whole floor had been covered in less than fifteen minutes.

After leaving Helga and Harold to collect the weapons and ammo, Sarge moved down to the next floor, where Riley watched his back. The occupants of the rooms turned out to be troopers like before, with the exception of a couple of females.

Sunday 25th January 2015 ... Crayfish, Team Two

James and Graham must have hit the jackpot with their house; the first piece of luck was finding a jeep in the driveway. Inside they found what looked to be a fairly high-ranking officer who was in bed with a young girl. They were both fast asleep.

She looked to be around thirteen or fourteen years old, and certainly couldn't have been much older than one of James's granddaughters. Unfortunately, as James stabbed the officer in the throat, a spray of arterial blood spurted out all over the girl. Woken suddenly like that, she was scared out of her mind, and started screaming loudly. He was frozen in place for a moment, but quickly jerked into action; placing his hand over her mouth to try and cut the noise. The girl bit him hard, making him recoil backwards. Jumping out of bed, she headed for the door.

Despite being seventy-five years old, James was still pretty fit. He took off after her, and somehow managed to beat her to the door, before clobbering her with the butt of his rifle. Graham's Type 68 bellowed out from the next room as the young girl slumped to the floor, and he realised that the game was up; probably because of all the noise he was causing!

He quickly ran the girl through the chest with his bayonet, then grabbed the weapons, the ammo and the officer's tunic and made a run for the jeep. No keys! Graham returned shaking his head after running back inside to try and find them. It turned out they were in the trooper's tunic pocket the whole time!

Sunday 25th January 2015 ... Bugle Hotel, Team One

At 0245, George and Eleanora met up with the rest of them in the car park of the Bugle Hotel. They apologised to the others for things getting a little noisy. The occupants of the last house were getting up as they'd entered, and they'd had no alternative but to shoot them.

George with his pistol didn't hold back. Eleanora was the same, as she gave the three men a burst with her rifle. As they loaded all the booty into the second jeep, they were pleased to find that the keys were still in the ignition. After pouring a couple of drums of fuel into the jeeps, they grabbed the four extra drums that had been sitting alongside the first jeep.

With George driving, Eleanora, Mick, Peter, Clinton, and David with the Ultimax 100 LMG on the back, disappeared down to Clan Bay to retrieve the weapons stash.

Sarge who was driving the other jeep, with Helga, William, Jack, Riley, and Harold on board decided to drive with the lights on; this was no time for moving slowly!

Sunday 25th January 2015 ... Crayfish, Team Two

Robert and Sid did okay until they came to house number six, where it all went horribly wrong. Sid missed the woman altogether with his bayonet, and had to use it like a knife, which caused her to scream loudly.

Her partner came to, managing to punch Sid in the face, and knocking him to the floor. Grabbing Sid's weapon, he then tried to shoot him; but being unfamiliar with the Indonesian LMG he couldn't find the safety in the dark.

After lunging at the man with his bayonet, Sid managed to bring him down, before retaking possession of the LMG just in time to see the woman jump at him; still screaming wildly. She clung to his back, punching him in the head the whole time. There was no way he could get his weapon around to shoot her, and he just couldn't get enough swing to stab her.

In the end he ran backwards, ramming her into the wall and making her fall off. In shear desperation he emptied five rounds into her out of the Ultimax.

The commotion next door had made it impossible for Robert to be quiet about anything. The occupant of his room was wide awake, so he just had to shoot him.

In the last bedroom Sid found three kids hiding under the bed. He knew he could show no mercy. One by one they came out and stood in a row, wondering who he was, and what he wanted. The Ultimax made short work of their little bodies; the noise was almost unbearable.

Sunday 25th January 2015 ... Clan Bay, Team One

After driving two kilometres towards New England, Sarge stopped at the old post office and sent George over the road to the shop to check whether anyone was living there. Sarge was pretty sure Dick had said there were no houses attached to either business, but he wanted to be sure.

They entered the post office by smashing the glass front door; quickly establishing that no one was living there. As they climbed back on board the jeep, they heard shots coming from across the road. George and Peter, who'd gone to check out the other shop, had been surprised when they came across two NK Nationals who had been sleeping in a makeshift bedroom at the back of the building.

The sound of the post office door shattering had woken them up, and they had armed themselves with huge kitchen knives. As they ran towards George and Peter, the two did what they needed to do.

Peter and Sarge pulled the two jeeps up next to each other.

"Lucky we checked Sarge! Otherwise, we would have missed those turkeys."

Sunday 25th January 2015 ... Crayfish, Team Two

By 0400, they'd cleared around forty houses. Dick regrouped team two, ready for the assault on the Crayfish Motel.

While Cedric and Bentley headed back to the *Fremantle* to get a .50 Calibre mounted onto the back of the jeep that Sid and Robert had acquired, the rest of them made their way into the car park of the motel.

With twenty rooms to cover, Dick thought the fastest way would be to do it himself, with the others watching his back. After commandeering a jeep which still had its keys in the ignition, he sent Johnny, Josh, Robert, Sid, James and Graham off to check the next area while it was still dark. This was on the road heading out of town towards the small town of Rex.

Tony, Mick and Jill watched Dick's back while he tried the first door, finding it locked. "Damn!" He knew if he smashed it, the whole lot would wake up. After that, all hell would break loose. Instead, he sent Jill to the office to try and find some duplicate keys. She returned five minutes later with a master key in her hand. Dick was impressed.

"I could kiss you!"

He opened the first door, then handed the master key to Jill, who went along the hall quietly unlocking all the doors. Dick followed after her, entering each room in turn and shooting everyone in the head at point blank range with the .22.

Sunday 25th January 2015... New England, Team One

0430. Once inside the New England penal site, Sarge sent George and his team down to the shop alongside the wharf to check if anyone was living there. The rest of his team cleared the two houses alongside the New England Motel.

This time he sent William in first, armed with his silenced SLR. He followed, ready to back up if required. It didn't take long to deal with the three troopers.

Back outside the motel Sarge whispered, "There are ten rooms all in a row outside, with maybe two or three inside. Will and Harold, you take the inside of the main building, while Jack and Riley, you start at the other end. We'll all meet in the middle."

Once Sarge had showed Helga how to cover the heads with a pillow to muffle the sounds, they worked quickly through the rooms. They approached each side of a bed in unison, both picking up a cushion off the lounge and using it to muffle the pistol blasts.

After reaching the middle, they met up with Jack and Riley, who were covered in blood. They had managed to despatch all their victims with the blade.

"We cheated Sarge; there was only one trooper in each room!"

Sarge grinned at the retired fisherman.

"So, does that mean you're saying that Helga and I got all the randy bastards?"

Sunday 25th January 2015 ... Crayfish, Team Two

Once Cedric and Bentley had pulled up on the Crayfish wharf, Jack and Annie got to work manhandling the pedestal for the .50 Calibre over the guard rail. Jack had made it up from some scrounged pipe and steel plate. Working under spotlights, and with the .50 Cal's attachment already in place, all he had to do was to fit it to the jeep's floor. He was hoping there would be holes, or maybe even a bracket already in place.

Cedric went up to the Bridge to report to Doc, Nari and Patch.

"All going well Skipper! We've made a few mistakes, but no one's been hurt so far."

Patch gave a sigh of relief.

Bentley, Jack and Annie were happy to discover a mounting block on the floor, and quickly marked the positions of the holes. Jack then blew them out with the oxy acetylene torch.

After loading up with four boxes of .50 calibre ammunition, the retired shipping agent and ex-chartered accountant took off back to the motel.

Sunday 25th January 2015 ... New England Motel, Team One

It was 0500 by the time William and Harold entered through the main bar. Surprisingly, they'd found it open. After searching the office, dining room and kitchen, they found another couple of rooms in another wing towards the front of the motel, overlooking the penal colony.

Daylight was creeping in across the bay, and the sun was just starting to show its head above the hills to the east. As they entered the first room; they found a single Alliance trooper; quickly executing him with the silenced SLR. Harold grabbed Will's arm, warning him to move quietly, as the pair heard voices coming from the last room. From the sounds of it, the room contained a man and a woman, who was giggling constantly.

Harold held up three fingers, then counted down two, then one, before kicking the locked door open. Upon entering, Will found a young female NK National in the hands and knees position on the bed facing the open blinds, with the male, in his more dominant position, thrusting from behind.

The sudden intrusion was so fast that the pair didn't have time to move apart before Will fired his four silenced rounds. The first one missed, while the second hit the male in the back at waist level, before travelling through his body and entering the female's head. It exited out of her right eye in a rush of blood. The third and fourth rounds hit the male in the buttocks, tearing straight through his body before entering the torso of the woman and then exiting out of her chest.

Sunday 25th January 2015 ... Crayfish, Team Two

0530. Dick, Tony, Mick, and Jill quickly ransacked the rooms of the Crayfish Motel, securing all the weapons and ammunition they could find as they went.

"Don't forget people, we are still looking for the keys to the other jeep. You'll need to search all their pockets, and also the bedside tables."

Dick didn't want to load the jeep with booty until he was sure they had the keys.

Cedric and Bentley arrived with their newly fitted .50 Calibre. As he inspected Jack's engineering feat, Dick commented, "That man is a genius! What he can't put out from the *Fremantle's* workshop is nobody's business!"

"Found them," yelled Tony, holding up a set of keys as he came out of room nine. They'd found two jeeps as well as two three-ton trucks; it wouldn't be too hard to work out which ones they fit.

"Found another set!" yelled Jill, who'd been ransacking the office.

"Try the trucks as well," said Dick. "Don't forget to check that they've all got fuel; it's getting lighter by the minute!"

While Mick got one of the trucks going, Tony and Jill found the extra fuel. Cedric and Bentley loaded all the weapons and ammo evenly between the two jeeps and one truck.

Dick addressed the group.

"Right team, we will finish the street out past the wharf; there are around ten houses to check. I know this road goes to Blue Beach, but we just haven't got the manpower right now to tackle the 120 homes there.

"Once the ten are done, we'll follow the rest of our team out on the Rex Road; hopefully by that time they'll be almost finished. After that, half of you will be deposited back at the *Fremantle*, along with half of team one. Hopefully, you'll next be off to Sand Alley.

"The remaining half of this team, under the command of Johnny, will head to New England and regroup with Sarge. After that you'll head north. You will need to get some rest and a feed before moving off towards Rex and Falcons Neck."

Tony asked, "Where are you off to, Dick?"

The retired concreter realised he was really going to miss Dick!

"Well Tony, I will head up the new team three at Sand Alley. The team will be made up of half of you, along with half of Sarge's team. If all goes well, we will catch up with you guys in the middle."

Sunday 25th January 2015 ... New England Motel, Team One

At 0530 George, Eleanora, Mick, Peter, Clinton, and David arrived in the New England car park just as Sarge was regrouping his team.

"Any trouble?" asked Sarge.

George was feeling guilty. As they'd searched the area around the shop, they'd heard the shots, and knew that Sarge and the rest of them were having trouble.

"There was nobody there, Sarge."

While the remaining weapons and ammo were being loaded, Sarge spoke to his team.

"We will split into the two teams now; we've still got around forty shacks to clear at Devils Bay, which is just a few clicks down the road. Once we've finished there, Mick, Peter, Clinton, William, Harold, and Riley will take the jeep and head straight to Crayfish, where you will join the *Fremantle*.

"Whatever happens, do not stop! I know you are going to pass homes and it will be daylight, but I'm hoping that, at the speed you'll be driving, anyone who sees you will think you're Alliance.

"Helga, Jack, David, George, and Eleanora will come with me to OH&S Cove and finish the nine homes there. BUT remember it is daylight now! We no longer have the luxury of stealth; they will shoot back if they are armed. Now, mount up!"

Sunday 25th January 2015 ... Crayfish to Rex Road, Team Two

It was already 0600. Dick, with Jill as passenger, drove one of the jeeps, closely followed by Mick and Tony in the truck. Cedric and Bentley in the other jeep caught up with Johnny, Josh, Robert, Sid, James, and Graham.

As they covered the last couple of homes, they came under fire from a trooper in the second last house. With no fire coming from the last house, they were pretty sure it was empty.

Not only was the trooper keeping them pinned down; but he still had time to send one off at the oncoming vehicles.

"Cocky bastard!" muttered Dick as he pulled up a few hundred yards behind the others.

James slumped to the ground, yelling out, "Fuck! I've been hit!"

Dick whistled up Cedric in the jeep and swapped places with Bentley. He leaned down to man the .50 Calibre.

"Are you up for this Cedric? Drive me past the house at say twenty kilometres an hour, while I pepper it with the .50. Then turn around and make another pass. After that we'll go in."

Cedric was really scared. His brain was saying 'This is stupid, I've never done anything like this in my life!' Ignoring his inner thoughts, he muttered nervously to Dick through a dry mouth,

"I'll do my best, Dick!"

Revving the engine, Cedric took off like a Le-Man's driver. Johnny could see what was about to happen.

"As soon as Dick starts firing, drag James back in behind the jeep."

A shot rang out, hitting Dick's jeep. Dick opened up with the .50; with both thumb triggers depressed he sent out a massive burst. With a rate of fire between 450 and 600 rounds per minute, it didn't take long for him to dispense half a box of Armour Piercing half inch rounds into the front room of the house. Cedric, who was grinning like a Cheshire cat, turned the jeep around.

Dick tapped him on the shoulder.

"I don't think we will need another run mate!"

Cedric looked at the front room, realising that half the wall was cut to ribbons. It was obvious that the trooper, or what was left of him, was dead. The armour piercing rounds had cut through the wall and studs; nothing had stopped it!

Johnny and Sid made their way into the house while Josh and Robert went next door.

Dick found James with a hole through his right hand. He'd had it resting just over his right hip, and the 7.62mm round had gone straight through.

Graham was doing a great job as he applied a pressure bandage to both wounds, after loading James into the truck, along with Jill, Josh, Sid, and Graham, Dick told the others to follow him back to the *Fremantle*, where hopefully those from Sarge's team would meet up with them.

Sunday 25th January 2015 ... New England to Crayfish Road, half of Team One

Mick, Peter, Clinton, William, Harold, and Riley barrelled up the New England to Crayfish Road at an average speed of eighty kilometres an hour. This was probably the fastest the old Alliance jeep had been pushed in its life. Mick was driving, with Peter riding shotgun, and the others in the back, with their weapons between their knees, were hanging on like grim death.

"Take it easy, Mick!" yelled Harold, nearly losing his Armalite out the back.

As they passed around two dozen farms, they could see the NK Nationals were starting to wake up.

"What will we do if they see us?" asked William.

"Just wave!" said Mick with a smile. "They won't have a fucking clue who we are."

By 0800, they made it to the Wharf.

"She's still here!"

They could see Dick in the truck, pulled up alongside the other three jeeps.

"With all the other vehicles on the wharf, it looks like quite a party!"

"Shit! It looks like someone has been wounded," yelled Harold.

"Isn't that the old fellow? You know; James, the architect?"

"Yeah, I was chatting to him at the backpackers; he's a nice guy!" returned Peter.

As they parked the truck and the jeep in the wharf's carpark and boarded the *Fremantle*, the new team three could already hear the rumble of the main engines. Johnny assembled what was left of team two in the three jeeps, ready for the return run to New England.

"There are about two dozen farms Johnny; spread a fair distance apart."

"Thanks Mick! And good luck."

Patch yelled out, "Wait! I've got a feed here for yours and Sarge's team!"

She ran along the wharf and handed Johnny a couple of large bags. Nari was close behind, sporting a case of cordial and bottled water. Mick Jones grinned as he took all the provisions from the two girls.

"Geez thanks Love! We really appreciate these!"

Johnny was on the brick phone calling Sarge, who confirmed the rendezvous.

Doc's voice came over the ship's broadcast.

"Slip all lines!"

Sunday 25th January 2015 ... Devil Bay, half of the new Team Four

At 0800, Sarge, Helga, Jack, David, George, and Eleanora waved goodbye to the others. Together, they had successfully cleared the forty shacks in Devil Bay.

"Record time, team! Only took just over two hours!" Sarge exclaimed.

As he surveyed the kill-hardened group, Sarge felt pretty proud of the way they'd conducted themselves. For ordinary people to have such brief training, and to then go on to kill the way they had, was quite remarkable.

There had been no real problems; as it turned out, half of the homes hadn't contained any troops. This was a sign that cracks were starting to show in the Alliance.

"Mount up team. We only have about nine homes to go, but their occupants will all be awake by now.

"I reckon we do it this way, we pull up before the farm and let David and George out to flank the house while we drive right up to the front door. Eleanora, Jack and Helga will stand on either side of the front door while I knock. When they open the door, I will despatch whoever opens, and then we'll enter.

"David and George will need to keep an eye out, just in case anyone exits the back door, but make sure it's not one of us!"

Sarge turned the key on the Mercedes look alike jeep and drove towards OH&S Cove. The first farm was on the left, just before the road went down the hill into the bay proper. The area was heavily overgrown with tea-trees. Letting David and George off was easy, they quickly punched through the light tea-tree scrub before coming to the back of the farm.

Once Sarge had pulled the jeep up at the front entrance, Jack went left, and Helga and Eleanora went right. After bashing on the door Sarge was met by an elderly woman around sixty years of age. He simply shot her between the eyes with his 9mm Browning.

As he entered the house, with Eleanora and Helga close behind him, they were confronted by an elderly man yelling abuse at them. Eleanora pulled the trigger on the assault rifle, bringing him down with a short burst.

Screams were coming from the back of the house. They heard the back-flyscreen door bang as someone exited quickly, followed by the sound of the Ultimax LMG opening up. As more screams sounded from behind him, old Jack fired his weapon into one of the front rooms.

Eleanora cleared another bedroom while Helga and Sarge entered the kitchen-living room. Hearing a noise behind him, Sarge ducked just as someone swung a frypan at his head. Helga quickly shot them with her Type 54 pistol.

Unfortunately, she only hit the woman in the shoulder, missing her vital organs, so she had to take another shot. Meanwhile Sarge fired his 9mm at the two men he'd found hiding in the corner of the living room.

"All clear!" yelled Sarge at last.

Jack echoed the call from the front of the house.

After giving David and George a wave, they searched the remaining area.

Sunday 25th January 2015 ... FCPB Fremantle, Crayfish, with the new Team Three on board

On board the FCPB, Doc shook Dick's hand. This was pretty difficult with Patch's arms wrapped around his neck.

"Glad you're back mate! But why did you park the vehicles in the carpark?"

Dick grinned as he held up the two sets of keys.

"You never know when we will need these again, Skipper!"

With Jack on the wheel, Doc went astern on port and ahead on starboard to screw the FCPB around to port, fending off the starboard quarter. With the bow now facing out into Monks Bay he moved to half ahead both.

"Head for the opening Chief."

Jack replied, "Roger that Skipper."

Doc broadcast, "Pull in all fenders and prepare for sea."

In the sickbay, Doctor Rob and Nari were hard at work on James; it looked like he had lost a fair bit of blood.

"Good thing with a thigh wound Nari, is that it's nowhere near any vital organs. All we have to do is stop the bleeding and close up the wound. How are you going with his hand?"

"Not so lucky there, Doc. The bullet smashed a lot of bones as it went through; I might need you to come back to it. For now, I'll just clean it up and dress it until you've finished with the thigh wound."

The eleven members of the new Team Three were in the mess enjoying a hot meal of sausages in gravy, mashed spud and carrots. Leaving them to enjoy a well-earned rest, Dick stepped up to the Bridge to consult the chart and get an ETA on Sand Alley.

"Slow ahead both, make for ten knots."

Jack acknowledged, "Roger that!"

Dick confirmed the ETA.

"What do you reckon? I think we should get to Sand Alley around midnight?"

"Yeah, sounds good Dick. We'll spin her first, and then go into the wharf astern, so it's closer to the bridge control box. Put your team ashore to connect up then open the bridge; hopefully with you and team three on the Peninsular side."

"Where do you want to lie over Skipper?"

Turning to the chart he pointed, "Right here!"

Patch looked at the chart.

"Strawberry Bay sounds nice!"

Sunday 25th January 2015 ... Devil Bay, half of the new Team Four

The next farm at OH&S Cove was on the right, opposite the beach. Just as they were about to turn into the drive, *Brrr ... Brrr ...*

"Great timing!" muttered Sarge.

After taking the call and confirming the rendezvous at the Horn Hotel, he headed up a driveway which turned out to be some 500 metres long. He stopped and let out George and David, and then approached the front door as before.

He could see someone moving around inside. Sarge thought it was probably a trooper. Hopefully he'd be the one to answer the door.

No such luck! As the door opened, a small child stood in front of him. The unexpected sight threw Sarge for a second; he hesitated, not sure whether to shoot first, which would alert the trooper, or just barge right in and then shoot.

He chose the latter option, pushing the child out of the way as he ran into the room with his 9mm drawn. He didn't see the rifle come down until it knocked the pistol out of his hand. This threw him off balance, and he stumbled over some furniture.

Helga was right behind him. In her panic at seeing Sarge go down, she pulled the trigger on her pistol too soon.

The trooper quickly worked out which one of them would be the biggest threat. The man swung and fired at Helga. The 7.62mm full metal jacket round found its mark as it entered Helga's chest below her right breast and exited through her back. This gave Sarge the split second he needed to regain possession of the 9mm Browning and get off two shots.

The first hit the trooper under the arm and went straight through his heart, while the other hit the child in the back as she tried to run away. He yelled to Eleanora.

"See to Helga!"

There was no time to think. Sarge beckoned Jack to join him as they cleared the next room. Once again, they heard the back-flyscreen bang and then the familiar sound of the Ultimax LMG as it let off a long burst, followed by the sound of George's F1. They cleared the farm, with a final body count of nine.

Sarge asked about Helga.

"How is she going El?"

"Not good Sarge! There's more wound than we can handle."

"Shit!"

Sarge returned to the jeep and dialled Johnny's number.

Brrr ... Brrr ...

"Well hello Sarge."

"Mate we have a man down! Don't turn left to the hotel; instead turn right and continue towards OH&S Cove. We will meet you halfway. You'll need to get her back to Strong Fort Bay and the medical team, ASAP!"

"Shit! Who is it? ... Right, we will be there in ten; just turning towards Devil Bay now."

"What's wrong Johnny," asked Robert, quite concerned at what he'd heard.

"Helga's been hit. We haven't got time to tell the others, so let's hope they can keep up."

Putting his foot to the floor, Johnny soon had the old Mercedes rattling along at ninety kilometres an hour. Robert took a look behind him.

"Well, they're keeping up mate."

After driving right through the sleepy area known as Devil Bay, then around past the turnoff to the children's penitentiary ruins on the left, they followed the road up over the hill where they met Sarge coming towards them.

"Let's hope the others are paying attention!"

Cedric and Bentley pulled up behind them, just ahead of Mick and Tony.

"Bloody hell Johnny! What got up your arse? You were driving like a fucking maniac!"

Bentley choked on his words as Sarge and Jack carried Helga over to Johnny's jeep.

"Take her straight to the track we found. Leave two jeeps just out of sight and all go in the last one over the dunes and get her to a hospital. We will finish these seven farms and meet you there. To make things easier, bring your jeep down the road to the tree; that will save us having to go all the way around the dunes."

Sunday 25th January 2015 ... FCPB Fremantle on route to Strawberry Bay, Team Three

The FCPB *Fremantle* cruised her way north along the western side of the Peninsular.

"Run up the ensign Patch; we might as well display who we are while travelling along the coast. You never know! We might find a few more survivors."

Doc was following his charted course around Tilt Island and Blue Head and into the very shallow Strawberry Bay, which was on the other side of Norfolk Bay, opposite Sand Alley.

Brrr ... Brrr ... Brrr ...

"Get that Dick, it might be important. Could be Sarge or Johnny."

Annie's ears pricked up at the mention of Sarge. She longed for him to be back with her; the four days while he'd been training had been hard enough, but this was excruciating.

"*Fremantle*, Dick Mann speaking."

"Hello this is an automated message, message reads, if you have survived the Alliance Invasion and are hiding ring 0189991236, we will find you and we will fight back to get our homes back, this will be saved on your phone."

Annie blurted out, "What the fuck was that! Oops, sorry!"

Dick looked around him at the others.

"That, my dear Annie, is our resident IT nut Vince. He's worked out how to break into all the old brick phones out there. Every phone, whether it is turned on or not, or even if it has flat batteries, or is sitting in a cupboard or whatever, will have broadcast that message."

Doc was smiling.

"Bloody brilliant?! Starboard twenty, steer *zero six five* Chief. We're entering the Flinders Channel."

As Dick returned below, he stuck his head into the sickbay to see how James was doing.

"Well, he'll never play the piano again Dick, but we did manage to plug the hole in his thigh. The hand caused alot more problems; we've done the best we could, given the equipment we have."

Dick entered the Junior Sailors Mess and addressed the team.

"Pick a bunk and get some rest; our ETA is midnight tonight."

Mick Swab spoke up.

"What's the plan Dick?"

"*Fremantle* will go in astern, making us starboard side to. We disembark, run the cable to the bridge control, and then scarper to the Peninsular side of the bridge. We then clear the Sand Alley Hotel, taking up defensive positions. *Freo* will open the bridge; then the crew will retrieve the cable and sail.

"We will clear the other couple of homes and acquire some vehicles. Hopefully, there will be some outside the hotel."

The others were listening intently. Thinking about how far these blokes had come in such a short time, Dick continued.

"We will leave snipers and two LMG's and one .50 at the hotel. So that's Mick and Sid on the LMG's, Will on the Sniper rifle and Riley on the .50 Calibre.

"That leaves Peter, Clinton, Harold, Jill, Josh, and Graham with me, hopefully in a couple of jeeps, to start the clearing and head down the Peninsular towards team four.

"Any questions?"

The group were pretty happy with Dick's plan. Most of them turned in; while those remaining just chilled out.

Sunday 25th January 2015 … OH&S Cove, half of the new Team Four

At 0940, Sarge, Jack, David, George, and Eleanora moved on to the next farm some two kilometres up the road and repeated their approach as before. This time there were no problems. The occupants were all up, and Sarge was greeted at the door by a rather stunning woman in her early twenties.

He chose a different tact this time, marching her into the kitchen, where he found the other four family members. Sarge shot her through the back whilst still holding on to her, then Jack and Eleanora made short work of the others in the room. Jack searched the rest of the house, shooting three children who were still in their beds. He admitted later that this was something he was not exactly proud of.

By now they were coming close to the end of the beach. The next four shacks were very small, more like humpies than farms or houses. Three of them were empty, while the fourth contained three men. Judging by their dress, Sarge put them down as being deserters.

They were playing cards when David and George burst into the little cabin; one went for a weapon but was stopped in his tracks by the Ultimax LMG.

The last two farms were right at the end of the road on either side.

The sight of the team pulling up in the middle of the road right outside, sort of gave the game away. The two women, who'd been gardening outside the left farm, quickly ran back inside yelling, closely followed by Sarge and Jack. David and George went to check out the farm on the right.

Having to shoot unarmed civilians was a hard thing to swallow. In order to keep themselves sane, the team constantly had to remind themselves that these people were part of a master plan to annihilate all Taswegians.

This was the reason why Sarge had left Eleanora watching the jeep. She had been having a hard time coming to grips with the killing. He'd expected this and had thought that more of them would have had the same trouble. The fact that, on the whole, they were coping so well had really surprised him.

Once inside, one of the two women reached for an assault rifle, but before she could bring it to bear, she was cut down by a short burst from Jack's Type 68.

The penny dropped, as Sarge realised the two women were alone on the farm.

"You know Jack, I reckon that two of the guys down the road probably live here; you know ... the deserters."

Jack agreed. The uniforms and ammo webbing they found in the bedroom confirmed their theory.

They could hear the sound of George's F1 from over the road, as well as frantic screaming from a woman. It sounded like she was just outside.

Running quickly outside, they watched as Eleanora took aim at a woman who was running full pelt back down the road. Set on semi auto, it took four shots to bring the escapee down.

"Well done girl," grinned Sarge.

George and David appeared and gave her a huge hug.

"Do you feel better El?"

Sunday 25th January 2015 ... Agnes Creek, other half of the new Team Four

By lunch time, Johnny, Robert, and Helga found themselves turning into Agnes Creek, closely followed by the other two jeeps.

As they stashed them out of sight Cedric asked, "Who are we afraid of? Why are we hiding the jeeps? We've bloody killed everyone already!"

"Not everyone," answered Johnny. "They could send an attachment down from Falcons Neck."

With everyone aboard, they made their way through the track that Sarge and Dick had reconnoitred earlier, following it up and over the sand dunes and on to Strong Fort Bay Beach. Helen and Trish were first to see them, and quickly alerted the others. There were smiles and screams of delight all round at first. Then they saw Helga.

"Get her into the medical room quickly," yelled Johnny.

Doctor Margaret was on hand to take her, assisted by Wendy and Joan. The three women quickly went about their business. The rest left them to it and went off to catch up with their families and fill them in about what had been happening.

Apparently, all was quiet in the Bay; the women had taken it in turns to guard the entrance but there had been no problems. Johnny explained what was happening with the *Fremantle*, and where they were with splitting the teams.

"Where is Sarge? Why is he not here?" asked Sarah.

"He's coming with the rest of what we now call team four. If we can get some tucker on for everyone that would be great."

Johnny hugged his family with joy; not really knowing whether he could ever tell them the true extent of what he and the others had been doing. He didn't even want to think about it for now, and he knew that the other members of the team would be thinking the same thing.

Tears flooded his eyes as he watched the children happily playing outside.

Helen gave him a hug.

"Is there anything I can do?"

"Shit! I nearly forgot. Can someone take the jeep down to the tree and pick up Sarge's lot?"

Mick Jones stood up.

"I'll do it mate. Do you have to change the guard while I'm going ladies?"

Taking the opportunity to swap watch keepers over, Ellen and Helen Crawfield went with him. They arrived just in time to see the weary team of Sarge, Jack, David, George, and Eleanora climbing over the tree.

"Mate, what a sight for sore eyes you lot are!" grinned Mick.

Sarge approached the medical room, where he was met by a sombre Joan.

"How is she, Love?" asked Sarge.

She shook her head, too distraught to speak. Looking at the tears in her eyes, he knew what he'd find before he entered the room, where he found Doctor Margaret placing a sheet over Helga's head. The ex-Benowa GP placed her hand on Sarge's shoulder.

"Sorry Sarge."

Sunday 25th January 2015 ... FCPB Fremantle, Strawberry Bay

1200.

"Starboard 30, steer *one six zero*, slow ahead. Make for five knots Chief. Can someone watch the depth sounder please; we don't have much water under us in here!"

"Roger that Skipper."

Jack was in his element.

"I'll get the sounder, Doc," called Dick.

The day was perfect, with a temperature of twenty degrees and blue skies. The sleek grey lines of the FCPB cut through the clear water like a sharp knife through butter. If things were different, they might have thought they were taking a cruise around the top end of Australia.

"Ease to starboard and stop both engines, let her glide. Depth please Dick?"

"Three-point five metres, Doc."

They got a shock as they rounded the point and found themselves confronted by the sight of an armada of small vessels. They counted at least seven yachts, as well as quite a few dinghies and a few kayaks.

"Three metres, Doc."

"Slow astern Chief, all stop."

"Two point five metres."

Taking all the way off, the grey war machine stirred up the sand as she came to a stop. With a draft of one point seven five metres there wasn't much water under the keel. The crew watched as people scurried about the different vessels.

"Drop anchor. Let's show them we mean them no harm."

Dick, Jack and Annie closed up to drop anchor. The rattle of the chain down the hawse pipe was so loud that it could be heard all around the sleepy bay. The pick finally came to rest on the sandy bottom, just a few metres below.

"Finished with main engines, Chief."

After switching the ship's broadcast to external speakers, Doc piped, "We are Taswegian survivors fighting back against the Alliance."

Dick looked through the binoculars but could see nothing. There was no movement at all.

"Maybe they don't believe us, Doc."

"What do you recommend we do mate?"

Dick looked at Patch. He knew how much she was looking forward to some down time with him before Sand Alley. He tickled her under the arms as he said, "Maybe we fire up the Barby!"

References

Fremantle Drawings- www.navy.gov.au
Fremantle photos- Compliments LS/PO ETP Gary Haig
Catamaran photo- www.incat.com
Weapons Statistics- www.en.wikipedia.org

By the Same Author

I hope you have enjoyed TOAST Book 2, 'Hells Salvation'
  Visit my Website and view all of my other books.
  Just copy and Paste this into your Browser
www.rickallencbooks.com

Tales of a Saddletramp
Saddlery Care and Maintenance

TOAST Book 1 : **The Ride to Hell**
TOAST Book 2 : **Hells Salvation**
TOAST Book 3 : **Hells Beach**
TOAST Book 4 : **Hells Retaliation**
TOAST Book 5 : **Hells Mission**
TOAST Book 6 : **Hells Victory**
TOAST Book 7 : **Return from Hell**

Cast of Main Characters

Twaddle Originals

Richard (Dick) Mann Ex-navy Chief Petty Officer Clearance Diver, weapons specialist, and demolition's expert. He started his navy career at HMAS Leeuwin as a Junior Recruit, then a Weapons Mechanic before becoming a CD. Sometimes appears grumpy but is really not, a gentle giant with a huge bite if provoked, six foot five, balding with a grey beard.

Beth (Patch) Mann Formally Beth McFarlane of Western Australia, expert in all things IT, married Dick on 23rd March 1979, has 5 children to him, has a heart of gold and would do anything to make it all right.

Jack Smouch Ex-navy Petty Officer Clearance Diver, specialist Sniper, a member of the 'Mile' club and world record with a confirmed kill at 2815 metres. Started his Navy career in the Marine Technical Propulsion (Stoker) branch. Deep down just wants to help his mates and would bend over backwards to do so.

April Smouch French sustainability expert, worked for the French Government, one child to abusive husband. Met Jack whilst he was on a holiday after 1st tour of Afghanistan. A gentle unassuming woman of great resolve.

Wayne (Sarge) Michaels Ex-Army Sapper, expert in small arms, explosives, and demolition, handy with his hands in more ways than one can imagine and would do anything for his mates.

Annie Palmer Expert Horsewoman, partner to Sarge, treated like a daughter by Dick and Patch, just loves everyone especially animals, well mainly horses.

Kings Town Hospital

Dr Roger (Doc) Johns Mate of Dick and Patch, ex Royal Australian Navy Reserve Captain, keen sailor and prominent Ear Nose and Throat (ENT) specialist. A survivor of a failed marriage with one daughter, loves sailing, a mild-mannered doctor at heart.

Nari Kim South Korean Triage Nurse on working holiday at Kings Town Hospital and now Doc's girlfriend, a passionate woman who would die for 'her man'

Dr Phil Brown Surgeon

Dr Ted Green Anaesthetist

Dr Les Solomon Cardiology

Dr Helen Smith Diagnostic Imaging, not really a doctor but at a suggestion by Doc it saves her life.

Dr Henry Swain ENT, the only doctor older than Doc, looked up to by everyone.

Dr Alex Wallace Endoscopy, escapes on his yacht 'Rumble'

Dr Rob Simpson Gynaecology, 55, moved to Benowa

Dr David Benson Haematology

Dr Lynda Browne Nephrology

Dr Bruce Charles Oncology

Dr Bob Silver Orthopaedics

Dr Patricia Collins Radiotherapy

Dr Dave Reddy Renal

Dr Reginald Miles Urology

Dr Julie Smith Paediatrician

Dr Michael Bane Gynaecology

Dr Christine Simmons Haematology

Dr Ian Walters Intensive Care.

High Head Originals

Belle   Flood Housewife, good friends to Patch and Dick, married to Ernie, one daughter, Nic. Lives in the High head Lighthouse.

Ernie   Flood Ex-Army Reservist, crane driver working at the Bull Bay terminal for Gary Town Cranes. Lives in the High head Lighthouse. Would give you the shirt of his back if need be.

Nic Walt Ernie and Belle's Daughter, Pilot Station Museum Curator, mother of Gaz and Boz. A wild child in her youth calmed somewhat by the robustly handsome Smokey.

Smokey Walt Chief River Pilot in charge of the Ramat River Pilot Station, ex-navy Coxswain, married to Nic, a take no prisoners kind of guy.

Gaz Walt Trainee River Pilot under his father Smokey, ex-Army Reservist

Boz Walt Trainee River Pilot under his father Smokey, ex-Army Reservist

Charlotte Platt Gary Town Senior Constable, married to Henry

Henry Platt Gary Town Senior Constable, married to Charlotte

Kylie Wiggins University student orphaned when the Alliance killed her parents.

Claudia Smith Locals found hiding from the alliance at Cimitiere Creek, usually a loner, found friends with Chris and Bill after the Holocaust.

Chris Smith Locals found hiding from the alliance at Cimitiere Creek, ex-Army reservist, worked for the Hydro Electric Commission in Lawn.

Bill Gates Locals found hiding from the alliance at Cimitiere Creek, ex-Army reservist, worked at the Gary Town Fish and Chip shop.

North Korean Alliance

General Jun Lee Sung North Korean General in charge of the whole invasion, a proud man and a career Army man, at sixty he was ecstatic when picked by the president to lead the invasion force.

Captain Li Chun Second in charge under the General and another career Army man who takes his position seriously.

Indonesian Alliance

Admiral Adi Atmadja Captain of the Super Tanker *Indo Maersk* and overall commander of all Indonesian Alliance, due to retire as soon as the Nationals are placed, and a suitable replacement can be found to take his place.

Nurul Atmadja Admirals wife, a very doting woman who in her own right had a promising career, giving this up to serve her husband and raise her children.

Huje Samira Major and the Admirals nephew

Raja Atmadja Captain

Lieutenant Colonel Raj Sumatro Indonesian Alliance Commander at Benowa, East Coast, proud to be picked to lead the Indonesians, a likely candidate to replace the Admiral as supreme commander.

Adina Sumatro Raj's wife

Ambar Adina's mother

Kevin Sumatro Raj's father

Indah Sumatro Raj's mother

Wayan Raj's grandfather, an ex-military man proud his grandson had made it onto the list to invade Taswegia sealing his longevity.

Patrol Boat Warrnambool

Commander Suprapto Commander, a short man in stature, career navy man, came up through the ranks and picked because of his humanity.

Lieutenant Joko Executive Officer second in command

Chief Ade Engineer.

Strong Fort Bay Originals

John Badman Julia Bay farmer, reluctant leader

Helen Badman John's wife

Trish Badman John's daughter

Billy Badman John's son

James Smythe Julia Bay Architect

Miriam Smythe James' wife retired schoolteacher

Robert Crawfield Dentist

Gina Crawfield Dental receptionist

Sid Crawfield Ex railway worker

Ellen Crawfield Sid's wife

Helen Crawfield Ellen and Sid's daughter

Craig Crawfield Ellen and Sid's son

Cedric Bilton Retired Shipping Agent

Aileen Bilton Self-employed Hairdresser

Mick Jones Farmer

Sarah Jones Mick's wife

Roger Jones Mick and Sarah's child

Jimmy Jones Mick and Sarah's child

Shelly Jones Mick and Sarah's child

Michael Jones Mick and Sarah's child

Graham Walton Courier Driver

Bentley Frank Chartered Accountant

Barbara Frank Bentley's wife

Josh Frank Bentley and Barbara's child

Jill Frank Bentley and Barbara's child

Blyth Frank Bentley and Barbara's child

Anna   Frank Bentley and Barbara's child

Tony Oglio Retired concreter and Pizza expert

Mary Oglio Retired Bank worker.

Christa Leanne Original Crew
Harry Montgomery Deckhand

Gary Montgomery Deckhand.

Black Ink Original Crew
Harold Patmore Skipper

Riley Patmore Deckhand.

Benowa Originals
George Black Benowa Schoolteacher

Wendy Black Benowa Nursing sister

Kelly Black Wendy and George's daughter

Rob Black Wendy and George's son

Mick Swab Benowa barman

Peter Howe Retired Fisherman

Brian Smith Benowa service station attendant

Yvonne Smith Benowa Medical Receptionist

Hilary   Smith Brian and Yvonne's daughter

Jack Davis Retired Fisherman

Joan Davis Retired Schoolteacher

David   Numa Benowa Motel staff

Eleanore Fame Self-employed Hairdresser

Clinton Ramon Invalid pensioner and ex butcher

William Green Wildlife attendant

Helga   Sven   Swedish Exchange Wildlife Attendant

Dr Margaret Bones GP.

Glossary

AEST- Australian Eastern Standard Time

AMPS- Advanced Mobile Phone System

Bangers- Sausages

BMND-SE- British Multinational Division Southeast

Broken Arrow- Term used to describe when the enemy has overrun the Base

Bum Nuts- Eggs

CDAT- Clearance Diving Acceptance Test

CD- Clearance Divers

CDT 3- Clearance Diving Team 3

CDT's- Clearance Diving Teams

Chow- Army Food

DDG- Guided Missile Destroyer

Dob- Tell tales on, report to the authorities

ENT- Ear Nose and Throat

EOD- Explosive Ordnance Disposal

FCPB- Fremantle Class Patrol Boat

Fid- Tool for splicing rope

Fo'c'sle- the Forecastle, forward part of the upper deck forward of the mast.

GSW- Gun Shot Wounds

Heads- Toilet

HF- High Frequency

HITS- Herrings in Tomato Sauce

ISIS- Militant group - (Islamic State of Iraq and Syria)

IT- Information Technology

Kai- pronounced Kye, a thick Hot Chocolate drink

Kip- Sleep

Local Bike- Woman of loose moral standards who everyone rides.

MCM- Mine Countermeasures

MHC- Mine Hunter Coastal

MIRV's- Multiple independently targetable re-entry vehicles.

MTO- Maritime Tactical Operations

Nigger's Bum- Old colloquial term meaning "Not fair". No longer considered appropriate.

NK- North Korean

NVG- Night Vision Goggles

OBG(W)- Overwatch Battle Group West

Pit or Rack- Bunk, Bed

PMG- Postmaster General

Pongos- Army (wherever the Army goes the pong goes)

Pot Mess- Scran rustled up out of whatever could be found in a tin.

PTSD- Post Traumatic Stress Disorder

Pusser's grip- Canvas carry bag issued when you joined

Pussers- Royal Australian Navy

RAA- Royal Australian Army

RAE- Royal Australian Engineers

RFDS- Royal Flying Doctor Service

Roger- Received

Roo- Kangaroo

ROV- Remote Operated Vehicles

RPG- Rocket Propelled Grenade

RSL- Returned Serviceman's League

Runt-Someone of small stature

Sangers- Sandwiches

SAS- Special Air Service

Scran- Shit Cooked by the Royal Australian Navy

Shake- To wake someone up

Slope- Derogatory term for Asian

SLR- Self Loading Rifle

Standard NATO Brew- (White with two sugars)

TAG (E)- Tactical Assault Group (East)

Tinned Cow- Condensed Milk

TPI- Totally and Permanently Incapacitated

UBDR- Underwater Battle Damage Repair

UHF- Ultra High Frequency

VHF- Very High Frequency

WM- Weapons Mechanic

Woolly Pully- The thick issue Navy jumper

WWI- World War One.

Weapons

NORTH KOREAN ALLIANCE WEAPONS

Type 54 pistols -

Chinese made Tokarev batches, the 54 pistol has a 7.62mm x 25mm or 38 Calibre super rounds.

This is a knock off of the Soviet Union made TT semi auto pistol and was issued with an 8-round magazine.

Short recoil actuated locked breech, single action, and semi-automatic.

Muzzle velocity 420m/s (1,378ft./s)
Effective firing range 50m

Type 68 assault rifle-

This is commonly called an AKM semi-automatic rifle and has a 7.62·39mm round.

With a M43 30 round magazine it fires 600 rounds a minute gas operated.

350 metre Effective range
Type 69 RPG   Type_69_Rocket Propelled Grenade

The Type 69 uses an 85mm rocket propelled grenade (RPG), made by Norinco, is a Chinese variant of the Soviet RPG-7. First introduced in 1972, the Type 69 is a common individual anti-tank weapon in service with the North Korea

Effective firing range   200m

INDONESIAN ALLIANCE WEAPONS

Pindad P2 Semi-automatic Pistol was the standard issue sidearm, a local copy of the Browning Hi-Power. Approximately 2,000 P2s manufactured.

Firing a 9·19mm Parabellum round. It is a firearms cartridge that was designed by Georg Luger and introduced in 1902 by the German weapons manufacturer Deutsche Waffen-und Munitionsfabriken (DWM) for their Luger semi-automatic.

The name Parabellum is derived from the Latin: Si Vis pacem, para bellum, which was the motto of DWM.

'A semi-automatic pistol is a type of pistol that is semi-automatic, meaning it uses the energy of the fired cartridge to cycle the action of the firearm and advance the next available cartridge into position for firing. One cartridge is fired each time the trigger of a semi-automatic pistol is pulled; the pistol's "disconnector" ensures this behaviour.'

The SS1-R5 Raider

Assault Rifles are used by the Indonesian Military Designed for Special Forces operations such as infiltration, short distance contact in jungle, mountain, marsh, sea and urban warfare.

SS1-R5 can be attached with bayonet and various types of telescopes.

It has Safe, Single and Full Automatic firing options.

The weapon fires a 5.56·45mm NATO round and is a rimless bottlenecked intermediate cartridge family developed in the late 1970s in Belgium by FN Herstal. The 5.56·45mm NATO cartridge family was derived from, but is not identical to the .223 Remington cartridge designed by Remington Arms in the early 1960s.

TASWEGIAN RESISTANCE FORCE WEAPONS

Browning 9mm Semi-Automatic Pistol-

9mm Hi Power pistols have a magazine capacity of 13 cartridges plus one in the chamber, for a total capacity of 14 cartridges. It was based on a design by American firearms inventor John Browning, firing a 7.65·21mm Parabellum round. Short recoil operated.

Rate of fire   Semi-automatic
Muzzle velocity   335m/s (1,100ft. /s)
Effective firing range   50m (54.7yd.)
Feed system Detachable box magazine; capacities 13 rounds.

9mm Glock-

The Glock is a series of polymer-framed, short recoil-operated, locked-breech semi-automatic pistols designed and produced by Austrian manufacturer Glock. The firearm entered Austrian military and police service by 1982 after it was the top performer in reliability and safety tests.

Despite initial resistance from the market to accept a perceived "plastic gun" due to concerns regarding durability and reliability which proved unfounded, as well as fears that its use of a polymer frame might bypass the detection of the metal detectors in airports, also unfounded. Glock pistols have become the company's most profitable line of products as well as supplying national armed forces, security agencies, and police forces in at least 48 countries.

With an effective firing range of 50 metres, a muzzle velocity of 375 metres per second and rate of fire of between 1100 and 1200 rounds per minute this is indeed a very formidable weapon.

Rounds 9mm x 19mm Parabellum (same as the Indonesian Pindad P2 Pistol).

The Bren gun-

Usually called simply the Bren, is a series of light machine guns (LMG) made by Britain in the 1930s and used in various roles until 1992.

Effective firing range   550m (600yd.)
Maximum firing range   1,690m (1,850 yd.)
Place of origin   Designed in Czechoslovakia

When the British Army adopted the 7.62mm NATO cartridge, the Bren was re-designed to 7.62mm calibre, fitted with a new bolt, barrel and magazine.

SLR-

The Australian L1A1 is also known as the "self-loading rifle" (SLR), and in fully automatic form - the "automatic rifle" (AR).

Cartridge   7.62·51mm NATO round
Action   Gas-operated, tilting breechblock
Rate of fire   Semi-automatic
Muzzle velocity   823m/s (2,700ft./s)
Effective firing range   800m (875yds.) (Effective range)
Feed system   20- or 30- round detachable box magazine
Sights   Aperture rear sight, post front sight.

F1 Sub Machine Gun-

The 9·19mm Parabellum F1 was a standard Australian submachine gun manufactured by the Lithgow Small Arms Factory. First issued to Australian troops in July 1963, it replaced the Owen machine carbine. Like the Owen, the F1 had a distinctive top mounted magazine.

Sights:	Offset iron sights,
Feed system:	34-round Sterling SMG compatible box magazine,
Effective firing range:	150m
Maximum firing range:	100–200m
Rate of fire:	600–640 rounds/min
Calibre:	9mm

Barrett's 50 calibre Snipers rifle-

The Barrett M82a1, standardised by the U.S. military as the M107, is a recoil-operated.

The Barrett M107 is a .50 calibre, shoulder-fired, semi-automatic Sniper rifle.

Like its predecessors, the rifle is said to have manageable recoil.

Effective firing range:	1,800m (1,969yd.)
Designer:	Ronnie Barrett
Cartridge:	.50 BMG .416 Barrett.

The Winchester Model 70-

243 is a bolt-action sporting rifle.

Introduced in 1936 earning the moniker "The Rifleman's Rifle."

The .243 produces a velocity of 2,960 feet (902.21m) per second with a 100-grain (6.6 gram) projectile commercially loaded, fired from a 24-inch (610mm) barrel.

12 Gauge Shotgun-

A shotgun (also known as a scattergun is a firearm that is usually designed to be fired from the shoulder, which uses the energy of a fixed shell to fire a number of small spherical pellets called shot, or a solid projectile called a slug.

Shotguns come in a wide variety of sizes, ranging from 5.5mm (.22 inch) bore up to 5cm (2.0in.) bore, and in a range of firearm operating mechanisms, including breech loading, single-barrelled, double or combination gun, pump-action, bolt, and lever-action, revolver, semi-automatic, and even fully automatic variants.

M16 Armalite-

Commonly called the M16 rifle, officially designated an Assault Rifle, Calibre 5.56mm.

M16 is a family of military rifles adapted from the Armalite AR-15 rifle for the United States military.

The original M16 rifle was a 5.56mm automatic rifle, limited twist rifling in the barrel to enable the rounds to tumble literally chopping through the jungle and with a 20-round magazine, later modifications included a 30-round curved magazine.

It had a rate of fire of 700-950 rounds per minute and a Muzzle velocity of 960 metres per second.